In the summer of 1381 this challenging couplet became a call to action in the English countryside. The peasants, for too long the chattels of their landlords, roused themselves in anger as mindless and overpowering as a forest fire. Hardship and suffering, their only inheritance, had grown past bearing, and from Essex and Kent they moved on London in irresistible and swelling force to demand a charter of rights from the King. Two very different men had fanned the spark which had smouldered for so long: Wat Tyler, a violent, masterful man of affairs and John Ball, a timid but immensely stubborn dreamer.

Against these men and their followers stood many. Among them the energetic and ruthless Walworth, Lord Mayor of London, and the subtle patriot, Lord Salisbury, tormented by doubts and world-weariness. The inevitable clash of these two opposing forces is charged with the kind of drama that can only arise when oppressed meets oppressor. And the reader is witness to all the harsh contrasts of life in medieval England as the misery of the peasant confronts the splendour of the Court.

In this novel of unusual power and scope the author brings to his task not only the gifts of a storyteller but a sense of historical and political analysis which shows how, as this great popular struggle for human rights developed, its leaders came to realize that time and circumstance would not permit success.

THE AUTHOR

Charles E. Israel was born in Evansville, Indiana, in 1920, brought up in Baltimore, Maryland, and attended schools in North Carolina and Ohio. He served in the Merchant Marine during World War II, in the Atlantic, Pacific and Mediterranean theatres of war. At the war's end he returned to Europe to work with displaced persons as a member of the U.N.R.R.A. staff and of other international organisations, and it was during an assignment in Germany that he met his wife, the former Verna Sweezey.

In 1950, en route to India, the Israels visited Hollywood, and remained for three years while he wrote for radio and television (they never continued their journey). Four scripts which he wrote at that time for the Ford Foundation series, *The Ways of Mankind*, were produced in Canada, and this resulted in a move in 1953 to Toronto, where he has been residing ever since. Today, Mr Israel is one of Canada's best-known writers for television as well as a distinguished novelist, the author of *The Mark* and *Rizpah*.

THIS is a massive novel about the Peasants' Revolt of 1381. The despairing peasants, suffering under the general conditions of villeinage and yoked by a draconic Poll Tax, are fired by two popular leaders — Wat Tyler and John Ball. Tyler is a violent, masterful man of affairs, Ball is a timid but immensely stubborn dreamer. His dreams become reality as the thousands of peasants gather, in Kent under Tyler and in Essex under Jack Straw, and march on London demanding a charter of rights.

Salisbury and Walworth, the two chief opponents of the Revolt, have much in common with the characters of Ball and Tyler respectively. Salisbury, a patriot tormented by doubts and world-weariness, is infinitely subtle but none the less gentle in many ways. Walworth, the energetic and bitter Lord Mayor of London, typifies the rising mercantile class; unlike his counterpart, Wat Tyler, he lacks the saving grace of compassion.

The historic confrontations of opposing forces at Mile End and Smithfield form the first great climax of the novel; the second is provided by the collapse of the Revolt as the initiative is quickly regained by the King and Council. There is a wealth of character colour, ranging from the rough, beery, good-hearted archetypal peasant, epitomised by Abel, to the sly intrigues of Courtenay, Bishop of London.

The narrative drama is matched by the historical and political analysis, which shows how, as the Revolt developed, its leaders came to realise that it was doomed to failure.

By the same author

HOW MANY ANGELS
THE MARK
RIZPAH

WHO WAS THEN THE GENTLEMAN?

A Novel

BY

CHARLES E. ISRAEL

TORONTO : 1963 : MACMILLAN

MACMILLAN AND COMPANY LIMITED
St Martin's Street London WC 2
also Bombay Calcutta Madras Melbourne

THE MACMILLAN COMPANY OF CANADA LIMITED
Toronto

PRINTED IN GREAT BRITAIN

JANUARY – JULY
A.D. 1381

JANUARY

I

THE sun edged over the crest of the hill, bathing the highroad in a pale and elusive radiance. To the traveller, a priest hurrying northeastward, the growing light brought scant comfort. If anything, the dark tangle of forest crouching on either side of the road seemed more sombre and threatening than it had moments before, when dawn had blurred and softened the lines of the bare branches.

The traveller shivered, tightened his cowl about his head and lengthened his stride until unawares he was almost running. His cassock billowed out behind him, then flapped in sharply about his legs. He caught his heel in the hem, pitched forward, and saved himself from falling by a series of ungainly flailing movements of his arms. Just as he had nearly recovered his balance, his foot struck a stone frozen at the bottom of a rut, and he went down heavily, skinning his cheek on the hard ground.

After a moment he picked himself up, breathing quickly, and stood nibbling at a fingernail, peering down short-sightedly at the stone which had tripped him. The weariness was working in him again, addling his sense of purpose, tempting him to rest. And then the sound of his breathing, harsh and erratic in the stillness, brought a return of fear. He glanced around furtively, not sure what he expected to see: a band of thieves, the Archbishop's bailiff in full armour, a demon. . . . There was no one.

He forced his lungs and the pounding of his heart under control and thought: I have nothing to be afraid of. And as if in echo he could hear Christiana's voice whispering: why are you afraid, you have nothing to be afraid of. Her laughter close to his ear in the darkness, at once fond and derisive: you're a priest, aren't you, I thought priests feared nothing. But then, in one of those lightning turnabouts of mood to which he had never become accustomed, her touch conveying concern, her voice verging on tears: I'm afraid for you, John.

3

He felt longing stir in him, powerful and more disturbing even than desire. As always when he was away from it, the memory of Christiana's house in Colchester grew constantly stronger and clearer, until the simple knowledge of its existence was like physical pain. He could see firelight shimmering over clean rushes carpeting the floor, the table where they ate, he carving pieces from the joint with the nicked and pitted knife he carried even now at his waist, the bed where they slept. He could hear the cries of itinerant jugglers and minstrels as they passed by on the steeply slanted street outside, gathering crowds like flies to spilled ale. He could feel the peace of waking with her breathing softly beside him, and lying quietly waiting for dawn to find its way through the single shuttered window.

Now, standing shivering and alone beside the highroad, for a few terrible moments he found he could not remember when he had last slept in the Colchester house. He made a desperate effort to order time. It was not easy. Living on the road bled days and even weeks of meaning. Villages and walled towns ran together in confused remembrance, seasons tumbled one into the other. This was January. December he recalled chiefly for the cold, November for the ceaseless rain which had turned highroads into rivers, rivers into vicious torrents. November was important for another, more ominous reason. It was the month when Parliament had met, and with arrogant deliberateness had ordered a poll tax to be set against every man, woman and child in England.

Slowly his mind traced its way, struggling backward out of bleak winter into the crisp, rime-frost freshness of October and finally coming to rest in a warm and cloudless September.

So it was September. Relieved, he allowed memory to linger among the hours of blessed ease. The mornings, with Christiana stirring porridge over the fire. When he was younger he had been accustomed to break his fast with a bowl of ale and some cheese or even a thick slab of roast pork, but advancing age had somehow, imperceptibly, lent porridge an aspect of soothing luxury.

He heard a sound in the underbrush and spun about quickly in time to see a great grey rabbit dart out of a space between two hawthorns. It regarded him from frightened, red-rimmed eyes for an instant before turning and diving back into the forest. The priest looked meditatively at the spot where the rabbit had disappeared. Once he had considered love the most powerful emotion in the world. Now he wondered if it was not fear.

He sighed. It was time to be moving on. Reluctantly he yielded his recollection of firelight and thick porridge and the warmth of

4

rough wool blankets. He fumbled in the pouch hanging from his belt, took out the scrap of bread he had been saving, began to munch it as he resumed his journey.

He walked along the Roman road in the direction of Chelmsford, his short-sighted gaze probing the trees to his right for the gap which would indicate the turnoff to Billericay.

The rays of the rising sun struck the branches of a massive chestnut, descended the trunk, and with breathtaking alchemy transformed it into a mass of flaming gold. The priest began to feel warmth flooding through him, easing the stiffness of his bones and muscles. And at least, he reflected, his spirits rising, today my hands will not be blue with cold. He held them up close to his face, surveyed the blunt, splayed fingers, nails bitten to the quick with a rim of grime around each cuticle, then repeated to himself with childish satisfaction: at least today they'll not be blue with cold. And spoke it aloud in rhythm with his steps, as if it were a formula whose repetition would ensure success for the task ahead.

The way to Billericay, which he located without difficulty before the sun was much higher, was little more than a footpath winding among thickets and occasionally emerging onto uncultivated fields rank with marsh vegetation or studded with giant, half-buried boulders. Often, crossing these open spaces, the track disappeared altogether, but the priest knew the way well and hesitated only briefly as he thrust aside the frost-stiffened reeds or clambered over the granular surface of the rocks. The landscape of Essex pleased him more than the gentle, river-laced contours of Kent. It was not as rugged as his native Yorkshire, but there was a hint of north country in the low-lying marshes which touched him with nostalgia.

Two miles from Billericay the track plunged again into dense forest. But now it was wide, and deeply rutted from the constant passage of carts, though none of these was now in sight. The priest regretted the abrupt reduction of sunlight, which pierced the overhanging canopy of branches only at rare intervals and reached the floor of the forest diffused, casting grotesque, half-limned shadows. But he was cheered by the knowledge that he had not far to go now, and he fell into the reverie, part contemplation, part dream, which he had found served to pass time on his journeys.

He thought of what he had done, and what he still had to do, and as always when he considered this, hope and weariness contended in his heart. And of late, he knew, the weariness had more often triumphed.

He thought of young King Richard, whom he had never seen,

of the Archbishop, whom he had seen once, and of the people of England, of whom he had seen incalculable numbers.

He was so absorbed that he failed to notice the man who had overtaken him and was now walking by his side. He finally sensed the man's presence in the core of his reverie, then, catching sight of him out of the corner of his eye, he stopped short, staring, knowing that his face must have gone ashen.

The man grinned, opening wide a mouth completely devoid of teeth. 'I've startled you,' he said happily.

'I was thinking,' the priest said, hearing his voice hoarse and shaky, stumbling over the words.

'I've startled you,' the man observed again, and the toothless smile waned, vanished.

It was then that the priest noticed the missing arm. The man's left sleeve dangled limply at his side. The priest let his glance travel over him, taking in the short woollen tunic, once perhaps scarlet, now faded to dirty russet, an attached hood, the edges of which were frayed and caked with grease, the hose, torn in a dozen places, badly patched in half as many more. He observed the grizzled stubble on the man's cheeks, the fact that he carried neither a long nor a short sword, only a dagger stuck carelessly through the belt encircling his waist. Clearly he was no bailiff, nor was it even remotely probable that he was in the service of a bailiff. The priest began to feel a little easier.

'You were looking at my arm,' said the man.

The priest calculated his reply with care. 'At the arm you have,' he asked slowly, 'or the arm you haven't?'

The man first snickered, then laughter spluttered from his hole of a mouth. 'The arm . . .' he began, and stopped, shaken by convulsive mirth. 'The arm . . .' Tears came into his eyes. 'By cock, there's a question for you.'

With frightening abruptness the laughter ceased. 'I'm no runaway serf,' he said, making it sound like an accusation.

'I didn't say you were.'

'You didn't say I was, and I'm not.' The man's eyes were hard now. 'You think I had my arm cut off for running away.'

'I didn't say . . .'

'If I thought that was in your mind . . .' He stopped, letting the menace hang between them. Then, 'No, you didn't say it, did you?' He lifted the edge of his tunic, extracted a filthy scrap of parchment from a pouch. 'Can you read?'

'I can.'

'You needn't turn your nose up. I've known a lot of you who

6

can't.' He fingered the parchment, turning it slowly over and over in his hand. 'A lot of you,' he repeated, looking up. 'I can't read myself, but I know what's on it. A thieving pardoner in Chelmsford read it to me, a groat he stole from my pouch for the favour. He read it over twice in that slimy voice of his and I learned it off straightaway. It's all here.' He tapped his head with the paper. 'All here. Poitiers, it says, nickety-nick. It says I was an archer at Poitiers. Twenty-five years ago, nickety-nick. Poitiers, it says. The year of our Lord thirteen hundred and fifty-six. Thirteen . . .'

The man's voice trailed off, and he was silent so long that the priest stirred restlessly. 'I must . . .' he began.

'Poitiers!' said the man, so vehemently that the priest recoiled. More quietly, 'The Frenchman's mace, the light of it flashing. . . .' His voice rising once more, 'Nickety-nick, the arrows flying into the sun. Three to one they outnumbered us, three to one they rode through us. We should all have died, by rights we should all be worms in French soil now. The Frenchman's mace . . .' He looked down at the parchment, fondled it with his fingers, shrugged and returned it to his pouch. He smiled at the priest, showing most of his lower gum. 'I've been waiting for you,' he said softly.

The priest had to clear his throat before he could speak. 'For me?' he managed to ask.

'For you or anyone else to keep me company to Billericay. Two are better than one in these woods. A score is better, but a pair will do.'

The priest sighed. He felt drained of strength, and as usual disgusted with himself the moment he realized his fears were groundless. But he knew he could not keep them from recurring. Often enough, just often enough, they were not groundless.

He continued on toward Billericay, the veteran of Poitiers beside him. The man seemed content merely to have the companionship of another human being and did not press conversation. Once he said savagely, 'They'll have the devil at them for this.' The priest did not ask the obvious question, and the man did not speak again until they reached the village.

Then he said, 'Good day, John Ball.'

The priest took a step backward, staring at him. 'How did you know my name?'

'Many do,' replied the man soberly. He walked away without looking back.

Billericay lay astride a narrow plateau dominating all the immediate countryside except a steep-rising outcrop just to the east, which was the site of the lord's manor house.

7

It had been summer when Ball had paid his last visit to the village, and the single curving street had been redolent then of warm-weather smells: the sweet-pungent odour of animal and human waste mingling with the spicy fragrance of nearby forest and the musky, more pervasive essence borne up from the marshland. The piles of refuse still lay outside each thatch-roofed house, seeming neither to have increased nor decreased in size, but frozen now, only beginning to thaw beneath the brilliant sunlight.

Ball was surprised to find the street practically empty, the doors of the houses closed. It was the time between early mass and the second service, and on a Sunday morning, particularly when the weather was clement, people were accustomed to lounge in front of their dwellings, leaning against the mud walls, gossiping, arguing, joking. Now there were only two very old men, gnarled as the sticks which supported them, facing each other motionless as church images, and a scabby child squatting dreamily beside a dung-heap.

He was about to speak to the old men, was already framing a discreetly anxious inquiry in his mind, when the wind shifted, bearing from the far end of the village the sound of laughter and a snatch of song. Ball hurried toward it, made his way along the rough stone wall surrounding the church and came out on an open square where marketplace and churchyard shared a common boundary.

The reason for the deserted street was apparent now. As nearly as he could tell, almost the whole population of Billericay was congregated in the square. In addition, there were a number of strangers. A juggler wearing a jaunty belled cap had three knives going in the air; his fingers fluttered like birds among the flashing blades. Three peddlers cried out raucously, plucking at the sleeves of all within reach, swearing to the excellence of a variety of goods they carried strapped to their backs: clothing, cutlasses, pewter pots. Ball's one-armed companion of the road was engaged in amiable discussion with a herbalist whose wares were tied by leather thongs to the outside of his motley cape.

The people appeared the same: the pinched and pallid faces, many of them bearing the peculiarly vacant expression of never-quite-satisfied hunger; the drab and threadbare garments, the tattered footwear. They appeared the same, yet at once he felt a difference in them. There was a feeling of excitement in the square, like that of a fair day but somehow more subdued. Young men lolled about, heads bare, hoods tucked in their belts. Girls drifted among them, covertly watching the youths while making a fetching show of demureness. There was steady traffic to and from the inn, distinguished from other houses by the long pole with a clump of

8

straw at the end projecting out from the doorway. Some boys had tied a mastiff to a gravestone in the churchyard and were pelting the animal with twigs and scraps of rubbish.

John Ball stood unobtrusively at the edge of the square. The moment he always dreaded had come. He glanced around, rubbing the raw ends of his fingers against the coarse cloth of his cassock. The festive air of the village puzzled and disquieted him, but he was reluctant to inquire about it. He knew from past experience that he should not attempt conversation until he had done what he came to do; otherwise, what courage he had would desert him. He strained his eyes, searching the crowd for the presence of danger: armed henchmen from the manor house, a bailiff or a bailiff's retainer. He smiled involuntarily with the thought that if the Archbishop had as many in his service as Ball's fears led him to look for, there would be more bailiffs in England than serfs. Yet he would always be aware of the prelate's far-reaching influence, and he knew it could assert itself when least expected. There had been ample proof of this.

His cursory survey of the square gave him no immediate cause for alarm, and he accepted the knowledge sourly. For this meant he could no longer delay.

He felt the weariness fermenting in him again, insidious and enervating, making his limbs heavy and blurring his already faulty vision. What kind of man am I? he asked himself despairingly, and stepped forward, goading himself to resolution before he should be forced to answer his question.

He sighed, a deep trembling expulsion of breath, and flung the cowl back from his head. The crowd, swimming before his eyes, steadied and came gradually into focus. A few of those nearest him had already turned in his direction, their glances mildly curious.

'My friends, draw close and hear me!'

There was a momentary hush in the square. He wished his voice were lower, less cracked; he wished he possessed the kind of magnetism which could draw them to him with a simple gesture, a commanding stance; he wished he were not there at all, but deep in a forest beside some still undiscovered stream with an eternity of oblivion before him.

'My friends . . .' His palms were sweating, and there was a bitter taste in his mouth. 'People of Billericay . . . people of England . . .'

The juggler, whose whirling knives had not missed a beat through all this, uttered a shrill cry and called out in effeminate but

9

uncannily accurate imitation, 'People of Billericay . . . people of England!'

Laughter rippled out from where the juggler stood, abashed and uncertain at first, gathering momentum. A peddler seized a pewter pot from his store of wares and waved it wildly above his head shouting, 'People of Billericay . . . the finest pewter in all England!' And at the same instant one of the boys baiting the dog hit him on the snout with a stick, making the beast howl with pain. The juggler let his knives fall to the ground and reeled about, hand clutching at his breast as if he had been mortally wounded. Men and women doubled up with laughter, pointing at the juggler, pummelling each other and screaming back and forth across the square.

Ball stood without moving, waiting for the laughter to abate. Suddenly he grew angry. The sight of the faces before him, distorted with mirth, released a caustic fury which flooded through his innards, dissolving fear and diffidence.

'You will listen when I speak!' he shouted. 'You will listen to me now!'

In the shocked silence that followed he could hear only the whimpering of the mastiff and his own tremulous breathing. He did not understand how he had done it, but they were facing him, all of them, attentive and chastened.

'My friends,' he continued, speaking gently to them now, as if to recalcitrant children, 'for you are my friends, just as all those who live in bondage are friends and brothers . . . I have spoken to you before about the most precious thing in our lives: our own freedom. I have come again to speak to you, more urgently now since time grows short.'

He never ceased to marvel at what happened to his voice, once he had begun to speak the words he had come to speak. It was low and resonant now, without a trace of the hoarse, cracked quality which plagued his ordinary speech. 'My good friends, matters cannot go well in England until all things be held in common, when there shall be neither vassals nor lords, when the lords shall be no more masters than ourselves.'

There was not a sound from his audience. The parish priest, a slim, delicate young man, came out of the church and stopped short when he saw Ball, his face reflecting apprehension and disapproval. Ball gave no sign that he had noticed the priest's presence.

'How ill the lords behave toward us. For what reason do they hold us in bondage? What can they show, or what reason can they give, why they should be more masters than ourselves?'

He had them now. He perceived it in their parted lips, their brows wrinkling with the effort of concentration. He felt the odd exultancy which took hold of him when he knew he was being heard, and understood. Nothing could stop him now: bailiffs, henchmen, not the Archbishop himself, even if he were accompanied by every soldier in the realm. And yet, as always in the midst of such triumph, he grew depressed. For in their eyes he saw only resignation, the patience that was cousin to hopelessness. Anger welled through him again, but it was no longer directed at those who stood before him.

'The lords,' he said, contempt edging his words, 'are clothed in velvet and rich stuffs, ornamented with ermine and other furs, while we are forced to wear poor clothing. They have wine, spices and fine bread, while we have only rye, and the refuse of the straw; and when we drink, it must be water. They have handsome seats and manors, while we must brave the wind and rain in our labours in the field. And it is only by our labours that they are able to support their pomp.'

'John Ball speaks the truth!' It was the one-armed veteran of Poitiers. 'By cock, he speaks the truth!'

He felt rather than heard the crowd echoing the man's words. Tension ran like a summer storm across the square, flickered around its periphery. The parish priest looked distressed. He took a half step forward as if to speak, thought better of it and stood with his eyes wide, watching.

'Are we not all descended from the same parents, Adam and Eve?'

Someone called out, 'When Adam delved and Eve span . . .'

A voice far back in the crowd finished it: ' . . . Who was then the gentleman?'

And now they all took it up, reciting it in unison with the lilt and roundness of a liturgical chant:

> When Adam delved and Eve span,
> Who was then the gentleman?

The parish priest retreated hastily into the church. No one seemed to hear the heavy door slam shut.

'We are called slaves, and if we do not perform our services we are beaten, and until now we have had no sovereign who was willing to hear us.' Ball paused, peering round him. 'But the time will soon be ripe. We shall go to the King and speak with him. This King is young, and through him we may obtain relief from our troubles.'

A woman asked hesitantly, 'And if he does not grant it?'

11

'If he does not,' Ball replied slowly, 'we must ourselves seek to relieve our condition.'

He stopped speaking. No one moved or made a sound. Then, shattering the quiet so suddenly that he and all those around him started violently, the church bell began ringing: steadily, heavily, in a peculiar pattern of strokes and pauses.

'The Burial Bell . . .' He heard the whisper spreading through the square, moving outward and in again. 'The Burial Bell. It's time!'

And in the distance he could now hear the sound of minstrels' pipes, floating toward the village from the direction of the lord's manor house.

Slowly at first, as if they were emerging from a trance, then more quickly until they were jostling each other in their haste, the people turned and left the square. The Poitiers veteran was last to go. He called out to Ball, his words reverberating from the walls of the church, 'Aren't you coming?'

'Coming where?'

'Don't you know? The lord's sister. She died on Friday. Today's the funeral. I thought you knew. There's roast ox and bread and drink and tuppence for every man who attends. Aren't you coming, John Ball?'

Ball shook his head. But the one-armed man had not waited for a reply. He was gone, calling back over his shoulder, 'Tuppence for every man . . .'

The church bell stopped tolling. Ball heard a plaintive moan and looked over at the mastiff, forgotten in the excitement, still bound to the gravestone. The dog's muzzle was bleeding; its eyes were filled with baffled submission.

The church door opened and thudded shut. Ball turned to see the priest walking in the direction the villagers had taken. He gave Ball a fleeting scornful glance, then averted his head.

2

H E HAD slept in Braintree, accepting the hospitality of a tanner who had recognized him as he wandered the streets at dusk searching for a place out of the wind where he could lie down. In the two weeks since the incident at Billericay, it was the only night he had spent under a roof. He was grateful for the straw pallet, and for the smoky warmth of the room, but he had lain awake for a long time, listening to the varied breathing of the tanner and his wife and their three children, before he had been able to fall asleep.

He left Braintree at the prime hour, as the Morrow Bell was ringing for dispersal of the watch and the convening of mass. Long before noon he had passed Coggeshall, but then fatigue began to gnaw at him, so that by the time he reached Marks Tey his steps were lagging. It was past mid-afternoon when he drew near the walls of Colchester.

On an impulse he avoided the Head Gate and followed the wall down Balkerne Lane. Just above the ruins of the old Roman gate he stopped, looking at the row of crumbling houses which faced the ancient brick rampart. Three of the warren-like buildings had been owned by Christiana's husband, and since his death had continued to be her source of income. He watched the snot-nosed children, their faces shrivelled with hunger, swirling like driven leaves in and out of the doors of the hovels. Every now and then a slatternly woman would emerge from one of the doors, squint savagely at the light, curse the children with repetitive fluency, then disappear back into the house. The women were old before their time; even the children seemed to have been born old; and the men, who would return at twilight, were a brutal travesty of what God had made when He created Adam. They were called free, and legally this was true, but the lives they led were even more stifling and squalid than those of the serfs in their village slavery.

He felt no pity for the people in the tenements. Long ago he had learned that pity is a futile emotion, wasted on the pitied and pitier alike. But as he stood looking at the houses, the foul mood which had dogged him since Billericay inexplicably evaporated.

He wished it had not left him, for irritability had given him strength, had made it possible for him to go speaking to people in village after village, addressing them with a brusqueness he had never before employed. Now, with this prop suddenly gone, he found himself so exhausted he could scarcely stand up.

Ball wanted to turn his back on the tenements and leave, but he made himself remain with the thought: if you cannot bear the knowledge that the haven you cherish in this city rests on the profits from this, then you must give up your haven. He knew he would not. He had not been able to give it up ten years before, in the first days of his life with Christiana. How much more difficult it would be now, with need stamped on his soul, indelible as a graven coin.

And against his will he began thinking about the lives the people led inside the tenements: the bodies packed together in fetid little rooms, the spoiled and often maggoty food, the surly joyless coupling of men and women. Did they ever recognize the extent to which life was cheating them, and would they ever learn to cry out against it, or was their apathy the only true defence, short of the grave, against life itself?

Speculation like this, he knew, was ridiculous, and as useless as pity, but without the awareness it kept alive in him, was there any sense in what he was attempting to do?

Was there any sense, after all?

He tried to put the question out of his mind as he descended the sharp incline of Balkerne Hill and followed the wall until it swung eastward almost at the edge of the sluggish river. The January afternoon was waning as he entered the city through the massive North Gate and trudged up the hill, threading his way through a network of narrow, tortuous lanes.

His joints ached, and he knew he could not spend many more winters in the open, walking mile after mile, sleeping wherever darkness overtook him. Summer was not too bad, but even then the ground on which he slept was often damp. There had been mornings this past year when he had thought he would be unable to get up.

Would there have to be another winter?

He could not answer this. Billericay had not been his first setback, far from it, but since then he had understood better than ever the enormity, and perhaps the folly, of what he and Tyler and the others were undertaking.

Christiana's house was one of a row of small but sturdy dwellings on West Stockwell Street. When he entered, he saw her kneeling by the fire, and it seemed to him he had never left this room.

There was no surprise in her eyes as she got up and came to him, only a quick flush of pleasure rising to her cheeks, completely transforming her even as she crossed the space between them. She possessed great natural beauty: elegant features, clear skin, a firm and well-formed body. But like many sensual women, she was often careless of her appearance to the point of contempt, seeming to take perverse delight in dowdiness. Yet, let her be touched by a moment of excitement or joy or anger, and it did not matter how drab a gown and girdle she was wearing, or how untidily the ends of her hair straggled from under her cap: she was again a beautiful woman. As she was now.

14

'You're tired,' she said, without any other greeting. Then, taking his hands in hers, 'And you're cold as well. Come sit down.'

He allowed her to lead him to a bench beside a table, made no protest as she removed his cowl, clucked disapprovingly over the shocking state of his fingernails and the several places where his cassock was ripped. She was in her early forties, fifteen years younger than he, but always in the first hour of his return she would become motherly. He never tried to stop her. Now he smiled, thinking that surely if a man could not remember his own mother . . .

'Why are you smiling?'

He shook his head.

She said softly, 'And if I want to act like a mother for a time, a little time . . .'

He looked up at her, startled and yet pleased as always when he first returned by her disturbing talent for divining his thoughts.

Christiana went to the hearth and removed the pot hanging over the embers. 'I was cooking some barley soup for my supper. We'll have that first, and later . . .'

He raised his hand wearily. 'Tomorrow. Tomorrow I'll eat more. The soup will do for now.'

She stood looking at him for a moment, then set the pot down and came back to him, slowly, with the easy indolent walk which had once made him tremble whenever he saw her and even now, after all this time of forbearance, could still stir him more deeply than he wished to admit. She took his head in her hands, let her fingers trail down his cheeks, linger on the lines of his jaw. But when she bent to kiss him, he held her away from him.

She could conceal neither her disappointment nor her hurt. Her hands dropped to her sides, and her expression grew petulant. 'Other priests have women,' she said.

'Other priests can do as they please.'

It was the opening gambit in an endless chess game, to be played through all the predetermined moves to inevitable stalemate.

'For six years . . . whenever you were here, which was seldom enough, let the Virgin be my witness to that . . . six years we lived together as man and wife. And now for the past four . . .'

'We were never man and wife. Nor can we ever be.'

He did not want to quarrel. But if they did, it would be his fault. He was saying the wrong things, and saying them with a smug self-righteousness he did not feel.

She looked at him, her full lips compressed in an angry line. 'If you don't want me, there are many who do.'

15

'Christiana . . .' He spoke her name as if it were a cry of pain.

Her manner changed, swiftly, as was her wont. She smiled and asked crooningly, 'Am I ugly? Have I become so unattractive?'

He smiled back thinly, not deceived. 'You know . . .' he began.

'Do I know?' she burst out. 'How would I know? To have a man who is not a man, who is not here most of the time even if he were a man . . .' She broke off, then said, spitting out the words, 'Your tonsure needs to be shaved.'

He blinked at her, not sure he had heard correctly, then began to laugh. She glared at him, but soon her expression softened, and her laughter joined his.

After a few moments she said, 'A man who always looks at me as if he didn't even see me,' but there was no longer any edge to her voice. 'Your tonsure does need to be shaved, you know. And your face.'

He touched the wiry growth on his cheeks, moved his hand upward to the top of his head. 'Yes,' he said, and sighed.

'Whenever you sigh like that,' she said, going to the cupboard and fetching a razor, 'you make me worry. I always think you have the ague.'

'I've been sighing like that for many years,' he said absently. He was looking at her: the lines of her figure; the softness of her hair, black, flecked here and there with grey; the way she moved.

'You've been . . .' she began, then, as she turned around and saw his expression, 'Thank you, John Ball,' she said quietly. 'Thank you very much.'

She filled a bowl with water out of a wooden bucket in the corner and brought it, together with the razor, to where he was sitting. When she touched him it was still with tenderness, but the quality of the contact was different now, somehow impersonal. The tension between them had withdrawn, only to wait its time, he knew, but it had withdrawn.

She shaved the top of his head carefully, deftly, as she did everything. He wondered what the Master of Novices would say if he could see one of his former charges being shaved by a woman. Once probably he would have been amused, but the Master of Novices was an abbot now, and exalted position was a frequent murderer of humour. Still . . . He chuckled.

'I wonder what they would say if they could see you now.'

He wanted to look up at her, but the razor was scraping his skull, and he remained still.

'What made you say that?' he asked after a while.

'Say what?' She had already forgotten it.

16

He shifted on the bench and knocked the bowl of water onto the floor. She made no comment to his murmured apology, but picked up the bowl and went for more water. Only when she had returned and resumed her task did she say, her voice low and concerned, 'This is why I fret so about you while you're away from me. You're so awkward and you don't see well and you're so—' she searched for the word, 'so trusting. I'm afraid for you, John. I'm afraid of what they'll do to you one day.'

'Nothing will happen to me.'

'How much longer will it go on?'

'I wish I knew.'

'Almost twenty-five years of your life . . . twenty-five years of wandering, of running away . . .'

'I haven't been wandering or running away all that time,' he said gently.

'No,' she said with sudden bitterness. 'You were able to spend three of those years in the Archbishop's prison.'

'I meant . . .'

'I know very well what you meant,' she interrupted impatiently. 'Sometimes I think you're a fool.'

'Sometimes I know I am.'

'And you're afraid, too. You've told me you are.'

'Yes,' he said, 'I'm afraid.'

'Then why do you have to do what you're doing? Do you think they want to change, those people? They're content enough with things as they are. They always will be.'

'Christiana . . .'

'You're not young any more. You need rest. You deserve some peace. Let the Virgin be my witness you do.'

He reached up to take the razor from her hand. 'I'll shave my beard.'

She stood beside him for a moment, then shrugged and moved off, her steps making a pleasant sibilant sound through the rushes.

He concentrated on shaving, and when he looked up again she had fastened the shutter over the oil-papered window. Two bowls of soup and some slabs of bread were on the table, together with a dish of flaming tallow which lighted the room fitfully.

The curfew bell began to ring from nearby St. Martin's. He had not realized it was so late.

They ate in silence. Halfway through the meal he sensed that she wanted to tell him something. Of the two of them she was more instinctively accurate about his thoughts, but they knew each other well.

17

He finished eating and waited. When he saw that she would not speak until she was prompted, he asked, 'What is it?'

She looked at him steadily. Often she was frivolous, just as often irrational, but where serious matters were concerned, she never played cat-and-mouse with him. He was sure this was serious, whatever it was.

She took a deep breath. 'Tyler was here, asking for you.'

He kept his voice even. 'When?'

'Yesterday. Between Angelus and Curfew.'

'Did he say he wanted to see me?'

'He said it was important for you to come to him as soon as you returned. He said to be careful no one saw you.'

'Why didn't you tell me earlier?'

'Because I suppose I'm selfish. After you've seen Tyler you'll probably have to go away again. I wanted you with me for a time.'

'Perhaps I won't have to go away at once.'

'Perhaps.'

'You should have told me sooner,' he said, getting up from the table. The fear was wakening softly, fluttering in his belly. 'Why didn't you?'

She stared at him an instant before replying. 'Because,' she said slowly, 'I didn't think you really wanted to hear.'

Anger flared up in him, was quickly gone. He sat down. 'I didn't.' He smiled sadly. 'Since you know so well how I felt, why did you tell me at all?'

'You had to know,' she said dully. She looked over at him. 'Where will it end, John?'

He did not reply. He was thinking, not of Tyler, but of Christiana. What right had he to do what he was doing to her? He could not marry her, and he would not leave her. He was a priest who was not a priest, a man who was not a man, sometimes a fugitive, sometimes only an outcast, a plotter who was not even sure of the value of what he was plotting. And for all these contradictions, all these uncertainties, she, not he, had to pay the penalty.

The sound of her voice made him look up. 'I would not have it any other way,' she was saying quietly. 'Now or before.'

Her eyes were faintly luminous, reflecting the flicker of the tallow lamp. He sighed and said, 'I love you, Christiana. More than my life I love you.'

'Then make me your wife.'

'You know . . .'

'Yes,' she said.

18

He got up. 'I must go.'

She was beside him in an instant, her hand on his arm urgent and restraining. He looked at her, puzzled until he heard the heavy footsteps of the watch approaching, passing the window.

When they died away, he touched her cheek briefly with his fingertips. Then he left the house.

3

WAT TYLER heard Curfew ringing just after he had climbed East Hill and was approaching the walls of the Castle. He could see the Great Tower of the Keep rising rounded in the darkness, its heights catching a few indistinct rays of torch-light from below.

He kept as close to the Castle wall as possible, listening for the watch, moving carefully so he would not stumble into a pile of refuse or over one of the stones that were always dropping out of the wall.

He had not far to go to reach his house. If he were stopped, he could always show the officer of the watch the tools he carried, and, begging his pardon, spill out some long and lying tale about being detained on an urgent job of carpentry by the rector of St. James's (where he had in fact been working that day, but not since mid-afternoon). He could touch his forehead obsequiously and play the dullard and swear he knew nothing about written passes, since this was the first time in all his life he had ever been out of his house after Curfew had tolled, and would the noble lord treat him kindly and set him in the proper direction, since it would seem he had lost his bearings in the darkness and he was a deal more than a little frightened. And he could bow again and shuffle his feet and reply to all questions with such a show of obtuseness that they would soon tire of him and be on their way.

All of this he could do. But he knew, even as he rehearsed the speeches in his mind, as he had done often before, that if he were stopped he would never use them. He had no temper for such pretence; his patience would run out with the first arrogant word, the first threatening gesture. He knew what he would actually do. If there were no more than two of them, he would use the mallet on one, the awl on the second, and be away before the rest of the swine arrived. If it happened that he was not carrying his tools,

19

bare hands would do; it would not be the first time he had cracked a pair of skulls by bashing them together.

But if there were more than two of them, he would not be so foolish as to run headlong against luck. He would rely then on his fleetness, and on his intimate knowledge of every turning in the city's lanes. They, following slow-footed, encumbered with weapons and torches, would never catch sight of him again after the first moment.

He turned to his left and plunged into the blackness of a gap barely wide enough to admit him. When he came out of the alleyway, he knew Holy Trinity would be to his right and home would be a few dozen steps away, hard against the city's south wall in Eld Lane.

He stopped, held himself rigid as he heard something stir at the end of the passage. He waited only long enough to be sure it was a rat, then hurried on. When we have won, he thought grimly, there will be no more of this skulking about in shadowed shame. There will be but one pass required: membership in the brotherhood of man, and the only scrutineer will be the eyes of freedom.

Until he came in sight of his house he did not realize how tightly he had been grasping the handle of the mallet. He shifted it to the other hand and flexed his fingers as he walked quickly across the lane.

He had to stoop to get through the doorway, and when he had closed the door behind him, he could at first see nothing but the light of the fire. It was the only illumination in the room; there was no money for candles or oil. Then his glance found Isabella, sitting huddled on a bench; she had apparently not even moved when he came in.

'You're late,' she said tonelessly.

He grunted, stripping off his outer tunic and tossing it and his tools into a corner. He crossed the room, flicking the straw mattress lightly out of the way with the toe of his boot, and stood warming his back at the fire.

'You could have been taken by the watch.'

He said, more loudly and angrily than he intended, 'I've not been taken yet,' and watched her shrink further into herself, hunching down on the bench like some frail and forlorn bird. He knew she was frightened by the quick flare of his temper, and this angered him more, but there was no fear in her voice as she said laconically, 'There's food.'

He left the fire and went toward the table where bread, salt herring and raw onion were waiting, but before he reached it he caught sight of the blood-soaked rag wrapped round her left hand. He was kneeling beside her in an instant.

'What have you done?'

'It's nothing. The knife slipped. . . .'

'You're an idiot. A clumsy misbegotten heedless idiot. . . .'

He was busy meanwhile unwinding the bandage with his quick, precise carpenter's fingers. There was a gash across the fleshy part of her palm, ugly but not too deep. He heard himself sigh with relief and shook his head, puzzled that the sound had come from him. He was still holding her hand. It was delicate and small-boned like the rest of her. He brooded a moment over its fragility, then looked up at her face. Her eyes were in the shadow, but the firelight played on her hair, glinted off the high sharp angle of her cheekbone.

He said huskily, scarcely conscious that he was speaking, 'You'll take care.' More insistently, 'You will . . .'

She shifted her head. He could see her eyes now, and in them was an expression which moved him strangely, and at the same time baffled him.

'Wat,' she said, 'I'm glad you're back safe.'

The way she spoke did something to his heart: he could feel it leap convulsively. And in that instant he felt a rare and terrible sense of panic take hold of him. He was sure that in another moment he would be trembling. He put her hand away from him with a curt dismissive gesture. 'It will heal,' he said harshly.

Her tone was a replica of his as she repeated, 'It will heal.'

She took the bloody cloth and began to bandage her hand again. Tyler got up and went to the table, rolled a herring around a chunk of onion and bit into it. He paced back and forth across the floor while he ate.

'There's ale,' she said.

The flatness of her voice made him feel more comfortable again. He grunted, watching her pour the thin brew out of a jug into a wooden cup. He took a long draught from it. By the time he set the cup down, he had almost forgotten his consternation of a moment ago.

When he had first seen Isabella seven years before, he had just returned from his tour of soldiering in France, and he had been looking for a wife. He was thirty-four then, and he had avoided marrying earlier mainly because of his aversion for the grubby importunities of the marriage brokers.

His parents had originally been serfs, their families bound to a

21

manor in Thaxted, in western Essex. They had wanted each other, but their parents lacked money for the marriage fine, and the lord had laughed at their request for permission to wed. Tyler's father was eighteen then, his mother a year younger. They had run away from the land and had managed to reach Colchester. For a year they lived lives of dark dread, scrabbling for enough work to earn them the scraps of food on which they existed, expecting every moment of the day and night to be confronted by the bailiff from Thaxted and dragged back to the manor, where they would be branded and perhaps mutilated as an example to others. But they had been fortunate. They had not been captured within the prescribed limit of a year and a day, and, in accordance with the law, they had been able to become freemen of the city where they had found refuge. Then, nine years after Tyler's birth, they had both died, victims of the Black Death. But they had left him the heritage of their freedom.

He had always felt, in some vague fashion, that he owed it to his parents to take a wife out of free choice, rather than allow matters to be arranged for him either by the brokers or one of his companions at work who happened to have a marriageable daughter.

Until his return from the wars he had found no one. Nor in truth had he sought too avidly. Women had seemed to fall in his path. He had picked them up, used them briefly and cast them aside. It was a satisfactory enough arrangement, and he had been content with it.

But, after two years in France, he had found himself possessed of a peculiar hunger that could not be assuaged by his former casual habits.

He had seen Isabella in the marketplace. She was the daughter of a mercer, not a rich man but well enough off. He had watched her helping her father at the stall, had covertly appraised her delicacy, the lightness of her movements as she folded the lengths of woollen material.

It had not been difficult to arrange a meeting. She had come to him secretly in the slow summer twilight, and he had urged her on with stumbling haste to one of the town's traditional trysting places, where the tree-lined Sheepen Road followed the curve of the river bank. She had offered no resistance to his love-making, and afterwards the sight of her lying beside him, frail and compliant, had sent him into a quick rage. He had called her a slut and a whore and had continued to heap abuse on her until finally he had run out of words and had lain back exhausted. She had listened to him without replying, her gaze fixed on his face. Then she had

22

got up and, calmly arranging the folds of her skirt, had said, 'We'll go now.' He had thought this was the end as far as she was concerned, but just before they parted she had turned to him and said matter-of-factly, 'We'll meet tomorrow night.'

He had met her again, part out of curiosity, part out of pique. She had been as acquiescent as before, and her frailness had again both intrigued and infuriated him. Had he been able to break her spirit then, he would have done so and left her without a moment's remorse. But suddenly he discovered in her a toughness that matched his own. He knew his outbursts of temper frightened her; he could see it in the hunching of her shoulders, the trembling of her hands. But then she would speak, and her voice would be quietly, doggedly defiant. He knew that although she was afraid of him, she would not surrender to her fear. He had found the knowledge comforting, though he had not known the reason then and still did not understand it.

When he had asked her to marry him, she had agreed at once, without the slightest hesitation, as if she had known all along it would be this way.

The mercer had promptly disinherited her, and she had never spoken of him again.

In the seven years of their marriage she had borne Tyler three sons, all dead at birth. He had stormed and cursed on each occasion, slamming his fist into his palm as he always did when he was upset, but Isabella had not displayed the slightest bit of emotion. Each time she had gone with him and watched dry-eyed while he buried the tiny corpse in St. Mary's Field, then had returned to the house and resumed whatever household task had been interrupted by her labour pains.

Sometimes Tyler felt that he did not know her any better now than he did on the first evening when they had walked together along the Sheepen Road.

He went to the fire and tossed a bramble root onto the coals. The flames licked up around it, died, then caught and burned brightly.

'We'll need more wood,' he said.

'I'll buy some tomorrow,' she replied, and added, 'It's up another ha'penny.'

He grumbled without much vehemence, 'They'll not be content till they starve us all.'

He finished eating the herring and wiped his hands on his tunic, then paced restlessly back and forth across the room. The smoke, unable to escape quickly enough through the hole in the roof, had descended, and the air was thick with it. Tyler's eyes smarted, but it did not seem to disturb Isabella. She went quietly about clearing up the remainder of the food, then spread out the straw mattress neatly on the floor.

Finally she asked, 'Where will you be working tomorrow?'

'St. James's again. Some of the crossbeams in the nave have gone rotten.'

'And after you've finished work?'

He shrugged. 'There'll be people to see.'

She nodded without comment.

There was a tapping at the door, staccato and insistent. Tyler stopped pacing. He and Isabella looked at each other, neither moving. The tapping ceased, began again more urgently.

Tyler crossed to the door, unbarred it and flung it open. John Ball stood framed in darkness, peering past him, blinking at the firelight. Tyler made a peremptory gesture; Ball took a hasty step forward, caught his foot on the threshold and sprawled face down on the floor. Isabella uttered a small cry and ran to him.

Ball turned over and sat up stiffly. 'I would probably have done better,' he said, 'to have tried a career as a jester or a fool. Who knows? With my great talents I might have risen to become the King's fool.'

'With your great talents,' Tyler said with heavy irony, 'you might very well still do it.' He fastened the wooden bar firmly across the door. 'Did you meet anyone on the way here?'

'Only a tippler turned out of some inn, singing and shouting loud enough to be heard in London.' He inspected his hands, stared ruefully at a long sliver of wood half-embedded in his thumb. 'Why is it that a sot can disturb the dead with his caterwauling and never even be noticed by the watch, while we . . .' He stopped speaking, tried without success to extract the splinter. He smiled up at Tyler 'Perhaps we're going about things the wrong way. With enough strong wine, we could plan our whole campaign in the streets.'

Isabella took Ball's hand gently in hers, pulled out the splinter. 'You're cold,' she said.

'Am I?' Ball shook his head wonderingly. 'It's sometimes hard to know any more.'

'You should not have come after Curfew. They might have . . .'

'Women and priests!' Tyler interrupted angrily. 'Neither of them any use to anyone.'

Isabella paid no attention to his outburst, but Ball looked up, his expression deeply wounded.

Tyler relented at once. He had never been able to prevent him-

24

self from hurting Ball, and always, the moment he had done so, he would be remorseful. He went to him and took his arm, helped him to his feet. 'Forgive me, John. You know I meant nothing by it.'

The priest smiled; his eyes lighted up. Tyler marvelled anew at the aura of warmth this slight, stooped man could emanate.

Six years before, in the churchyard of a village not far from Colchester, he had first heard Ball preach. As he had listened and felt the intensity of the words touching off some deep-coiled power within him, he had known even then that Ball's cause would become his. So it had, and so had his affection for him grown, until it too was part of the fibre of his life.

He noticed now how markedly the priest had aged in this past year. Ball was peering about him, a little dazedly, his deepset eyes red-rimmed with exhaustion. He let his hand wander up to his mouth in a childish and somehow pathetic gesture, and began to chew at the nail of his forefinger.

He seemed so lost and vulnerable that Tyler felt his breath catch. Isabella looked in his direction, and he said hurriedly to Ball, 'When did you return?'

'This evening.'

'You need not have come tonight. Morning would have been time enough.'

Ball said simply, 'The message was to come as soon as I arrived.'

And Tyler was aware of having once again underestimated the priest. Beneath the awkwardness, the seeming lack of any defence, lived an iron stamina, indomitable and tireless.

Isabella got up from where she had been kneeling and moved to the bench, sat down among the shadows. Tyler realized suddenly how alike they were, the priest and his wife. And he found himself wondering: must I only care for what I cannot break? But the question confused him, and he dismissed it with relief.

'A man named Farringdon came from London,' he said brusquely. 'Night before last.'

'I've heard of him,' observed Ball. 'They say he has influence there.'

'He seemed less interested in the cause than in getting back some tenements he claimed were stolen from him.'

Tyler saw Ball wince at the mention of tenements and was again annoyed with him. Why did the man squirm so over trifles? You recognized things as they were, and you accepted or rejected them; nothing could be simpler. There was no point in worrying them, like a dog turning a bone over and over long after it was picked clean.

25

'I've heard,' Ball was saying again, lamely, as if he were making conversation, 'that Farringdon has influence in London.'

'He says sympathy for us is rising there. He says the bees are flocking to the hive, more every day. Soon, he says, there'll be so many that the hive will fall and break open, and the golden honey will be there for the taking.'

'He speaks colourfully, your Farringdon,' said Ball, 'if a jot obscurely.'

'Maybe that wasn't exactly the way he put it,' Tyler said impatiently. 'The gist of his words was that the time would soon be ripe.'

'And you agree with him.'

'I think we should begin to move with the first breath of spring. Wrawe has sent word that Suffolk is growing restive. The people are talking about not paying the poll tax. To me that's a sign we should act. March would not be too soon.'

Ball straightened up. 'We'll wait,' he said in a quiet, clear voice.

Tyler felt exasperation stirring in him. 'Wait for what? For the bailiffs to ride into every town and village in England and rob people of what little money they have, money they've sweated to earn. . . .'

'Just that,' said Ball mildly. 'Until it becomes an intolerable burden, the poll tax is just another phase. And it cannot become a burden until the bailiffs begin to collect it.'

'They're beginning now.'

'They'll fail,' said Ball. 'Then they'll try to repair their failure with cruelty. We'll wait until then.'

Tyler glared at the priest. What Ball said was logical. But now that they had come so far, he found logic distasteful and waiting intolerable. He was developing an insatiable thirst for action.

'We'll act!' he shouted, slamming his fist into his palm. 'Now!'

Ball took a step backward and Isabella moaned softly. Neither spoke.

In the silence, Tyler looked down at his hands, let them drop slowly to his sides. He began to cast about for logic with which to answer Ball's logic.

'Jack Straw says . . .'

Ball interrupted quietly, with ease. 'Straw sits on his hilltop in Fobbing, looking down on his fishermen, breathing fire through the windows of his church. He says we're ready. Does he know the temper of people in Kent and Sussex and Surrey? Does he know the state of courage in Hertford?'

'Do you?'

'I shall learn it.'

Tyler strode back and forth. The walls of the room pressed in on him, confining, frustrating. He seized the earthenware jug and smashed it on the floor. A few drops of ale flew into the fire, sizzling; the rest puddled out around the broken jug. Isabella got up and without a word began to gather the pieces together.

Tyler said through clenched teeth, 'That's the way we'll smash them when we do act.' Then his jaw muscles slackened. He felt better and added, 'If we ever do,' in a low voice, looking from Ball to Isabella with a sheepish smile.

Ball did not return the smile. 'Sometimes, Wat,' he said, 'I fear what your anger will do to us.'

'Sometimes I fear it will not do enough for us.'

The priest's shoulders slumped suddenly. He seemed to be shrinking into himself. 'Wat,' he said, 'does it never trouble you . . . the hopes we're setting in men's minds . . . the fires we're kindling in their breasts. . . .'

'Only,' said Tyler, 'that the fire will not be hot enough.'

Ball sighed. 'We have agreed that there will be no killing.'

'We have agreed on nothing of the sort,' replied Tyler, his temper rising again. 'There'll be killing, John Ball, whether you wish it or not. Do you expect peasants to deal gently with men who have starved and beaten them, who've robbed them of their birthright as human beings?'

'There's no need to throw my own words back at me.'

'Then take responsibility for them.'

Ball sighed once more, tremulously, and said, 'I must go.' At the door he turned. 'I shall travel to Kent as soon as I can. Perhaps between the poll tax and my preaching . . .' He shrugged, began to fumble with the bar of the door.

Tyler came to help him. 'It will go well,' he said warmly. 'Of this I'm sure.'

'Once . . .' said Ball, and let his voice die away. It seemed that the single word falling into the smoke-filled room was at the same time a wish and a confession.

Ball raised his head until he was looking into Tyler's eyes. 'Sometimes,' he said, 'when I pass a village and see the houses lying peacefully under the sunset . . .' He fell silent, and when he spoke again his tone was bitter. 'Loneliness, plotting, stirring up strife. . . . Are we right, after all? Have we ever been right?'

Tyler struggled to find words to say what was in his heart. He was only able to grip Ball's shoulders and whisper gruffly, 'When we've won. . . .'

Ball moistened his lips. 'God bless you, Wat. God bless your strength and my weakness.'

Tyler opened the door. The priest slipped past him and out into the darkness.

As he dropped the bar into place, Isabella drifted toward him, her hand raised in an oddly suppliant gesture. 'What will happen to him?' she asked. 'What will happen to us all?'

She never complained openly, but sometimes her resigned manner was so akin to complaint that it maddened him.

As it did now. He was beside her in two swift steps, his hands closing so tightly around her arms that she gasped with pain. The fire was almost out, but he could still see her face: eyes wide, mouth slightly open, the faintest hint of cheek-down golden in the dying light. Her beauty set an unreasoning rage storming into his blood. He threw her onto the mattress, plunged down beside her. There was no pleasure and little relief in his taking her. The cries which burst from her lips were like those of a small animal hunted through the forest: plaintive and desperate. He heard them as from some great distance.

After a time they lay quiet, separate from each other. He knew that she was also awake. Her breathing was ragged, restless, close to tears. He wanted to speak to her, or simply to reach out and touch her. But somehow it seemed impossible.

FEBRUARY

I

THE wind plucking at the thatched roofs was shrill and capricious, but as it swooped down to corrugate the pools of water dotting the village street, its tone would now and then change subtly, and there would be an instant's promise of spring.

Abel Threder felt it, making his way through the twilight toward the inn, and mistrusted it. Spring sent no harbingers in the middle of February, unless they had come by way of the devil. His scepticism did not prevent him, however, from enjoying the vagrant softness in the air, nor did he try to undeceive his loins, which always responded with the pertinacity of a stud bull to the high sweet call of spring.

Soon in truth it would be ploughing time, then seeding, and before one knew it, reaping and threshing. He would divide his labour between the lord's land and the land he called his own, and so spring would deepen to summer, and summer to melancholy autumn.

It was sufficient to make a man weep, the way the seasons flew, and to prove his point he shed two tears, let them roll down his cheeks. But when two more followed he said out loud, 'Enough,' and thought: to tithe from a fund of sadness is fair and as things should be, but there's no sense doling out more of anything than is required, even to the Almighty.

He wiped away the traces of moisture with a corner of his hood, pausing under the signpole of the inn to do so. Not that the habitués inside would ever suspect him of having wept in the street. He knew that laughter would greet his appearance in the doorway, would gather volume as soon as he spoke his first words, no matter what they might be. He had come to expect it; the forty-two years of his life had been spent in this village, and for most of these his reputation as a clown had been building.

Forty-two less, of course, the enforced three he had spent abroad as part of the Black Prince's army. But even during those years his role had not greatly changed. There had been a night in Castile when the Black Prince himself, already ill and morose, had appeared in the circle of firelight where he and some of the other archers were lounging. And Abel had felt a rush of sympathy for the sombre nobleman with his great black drooping moustaches and his fever-haunted eyes. He had broken through the sudden hush of his comrades in the presence of royalty to perform an antic dance and sing an antic song which made the Prince first smile, then laugh aloud. He had earned a groat for his boldness.

Perhaps, he thought as he entered the inn, tonight I'll make some well-heeled traveller here laugh hard enough to shake silver out of his pouch for ale all round. The rich, nut-brown brew, naturally, not the pale bullock-piss he and his friends were accustomed to drink, nursing a single cup of it through an evening.

He could scarcely make out anyone in the room at first, the smoke was so thick. But they saw him, and at the initial heralding shout of mirth he doffed his hood and made a deep mock-bow. As luck would have it, and somehow luck always had it, the perigee of his bow brought his nose within inches of the most massive mound of dog turds he had ever seen. It lay fresh and firmly formed, enthroned in noisome splendour on a criss-cross of bedraggled rushes. Truly awed at first, he remained transfixed, his eyes bugging. Then slowly, amid a chorus of snickers gently gathering, he straightened up, walked round and round the monumental pile, inspecting it. He backed away from it; he came close again, forcing his eyes to cross. He shook his head reverently. Then he looked around.

'Nicholas!' he bawled. 'Nicholas, come here at once!'

The innkeeper barged forward, a great beef of a man, his face shiny with sweat, oozing obsequiousness as his part of the game, receptive through long practice to Abel's next move, whatever it would be.

'Nicholas,' said Abel, pointing toward the spot with eyes averted, nostrils quivering with indignation. 'Tell me truly, Nicholas. Don't you think your mice are getting a trifle out of hand?'

The innkeeper's laughter boomed out louder than the rest. He roared with such gusto and extravagance of gesture that he lost his balance, and after teetering above it for an exquisitely desperate instant, plunked his foot squarely into the mess.

The sight of his expression loosed true bedlam. Hilarity billowed out, swirled up among the low-hanging rafters. When the laughter had abated a little, a pockmarked merchant, swathed in furs, called out from his place in a corner, 'Ale, innkeeper. The best ale for that fellow.'

'If you mean me, sir, I'm grateful,' Abel said with dignity. 'But the surgeon has told me that to drink good ale alone is to invite quinsy.'

'I'll drink with you,' retorted the merchant.

'Gladly, sir. But I've heard it said the devil walks through empty cups. Would you have all these jolly topers bedevilled by our surfeit?'

The merchant hesitated, then, making a wry face, spread out his hands in grudging agreement. A wayfaring minstrel picked up his zither and began to play. The normal rhythm of conversation reasserted itself. Abel saw his young friend Roger atte Well signalling from across the room that he wanted to speak to him. He nodded and squeezed between a peddler and Old Elias Roper, who was fat and miserly and on his way to becoming tipsy. Before he could reach Roger's side, Abel's cup of ale came. The first sip afforded him so much pleasure that he seized the minstrel's zither and strummed inexpertly but with abandon as he sang:

> Back and side, go bare, go bare,
> Both hand and foot go cold.
> But belly, God send thee good ale enough,
> Whether it be new or old.

Old Elias (why old, Abel suddenly wondered, seeing as he's no more than five years my senior, then remembering once more with a pang the saddening passage of time which had caused his earlier tears) applauded louder than the rest, drained his cup, then clapped his free hand down on the shoulder of the peddler.

'How?' he asked loudly. 'How are they going to avoid paying the poll tax?'

The rest of the talk in the room dropped away, leaving Elias's question stark as a winter-stripped tree.

The peddler, a wisp of a man with a long, prominent jaw and thin lips, glanced round him, savouring the silence, a flicker of appreciation for it animating his otherwise cold eyes. 'This morning I was in Gravesend,' he said. 'In the past two months I have travelled over most of Kent. Everywhere it was the same.'

Abel, who always found political talk boring, yawned and belched at the same time, was rewarded with a single explosive guffaw from the minstrel. The peddler regarded both of them briefly with an expression of annoyance, then let his face go impassive again.

31

'Everywhere it was the same,' he repeated. His lips barely moved as he spoke. 'Villages, towns, even some of the walled cities are falsifying their returns.'

'How's that, how's that?' asked Old Elias. His speech was becoming somewhat slurred, and he seemed to be having trouble keeping his head from listing to one side. 'I don't understand what . . . what . . .' He gave up and beckoned Nicholas to refill his cup.

'If there are two hundred souls in a town,' the peddler explained patiently, 'the town elders report only a hundred. When the bailiffs come, they collect only on the basis of the report.'

'Ah,' said Elias. He showed surprisingly white and regular teeth in a beatific grin. 'Ah,' he said again, and emptied half the contents of the cup Nicholas brought him.

'It's too much trouble by far,' said Abel. 'I say we should pay what they ask and put a curse on the coin. I know at least one shilling in this village would give them a pox after where it's been hidden.'

He looked around, disappointed because no one laughed, or even smiled.

Robert Ogden, who lived with his wife and six children in the hut next to Abel's, spat on the floor. 'It's well enough for you to talk of paying,' he grumbled. 'Some of us are saving all we can lay hands on to buy our freedom. If they keep taking it from us . . .' He spat again.

'And,' interjected Old Elias unctuously, 'some of us have families to support.'

At last there was laughter. Everyone knew how the marriage bargain Elias had made rankled in him. When he had taken a wife over twenty years younger than himself, he had also been compelled to house her mother and sister.

The laughter was short-lived. Little stubble-fires of talk broke out, went smouldering round the room. One man said, 'But if they find us out . . .' and another replied harshly, 'They won't,' even as he looked apprehensively over his shoulder at the door.

The separate groups began to draw closer together; their words became inaudible to Abel. He saw Elias rubbing his big belly excitedly and clutching with his free hand at the peddler's sleeve.

A hand was touching his own arm. He turned to find Roger at his side, looking at him with the bland innocence that only wide-open blue eyes in a very young face can produce.

'God be thanked,' said Abel. 'I was beginning to wonder if

everyone had gone mad with all this talk of money and no money.'

Roger ignored the remark and inclined his head curtly toward Old Elias. 'He's getting drunk.'

Abel turned and regarded their fat neighbour with an appraising eye. 'As drunk as Father Noah,' he agreed.

'Then,' said Roger, his eyes widening even more and growing very bright, 'it will soon be time.'

'It's always time,' Abel said sagely. But when Roger smiled a slow, secretive smile he asked, a little anxiously, 'Time for what?'

'If he keeps on like this, in an hour his bed will be shaking with me and Barbara in it, and you'll be raising her sister's skirts.'

Abel looked at him speculatively. 'You're an evil lad,' he said. 'Who put such terrible ideas in your head?'

'Come after dark, she said. Come after dark and bring a friend. When he's gone drunk and Mother's abed. That's what she said.'

'I shall always wonder,' Abel said, 'which one of you passion filled with such a tender gift for rhyme.'

'You'll come with me?'

'Evil churl . . . your love's sister . . .'

'Peg's a pretty piece . . .'

'So the poetry's yours. Listen. I remember that girl's christening. Not eighteen years ago it was, maybe less. I was present in the church.'

'You'll not be present at her deflowering. That I can warrant.'

'It's a wicked, wicked world,' said Abel, sighing piously.

'The door will be unbarred. She's left it that way each night for two weeks, just on the chance . . .'

'And the cuckold here, sprouting horns long enough to curl round Nicholas's rafters.'

There was a sudden commotion as Elias rose to his feet, overturning his cup, and stood swaying, glaring balefully at the peddler. 'You'll not speak to me that way!' he roared. 'I've been reeve of this village six years running, and hayward more times than I can count. By the bailiff's beard, you'll not . . .'

'I spoke no word against you,' said the peddler, also getting up.

Elias hiccupped. 'You said . . .' He did not wait to finish, but lunged at the peddler, who stepped nimbly out of reach. Elias, breathing heavily through his nose, was collecting himself for another charge when Nicholas came forward, a black cloak in his beefy hands, and threw it over Elias's head. Two or three of the others helped the innkeeper hustle the shrouded figure up and down the room. After several turns his muffled cries began to subside. Nicholas held up his hand, and they all stopped walking.

'Now, Elias, have you taken enough exercise for the night?'

There was no reply. Nicholas removed the cloak.

Elias looked all round the room, slowly and meditatively. 'By the bailiff's beard,' he said. He smiled, beautifully, showing most of his fine white teeth. Then his eyes rolled up into his head and he toppled majestically onto the rush-covered floor, just missing a sleeping dog. Nicholas kicked the dog out of the way, picked up Elias, carried him across the room and deposited him tenderly against the wall.

Conversation resumed as if nothing had happened.

Roger took Abel's arm, saying, 'Come, let's hurry!'

'Softly, lad. You'll scratch your itch soon enough.' But he followed Roger toward the door.

The wind was still gusting along the street. They breathed deeply to clear their lungs of smoke. A spray of rain flung itself past them, rattled against the shutters of the inn. Roger skipped ahead of him, ran back to pull at Abel, skipped away again into the darkness.

There was no fear of the watch in their village. The single watchman was half-blind and crippled with gout. On the rare occasions when a hue and cry was raised, he was the last to hear it.

Abel, plodding along with his head down, stepped across a puddle and collided with Roger.

'What now, boy? Forgotten something?'

'Abel . . .' He could not see the young man's face, but he was sure it must look terribly earnest. 'Abel, is it true that demons haunt any man who commits adultery?'

Abel threw back his head and laughed soundlessly, but he kept his voice grave and deliberate. 'I've heard it said.'

'It's a thing to think about,' Roger said indecisively. 'But then, God knows when he'll be this drunk again.'

'And God knows all your talk has finally succeeded in heating up my breeches. Let's not delay. . . .'

He walloped Roger between the shoulders and they loped along the street, heedless now of mudholes, not slowing down till the front of Elias's house rose before them, its white wall gleaming palely.

Like them, Elias was a serf, but he had managed to achieve some prosperity over the years as a result of shrewd dealing in cattle. His house was the only building made of stone in the entire village, and also the only one to contain two stories.

34

Roger hesitated before the door. 'Barbara sleeps upstairs,' he said in a low voice. 'Peg has her bed off the common room.'

'Truly interesting. And will you stay here prattling the whole night?'

He was more excited than he wanted to admit even to himself. Roger had not lied when he called Peg a pretty piece. Abel had not taken much notice of her before, having regarded her as a child, which she obviously no longer was. Now he remembered her soft-rising bosom, her slimness, the twinkle of her high-laced shoes as she tripped along the village street. How could he have been blind to anything so delightful?

Roger leaned against the door and breathed a small explosive sound of triumph as it gave beneath the pressure. They stepped into the common room. The blackness when Roger closed the door behind them was complete.

He heard Roger's footsteps groping their way across the room and began his own uncertain essay inward from the door. He stopped as a latch clicked somewhere deep in the house. The wind howled suddenly, and the trees outside clattered their branches. He heard the stairs creak.

Or thought he did. For a hand grasped his wrist at the same time as Roger's lovelorn voice cried out softly, 'Barbara, sweet . . .'

'The demon,' he replied in a sepulchral whisper. 'The demon come to collect his tariff of blood from an adulterer.'

Roger released his wrist with a frightened little yelp and shrank away. Abel tried to smother his laughter, but it leaked through his fingers. Roger swore, then said plaintively, 'I can't find the stairs.'

He must have though, for in a moment Abel heard them creak under stealthy ascending steps. And in an amazingly short time there was another sound, regular and rhythmic. One part of Roger's prediction had come to pass. The bed was shaking, right enough. She must have been waiting, all cocked and ready, the saucy bitch.

He stood in the darkness, wishing he had thought to ask exactly where the sister's room was. Well, he'd find it soon enough. He moved cautiously across the floor, but not cautiously enough to avoid barking his shin on a bench.

Over his own exclamation of pain he heard the quick rustle of rushes. 'Peg,' he called out quietly. 'I'm here, love. Here I am.'

There was no reply. The rustling seemed to flit about, now coming from one corner, now another. And the wind rose again,

35

soughing through the trees, moaning about the eaves. He began to feel uneasy. The devil assumed a thousand forms, he had heard a priest say, and no sinner was safe from him once the protective hand of God had departed. The rustling came closer. He wished now he could find his way to the door. He'd be away from this demon whoever and whatever it was, and he'd never again even think of . . .

His mounting terror receded suddenly in mid-resolution. He had caught a faint and provocative whiff of lavender. Lavender, by the Almighty, and the sweet musky scent of a woman's body. If this was the devil he'd take his chances and die happy. 'Here, love,' he ventured again. 'I'm here.'

The lavender enveloped him. He could hear her breathing now. Tentatively, he reached out, and his fingers encountered the living warmth of human flesh. Bald-ass naked, by Alfred the wench was naked. A moment and her breath was hot in his ear.

He wasted no more time. If this was the way she wanted it, he was the man to oblige her. They rolled down together on the common-room floor. He gave himself up to the lucky bliss of it all. . . .

The smack he received on his bare bottom was far from gentle. Indignantly, and with considerable difficulty, he managed to manœuvre himself into a sitting position.

He stared and rubbed his eyes. Standing before him holding a candle, demurely clad in nightdress, was Peg, her expression stony with contempt. He shook his head, trying to clear it, not daring to look down beside him. Perhaps the devil. . . .

'I'll raise a hue and cry against you,' the girl was saying. 'Raping my mother. . . .'

'Your mother!'

'Raping her! Have you no shame? No pity for an old lady's grey hair?'

'Child, child,' murmured a voice from the floor, 'go back to bed and stop meddling. What can you do? A rape is a rape. . . .'

Suddenly Peg's face crinkled, and her lips let go a cascade of tinkling laughter.

'I'll have you,' Abel said angrily. 'I'll turn that laugh to something else. . . .'

'Another night,' she said merrily.

'Go back to bed, child,' said the mother.

And there was Roger, clumping down the stairs, Barbara floating along behind him pleased as a fat cat, the two of them taking in the situation and also beginning to howl with laughter.

36

'Another night,' Peg said again, only smiling now, bending over to kiss him on the top of the head.

'Child, child,' said the mother.

Above the sound of the wind they heard another, the unmistakable voice of Elias raised in off-key song, coming closer.

Never, even when the Black Prince's army was entering battle, had he witnessed such swift and well-co-ordinated activity as that which followed. Barbara stripped off her outer robe, gave it to her mother, then raced upstairs to fetch another for herself. The old lady draped the robe about her and stood quietly near the door, a portrait of propriety. Peg herded Roger and Abel from the common room, pointed to a window opening out of the back of the house.

'There,' she said, brushed her lips against Abel's, and was gone.

They heard the front door burst open and the voices of the men who had brought Old Elias home mingling with his sporadic attempts at song.

'Alack and alas,' Abel could hear Barbara saying, her voice dripping with solicitude. 'My poor husband.'

'Alack and alas,' echoed Peg.

'The poor, poor man,' said the mother. 'Just put him here.'

Abel and Roger eased through the window and into the night.

The sky was completely clear, except for a tiny cloud drifting away to the east. Over everything rode the moon, a serene crescent.

Perhaps, thought Abel, spring is truly in the offing, after all.

MARCH

I

SALISBURY's squire saw it before he did.

They were riding through the bottom land fringing the ascent to the town of St. Albans. Since dawn they had been pushing the horses hard to assure themselves of reaching the Abbey before dark. Now that the town was less than an hour away, with night a good two hours off, Salisbury had slowed his pace to let his lather-flecked mount have a breather. Thomas had followed suit, reluctantly; the lad enjoyed hard riding; it gave him the feeling, Salisbury sensed, of performing a mission of great urgency and importance.

The matter that had sent them north from London three days before was neither urgent nor important: some stupid snarl involving one of the King's estates near Cambridge, which Richard had insisted only Salisbury could unravel. It could have waited a month, or even six. Knowing he would have to be back in London for the Council meeting at the end of the week, Salisbury had tried to postpone the trip or call it off altogether. But the boy could be wilful, and when he was, it was useless to attempt to thwart him. Richard's smooth oval face would wrinkle like that of a baby with colic; his eyes would absorb slyness and seem to draw closer together; he would stick out his pointed chin and speak in that thin reedy voice.

An unattractive picture, always, on the face of it, and yet there was something oddly appealing about the boy's fits of pique. Perhaps because in the flaring nostrils, the cold fury with its latent fire, there was ever a hint of his mother. Perhaps.

So he had ridden off to the north: fatigued, disgruntled, feeling put upon. The trip had done nothing to improve his disposition: England in the month of March often left much to be desired.

The day's dampness and his own sweat had already made him uncomfortable, and with the approach of evening the moisture in the air was becoming palpable, gathering in a clammy mist close

39

above the treetops. He was sure he was working up to a chill. He wished he were home; even Elizabeth's nervous and excessive concern would be more bearable than a night in one of the draughty Abbey apartments. But in an unthinking moment he had promised the Abbot that he would stop over on his way back to London, and these days it was not wise for an adviser of the King to offend de la Mare. Or anyone else of means or power.

His horse was ambling along, and he let his head loll forward, soothed to half-sleep by the monotonous squeak of his saddle accompanying the regular slap-thud of the sword against his thigh.

It was then that his squire saw it.

'Mother of God,' exclaimed Thomas softly.

The lad was given to oaths but not as a rule to awe, so Salisbury looked up sharply. A hundred paces ahead of them, half-obscured by mist, barring the way to a ford across a shallow stream, was a knight, one of the tallest men Salisbury had ever seen. He sat his horse arrayed in full battle armour. His visor was down, his lance levelled directly at them.

It was an impressive sight, rendered more so by the hollow voice which issued out of the visored helmet. 'Hold, Devereau!' it said, ringing clear above the sound of the stream and their horses' hooves.

Salisbury and Thomas exchanged a puzzled glance. Then Salisbury shrugged, and they continued to ride forward.

The voice said again, on a slight rising note, 'Hold, Devereau,' and the lance came up a few inches, targeting in on the centre of Salisbury's chest. He reached wearily for his sword, half-drew it, then returned it slowly to its scabbard. They were close enough now for him to see that the knight's helmet was rusty, his breastplate spotted with greenish mould, and his lance shaft badly split.

They stopped two horse-lengths away from the apparition. Thomas grew tired of waiting for his master to speak and said with ill-concealed surliness, 'You're squatting in our path, knight.'

(Would the lad never learn even the rudiments of diplomacy, Salisbury wondered, even after all his attempts to teach him?)

'You shall not pass,' said the knight. He thrust the lance toward Salisbury. 'It is not every afternoon I am so fortunate as to meet a Devereau. Prepare to meet your Maker, Devereau.'

'There must be some error, good knight,' said Salisbury, pleased to note that despite his incipient chill his voice was at its most mellifluous and authoritative. 'My name is not Devereau.'

The knight lifted a battered gauntlet. His visor rasped open, revealing two troubled and confused eyes, grey skin pouched beneath them. 'Not Devereau?' he asked uncertainly. 'Not Sir John Devereau?'

'You are addressing,' said Thomas in his most imperious accents, 'His Lordship William Montagu, Earl of Salisbury.'

The knight shook his head, muttering, 'Not Devereau. . . .' Salisbury saw Thomas about to administer a scathing retort, signed him to be still. 'Perhaps,' said the knight in a bereft voice, 'if I could accompany you a small part of your way . . . perhaps if I describe the Devereaus, you could tell me if you have seen . . .' He stopped, looking confused.

Salisbury smothered a moment's irritation and said gently, 'Come along.' They wheeled their horses, plunged through the ford and climbed a hill just beginning to show a trace of spring greenery.

The knight rode beside Salisbury. Suddenly, without preamble, he was saying, 'You see, the Devereaus killed the father of the lady I have the good fortune to love. I have vowed by all the rules of chivalry to seek every one of their family out and kill them. Then, and only then, may I wed the lady I have the good fortune to love. Ten years now I have sought them, and ten years longer shall I seek if it becomes necessary.'

Salisbury, schooled to maintain the impassive countenance of the diplomat, still could not repress a shudder, compounded of disbelief and a slight sickish feeling. The knight, however, was oblivious of it and went on chattily, 'You, sir. I am sure you have loved a lady.'

'Yes,' replied Salisbury, his voice more bitter than he intended, 'I have loved a lady.'

'A sweet and pure lady, of course.'

That, reflected Salisbury, is a somewhat moot point.

The knight drew up his horse abruptly and stared open-mouthed at Salisbury, who reined in and returned his gaze. 'My lord,' the man stammered, 'my lord . . . he said . . . I have only now realized . . . he said you were an earl.'

Behind them Thomas snickered. Salisbury flashed his squire a reproachful scowl.

'But, my lord, I have been false to the first rule of chivalry. I am ashamed, my lord, not to have dismounted and made proper obeisance.'

'It's not necessary . . .'

'How can you even think such a thing, my lord? It is expressly prescribed in the code of chivalry. What if the King and his lovely Queen should hear of such a breach of honour and deportment?'

Despite his sympathy for the other's manifest madness, Salisbury was beginning to find the exchange tiresome. 'The King is a young boy,' he said shortly.

The knight made a soft and deprecatory movement with his gauntleted hand. 'Edward a young boy, my lord? Surely you are joking. Edward, the protector of England, the champion of knighthood, the upholder of the grace and glory of all chivalry . . .'

Salisbury stirred uneasily. 'Edward has been dead four years.'

He thought the knight was going to topple from his horse. The part of his face visible through the open visor was ashen. He swayed and held himself upright with difficulty. 'Dead?' he moaned. 'Our beloved Edward dead? It is not possible . . . not possible . . .'

Often when Salisbury was agitated his speech became pompous. He knew it and there was nothing he could do about it. He said now, 'My good man, I can only assure you . . .'

'Dead,' said the knight. 'Four years dead. What will become of England now? The realm will disintegrate and there will be no man to . . . What will become of England?'

The question was much too close to one Salisbury had asked himself four years ago, and had not been able to answer since. But he would not hear it from a madman. 'England,' he began, speaking with a deliberate, patronizing languor, 'will always be sound and strong, just as it has been and . . .'

The knight did not hear him. He had turned and was galloping full speed in the direction from which they had come. Drifting back to them came a cry of grief so terrible and so anguished that Salisbury shivered.

'Mother of God,' said Thomas softly, after a moment.

Salisbury made no comment. As they rode on, he felt an almost irresistible urge to flee, as fast and as far as he could. But night was approaching, and ahead of them lay St. Albans.

They had just passed through the town gate and were pressing their horses up the hill toward the Abbey. Salisbury could see the Norman tower climbing into the twilight sky. Something, he was never sure what, drew his gaze back to the street and he stared, unbelieving.

She was there. Just as she looked when he had first seen her, years before. The flawless skin touched with the faint flush it took on when she was pleased, the flaring nostrils, the tiny white teeth nibbling at the lower lip, the grey eyes contemplating him with that mixture of caprice and promise.

The illusion spent itself after an instant. She was only a peasant girl dressed in rough shapeless wool, moving clumsy-gaited along the uneven surface of the street.

42

But suddenly the girl's expression went sulky, and the likeness to Joan returned so sharply, so poignantly, that it was all he could do to refrain from calling out to her.

Thomas asked anxiously, 'Are you quite well, my lord?'

'Quite well.'

'You're pale. If . . .'

'I'm quite well.'

But of course he was not. And as long as he and Joan both lived, it was doubtful whether he would be.

The subtlety arrived at the table, a huge pastry veined with jelly and calcimined with an appalling thickness of coloured sugar, carried aloft by two pages. But, Salisbury reflected a little grimly, the conversation of the Abbot contained no similarity to the name of the dessert.

Long before the second course was served, a bream poached in ale and flavoured with saffron and almond milk, he had understood the reason for his host's insistence on his visiting St. Albans.

De la Mare was florid-faced, with a snub nose and a natural tonsure formed by a gleaming bald spot: a corrupt replica of one of the gargoyles Salisbury remembered seeing on the cathedral in Paris. The Abbot fancied himself a skilled diplomat, and he was shrewd enough after a fashion, but in spite of his carefully nurtured London accent he was really only a heavy-handed provincial bumpkin.

'My dear Lord Salisbury,' he had said while the *joutes* were being served, 'you and I are aware, as perhaps few are, of the pressing need our dear young King has for friends about him, particularly at this critical moment in the history of our dear kingdom.'

Salisbury had dipped his spoon into the mixture before him and stirred it about. The years in France had played havoc with his digestion; since then he could only abide the simplest foods. This was one he could not stomach: borage, violet, mallow, parsley, cabbage and a few other indigestibles, boiled in ox-marrow broth and served with a slab of fat bacon. 'My lord Abbot,' he had said, making his voice deep and melodious (it was one of his two vanities, the other being his physical grace, and he displayed them often), 'the King is indeed fortunate to have such a staunch friend and supporter as yourself, and I can assure you that His Majesty is most grateful for your oft-demonstrated loyalty.'

He had felt unutterably weary, waiting for the next ploy, knowing what it would be. The Abbot had not come out with it at once, though. Instead he had cast a vacuous smile the length of the great

43

hall, then laughed aloud at some pitiful sally of the jester, who was becoming hopelessly entangled in a conceit he was attempting. Salisbury had looked down from the high table to where Thomas was preening before a couple of young monks, regaling them, he was sure, with some grossly exaggerated tale of the royal court.

To fill in the conversational break which he knew the Abbot was counting on to make him uncomfortable, he had extravagantly admired the *nef* set between him and de la Mare. He praised the quality of the jewels in the model of the ship containing spices which would have robbed him of sleep for nights, had he been forced to sample them. The roast peacock had been carried in, resplendent, having been returned to its own skin and feathers after cooking.

'There are many in the realm,' the Abbot had said then, 'motivated by a desire to see our dear country preserve its stability, who feel, quite wrongly let me assure you, that perhaps the presence on the throne of a more mature person would supply that stability. For myself, I can say that my devotion to our dear young King is complete and will continue forever. . . .' He had stopped and smiled again.

Mother of God, Salisbury had thought, in conscious parody of Thomas, why can none of us ever be honest? Why will he not say right out that he'll throw his support to the King's uncle, John of Gaunt, and even stir up trouble presently quiescent if we don't promise him something he wants? Then he had become annoyed with himself for even thinking such naïve thoughts and had continued to play, as he had done for years, the excruciating game of double tongue, triple heart and quadruple soul which went under the name of diplomacy.

He had learned quickly, skilfully, what the Abbot's price was for continued loyalty. It was not high: a piece of ground some two hundred acres in size adjoining land already church-owned. He had assured the Abbot that he would urge His Majesty strongly, and so forth and so forth, through all the prescribed ornate forms of consent to extortion.

All this before the arrival of the subtlety.

The Abbot, cramming his mouth full of pastry now, could not conceal his joy over a victory he considered so easily won. If he only knew, thought Salisbury, how much more of this bereft and bankrupt kingdom he could have merely for the asking.

The musicians entered, a kettle drummer and violist, and their playing drove the jester to frenzy. He must have been aware of how unenthusiastically his attempts at wit had been received by all but the Abbot. Now he began chasing the fool around the room, finally trapped the luckless and vacant-eyed idiot between

44

two tables and sent him sprawling among the rushes. The fool got up squealing and promptly pulled a dog's tail, sending the beast shrieking across the hall, the whole cacophony mingling and inexplicably harmonizing with the efforts of the musicians.

The Abbot roared with laughter, nearly choking over a mouthful of subtlety, turned to Salisbury, who smiled dutifully.

A pair of hooded monks pulled down the crossed beams which held the candles and replaced those which were guttering.

De la Mare, his mirth evaporating abruptly, rose and led the monks in the flowing, chanted Latin of the grace following meals.

When he sat down again, he resumed his smile as if it were a cloak he had put off for a moment.

The *hippocras* came, the wine laced with honey and delicate spices which marked the end of a banquet.

Salisbury was growing sleepy. Without thinking of the import of his words, he said to de la Mare, 'My lord Abbot must find it difficult, as everyone does these days, to retain enough help to work his lands.'

De la Mare turned to him with an expression so brutal and hostile that he recoiled. Realizing his mistake at once, Salisbury said smoothly, 'I was inquiring, of course, only in my lord Abbot's interest. Since it is likely he will soon have additional land as a gift from the King, perhaps His Majesty could also arrange for the binding over of extra peasants. . . .'

Somewhat mollified, but still scowling, the Abbot said, 'We have enough peasants.'

'Then my lord Abbot is fortunate. Since the Black Death, as my lord Abbot knows well, there has been an extreme shortage of labour. Many of the serfs dead, freemen charging exorbitant — and, of course, illegal — wages, peasants leaving the land. . . .'

The Abbot's lips curled back from his teeth. His eyes slitted. 'If any of my peasants dare to run away from the land,' he said in a grating voice, 'they will have good cause to regret it. We have already recaptured and hanged the few who have tried. If I thought that a serf was even considering such folly, he would swing from a gibbet till his flesh rotted from the bones.'

Salisbury said, 'Everyone knows that my lord Abbot's lands are a model of efficient administration. If others in England would follow his example . . .'

'My dear Lord Salisbury,' said de la Mare, suddenly all smiles again, 'my example is not so difficult to follow. But if it is not followed, there may be difficulties.' He chuckled over his little play on words.

Salisbury realized anew how dangerous it was to believe you knew a man simply because you could anticipate him on one level.

The Abbot raised his cup. 'May the Almighty God, full of grace and loving-kindness, protect and watch over our dear young King Richard.'

Amen and amen and amen, thought Salisbury, sipping the warm sweet wine.

And later in his apartment, just when he was sure he would finally fall asleep, the impulse to flee, which he had experienced and conquered earlier in the day, returned. But there was the knowledge that no matter how far he fled, it would never be far enough.

2

'YOU can tell right enough,' Walworth said, 'what a woman will be like, just by looking at her, before you ever take her between the covers.'

Agnes asked, 'And how can you do that, Lord Mayor?'

He hesitated, knowing from her expression she was leading him on, but unable to resist expounding his favourite subject. 'Every woman,' he said, 'tells you the instant you see her, in a thousand ways, without speaking a word. You know by the shape of her lips, the texture of her hair, the curve of her neck. . . .'

'If a woman is gap-toothed,' said Agnes, 'it's a sure sign she'll be ever so passionate.'

'You're ignorant and superstitious,' said Walworth, nettled.

Agnes laughed, a little tipsily. She poured wine for both of them, dribbling some from the jug onto the table top. 'I'm also an evil old woman,' she said. 'Evil as Lucifer. If I wasn't, the Lord Mayor wouldn't have put me in charge of all his brothels, now would you, Lord Mayor?'

He watched her drink, reflecting on the terrible trick fortune had played her: to ravage her face so that all her life's debauchery was traced there, and yet to leave her figure sleek and slim as a young girl's.

'I once heard a man say what you said about women.'

He caught the mocking note in her voice and stiffened, but he knew he would not stop her.

'He was an ox of a man, this fellow,' she went on. 'About the size of you. And when he'd come in here he'd talk talk talk, about

46

the shows he'd put on and how he could foretell a woman's way in bed down to the last roll and gasp just by looking at her. Only he'd never go with anybody. Then one night . . .' She began to whoop with laughter. 'One night . . . three of my girls . . . tickling him and down on the rushes before he . . . stripped him bald-ass bare . . . great ox of a man and no . . . you could scarcely see . . . tiny tiny tiny . . . Oh my. . . .' She brought her laughter gradually under control. 'Oh my. . . .'

She leaned toward him, still laughing a little, and rested a small, beautifully formed hand on his arm. He struck it away so violently that she rolled off the bench onto the floor. She picked herself up, quite unperturbed, and came back to her seat. She paid about as much heed to his angers as he did to her taunting. They understood each other perfectly.

'Get the accounts for me,' he said.

She ignored his command and studied him, her wrecked features twitching. 'At least, Lord Mayor, my girls and I know you're not like that ox of a man who used to come in here. If the people of London ever want witness to the prowess of their mayor . . .'

'Never mind that. Give me the accounts. I have to leave.'

Agnes clapped her hands loudly, twice. They were in her private room in the largest of his four houses on the south side of the river. All of them were disguised as stews where Londoners could come to have steambaths. It was forever amusing Agnes when some merchant from the north country, not knowing his way about the City, would knock on the door and actually ask if he could have a bath. It was her boast that every one of them quickly forgot what he had come for.

A girl wearing the prostitute's striped hood appeared, switching the bushy foxtail which was sewn to the seat of her gown, smiling at Walworth. Agnes sent her for the papers she needed, then said to the Lord Mayor, 'Will you not stay the night?'

'I have business in the morning, and a meeting of the King's Council at noon.'

'And I have two new girls. One from Flanders. Not yet sixteen, and already she knows more tricks than I knew when I was twice her age.'

'You knew every trick the serpent taught Eve while you were still in your cradle. What about the other girl?'

'From Coventry. She was caught four times there and had to leave. You know what happens. The pillory for the first two offences. Hair shorn for the third. And the fourth . . .' She raised lovely tapering fingers to touch her wrinkled mouth. 'The fourth

47

time they cut off her upper lip. But do you know . . .' She laughed sharply. 'She has more men ask for her than for any two of my girls.'

'*My* girls,' he said.

Agnes shrugged. 'Your girls, of course, Lord Mayor. You'll not stay?'

He shook his head. When the accounts came, he tucked them into his pouch, stood up and buckled on his sword.

'You're a fine-looking man, Lord Mayor.'

He knew she was flattering him, but he could not help being pleased. He took pride in his dress: in the richness of his wide-sleeved over-tunics, the colours of his long-toed shoes; he expected attention to be paid them.

'If my face was still like my body, I'd take you away from that prissy wench who lives in your house.'

'Never mind about her,' he said warningly.

'I might in any case. My bed is warm of nights.'

'I told you . . .'

'Yes,' she said. Then, after a moment, 'Do you want to hear what I've heard?'

'About Margaret?'

'A pox on Margaret. Rumours are what I've heard.'

'Rumours are cheap in a whorehouse.'

'Cheaper than the whores, God be thanked. They're saying there'll be trouble.'

'What kind of trouble?'

'There's talk of a rising.'

He looked at her incredulously. 'A rising? In my city?' He took a threatening step toward her. 'Don't you ever say a thing like that about my city.'

Her anger came to meet his. She opened her mouth soundlessly. For an instant he was reminded of the fury of his peregrine, striking with her beak at the gauntlet. Then she laughed, a warm rich release of gaiety. 'Good night, Lord Mayor.'

At the door he turned. She was drinking from the jug. The red wine overflowed, ran along the creases of her jowls and dropped onto the fine curve of her bosom.

Agnes's man stood in the torchlight beside Walworth's horse, droplets of mist in his beard, concern in his eyes.

He stammered slightly. 'The horse, Lord Mayor . . .'

'What's the matter with him?'

'Lame.'

48

'He wasn't lame earlier when I rode across.'

The servant backed away. 'When I came out just now, I saw
. . . lame.'

And in truth the stallion was pawing the ground with his right
forehoof, in tentative and confused fashion. He whinnied complainingly when Walworth touched the leg.

'A stone perhaps, Lord Mayor.' The man was babbling. 'A pot-
hole, some stiffness only now come up. We have no horse to give
you, Lord Mayor. But I can light you home if you wish.'

The man's stammer vexed Walworth. 'Since when,' he asked
irritably, 'must I be lighted home in my own city?' He turned
and strode away, calling back toward the torchlight, 'I'll send my
man to look after the horse in the morning.'

At once the fog steaming up from Lambeth Marsh enveloped him.
He walked quickly, undismayed at not being able to see the path.
Southwark was no less familiar to him than the lanes of London.
To his left he could feel the presence of the river, rank and turbid,
and beyond it the City, shrouded in darkness but still so vital and
alive he could almost hear its powerful heartbeat.

The curtain of mist parted briefly, revealing the gloomy shadow
of St. Mary Overy, turreted and aloof amid an encroaching cluster
of houses. In the distance he could just make out the twin flares
flanking the Bridge Gate.

He sniffed the air. A March smell. Dead winter borne in slow
procession toward the shrine of virgin spring. Lovekyn had always
said March was his favourite London month. A time of hope, he
had called it, distaste for his own sentimentality showing in his wise
old eyes. It was Lovekyn who had taught him to love London as a
woman should be loved: with lust, with heartsblood, with a tenderness born of honest knowledge. Lovekyn my mentor: friend, enemy,
father.

The guards at the Bridge Gate challenged him, then flocked
round him on recognition, tussling with one another to reach his
side and receive the blessing he would bestow on them: the amiable
clout alongside the head, the jest spoken out of the corner of the
mouth. Walworth tarried while one of the men ran ahead to call
for the drawbridge to be lowered. While he waited, he glanced
up above the arch at the heads of criminals impaled on pikes, dimly
illumined, a crop of jesters leering their appreciation of a last ironic
joke.

He crossed the bridge with the confident gait of a proprietor; listening with a critical ear to the gurgling of the river against the pilings,
as if he would chide it for a false note; waving back to the last guard

and the dying rumble of the drawbridge ascending before he let himself be swallowed up by darkness.

Now he was again in his city.

He heard a sharp cry, followed by a hollow tumbling bumping, followed by raucous laughter; knew it for roisterers rolling an ale keg filled with stones down the steep pitch of Drinkwater Wharf. He smiled to himself, thinking: the watch will have you, lads, and there'll be sour mouths and throbbing heads in The Bailey come the morrow when the fine is drawn from your pouches.

He paused at the intersection of Bridge and Thames Streets, the crossroads of his life. To the right lay his past: the fish-stinking hovel near Billingsgate from which Lovekyn had plucked him; the house Lovekyn had occupied before he became Lord Mayor, and which Walworth had taken over. He turned resolutely left, for this was the present: Lovekyn's grand dwelling of his latter years, which at his death had also gone to Walworth.

He stopped again, listening, at the foot of Oyster Hill, sure suddenly he was being followed. He was not alarmed; little frightened him on these streets. Nonetheless he drew his sword and waited. If footpads were after him, it would be better for him to be able to hear them than the other way round. There was a sly sibilance of footsteps, the muffled fragment of a word, silence.

He was right then. The innocent were not abroad; the drunken would have staggered by, glorying in clamour; there remained only the sinister, bent on violence.

Another rush of steps, rodent-quick in the] darkness. There were two of them by the sound. Walworth executed a stealthy manœuvre designed to place his back against the nearest house-wall. Above him he could sense solid masonry, one of the many solars spanning the street in low-flung overhang.

Two of them: this he confirmed now; approaching first together, then one of them veering off to work toward him from another angle. He remained stock-still, alert, his mouth filled with the acrid taste he had known before street brawls in his youth.

They were on him then, the only warning being a single sharp gasp from one of them. And that intake of breath gave him added strength, for it contained fear, and he felt more indignant than afraid.

He slashed twice into empty air before he felt the knife go home in his right arm. Shifting the sword to his other hand he swung again and knew the exhilaration of contact. There was a stifled cry, and a disembodied voice shrilling a jumble of words ending with his own name called in agony and hatred.

He was locked in close struggle with the other now, the two of them grunting and shuffling, vying for solid foothold in the slimy street. Shutters above them rattled open, candles shed a faltering light, and someone began to raise the hue and cry. Walworth had a glimpse of a pair of glittering eyes beneath a hood, a mouth suddenly twisted with effort, and his opponent was gone.

The other lay on the ground, face down, blood running from a wound in his side, feet pounding the earth in impotent tattoo resembling a child in a tantrum. Above them in the solar a voice was still bleating for the watch.

Walworth raised his sword and began to hack with frantic savagery at the prostrate form of his erstwhile assailant. After the first few blows he lost all sense of time and place.

When the watchmen pulled him back he looked at them blankly, until reason returned, blossomed over-bright and clear. He stared down at his bloody handiwork, at the sheen reflecting darkly off the blade of his sword.

The watch officer was young. He swallowed hard and said, 'You're hurt, Lord Mayor.'

'No,' said Walworth.

'Your arm.' Then, when there was no reply, 'Were they thieves?'

'Thieves,' said Walworth.

His brain was racing far ahead of his dull tongue. If they were thieves, how had they known his name? He remembered, with an odd pang of discomfort, Agnes's words about a rising, rejected them peremptorily. Members of a rival guild they must have been, plotting mischief against his own fishmongers' guild. So it had been for years, so it would be. But even this he was reluctant to accept.

'Thieves,' he repeated.

'We'll light you home, Lord Mayor.'

'No,' said Walworth, and when the officer opened his mouth to remonstrate, 'No,' he said again, more loudly. And, 'Thieves,' he stated for the third time, firmly, before he walked away, still carrying his bloody sword unsheathed.

Margaret dressed his wound. Her hair shimmered in the candle-light, pale gold.

She did not ask questions; she seldom did, as he seldom volunteered information. Even her frown of concentration as she wound the cloth about his arm was impersonal, accepting, dutiful.

He took comfort, as he often did, from the sight of the jagged scar on the back of her right hand, the relic of a childhood encounter with an iron-shod cartwheel. That must have caused her pain; that must have made her cry out.

She raised her head. The gemlike beauty of her features was breathtaking. He had always found it so, but he had never been able to tell her. Their marriage, arranged ten years before, had been a well-kept pact of mutual benefit. He provided; she was useful and ornamental.

'I've brought the accounts from Southwark,' he said.

'I'll begin work on them in the morning.' She was silent a moment, then said, 'The woman cheats you.'

'No more than another would.'

Margaret moved her shoulders in an almost imperceptible shrug and went on with the bandaging. When she had finished he went to the table and poured himself a cup of wine.

The first sip had a strange effect on him. It was as if all the wine he had ever drunk had suddenly flown to his head, encountering there the bloody chaos of this evening.

And it was Lovekyn's death which haunted him now as it had not in the thirteen years since he had buried the old man. The futile phrases attendant on death: if only I had had a chance to say or do such-and-such before he died, if only. The bitter-sweet nostalgia of familiar locales shared: Lovekyn in this very room, Lovekyn laughing in a tavern, Lovekyn dying. And the heaviest word known to man, the watchword of death: never.

He felt the tears start to his eyes and in chagrin turned, as if by doing so he could escape them.

And faced Margaret, whose lips parted, closed again as her eyes watched him, expressionless.

Slow fury was growing in him, fury with himself for having permitted the hint of tears, with her for having seen them.

He seized a candle from the table, marched with angry steps out of the house, across the narrow courtyard to the hawk shed.

The helper was asleep. Walworth set the candle down, breathed in air thick with the smell of ordure and rotten meat.

A merlin fluttered its wings; a tiercel cried out; the helper awoke, muttering. Only the peregrine falcon slept on, head tucked down on her spotted breast.

'Lord Mayor,' said the helper.

'Get out,' said Walworth.

The man rose, fearful, stupid with sleep, and crept out of the shed.

Then the falcon awoke, lifted her head and stared at Walworth, her eyes hard and unwavering. For a long time they looked at each other. She tightened her talons on the perch.

Walworth walked slowly toward the bird, his hand extended. She waited, watchful.

52

Swiftly, with a wild piercing cry, she struck at him, the deadly hooked beak flashing. He snatched his hand away just in time, but she did not appear to notice. Again and again she struck, shrilling her cry of rage.

And Walworth's own voice, raised in exultancy, was one with the falcon's.

3

As SALISBURY eased his horse onto the causeway across the Tower moat, he was still remembering the pair of altercations he had witnessed a few moments before: one involving some beggars, the other a couple of fishmongers. Both had taken place at Billingsgate, in a backwash of the teeming fish market. A blind beggar had gouged the eye out of another in a struggle over a farthing, and was set on in turn by a horde of his comrades, who baited him as if he were a bear. The fishmongers were quarrelling over an eel, still alive, tugging at it until the creature was torn in two, leaving each man in possession of a grisly segment.

Unimportant, ordinary episodes in themselves, the kind one saw a hundred times a day on the streets of London. But since his stay at St. Albans the night before, he had found himself endowing even the smallest events with a portentous symbolism.

He would have thought more about this, but as he came off the causeway at the Byward Tower, he was saluted by one of the mercenaries, a leathery soldier who had fought the rearguard action with him at Poitiers.

'You're well, my lord?'

'Quite well. You seem fit.'

It was their customary greeting, unvarying as the exchange that followed.

'Fine fighting weather, my lord. Just like the day we had at Poitiers.'

This no matter what the day was like: cloudless clear, murky with showers, miserable with sleet.

'Just like the day we had at Poitiers.'

He rode on. His conversation with the mercenary was indicative of how unchanging and wearisome his life had become. It seemed that he was able to predict and anticipate everything that would happen to him.

Except that now a new thread was weaving itself into the fabric of his life: the presentiment of doom which was plaguing him, sharp and enigmatic, growing more intense day by day.

He had felt a premonition before Poitiers. But that was of danger, not of doom. Then it was hardly surprising. The French had outnumbered them by more than three to one. And he, with all his aversion to violence, had fought with a viciousness he still could not understand, a thirst for blood which had led his men, in the flush of victory, to call him The Lion.

There would never again be a Poitiers for him. Of this he was sure.

Never for him, and perhaps never for England.

He entered the garden through the gate at the Wakefield Tower, pulled his horse up sharply as he emerged onto the green.

Though the day was damp, she was strolling in the company of her ladies. He watched her for a moment. For more than twenty years of his life the sight of her had always sent the blood rushing to his head; now he knew it would only upset his digestion for the balance of the day.

He dismounted, hailed a groom and turned the horse over to him. She looked round at the sound of his voice and waited, smiling, for him to approach her. The ladies retreated a little distance with languid tact, petals falling from a fading rose.

'My lady Joan. . . .'

'How pleasant to see my Lord Salisbury.'

The breathless quality which had always made her simplest utterance so appealing was distressing now. She could scarcely talk without gasping. She was stout, very nearly obese, and her sallow lifeless skin hinted at some gnawing internal illness.

'My lord has enjoyed a successful journey to the north?'

'Successful, madam. I am in hopes the King will be pleased with the settlement I have effected.'

'My son is always well pleased with all of my lord Salisbury's efforts on his behalf.'

How circumspect they were, how easily their tongues slid round the inanities of court language. How far away the moments when he had held her close, a vibrant lissome girl, in gardens jewelled with dew. How little in their sterile dialogue to suggest that he and she had once been the centre of a scandal whose echoes had reverberated all the way to the papal palace at Avignon.

Time had long since dried up the juices of gossip, which had once been savoured in half the halls of England, laved over conversation like a succulent sauce.

They had called her the Fair Maid of Kent then, half in snideness, half in tribute. Salisbury had been only one in a succession of lovers: among others Thomas Holland, then he, then Holland again. And a scant two months after Holland's death there had been her precipitous marriage to the Black Prince. But it had been Salisbury alone who bore the official disapproval of His Holiness in Avignon.

He would have liked to believe that because of this he had been the most important person in her life. But like any good diplomat he was a realist, and he understood that even during the two years of their marriage she was no stranger to other men. And each time he had taken her in his arms he had known he was scarring himself with her forever.

He often wished, of course, that he could hate her, for in hatred there would be healing. He had hoped that when she began to age, and to shed her beauty, the chains which shackled him would also drop away.

But she had only to smile, or touch his arm, and these hopes would vanish. There is never any escape from a love which contains no illusion.

She was smiling now, touching his arm, but her eyes were troubled. 'Please,' she was saying, 'you will protect my son. Tell me you will.'

He was suddenly wary, wondering if there were something she had heard, or sensed. . . . 'Surely, madam, you have no cause to believe he is in danger?'

She shook her head, vaguely.

'Please,' she said again.

The Bishop of London was alone in the council chamber, already seated at the long table, when Salisbury entered. He rose and murmured a greeting, his restless hand smoothing the rich cloth of his habit.

William Courtenay had been young when he assumed his powerful office. He was still under forty. On his well-fleshed face with its deep chin-dimple he wore the perpetual expression of a man in confident control of his destiny.

'I am informed,' he said, coming close to Salisbury, 'that the purpose of our meeting today is to discover why our peasant population has been suddenly decreased by half.'

'They've falsified returns,' Salisbury said shortly, 'to evade poll-tax payment,' and cursed himself, noting the Bishop's smile. Courtenay was one of the few men he knew who could rob him of his diplomat's façade and make him commit the sin of obviousness.

55

He was usually cautious in the Bishop's presence, but it always took him a few moments to adjust to the man's shrewd and waspish manner.

Courtenay reached out and fingered a button on Salisbury's doublet. 'I am sure,' he said, 'that our Chancellor, the capable Archbishop, will discharge this problem with his customary efficiency.'

Salisbury moved ever so slightly away from the Bishop, and Courtenay withdrew his hand smoothly, elegantly.

'The Chancellor,' said Salisbury, 'will have our full support in this as in all matters, will he not, Your Grace?'

Courtenay smiled. 'Of course, of course,' he murmured, then added, 'But there are times when I am forced to believe that our Chancellor lacks . . . only by reason of his preoccupation with Godly matters, naturally . . . a full knowledge of practical affairs. In times like these, that can be dangerous. I might even say perilous.'

'Perilous?' asked Salisbury quickly.

'Catastrophe is in the air,' said Courtenay, his voice more silky than ever. 'Catastrophe. . . .'

Salisbury opened his mouth to reply, but stopped as Walworth entered the chamber, exuding his usual earthy vitality and dressed as always, Salisbury observed, in finery a little too well-cut. They bowed to each other, neither troubling to conceal his feelings of mutual dislike.

Salisbury noticed that Walworth was carrying his right arm stiffly. He nodded toward it. 'An injury, Lord Mayor?'

'Nothing,' said Walworth, turning his back.

Salisbury ignored Courtenay's raised eyebrows and sauntered to one of the tiny windows. The council chamber was located in the White Tower, encapsulated so firmly in the thick stone walls of the keep that even in midsummer the atmosphere was dank. Salisbury felt the chill, which had abated after he left St. Albans, settling back into his bones.

Walworth and Courtenay had begun a quiet conversation as the Chancellor sidled into the room, moved with his self-effacing crablike gait to a place at the right of the King's chair.

He was followed by Sir Robert Hales, Prior of the Order of St. John of Jerusalem and Treasurer of the realm. Hales was laughing his high, whinnying chuckle at nothing in particular and glancing about him, flabby jowls flapping, shiny black eyes gleaming. 'Well well,' he said. Talk stopped, and everyone looked at him expectantly; he possessed a peculiar power for being able to gain instant attention whenever he spoke. But most often, when he obtained it, he had nothing to say. 'Well well,' he repeated, looking round and chortling.

The Chancellor cleared his throat and said, 'The King.' They all turned to the door, where Richard stood, gorgeously arrayed in scarlet and white, the colour effect somewhat marred by brown gravy stains down the front of his over-tunic. 'Good afternoon, my uncles,' he said, frowning as he marched toward his chair. 'I can see I was not expected so soon.'

His advisers, who had bowed dutifully as soon as they saw him, exchanged uncomfortable glances and said nothing. 'My uncles?' said Richard sharply.

Truly now, thought Salisbury, does the boy expect us to stand like statues, facing the door, waiting with drawn breath for him to appear? But he heard himself saying, 'Your presence, sire, was not only expected, it was eagerly awaited.' He averted his eyes from Courtenay's amused glance.

Richard mumbled something unintelligible and sat down, immediately lost himself in a painstaking inspection of his nails.

The Chancellor again cleared his throat. Simon Sudbury had wanted to be neither Chancellor nor Archbishop of Canterbury. Both positions had been thrust upon him, and he always appeared to be blinking in the glare of some indecent exposure. He rubbed his bald pate, plucked uncertainly at his thin fringe of greying hair and said, 'I believe we intended to discuss the poll tax.' He looked around quickly. 'It was the poll tax, was it not?'

'The poll tax, my lord Chancellor,' said Courtenay suavely, exploring the dimple in his chin with his forefinger. 'The poll tax indeed.'

Hales whinnied emptily and Walworth growled, 'They lied to us. The scum lied and they should be punished.'

'Whom shall we punish, Lord Mayor?' asked Salisbury gently. 'Every peasant in England?'

'If necessary.'

'That might prove somewhat difficult.'

'Not if those who apply the punishment are men. True, Hales?'

Hales looked up slowly. His eyes narrowed; he moved his lips in a cruel, sleepy smile. 'True,' he said.

Sudbury coughed apologetically and blinked around the room. 'I cannot understand,' he said. 'I know the peasants. I've talked to many of them. They're simple people, all of them, good but simple. Why, I asked one of them in a village . . . tell me, my good man, I said, do you know the Faith? Yes, he replied.' Sudbury's voice was sure now, his eyes bright; relating anecdotes was one of his

57

chief pleasures. 'Do you know the Father, the Son and the Holy Ghost, I asked. The father and the son I know well, he answered, for I tend their sheep. But I don't know that third fellow: there's none of his name in the village.' He looked around, his glowing smile waning when no one responded. 'Good people,' he said. 'Good simple people, worthy of God's love. . . .' He hesitated. 'And ours.'

Richard, continuing to look at his nails, said in his thin voice, 'It would seem to me, my uncles, that the fault in this case does not lie with the peasants. If those entrusted with the task of collecting the tax have proved themselves incapable of doing so, we should dismiss them and appoint new collectors. Only this time we should place my Treasurer Hales in direct control. . . .' He looked up, glanced around, then resumed the study of his nails.

Salisbury laughed inwardly at Courtenay's small start of surprise. He thought: your fatal flaw, my friend, is that for all your shrewdness, you will forever underestimate others.

'His Majesty is right,' said Walworth. 'If we . . .'

'Indeed,' said Courtenay, recovering rapidly and taking over. 'As always, the King has demonstrated his insight and astuteness. We shall appoint a new commission at once.'

Hales was instructed by the Council to use whatever measures were required, no matter how stringent: first, to obtain a true enumeration of those subject to the tax, then to collect it.

Sudbury adjourned the meeting with visible relief. After the King had departed, he sat down again in his chair with such a forlorn expression that Salisbury, about to follow the others out, reconsidered and went to the Chancellor's side. The old man looked up and smiled bleakly. 'They're good people, my lord Salisbury,' he said. 'Good simple people. I cannot understand this show of resistance. The tax is not a great deal, you know. Only a shilling from each person.'

'A shilling,' said Salisbury, 'can be a great deal if you do not have it.'

'They have it,' said a voice behind them.

Salisbury turned to see Courtenay approaching. 'Even if they do not have it,' he continued, 'they must find it. If we allow them to evade payment now, there will be trouble.'

'There will be trouble no matter what,' said Salisbury.

'Yes,' said Courtenay, after a pause. He placed his hand on Salisbury's shoulder. 'I trust I am not intruding.'

'Oh no, my son,' Sudbury replied.

Salisbury could not restrain himself from squirming under the pressure of Courtenay's hand. The Bishop stepped gracefully away and said, 'There is a matter I should like to bring to my lord Chancellor's attention.' He hesitated. 'Of course, it is not exactly within my authority . . .'

Sudbury rubbed his pate. 'Anything you wish to discuss with me is your right, my son,' he said warmly.

Courtenay smiled, a token deference quickly spent, and said, 'Then I shall come at once to the point. There is a man who calls himself a priest, John Ball by name.'

'I know him.'

'So do many others in Southern England, my lord Chancellor. He is a dangerous man.'

Salisbury, who had been again on the point of leaving, stopped to listen.

'Dangerous?' Sudbury asked lightly. 'I hardly think so. A lunatic, perhaps, but harmless.'

'Did you yourself not excommunicate and imprison him, my lord?'

'Of course. He was behaving badly, and I had to teach him a lesson. I forbade him ever to preach again and kept him in prison a year, two years, I'm not certain exactly how long. . . .'

'Seventeen months, my lord.'

'Oh yes, seventeen months. But that was several years ago. Surely . . .'

'Surely my lord knows he is preaching again?' said Courtenay, with all the swift smooth savagery of a great cat. 'Surely my lord is aware that he is exhorting people not to pay the poll tax, that he is urging them on to acts of open resistance?'

Sudbury seemed all at once to become very small in his chair. 'The people are good,' he said falteringly. 'They're simple. They will not listen. . . .' He looked up at Courtenay. 'They do not listen, do they, my son?'

'They listen,' replied the Bishop. 'My informants . . .' He broke off. 'They listen,' he said again, and his tone was very cold.

The old man spread out his hands. He looked from Courtenay to Salisbury. 'What shall I do then?'

Courtenay's manner changed, became at once deferential. 'I trust my lord will not consider me presumptuous. But if he would allow me to have Ball dealt with . . .'

Alarm sprang into Sudbury's eyes. 'You'll not . . .'

'No, my lord. He will not be made a martyr.'

'Then you have my permission.'

He rose even as he was speaking, slipped from the room softly as a wraith.

Courtenay said to Salisbury, 'You spoke of trouble.'

'No, Your Grace. You did.'

'But you agreed that there would be trouble.'

'It was only a feeling.'

'A man of your acumen, my lord Salisbury, does not have feelings.' He smiled fleetingly. 'There was no double meaning intended. Have you heard something which might...' He stopped, waiting.

'No,' said Salisbury. 'Have you?'

Courtenay looked at him for a long moment. Then, 'No,' he said. 'Nothing at all.'

APRIL

I

ABEL heard the sound of horses' hooves approaching from the distance, but for a time he thought it was part of his dream. He had spent the day on manor land, ploughing the lord's acres as part of his boon-work. At dusk he had brought the bullock back to the lord's barn, and was preparing to go home when the chief cook called out to him from the courtyard. The kitchen wood supply was low, said the cook, and three of his helpers were ill with fever. There was bread to be baked for tomorrow; he would let Abel know when he had cut enough wood.

So he had gone on working through the gentle twilight, and it was nearly dark when he was finally permitted to return to the village. He did not mind; the cook had allowed him, in accordance with custom, as much wood for himself as he could stack onto one outstretched arm. He had managed to take up a liberal amount, balancing it precisely from long practice. But he had had to be careful. If he dropped so much as one piece of wood while walking the first twenty paces, he would not only have to forfeit all he had gathered, but pay a small fine as well; this was also the custom. He had walked away, feeling the cook's eyes on him, and just after the twentieth step a single stick had fallen to the ground. He had picked it up triumphantly, settled the load comfortably in both arms, shouted a gay epithet back into the darkness gathering round the manor house, and begun to stride along the path toward the village.

It had taken him over an hour to make the trip, but he had not minded that, either. True, he was always somewhat uneasy when he was abroad alone after nightfall, but what man was not? And the spring air was cool and caressing, soft as a woman's touch against the sweaty warmth of his face.

He had thought then of Peg, had planned while he was walking to go to Old Elias's house as soon as he reached the village, and to tap on her window in the signal they had arranged. He remembered the way it was the last time: she deliciously fuddled with sleep as he carried her across the brook and into the shadows of Broad Field, where they had remained half the night.

But this evening, when he had at last reached the door of his hut, he had been too weary even to walk the extra distance to Elias's house, much less cope with the girl. He had stood in his doorway, watching the disappearance of the last tender shoot of daylight in the sky toward Gravesend, and had tried to remember a proverb he once knew about an old fox and a young vixen. But even this required too much effort. Another night, he had thought, another night, smiling at the memory the phrase conjured up.

He had entered the hut and, dropping the load of wood onto the mud floor, had fumbled about in the stale darkness for the chunk of bread and the bit of cheese he had put away against supper. He had chewed on them meditatively, listening to the rustle of mice in the heart of the thatch, thinking it would soon be time for them to desert him for the fields and the more profitable forage they would find there.

Then he had fallen onto his pallet and dreamed, as he often did, with mingled fear and elation, of marching with the Black Prince's army in Spain, and the thunder of the knights' horses across the parched Castilian plain.

So it was not until he heard the shouts in the street that he awoke fully and realized that this time the sound of horses had been only part dream.

He got up and went out of the door, conscious of the fact that other villagers were also coming out of their huts, showing signs of having dressed hastily, mumbling to one another while they peered around for the cause of the disturbance.

They had not far to look. The bailiff and four henchmen from the manor, all carrying torches, were standing by their horses, grouped near the doorway of Robert, Abel's neighbour. Robert's face, pale at all times, was now the colour of pure whey. He was opening and closing his mouth like a fish, but no sound was coming from his lips. Behind him stood his wife. She had always had some trouble with her nose, and when she became excited, she snorted like a rooting sow. In the background flitted five of their six children, goblins and geese to the torchlight's folly.

Robert's wife loosed a particularly loud snort. One of the henchmen farted and the other three laughed. The bailiff swore softly at them, then turned back to the hut. 'Robert Ogden,' he said, 'show me your eldest daughter.'

The villagers murmured for a moment among themselves, then

62

were still. Robert's lips stopped moving; his face appeared even more bloodless. The bailiff surveyed him with contempt. 'Search for her,' he said to the henchmen.

'She's not here,' the wife cried out.

The henchmen paid no attention to her. They swaggered to the doorway, and instead of filing in through the door, they kicked out enough of the mud wall so they could enter four abreast. Pallets and pieces of earthen crockery soon began flying through the hole into the street, as though they were being vomited from a great jagged maw. Robert's lips began again to make their inarticulate fish-movements. His wife wept, the sow-like sounds still rising from her throat.

Abel felt someone come up beside him. He turned to see Roger atte Well, blond head bare, eyes wide. 'I told him not to let her go,' he said.

'Could he have stopped her?' asked Abel.

The henchmen came out of the house. One of them handed the bailiff a threshing flail. The bailiff said quietly to Robert, 'I know your daughter ran away. Not only has she left her own village, but she has married a serf from another manor. The lord is highly displeased, but because you have always been a peaceable man and a good worker, he has ordered me to be lenient with you. The marriage fine will be three shillings, and the price for her running away will be another five.'

Robert found his voice and said, 'I have no money.'

'Come now, Robert,' said the bailiff, his tone growing more and more gentle. 'Eight shillings. Of course, if you prefer to face the manor court, it will likely come to ten. Perhaps more.'

'I have no money,' repeated Robert. His lips moved without sound for another moment. Then he managed to say, 'When they came back a second time . . . when they made us pay the bigger poll tax . . .' He was gazing at the bailiff's face, seemingly fascinated by what he saw there. 'They took it all, they took it all . . .' he finished tonelessly.

His wife sobbed and snorted at the same time. The henchmen laughed. 'Burn his barn,' said the bailiff, and the henchmen stopped laughing. Two of them went with their torches toward the field at the back of the house.

Abel began to breathe more quickly. He knew the tiny shed contained the seed with which Robert planned to start this year's crop. He studied his feet, scuffing them noiselessly in the dirt.

Old Elias was pushing his way through the villagers. He reached the bailiff's side and said, 'As reeve of the village . . .' The bailiff did not even glance at him. He placed one hand against Elias's massive paunch and gave him a hard shove. Elias staggered back a few steps as flames shot up from Robert's barn. Robert cried out, and Elias started forward again. This time the bailiff turned to look at him. When Elias got close enough, the bailiff kicked him in the groin. Elias dropped to the ground, writhing. A moan went up from the villagers, but no one stirred.

The bailiff turned suddenly, took hold of the loose garment Robert's wife was wearing, ripped it off her. The woman stood naked, weeping and snorting, while the bailiff struck her eight times with the threshing flail.

At the sound of the third blow, Roger atte Well took a step toward the bailiff. Abel seized him and said in his ear, 'Fool, be still. They'll go soon and leave us in peace.'

They did go. But first the bailiff said to Robert, in a voice so quiet Abel could hardly hear him, 'You have three other daughters. When they are old enough to let a man between their legs, make certain they marry a serf from this manor. That way you'll have only the marriage fine to pay, and no one will lose sleep as we all have tonight.' He paused briefly, then added, 'You still owe the lord eight shillings. He'll not make it difficult for you. After harvest will be time enough.'

The sound of the cantering horses receded; one after another the five torches disappeared over the hill in the direction of the manor house. But the flames rising from the barn in the field gave off enough light so that the villagers could still see each other.

Elias struggled to his feet and limped toward his house. The people made way for him silently. Barbara, Peg and their mother were standing in front of the door. Just as he reached them, Elias spun half-around, showed his white teeth in a flashing grimace and collapsed. The three women took hold of him and dragged him into the house.

Without speaking, the rest of the villagers began to return to their huts. Abel walked over to where Robert's wife still stood naked and snorting before the gaping ruin of their doorway. He picked up the torn chemise and tried to put it round her, but he could not get it to stay on. One of the children burst into tears, wept for a few moments and was just as abruptly quiet.

'Tomorrow,' Abel said to Robert, 'tomorrow we'll fix the wall.'

Robert nodded solemnly, and kept on nodding. He did not seem to be able to stop.

64

H_E would have passed the church by, had his attention not been attracted by the priest.

Ball hesitated, looking at him. He was expected in Chartham by noon, little more than an hour from now; he had come from Ashford that morning and still had over three miles to walk.

A fine drizzle was falling, warm and gentle, the kind of rain one had to expect in Kent at this time of year.

The church itself was in bad repair. A corner of the building was crumbling, and the heavy oak door sagged drunkenly from one hinge.

There was nothing unusual about a dilapidated church; he had seen many. But the sight of a cleric seated cross-legged in the churchyard mud was a good deal less common. The priest's habit was stretched tight across his back, clung soddenly to his bowed shoulders. He did not look up or even stir as Ball left the highroad and splashed toward him across the soggy green. Two wild pigs nosing about among the tombstones stopped their investigations, surveyed him with hostility and retreated to the shelter of a spreading oak.

Ball squatted beside the priest and touched his arm. The man's head came up slowly and Ball withdrew his hand, shocked. He had seldom seen so much despair in the eyes of any creature.

'Come into the church, out of the rain,' Ball said quietly.

The priest opened his mouth, and from it, like a devil's tocsin, poured forth peal after peal of miserable, raucous laughter. The wild pigs squealed, and lumbered away into the maze of tombstones.

Ball took the priest's head between his hands. 'Stop now,' he said. The laughter subsided, and the priest stared at him again.

'The roof has fallen in,' he said suddenly, in a perfectly rational voice. 'All winter, no matter where I moved the font, I could not keep it from being filled with rainwater. This morning the roof fell into the chancel.'

'Can the people not . . .'

'People? No one has come here in close on a year. People . . .'

'The rector . . .'

'In London, they say. They say he has grown wealthy singing paid masses at St. Paul's. They say he is the chaplain for a rich guild.'

'Who says?'

'They say . . .' answered the priest indecisively.

'Why do you not go away?'

Anguish crept back into the man's eyes. 'Go away?' A drop of moisture formed at the end of his nose, fattened, fell to the ground. 'I paid all I owned to the rector for this benefice.' He repeated the word, 'Benefice . . .' in a lingering, despairing drawl.

'There are other parishes. You could . . .'

'No!' Then, pathetically, in the quavery tones of a child or a very old man, 'I do not know the Latin. I cannot even read.' He was whispering now. 'But always, always I dreamed of being a priest. I memorized . . . the rector said the living . . .' He looked around distractedly. 'They say it will be different soon. They say everything will be different in England. That's what they say, but I don't believe them.'

'Who says?' asked Ball again, feeling that he was reopening the portals of a futile, circular catechism.

'They say . . .'

The priest struggled to get up off the ground; Ball assisted him. 'I must go and clear the chancel. I must have it ready for Vespers . . . perhaps if I hurry . . .'

Ball made an involuntary movement to accompany him. The priest shook his head. 'No,' he said. 'It is for me alone.'

As he entered the church, the pigs advanced cautiously and took up a stand just outside the sagging door.

There was the usual struggle to begin.

It did not seem to matter that the people gathered around him had grown attentive and expectant from the instant they spied him. This had been happening for almost a month now, ever since the new poll-tax collectors had begun their circuits through the shires.

It did not even seem to matter that the rain had ceased, leaving the market square at Chartham bathed in sunlight almost too warm for April.

There was still the heart-stopping moment before he could speak: the quick fearful survey of the square, probing outer edges blurred to his eyes for the glint of armour, the hand resting on the sword of authority. There was still the agony of choosing the first words, of urging them out of his constricted throat.

66

He took one last look at the grim, intent faces surrounding him, then said, 'In the beginning we were all created equal. . . .'

There was something disquieting in the immediate nods of approval, the restless stir of voices resembling nothing so much as a concerted growl.

He went on, 'Now we are in servitude. Serfs they call us and use us only for their gain. It is the tyranny of perverse men which has set our servitude upon us, in spite of God's law. . . .'

Then he heard the words of the couplet, much sooner than he had thought they would come, flung across the square by a woman's clear voice:

> *When Adam delved and Eve span,*
> *Who was then the gentleman?*

To be taken up at once by the whole assemblage, chanted over and over again, gathering volume, radiating anger, until after a few moments he was unable to distinguish the words. Here and there some clenched fists were raised. Soon the square was rife with upraised arms, a rich stand of rage.

And Ball became fearful again, not for himself now, but for what he had done. This crop was his; he had planted and nurtured it. He had sown the wind; he had laboured to reap a whirlwind. But now that he felt the first hot blast of its breath, he only wanted to run from it. In all the arduous years of cultivation, he had never truly reckoned with the nature of the harvest.

Ball lifted both hands high above his head, fingers outspread. The silence was immediate and complete. He felt himself breathing more easily. As long as they would listen to him, there would be no danger. They would seek success by peaceful means, and in peace they would put their victory to work.

'Be patient, my friends, only be patient. Soon the signal will be given, and we shall go to face the King.'

'When, John Ball? When shall we march?'

There was an edge of irritation in the voice, a frustration bordering on hysteria. He could feel it spreading through the crowd. Once more he raised his hands; once more they fell silent.

'Soon,' he said, surprised at how firm and calm his voice was, 'very soon. If we are to win, we must be patient. Otherwise we shall lose before we begin.'

They were not satisfied with his words, this he knew. But they accepted them, and for the time being that was all that was necessary.

They dispersed quickly, trooping out of the square back to tools laid down in the fields at the word that he had arrived.

Since it was not a market day, there were only a few left in the square when the man approached him.

'I have an important matter to discuss with you, John Ball.'

He squinted at the speaker, not recognizing him, but wondering at the sweet-voiced irony, the preciseness of his enunciation, which did not fit in with the shabby garb, the stubbled, dust-caked face.

'I am a priest,' said the man, 'like yourself.'

'Are you ashamed to wear the habit of the Church?'

The man glanced around. His eyes contained the same irony as his voice. 'It's better if I remain unknown here.' He drew in his breath. 'I come from the Abbot.'

'There are many abbots.'

'Do you know any other than the one who was once your Master of Novices?'

'You've come from York?' There was a betraying eagerness in Ball's tone, and he perceived that the other had noticed it.

'From London,' he said smilingly. 'The Abbot is visiting in London now.' Again he breathed in, a peculiar inverse sigh. 'He wishes to see you.'

'How did the Abbot know where I could be found?'

The man raised one shoulder in a hint of a shrug. 'That is not so difficult nowadays.' He came closer to Ball. 'He has grown old these past few years. He requests your presence as a special favour.'

'The Abbot begs a favour from me?' He tried, but he could not keep the wistful overtones out of his voice.

'Will you meet with him?'

Ball smiled. 'No, my friend. I'm older than I once was, and, I think, wiser. I've learned, when anyone wishes to see me urgently enough to send for me .'

'The Abbot loves you as if you were his own younger brother.' He was speaking earnestly now, the irony put from him. 'He said you would know this.'

'I thought I knew it once. But that was many years ago.'

'The meeting place could be of your own choosing.'

'Then let the Abbot come here and meet me among my people.'

The emissary inhaled so sharply that his breath whistled between his teeth. 'Don't jest.'

'Very well. I shall meet the Abbot in a church.'

'A church?'

'Does it surprise you that a priest would wish to see his old teacher in a house of God?'

68

'Which also happens to afford sanctuary.' The irony returned, delicate but pointed. 'He said you might be suspicious, and clever as well. You have nothing to fear.'

'All the same, you may tell the Abbot if he wishes to meet me, it will be in a church.' His glance travelled across the square to St. Mary's. 'Here in Chartham.'

The man turned slowly to regard the heavy, buttressed flint walls. 'At midnight, then. Three nights from now.' He swung round to face Ball again. 'He will be happy to see you. It will be difficult for you to believe how much he has aged.'

'That,' replied Ball gently, 'is something we shall have in common.'

3

THE indentation in the hills which held the village of Chartham was shaped like a lamp-bowl, the church tower now catching rays of moonlight its wick, glowing and giving off a soft lustre. Ball came down the hillside and approached the church cautiously. He was not sure the Abbot would be there. Nor was he certain that if the Abbot was there he would be alone.

Excitement tugged at his caution. He had not seen his teacher for fifteen years, and then only briefly, under circumstances which had bred bitterness, but that had long since burned away, leaving the love he had once borne the man clean and pure.

The village street was deserted, the churchyard so still that his footsteps, grown stealthy as he neared the church, sounded thunderous in his ears. He slipped into an alcove between two buttresses, leaned against the cold stone, listening, then made his way along the wall, around the transept to the porch.

The door gave easily, with none of the squeaking he had expected, and the very noiselessness made him tremble for the first time since he had descended into the village. He waited, recovering his resolution, then made his way up the brightly moonlit nave toward the solitary figure standing in the chancel.

'John?'

The voice was the same, deep and firm; at least the years had not altered that.

'John Ball?'

'My lord Abbot . . .'

Ball could see him clearly at last. As the emissary had promised, his appearance had indeed changed. The bold, darkly handsome features had become blurred, submerged in a fretwork of wrinkles. But somewhere in the play of eyes and mouth the force and warmth of the man still lived.

He embraced Ball, who experienced an emotion so strong and so confusing he could not deal with it, and therefore retreated into the anger surrounding their last meeting.

He asked coldly, 'What is it you want from me, my lord Abbot?'

'You speak to me as though I were a stranger.'

He could feel the pain behind the older man's words, and deliberately delved further into his anger to find strength to face it. 'You know when our friendship ended,' he said. 'Fifteen years ago, the first time they cast me into prison, I was weak and foolish enough to appeal to you for help.'

'I came to you at once.'

Ball laughed, a dry, brittle sound in the silence. 'You came, my lord Abbot. All the way from York, and I was grateful. But you did nothing. One word from you to the Archbishop would have freed me. You would not speak that word.'

'I had no choice.'

And suddenly Ball understood now what he should have known years before. Success was a necessity for the Abbot, as strong drink was for others. He had climbed, steadily and painstakingly, from lowly service to a major pinnacle of the Church. The acquiescence, the sycophancy, the espousal of tenets he neither believed in nor cared for were all part of the price. Some men had a choice as to whether they would pay or not; this man had none. He would climb still higher. As long as he lived he would have success by his side, both as companion and captor.

Ball's anger left him and he said simply, 'You had no choice.' He was grateful when the Abbot did not go on to explain or justify. They had known much of each other once; the bond had not altogether vanished. Ball asked, 'Did your man not come with you from London?'

'I sent him on to Canterbury. I shall go there myself when we have finished speaking.'

He knew he should maintain his formal tone, that he should ask again why the Abbot wished to see him and be done with whatever it was; he was sure the other expected him to do so. Instead he said, almost to himself, 'Do you remember how we used to get round the rule about not eating meat?'

'We still manage to get round it.'

'In the same way?'

70

'We've not found anything more effective.'

Ball chuckled. 'We were so pious and straight-faced, knowing the rule didn't apply to the sick, pretending we were ill and being sent to the infirmary and staying there just long enough to gobble as much meat as we could lay hands on. . . .'

'And Brother Alan never able to understand how there could be such a spate of illness and rapid recovery. . . .'

They began to laugh, unrestrainedly, slapping each other's shoulders, their hilarity echoing loudly up and down the long nave.

After a time the Abbot wiped his eyes on the sleeve of his cassock. Ball noticed that the habit was of velvet, liberally embroidered with what he was certain were threads of gold.

'I'm glad you came, John.'

'Thirty years,' said Ball. 'Thirty years since we've talked together.'

'You're forgetting the other time between . . .' His voice was sorrowing. 'The time you wanted help and I failed you.'

'We've already agreed you had no choice.'

'I suppose that's why I've come to look like such a wrinkled ancient, as if I'd spent a lifetime in debauchery. Perhaps I have. There's more than one kind of depravity.'

'You judge yourself too harshly.'

'Not harshly enough.' He grasped Ball's hands. 'Let me look at you, John. Looking at you gives me some indulgent illusion of youth regained, as if . . .' He smiled. 'Do you remember the night you woke me before dawn, the night you told me . . .'

There was no need for him to be more explicit. Ball recalled it well. He had been assigned that evening to minister in the hospitium, the chamber where wayfarers were fed and received shelter. The room, a jumble of tables and pallets, had been hot and crowded: ugglers and minstrels trading crude stories of the road; merchants crouching watchfully over their pouches, fearful of being robbed by the jugglers or each other. There was also a trio of knights who made a living by travelling from castle to castle and performing in tourneys. They were stripped to their waists and were showing off their scars (it was here Sir Oswald had at me well, and here, look, Sir Geoffrey nearly did me in, I'll not be matched against him for a time, I can say for certain, he cares only for blood).

And in the hospitium the restlessness, which had been festering in him for months, seemed to be drawing itself to a head. He had heard the conversations around him clearly: the minstrel telling of a miller who had tried to cheat him, a merchant decrying the shocking price of wool, one of the knights laughing now about a certain lady who was known to bestow her favours only on tournament victors, and then only when they had been wounded, so that this at times posed something of a dilemma. And while the talk had seemed to have no bearing on what he was thinking, it had inflamed his restlessness and robbed him of sleep. Finally, he had no longer been able to endure the turmoil of mind and heart. He had left the hospitium, with its litany of multi-toned snoring and little cries denoting troubled dreams, and had sought the cell of the Abbot, then the Prior.

'I understood why you had come,' the Abbot was saying. 'I had seen it growing in you, but I could say nothing until you spoke to me. When you did, I knew I could only advise you to leave the Abbey. Perhaps if I had been a stronger person I might have joined you.'

'Perhaps,' said Ball, staring up at the dark outlines of the wooden vaulting under the roof, 'if I had been stronger, I might have stayed.' Beside him he could feel the Abbot stir suddenly, about to speak. Ball brought his head down quickly. 'No . . . that's not true.'

'I understood then,' said the Abbot after a pause, 'why it was necessary for you to go. Some, at a certain stage of their lives, need to be in closer touch with people, to preach God's word among more than one may reach within cloistered walls. But I do not understand, and I have thought about it often, more often than you can imagine, why you finally took the course you did. Once you preached God's love, the value of morality, the essence of the bond between man and his Creator. Now your message contains only the gall and wormwood of the Scriptures, a doctrine of discontent.'

Ball said stiffly, 'You said earlier, and I agreed: you have no choice. Nor have I. While injustice exists, I must speak out against it.'

'Injustice?' The Abbot's tone was gently incredulous. 'If what you are advocating ever came to be, it would perpetrate the most monstrous injustice ever witnessed under heaven's eye.' He looked directly at Ball. 'The way we live has gone on for a long time, John.'

'Does that excuse it?'

'If it were wrong, God would change it.'

'Do you truly believe that?'

'I do.'

Ball sighed, and plucked at a fold of his cassock.

72

'You're weary, John.'

'Yes.'

'And lonely. Only God can know how truly lonely you must have been these many years. I feel the loneliness from you.' He turned a little away. 'I shall say what I must, and I'll be brief about it. I respect you too much to do otherwise. The post of Sub-prior of the Abbey is vacant. I would be gratified if you would accept it.'

'Why?'

'Do you think I have forgotten your capabilities? I would not make the offer if I didn't believe in them still.'

'After all these years . . .'

'There is also my affection for you.'

The Abbot was silent, studying Ball. He took a step forward, spoke in an urgent whisper. 'You are in danger, John. Great danger. If you continue with what you are doing, they will hunt you down. I know what I say is true. It is no problem for them to find you any time they wish. They will hunt you down and kill you. John . . .'

He broke off, struggling with emotion, and Ball felt the throbbing of his heart quicken. It was as if the Abbot's words had torn aside a curtain, revealing a tableau of death so horrible that he could not bear to contemplate it. Yet it was there, his own death, before him in all the stark simplicity of violence.

After a moment the Abbot went on, 'John, come with me. Neither of us is young any longer, but you have more years ahead than I. Use them, John. Use them in peace, in reflection, in teaching.'

Ball opened his mouth, but he was unable to speak the words of refusal. The enticement of quiet, of leisure, of the absence of fear, was too powerful. All the things he had longed for so intensely were within reach, only awaiting assent. He would even be able to have Christiana near him; such matters, he knew, were not difficult to arrange. And the crowning bafflement was this: had he been tempted in the bleak days when cold and hunger were constant companions, when doubts had plagued him without respite, he could have understood his indecision; but now, on the threshold of achievement, when the dream he and Tyler and the others had fashioned seemed sure of bursting into reality, why did he hesitate now?

'John?'

The wrinkled face, turned full into the moonlight, anxious, waiting, concerned. If he did not say it now . . .

He sighed. 'Goodbye, my lord Abbot.'

The older man stared at him. A tremor began at his left temple, ran down toward his mouth, was swallowed up in the folds of skin. He spoke in a hoarse voice. 'John, please. Consider what I have said.'

'I considered it many years ago.'

'Why . . . I cannot understand why . . .'

He wished he could explain. He owed an explanation to a man who, despite the many barriers lying between them, was surely his friend. But at the moment it was impossible to impart reasons for what he had done in the past and what he was doing now. He was not even certain that he understood the reasons himself. Again he said, 'Goodbye.'

They walked together back down the nave. At the door the Abbot said, 'At least let me offer you hospitality for the rest of the night. It's only a short distance to Canterbury. I brought an extra horse. . . .'

Ball turned to him quickly. The Abbot smiled and said, 'Yes, I was so certain of my powers of persuasion.'

There was a chill in the air. The moonlight made lacy brilliance of the trees just beyond the porch. Ball rested his hand lightly on the Abbot's arm, then set out across the churchyard.

He had almost reached the street when the soldiers surrounded him, nine or ten of them, drawn swords gleaming dully. Two took hold of Ball. A third uncoiled a rope he was carrying.

'See you bind him well,' said another, evidently their officer.

Ball recovered quickly from his surprise. One could not expect a thing for so many years and still register astonishment when it actually happened; terror had lain in not knowing time or place. He found himself curiously resigned.

The Abbot hurried forward, trembling with indignation. 'What is the meaning of this?' Ball had never heard such fury in the deep voice.

'This man is under arrest, my lord Abbot,' the officer said respectfully.

'By whose order?'

'My instructions were to take him unless you and he left the church together.'

'By whose order do you take him?'

'By order of the Archbishop, my lord.'

The Abbot's anger ceased in full flow. He looked from the officer to Ball, confused.

'John, you must understand.' He shook his head childishly. 'I didn't know they were here.'

Ball sighed. 'Will you tell them to release me?'

The Abbot hesitated, suffering in his eyes and in the abortive movement of his hand upward in a gesture of authority and down again, a wounded bird's plummeting. 'I wish I could. But you must believe me. I didn't know of this. I didn't summon them.'

'Does it matter?'

'No,' said the Abbot slowly. 'I don't suppose it does.'

As the soldiers led him away Ball saw the Abbot sinking to his knees in the churchyard, whether in prayer or despondency he could not be sure.

4

THE jailer was eating when the soldiers brought Ball to him. He was in no hurry to finish. His right hand held a greasy mutton bone on which he was gnawing; with his left hand he was scratching himself, thoroughly, with great attention to detail, in various recesses of his body. The soldier, becoming impatient, growled, 'Be quick. We ride to London this morning.'

'We, my lad? I ride with you?'

The soldier said without much feeling, 'You're a pimple-headed fart.'

'Aye,' agreed the jailer amiably. 'Pimple-headed to be sure. As to the other, I'd be glad of your advice. Rosewater, nutmeg, lily and rhubarb juice, I've taken them all in quantity. Nothing seems to help.'

'Do you receive charge of the prisoner?'

'Aye.' The jailer subjected Ball to a rapid scrutiny. 'Leave him. He'll not run far.'

'See he doesn't.'

The jailer spat out a piece of gristle. 'It's a strange world, it is. He's the prisoner and I'm the imprisoned. If the prisoner prisons the prisonkeeper, who's in prison at all? To put it a bit different, if I was the one in the cell and him here eating mutton . . .' The soldier had gone. 'Ah well, what difference? It was not a path to wisdom I was treading. You there, Sir Priest. Speak to me.'

'Good morning,' said Ball.

The jailer loosed a single bolt of laughter from far back in his throat and went on eating.

There was a latticed window behind the bench where the jailer was sitting. Through it Ball could see the quiet Medway, mist

75

hovering close to the water's surface. His captors and he had ridden hard for what remained of the night after leaving Chartham. Daybreak had met them at Charing. They had untied his feet from the stirrups then, satisfied he would not try to escape. Two hours later they had reached Maidstone, had trotted through the streets toward the Archbishop's prison, a pile of grey rock on the bank of the river. The few townspeople who witnessed their passage had stared at them without expression.

'Have you had your food?' asked the jailer, and before Ball could reply he tossed the mutton shank at him. It struck Ball's shoulder and fell at his feet. 'Pity you're so choosy. Last bit of meat you'll have till heaven takes charge of you.' He belched. 'That's not right, is it? A priest in prison is sure to roast in hell. Ah well.' He laughed at his rhyme, licked his hand, wiped it off on his tunic and picked up a ring of keys.

'Aye,' he said as he pushed Ball ahead of him along a narrow corridor, 'it's a long time since we had such fine company with us. A priest in my jail. Speak to me, Sir Priest.'

Ball continued to walk silently ahead of him.

'Lost your tongue, have you? You'll find it soon enough when the mice begin to gnaw at your flesh. They say we've got the finest mice in all England, and I'm inclined to believe it, I am. Mice and lice. Lice as big as mice, mice as big as rats, rats as big as cats, but we have no cats. Speak to me, Sir Priest.'

Ball stopped walking and turned to the jailer. He felt curiously lightheaded, beyond both fear and involvement, as though by being captured he himself had made some weighty decision. 'Twenty thousand men,' he said slowly, 'twenty thousand men will come here to free me.'

Something troubled sprang into the jailer's eyes, spread briefly across his face before vanishing. Then he laughed. 'Well now. Will they free me, too?' He gave Ball a shove that sent him stumbling down the passageway, overtook him in front of a massive wooden door, which he then unlocked and opened. He placed his foot against Ball's rump, propelled him into the malodorous gloom, slammed the door shut behind him.

The only light came from a small circular window at the top of one sweating stone wall. It was a larger cell, Ball noticed, than the one he had occupied in London fifteen years before, not so large as the one he had inhabited more recently in Canterbury.

He stood, his gaze fixed on the circle of light, pondering the boast he had made to the jailer about twenty thousand men. Surely it was as empty as his hopes had been for all the years of his

76

preaching. Then he reminded himself that this was no longer so. There was the temper of the crowd at Chartham, the anger he had seen smouldering in a dozen other Kentish towns and villages, Tyler's passion and the unpredictable choler of Straw.

There would be killing, Tyler had said, and now for the first time he admitted to himself that there could be. If they did come to release him, whether the number was twenty thousand or only a score, would their hands already be stained with blood, their hearts committed to carnage? Would they in fact come to release him at all?

He heard a light scamper of footsteps, and before he understood clearly that he was not alone in the cell someone was pummelling him, raining blows against his back. They did not hurt; there was not enough strength behind them. Ball managed to turn, and between instinctively raised arms saw a tiny man with long, dishevelled hair. 'Priest!' cried his assailant. 'Priest priest priest!' The single word rolling in rapid succession into the quiet was at once entreaty and curse.

The man's energy was soon spent. He let his hands fall and stood panting, an incredibly wispy creature with bright, angry eyes. 'Priest,' he said once more, firmly, with the air of one announcing a decision.

'Why did you strike me?' Ball asked calmly.

'I had no choice,' answered the man with equal calmness, and the effect of hearing an echo of the sentence endowed with so much significance only a few hours before sent Ball into a sudden paroxysm of mirth.

'Am I so ridiculous?' the man asked mournfully.

'No,' Ball replied, controlling his laughter, 'you are not, and I apologize. I was not laughing at you.'

'I hate priests, you see.'

'You have reasons, I'm sure.'

'Yes,' replied the other. 'Though they think not. They think I'm mad. Mad Simon they call me, and each time they lock me up here.'

'Each time?'

Simon ignored the question. 'When my wife died thirty-two years ago . . . she died during the Great Plague . . . and all the time she was dying I tried to get a priest to come and confess her, but not one would come.'

'Perhaps,' suggested Ball, recalling his own experiences in York while the Black Death was raging, 'perhaps they weren't able to come. Priests often had more than they could do. . . .'

'They could have come,' Simon said shortly. 'One was eating, two more were sitting down to jugs of ale . . . they could have come, but they didn't care. They didn't care about anything. It was a terrible time. People dropping in the streets, the living vomiting out their lives among the dead, the bells tolling all day and night. The fires where they threw the corpses, and the smell. We joined the dancers, my wife and I.'

Ball remembered how it was then, when he would leave the Abbey to go among the dead and dying. He could picture the dancers well even now, the companies of men and women driven beyond hope to the extreme outer edges of terror, seeking escape from the inexorable: skittering in mad serpentine processions through charnel streets, weeping, shouting, cursing, praying, collapsing, then rising to resume the desperate travesty of some dimly recollected gaiety.

'We joined the dancers,' Simon said again, 'but it was no use. One night my wife's knees gave way and she couldn't get up again. At first I thought she was exhausted, as I was myself, but then I felt the swellings on her body, and I knew. I carried her to our house. To this day I don't know how. She was taller than I, and heavier.' His voice softened. 'She was also very beautiful. In all my life, before or since, I have never known such beauty. . . .'

He stopped, making a helpless, grieving gesture, then went on. 'For eight days and nights I stayed by her side. I wiped the sweat from her face, the sickness from her lips, the filth from her body. I vowed that if she had to die, she would not be like the others I had seen, so encrusted with vileness you could hardly tell they were human. And when she screamed with pain, I remember that I screamed, too.' He was silent, seeming to re-live the nightmare, then continued quietly, 'On the ninth day the fever broke, you could almost see it crumbling. From then on she began getting better, and two weeks later she was completely well.'

Ball said, puzzled, 'But you told me she died. . . .'

'She did, priest,' Simon said sharply. 'A month after that, early morning, we had got up not long before, the end of Morrow Mass was ringing. She was getting ready to leave the house. There were a few market wares one could buy. I was a baker, and though there wasn't much flour, there was some and I was bending over my oven. She turned just as she reached the door to call something back to me. I never found out what it was. She lost her balance and stumbled, fell over the step and broke her neck.'

Once again Ball felt himself buffeted by the impulse to wild laughter, which he now stifled only with difficulty.

78

'She was half a day dying, and in all those hours not one priest would come.'

Simon stood thoughtfully in the centre of the cell. Suddenly he beckoned to Ball, who came close to the little man, heard him whisper, 'Do you want to know how you can escape from here?'

Ball drew back, startled. Simon motioned to him again. 'In that wall,' he said, pointing covertly, 'two of the stones are loose. If you can get them out, there'll be space enough for a man to crawl through. There's a passage leading down to the river.'

'Why haven't you already . . .'

'I'm not strong enough. But you are. We could both go, couldn't we?'

Ball crossed to the wall, haste making him trip over his feet, hearing Simon whisper once more, 'Couldn't we . . .'

He dug his fingers into a crevice, tore at a stone. It remained solidly in place. He tried another, scrabbling frantically at the mortar, wishing his nails had not been bitten useless.

Then he heard mewing, malicious laughter behind him and turned, realizing reluctantly he had been hoaxed.

'Why did you . . .' He shrugged hopelessly.

Simon's laughter ceased. He hung his head, backed away when Ball came toward him.

'I'll not harm you,' said Ball. 'I don't blame you for doing it.'

'Don't be kind to me,' shrilled Simon. 'I won't have you being kind to me.'

'Would it help either of us if I struck you?'

'I hate priests. I hate them!' He kicked at the filth-laden straw covering the floor. Then, his mood changing, he said, 'I want to get out of here. I want to be free more than anything I've ever wanted. Except, of course, to have her alive again.' His face puckered up, bright eyes almost disappearing. 'I've wondered . . . there's been time for wondering, in here, outside . . . with all the pleasure and joy it can bring, why must love be so terrible?'

Ball did not answer. He was thinking of Christiana, remembering how he had first seen her when he was preaching in the market-place in Colchester (he was bolder in those days; not since his last imprisonment had he dared speak within the walls of a city). She had waited for him after the rest of his audience dispersed, had made it plain, with the lack of pretence which characterized her, that she was waiting for him. He could not remember what they said to each other then, but he recalled having reflected how ironic it was that his sermons for several years after leaving the Abbey had been dedicated mainly to morality: the sanctity of marriage

79

and the sinfulness of any relationship outside wedlock, and here he was, a priest. . . . For he had known, both of them had known, after the first few moments, how it would be with them.

There had been the joy and the pleasure of which Simon spoke. There had also been understanding: she had known the hopes he nourished for what he was doing, and while she could not make his beliefs her own, she had nonetheless bestowed on them the gift of her respect. There had been trust, and peace. Yet in all these things, compounding to love, there had been and still were the seeds of pain. He had made her suffer through his own suffering, had made her share with him a burden which could have little value for her and which he himself, more often than not, longed to reject.

Simon had evidently forgotten his question about love and was now looking up at the little circular window. 'Soon,' he said musingly, 'he'll come to feed us, and soon after that it will be dark outside. And the dark will creep in here. Why is it not possible . . . if you shut out light, it remains dark. If you shut out the dark, then, could it not remain light?' He shook his head, perplexed. 'Are you really a priest?'

'Yes.'

'Why have they put you in here?'

'They say I speak dangerous words.'

'They say I'm mad. Mad mad Simon. They let me out now and again, and each time I do what I must do. I go into a church and I defile it. In the font. In the chancel. Feeling as I do, I would be a false man if I did otherwise. Can you understand that?'

'I can,' said Ball.

'I find it very confusing to be speaking to you like this. You're a priest and I hate priests and yet I'm talking to you as I've talked to no one since my wife died.'

Simon's eyes filled with tears. 'I want to be free. So much I want to be free. I want to see the sky and the sun and hear birds. I want to smell the goodness of loaves I have kneaded baking in an oven. But I know, the moment they release me . . .' He spread out his hands. 'Why do you not tell me my bitterness is a sin, that after all these years I have no right to distil hatred in my heart like venom? Why do you not point out that my revenge against the church is disgusting and futile, that because a few neglected their duty to my wife . . . Will you not tell me all these things before long?'

Ball shook his head.

'Perhaps you're not much of a priest after all then. It's just as well. I should never be able to promise . . .' The tears overflowed his eyes, wandered down his cheeks. 'But I do want to be free.'

And something in Simon's tone, in the quiet despair of his words, set a frenzy bubbling inside Ball. He felt suddenly certain that the people would rise, that they would cast off the yoke they had worn so long and march to the King, not as slaves, but as free men seeking to make their liberty lasting. They would rise, and he had to be with them when they did. For if he were not . . .

He ran to the door and pounded on it. 'Jailer!' he cried. 'Jailer! Unlock the door!' He paused, and when there was no sound he began to scream, 'Let me out! I must get out! I must be free! Jailer . . .'

He did not know how long he continued to pound on the door. When he finally turned from it, voice broken, knuckles torn and bleeding, he saw Simon coming toward him. He felt the little man's hand touch his forehead, cool and comforting.

Simon helped him lie down on the straw, left him to rummage in some dim corner of the cell. He returned with an armful of rags which he crushed together to form a pillow.

After a desperately lucid moment, during which he resigned himself to rotting and dying a prisoner, Ball slept.

MAY

I

How it actually started Abel was never sure, though the story was it began with words between Peg's mother and Robert's wife while they were waiting for their bread to be baked in the village oven.

Just the night before, almost everyone had been at the inn, which was unusual in itself, since the month of May always demanded heavy attention to the fields, from dawn to dark. But for some reason, on this particular evening no one had felt like working. Almost everyone had drifted to the inn. And everyone began agreeing that it was the worst spring any of them had known.

There had been the second visit of the poll-tax collectors, foiling the village's plans for evasion of the tax. This had been followed by the bailiff's raid and the burning of Robert Ogden's barn. Then the lord had imposed an extra day a week of boon-work on his acres. Nicholas had said the tax for brewing beer was going to be increased, he'd had it first-hand from the valet of the lord's steward. And Old Elias had chimed in with the news he'd heard as reeve, that both the tallage and the tax for corn-grinding would be up come summer. They'd all had more trouble than ever before with doves from the lord's cote, which were playing havoc with the young shoots of grain. But let any man take down his longbow and send an arrow through one of them, or set a snare, and there'd be fines or flogging or both.

To crown all this, the chance-sheep had escaped. It was the custom every year for the lord's steward to set a fat ewe on peasant land adjoining some part of manor land. If the sheep stayed where it was while the steward counted out loud to a hundred, it belonged to the villagers. However, if it strayed back onto the lord's land, the steward repossessed it. Every year for the past seven the chance-sheep had remained grazing contentedly on peasant soil, and there had been mutton turning on a spit in the evening. This spring, the ewe had bucketed over to the manor acres before the steward's count had even reached thirty.

It was, everyone had agreed, a black spring.

To which Abel had replied with a jaunty song about a black cock crowing of a black noon because the chicks of his black hen had all hatched out white. And everyone had laughed, but not as heartily as usual. Soon afterward, long before their normal departure time, they had trooped off to their huts, without any man bidding his neighbour so much as a goodnight.

The next evening, just before sundown, while they were starting back from the fields, the thing was beginning in the village.

Robert's wife and Matilda, Peg's mother, according to the story that was told later, were still at the bake-oven. Neither was in a very good temper, having waited all day for her turn, and now the heat was really too low for good baking, and Jack the Baker, a grumbling contrary man at best, refused to throw on more wood, saying it was far too late to fire up for a trifling matter of seven loaves.

But the bread was already baking, so there was nothing they could do but wait for it to be done.

Robert's wife sighed. 'It's been a black spring.'

'It'll be a blacker summer,' replied Matilda.

'Well enough for you to be complacent. You're the reeve's mother-in-law. What about us? Our barn burned with all our seed-crop. . . .'

'You got seed, didn't you?'

'Through no generosity of your son-in-law, I'll be bound. If it hadn't been for Abel Threder and one or two of the others . . .'

'Old Elias gives his tithe to the church,' snapped Peg's mother.

'Under compulsion like us all . . .'

'He's not obliged to hand over alms to every pauper who gets into trouble because he lets his daughter run away.'

Surprisingly, Robert's wife did not reply directly to this. Instead she sighed again and said, 'What will become of us? Three loaves to feed a family of seven for a week. . . .'

'Three loaves!' Matilda sang out, as if she'd sat on one of Jack's hot stones.

'Three loaves,' repeated Robert's wife, her voice mournful as wind through ripening barley. 'Not nearly enough for a family of seven. . . .'

'Five of those loaves are mine. If you dare touch one of them . . .'

'Do you know what's the boldest thing in the world?' asked

Robert's wife, beginning to snort softly. And without waiting for a reply, she answered her own riddle. 'A reeve's shirt, because every day it clasps a thief by the throat.'

'I'll have my five loaves now,' Matilda called to the baker.

'Not ready yet,' mumbled Jack.

'What I said goes for everyone who lives in the reeve's house as well,' Robert's wife commented snidely. 'If they're not thieving bread, they're stealing men.'

Peg's mother seized the rake from slow-witted Jack, dragged five loaves from the oven. Robert's wife grabbed one, but it was so hot she dropped it. By now she was snorting loudly in quick-time. When Matilda leaned over to pick up the loaf, she booted her so hard that Peg's mother plunged head-first into a pile of ashes Jack had removed from the pit. Matilda came up flailing, spitting out ash, gasping, 'Give me my loaf.'

She was asking for it, of course, and Robert's wife was ready enough to comply. She seized the mound of bread, which was still quite soft in the middle, and pushed it into Matilda's face, with a dead-centre aim on the mouth and nose.

Snorting triumphantly, she was about to follow up her advantage when Jack finally came to his senses and separated the women. The unspoiled bread went back into the oven, and under the baker's glowering surveillance was baked more or less in peace. The rivals did not even quarrel over the allocation of the finished loaves. Robert's wife took two, and Matilda maintained a dignified silence as she picked up the other four.

When she arrived at Elias's house, she told her daughters about the battle of the bake oven. Barbara immediately went to the door and rammed the bolt home.

By this time the sun was sinking red, betokening a spell of hot, clear weather. Old Elias, weary from a day of sweating in his fields, was just coming up the hill to his house, whistling to himself and thinking of supper. He reached the door, tried it, scratched himself puzzledly, tried it again.

'Barbara,' he called. 'Are you home, Barbara? Peg . . . Matilda . . .'

When there was no answer, he whistled through his teeth for a moment, then shouted, so loudly that everyone in the village heard him, even Nicholas, who came out of the inn, looking around and rubbing his beefy arms.

'Barbara! Open that door!'

From the other side of the heavy oak slab Barbara answered in her sweetest tones, 'You'll not get in here tonight, Elias Roper.'

'And why in the name of the Holy Ghost not?' roared Elias, bringing more villagers out of their huts. 'I'm tired and I'm hungry and I want to take you to bed.'

'Shame!' called Barbara. 'You let my mother be insulted because of you, and now you stand out there noising like a rutting boar!'

'Barbara!' shrieked Elias, as Abel came along the street with Roger and Robert.

They stood and watched as Elias ran back a few steps, then charged forward and butted the door with his paunch. The timbers shuddered but held. Once more he threw his weight at it, and still again. Then, puffing and wheezing, he rushed around to the rear of the house. Abel, following, turned the corner in time to see Elias, with a triumphant bellow, dive for the open window just as Peg reached out and slammed the shutters, catching Elias's fingers. The bellow changed to a wail of pure pain. He managed to extricate his hand, and, turning, saw Abel. Upon which he lowered his head and rushed straight at him, fists swinging like a pair of battle rams. Abel, caught off guard for only an instant, swung back, and the two of them, pounding each other, grunting and cursing, fought their way back to the street.

Nicholas, running up in the gathering dusk to see what the commotion was, collided with Roger, punched him and got back a blow in turn. In a moment all four men were rolling about in the dust. Robert danced about excitedly, opening and closing his mouth, kicking anyone who happened in range of his feet.

Another villager raised the hue and cry, and for the first time in anyone's memory the lame and half-blind watchman answered the alarm at once, limping along the street with unbelievable speed.

'Hue and cry, hue and cry!' he called. 'Thieves, brigands, bandits!' He raised his club in the air. 'Hue and cry!' he called again, rushed belligerently at the wall of Elias's house, and knocked himself senseless.

The door of the house opened. Barbara and Peg appeared, each rolling a wooden keg before them. Somehow Elias saw them. 'My wine!' he screamed, tearing himself out of Abel's grasp. 'My wine!' he cried again, rushing at Barbara and Peg. 'Sluttish thieving sows!'

The girls fled squealing, leaving the kegs unguarded. Elias picked up one, and Robert pushed him backward over the other.

Everyone crowded around. Two or three at a time took turns sitting on the frenzied Elias, while the others, having knocked the bungs out of the kegs, gulped wine, some in their cupped hands, some straight from the barrels.

The watchman revived and hurried over to join them. Abel held one keg up so the old man could drink, which he did, deeply and with gusto.

Matilda, venturing out of the house like an owl poised for the first flight of evening, spied Robert's wife, leaped on her and began enthusiastically to scratch and pull hair. Two or three other women pitched into the fray. Barbara and Peg went to the aid of their mother.

Matilda grabbed hold of Robert's wife's gown, ripped it from top to bottom, screamed with laughter at the other's nakedness. Her victory was short-lived. Robert's wife snorted, one long wrathful inhalation, seized Matilda's gown in both hands, and evened the score. Just as she did so, Jack the Baker came bumbling past them, oblivious of everything except reaching the wine kegs. He never did. The two women, in a wordless accord of exultant rage, fell on him, began punching and kicking him so ferociously that the luckless man gave a single despondent cry and fled, hotly pursued by all the women, with Matilda and Robert's wife in all their naked glory forming the vanguard.

The wine was gone. Elias's captors released him, which turned out to be an unwise move. He immediately picked up an empty keg, and grasping it by the bunghole, spun round and round, bowling over three or four villagers before Abel could bring the other keg down on his skull. Old Elias showed his gleaming teeth and settled, gently as a floating feather, onto the wine-stained dust.

The combat had become general now. Abel found himself side by side with Roger, battling two others, men he had known all his life and in this moment did not even recognize. When they had disposed of their two opponents, Abel and Roger turned on each other and continued fighting with unabated zeal.

The watchman hiccupped twice, so loudly he could be heard above all the din. 'Hue and cry!' he shrieked, then galloped down the street as if demons were chasing him.

Someone clouted Nicholas, knocking him flat on his face. As the innkeeper was getting up onto all fours, Robert, in a transport of excitement, planted a kick on his buttocks. He decamped at the other's first outburst of rage, ran fleetly the length of the street to his hut, slammed and bolted the door behind him. Nicholas lumbered in pursuit, purposeful as doom. He did not bother trying Robert's door, but began battering at the wall with his feet so effectively that he had soon opened a hole large enough for three to pass through.

Robert plunged nimbly past him, darted over to the inn, clambered up the door frame and broke off the projecting inn pole. Brandishing it like a lance, he advanced on Nicholas, who turned and prepared to charge. But before he could, Robert thrust the bundle of straw at the end of the pole directly into his face. The innkeeper recoiled, sneezed mightily several times, bending double with each explosion. Which gave Robert an opportunity to swat him repeatedly with the pole, until he was so fatigued he could swing no more. Then he simply sat down. Nicholas sank beside him. They both sighed.

It was all over in less than an hour, before the light was fully gone from the sky. The men began picking themselves up off the ground, feeling for broken bones, of which there were a few. The women returned from their pursuit of the baker, murmuring quietly to each other, seeking their men. Barbara and Peg dragged Elias into the house, dumped a jug of water in his face. He came to, smiling affably, apparently none the worse for his encounter with the wine keg. Barbara retired with him to their bedroom.

Matilda and Robert's wife picked up their gowns, surveyed each other sheepishly. Matilda invited the other woman into the house, where they lighted candles and began to mend their garments.

Abel and Roger sat on the ground grinning at each other. Abel's face was bruised and scraped; otherwise he felt extremely well. One of Roger's large blue eyes was almost closed, converting his customary expression of bland innocence to a cynical grimace.

Without speaking, they walked arm in arm out of the village to the brook, where they bathed their swollen faces.

Roger looked up, water dripping from his chin. 'Will we see if we can pry Barbara and Peg out of the house?'

'There's still enough heat in your breeches for that?'

'Only the thought,' replied Roger, laughing.

'Besides,' said Abel, 'this is one time, I think, Barbara will share Old Elias's bed the whole night.'

'I'll give him one thing. He has good wine. I wish there was more.'

'There was enough,' said Abel, touching his face gingerly.

They splashed across the brook and skirted the Broad Field. Abel sang as they walked, a ballad he had learned in Spain. He had no idea what the words meant, but the melody had always haunted him, as had the faces of the Castilians; their eyes and their songs alike seemed filled with perfumed sunlight and sadness.

'Remember when we took the deer from the lord's forest?' asked Roger.

'And the fish from his stream. When I think of how many times we could have been swinging from a pair of gibbets . . .'

'Is it right that they should have the privilege of hanging us for filling our empty bellies? . . . Abel?'

'It's the way things are. The deer and the fish are the lord's. We steal them if we can. If we're caught, we're spared the worry over whether it's right.'

'I've been thinking,' Roger said slowly, 'that one day I might leave the village. If I could reach a city or a town far enough away, and live there a year without being caught, and so become free . . . Have you never thought of running away, Abel?'

'Once. When I returned from serving with the Black Prince. For a few days . . .' He stopped speaking and shrugged. 'Then it was time for ploughing and sowing, and then reaping, and the summer was gone. So was the thought.'

'There's nothing to tie either of us. . . .'

'My father and grandfather were born and died here,' said Abel hotly. 'And more before them. I . . .' He paused, wondering at the force of his words. 'If you had talked to me yesterday about running away . . .' He groaned. 'Tonight . . .'

'All the same . . .'

'All the same, my bones are beginning to ache.'

They turned and walked back toward the village.

In the street they were accosted by the watchman. He put his face close to each of theirs in turn.

'Must see . . .' he said. 'Must see . . . no strangers in street, looking to do evil. You'd best be off home. Long since Curfew.'

He hiccupped. The sour vestige of Elias's wine floated about them.

'Goodnight, lads,' he said, and limped away.

'Yes,' said Abel softly. 'It was a good night.'

2

'ARE you so proud of your anger?' Isabella asked, her own voice fierce with a passion he had never heard in it. 'Does the strength in your hands make you so arrogant that you must smash whatever you touch?'

Tyler looked at his wife's face, its expression, normally so quiescent, secretive even, open and flaming now with unchecked emotion. His glance travelled past her to the bench lying in splintered shambles among the rushes, fragments strewn the length of the room.

He clenched his fist. She should not make him feel shame for what he had done. 'Am I to accept such news lightly?' he asked. 'Am I to sit down like some noble's chaplain, sweetly folding my hands and lisping pious words?' He mimicked ferociously. 'It is the will of God, I say, the will of the Almighty for man to accept the adversity inflicted on him without complaint . . .' He spat out the words. 'If this is the will of God, then let God burn in hell!'

She touched him in sudden alarm. 'Wat . . .'

He stifled his own apprehension over what he had said. 'Would you rather I ran out and tried to pull down the Castle with my bare hands?' he asked, then added more quietly, 'It's only a broken bench. I'll make another.'

'Will you also remake the jugs you've smashed other nights, the tunics you've torn? Soon we'll have nothing to wear or drink from, and then you need only take apart the house, timber by timber.'

Her voice had turned taunting, but there was something else in it that made him look sharply at her again. She twisted away from his gaze; not, however, before he had seen tears in her eyes. The sight of them made him angry once more, but now he could release his anger in another way.

'They have the hearts of chickens,' he raged. 'Why did they not . . .'

'Oh, Wat,' she said, still facing away from him. 'What could they do?'

The messenger had come and gone only a few moments before. He had stood in the doorway, dressed in the garb of a pardoner, great pouch hanging outside his cloak, cowl slightly awry. 'I bring news,' he said, shifting from one foot to the other, obviously anxious to be gone before Curfew. 'News of John Ball.'

Tyler had taken him by the arm and pulled him into the house. Isabella, busy at the hearth, had scarcely looked up. Both of them were accustomed to the arrival of messages from Ball during his absences from Colchester. Often they were verbal, but sometimes they came in the form of letters which Tyler was expected to have copied and circulated through the shires to all those who worked with them. Peculiar rhyming missives they were, which Tyler had once been inclined to ridicule, but had come to accept when he saw how they were treasured as talismans by those who believed in the cause. The language was always odd, not in the least like Ball's ordinary speech, or the clear and straightforward words he employed when addressing crowds. 'John the Miller has ground small, small, small,' one of them read. 'The King's son of heaven shall pay for all. Beware or ye be woe. Know your friend from your foe. Have enough and say ho! And do well and better and flee sin, and seek peace and hold you therein. And pray for John Trueman and all his fellows.'

After one read several of these, the words became less obscure, the meaning pointed and urgent, a message of hope and instruction for all bearing the strain of waiting and working in secret.

But there had been none of the letters for over a year, and Tyler had come to the conclusion, without ever questioning his friend, that he had abandoned this form of communication for more direct contact now that the time for action was imminent.

Still, he had asked the messenger, 'Have you a letter from Ball?'

'I have news,' the man had replied.

'What news?' Tyler had asked with unwonted patience, and Isabella had looked up from the fire.

'He's been arrested. They've put him in Maidstone Jail.'

'When?' asked Tyler, again forcing himself to almost excessive restraint.

'The end of April.'

'A month ago,' said Tyler, and the man had nodded, yawning.

'A month,' he had repeated. Then, able to contain himself no longer, he had picked up the bench and smashed it on the floor. 'A month! And all this time they've done nothing!' The messenger had emitted a startled goat's cry and fled the house.

Isabella had come to him then, anger blazing.

There was no anger in her now.

'What could they do?' she asked again.

'They could have burst the prison open. They could have set him free and killed those who held him. They could have hanged them and set their heads on pikes. . . .'

He stopped for breath.

'And then what?' she asked impassively.

Tyler swore an obscene oath and said, 'When we've won . . .'

She turned back to him, her face pale. 'He's not young any more, Wat.'

'He's had their prisons before.'

'He's too old. He'll be cold and sick . . .'

'We'll get him out,' Tyler said grimly.

91

'Someone should tell her,' said Isabella. 'She has a right to know.' Tyler nodded absently and she murmured, 'I'll go to-morrow.'

He could see Ball clearly: the red-rimmed eyes, the mouth trembling with fatigue, the ageing skin of the hands with nails bitten down far past the fingertips. He could hear the voice: hoarse and cracked, holding its perpetual note of doubt and fear, but at the same time warm and indomitable.

'If they hurt him . . .' said Tyler. His voice rose to a shout. 'If they so much as touch him, I'll kill every one of them. I'll hack them into pieces even the birds won't touch . . .' He broke off, clenching his fist again.

'You *are* proud of your anger,' she said despairingly. 'You wear it like a garland.'

'No,' he said. 'Anger is a weapon, to be kept sharp and used when it's needed.'

'Then use it only when it's needed,' she replied tartly.

'It soon will be.'

'Wat . . .'

'There's a proverb,' he said. 'Three things drive a man from his home: a leaking roof, a smoking chimney, and a nagging wife . . .'

She looked at him defiantly, but there was hurt in her voice. 'The roof might leak and the chimney smoke. You'll not have the third reason for leaving.' Her tone grew flat. 'Will you want ale?'

'None,' he replied.

'I'll put out the mattress.'

He nodded.

They were settling back into the laconic manner they employed with each other. Usually he would have been content to see it return. But tonight the news of Ball, touching the feeling they both had for him, had breached for a few moments the wall they tended between them.

He felt a pang of regret that it was so easy to rebuild.

When the knocking wakened him, he found himself far over on Isabella's side of the mattress, one arm about her. He lay quietly, not wishing to move, his hand nestling in the smooth warm hollow between her shoulder and the rise of her breast. She moaned, stirred, pressed closer to him. He floated gently in the sweet current between sleep and desire.

The knocking resumed, energetic and peremptory. Isabella awoke with a sharp cry of terror which found a momentary response in Tyler. He put her from him roughly, searched unsuccessfully for his dagger, settled for the mallet and awl, which he kept by him as he dressed. All the while the knocking continued, a ceaseless summons filling the room with its insistence.

'Wat . . .' Isabella's whispering voice, frightened but steady.

Tyler grunted and crossed to the door, removed the bar and opened it, stepping back smoothly to wait, awl and mallet at the ready.

The dimly silhouetted figure advanced into the house, brushing past Tyler with an angry shrug, saying, 'You took long enough. Are you besotted, or do you not care?'

Tyler recognized the voice even as he was raising the mallet. 'Straw?' he said tentatively.

'Yes, yes, Straw. Close the door, close the door, do you want all Colchester in here?'

His own ire rising, Tyler said, 'If they don't come, it will be no fault of yours. Have you no more sense than to pound . . .'

'No time for argument, close the door.'

'Close it yourself,' said Tyler. 'Isabella, light the fire.'

He heard the mattress rustle as she got up and draped the blanket about her. Soft footsteps moved to the hearth.

Straw, having shut the door, came close to him. 'News,' he said, 'there's news from Brentwood.' Saliva sprayed against Tyler's cheek. He wiped it away in quick annoyance.

'I've had my share of news tonight. Ball is in Maidstone Jail.'

Tyler could not see Straw, but he felt the other's impatient gesture of dismissal. 'Ball? No matter, no matter at all. He'll be out soon. There are more important things now.'

A sliver of flame shot up from the embers, climbed into the tent of twigs Isabella was placing around it. Straw was suddenly visible in the growing circle of light, thin lips pressed together, eyes filled with a terrible intensity. The skirt of his priest's habit was caked with dried mud.

'We've done it, Tyler,' he said. 'The rising has begun.'

Out of the corner of his eye Tyler saw Isabella throw part of the wrecked bench onto the fire. The dry wood crackled.

'Tell me what happened,' he said calmly.

'They'll not stop us now. We'll have their heads, every one of the filthy dogs. . . . If only I'd been there. We'd have killed the ones who were in Brentwood today.'

Tyler took a swift step toward him. 'Just tell me what happened.'

Straw, unperturbed and standing his ground, said, 'The tax collectors, they came to Brentwood, wanting us to pay more than we had already paid. . . .'

The commission, headed by a man named Bampton, had ridden into the town of Brentwood with a small company of clerks and soldiers. The townspeople had been informed of their coming and had been waiting two days, together with farmers and fishermen from the marsh villages of Fobbing, Stanford-le-hope and Corringham. All were armed with sticks, flails and longbows. They had been resolved not to pay one farthing more in taxes. Jack Straw, though he had been instrumental in organizing the resistance, had not expected the commission so early that day and had been out rounding up additional supporters.

A man from Straw's parish of Fobbing had refused to pay, in the name of all those assembled, and Bampton had ordered his arrest. The mob had pressed in around the commission, shouting and brandishing their makeshift weapons. Bampton had fled first, spurring his horse through the crowd and making for the London highroad. The soldiers and clerks, seeing their leader in retreat, had wasted no time in following him.

'But they'll return,' said Straw. He leaned toward Tyler. 'And this time you and I will be there to see they are dealt with properly. We've begun, Tyler.'

Isabella threw another section of the bench onto the fire.

'I'll see that the area around Colchester is alerted,' said Tyler.

Straw began to stride about the room, restlessly, aimlessly. 'The whole of England will be alerted now.'

'We'll move carefully. This must be done . . .'

'Carefully? There's no time for care. It's what we've been waiting for. We must show them our strength. We'll storm the manors, and when the commission returns . . .'

'You'll storm no manors until I give the word.'

Straw swung about and glared at Tyler. A fleck of saliva appeared in one corner of his mouth. 'The people of the marsh are mine,' he said. 'They do what I tell them.'

'Good. Go back to Fobbing and tell them to be ready. I'll meet you in Brentwood tomorrow night.'

The priest was quivering with anger and excitement. For an instant Tyler thought Straw would attempt to strike him. But he merely said, 'Brentwood, tomorrow night,' in a harsh voice, wheeled and went out of the door.

Tyler crossed to a corner, found what he had not been able to

94

locate before, a long, sharp dagger in a leather sheath. He ran his belt through it, strapped it round his waist.

'Where?' asked Isabella tonelessly.

'The villages nearby first.'

'Will you be back before you go to Brentwood?'

He shook his head. They looked at each other without speaking for a long moment. Then Tyler left the house.

He reached Stanway at sunrise, having visited three other villages in darkness, rousing the leaders, informing them of what had happened, exhorting them to be prepared to march when the signal was given. A mile farther on, in Marks Tey, he planned to obtain a horse and ride to Brentwood. It would be a hard journey, over byroads and paths, and he was anxious to be on his way. First, however, he wanted to meet with one more of his lieutenants, a peasant farmer named Sesson.

Tyler found him seated comfortably before his fire, spooning down porridge before going out to his field. Sesson was a tall man, somewhat flabby, with a shock of thick grey hair. As Tyler entered the hut, the man's wife drew in her breath and looked over at him, her eyes widening.

'We're ready,' said Tyler brusquely. 'They've risen at Brentwood.'

Sesson took another mouthful of porridge and nodded ruminatively.

'You'll tell the others?'

Sesson swallowed, nodded again.

'You know the signal.'

'I know the signal.'

Something was wrong. The woman was fluttering about, hands shaking, casting enigmatic glances at her husband.

'Today is Friday. You should be ready to march by Tuesday. Wednesday at the latest.'

'I'm not marching,' said Sesson.

His wife made a whimpering sound, half relief, half fear. Tyler said, keeping his voice under control, 'Why not?'

'There's no reason any more.'

'No reason?'

Sesson put down the bowl. His wife rushed over to pick it up and with trembling fingers began to refill it. Sesson motioned that he wanted no more. The woman started to eat what she had dished out, greedily, obsessively.

Sesson said, 'The steward of the manor has been kind to us this spring.'

95

'That isn't what you told me when I was here last. You were all fire and zeal then, and the manor lord was a brutal tyrant.'

'You've not been here since February.'

'The feast,' his wife said, 'don't forget to tell him about the feast.'

'The steward,' said Sesson, ignoring his wife's interjection, 'has promised us we can fish in the lord's stream.'

Tyler's wrath finally exploded. 'Promised!'

'He's said he'll give even more in the future.'

'The feast, the feast,' said his wife, clanking the spoon in the empty bowl.

'How much do you think promises like that are worth? How many times before have there been promises . . .'

'The feast,' said the woman.

'They've granted fishing rights. That's something.'

'They grant nothing they can't take back. Only the King . . .'

'When Alan Tanner's wife was carrying her child, the steward gave them extra firewood.'

Sesson's wife could no longer restrict herself to prompting. 'And they're going to give us a feast next week,' she burst out excitedly. 'Two roast sheep, and bread made from fine flour, and wine . . .'

Sesson, looking at Tyler's face, said sharply, 'Silence!' The woman stopped speaking and clanked the spoon in the empty porridge bowl.

Tyler lunged at Sesson, hauled him to his feet by his shirt. 'I trusted you!' he shouted. Sesson made a futile effort to strike him, and Tyler tightened his grip on the shirt. The woman was making little strangled sounds as if she were the one being assaulted.

Finally Tyler's rage ran out. He released Sesson, who stood motionless, hands at his sides. 'Things are better,' he said, breathing raggedly, 'It's not necessary to act now. If we wait . . .'

'We'll wait no longer!'

'This year fishing rights, next year . . .'

'You're afraid, aren't you?' Tyler asked quietly.

Sesson hesitated, then nodded.

Tyler turned toward the door.

'They'll kill you, Tyler,' Sesson said.

'Kill . . .' echoed the woman.

At the door Tyler swung around. 'Do you not think the others are frightened?'

Sesson's eyes were tortured. 'I don't care about the others. I don't want to die.'

Tyler was about to retort sharply, to lash out at the man for his cowardice, but he found suddenly he could not. He made a half-gesture toward Sesson: of sympathy, of understanding, he was not certain what. Then the mood was gone, and he withdrew his hand angrily.

He left the hut without speaking again, and as he closed the door he could hear the woman crying out in a high, hysterical voice, 'They'll kill you.'

It was long past noon before he was able to shut the words out of his mind.

JUNE

I

COURTENAY rode beside Walworth now that they had emerged from the narrower lanes onto Lombard Street. Margaret followed them, dressed in a russet hawking costume, sitting her horse like a man. The helpers brought up the rear, one of them balancing with practised skill the perch holding two birds: a merlin for Margaret and the tiercel for Courtenay. Walworth carried the peregrine falcon on his gloved left hand. Outside the shed where she was kept when not hunting he allowed no one else to handle her.

The falcon screamed and dug her talons viciously into the thick leather of the glove. 'I see she has spirit,' observed Courtenay in an accent of faint repugnance.

'Temper, Your Grace,' said Walworth proudly.

'It was my impression that falcons were easy to tame.'

'She obeys instruction well, but she's never been tamed.' He added, 'I prefer it so,' and saw Courtenay's head turn toward him in a slow, appraising stare.

Walworth wondered why the Bishop had accompanied them; it was known he had no great love for this sport. But when Courtenay had sent a message saying he wished to call this afternoon, Walworth had been reluctant to give up his plans for hawking and had replied with an invitation for the Bishop to ride with them. Courtenay, he was aware, rarely did anything without a purpose; no doubt there was a reason now.

Margaret began to sing, a gentle, melancholy melody about a knight who had been away from England on a crusade and returned to find his lady dead. Walworth knew without looking back that his wife would be smiling enigmatically as she sang, and that if he did turn to look at her, the smile would deepen without becoming warmer.

'My lady sings very beautifully,' said Courtenay suavely.

'Thank you, Your Grace.'

99

He knew, again without turning, the slow inclination of her head, the disconcerting hazel eyes touched ever so lightly with mockery, her customary reaction to flattery.

They were approaching Poultry Street. A trio of ravens flopped down just ahead of them to peck at some refuse, and the falcon strained to be free. 'No carrion pickers for you,' he said. 'Soon enough, soon enough, my sweet.' And again he saw Courtenay studying him.

A couple of carts rolling abreast clattered toward them from the Cheapside, pulled by a pair of wild-eyed horses whipped up to frenzy by their drivers. It was obviously a race, and the hawking group had to press close to one wall to avoid being run down.

Walworth laughed, calling encouragement to both drivers, who waved back as they plunged past toward the Cornhill. Courtenay said, 'I was under the impression, Lord Mayor, that cart racing was illegal in the streets of London.'

'So it is, Your Grace. But my old master John Lovekyn used to say: to be able to see everything is merely proof of good eyesight, but to be able not to see some things is the beginning of understanding.'

'Ah yes, Lovekyn,' said the Bishop.

Courtenay was looking straight ahead. Walworth could only see half of the wide mouth, curved in a sleek smile. For a moment he had a strange notion that the other half of the Bishop's face would not be smiling at all. This disturbed him, for in a way it summed up his feelings about the younger man. One side of Courtenay's character contained little illusion for Walworth. Together with Agnes he had spied on countless clients who made their way secretly to Southwark seeking gratification of a variety of voluptuous tastes. But even if Courtenay had fallen neatly into this classification, which he did not, there was still a part of him Walworth could not fathom. With such a man, Lovekyn would have said, determine what he wants, and be cautious. Walworth was aware of the Bishop's cleverness and ambition, the power and wealth he had accumulated. But Walworth also knew his own chief resources: the shrewdness and the driving physical force which had helped to place him where he was.

'Lovekyn,' Courtenay was saying again, musingly. 'He was knighted, was he not, while he was Lord Mayor.'

Walworth was irritated by the pointed reference to the fact that he was the only member of the King's Council of common birth. He was tempted to reply sharply, and ordinarily he would have done so, but he was sure the Bishop had a reason for saying what he had said. With difficulty Walworth observed Lovekyn's maxim: when in doubt, say nothing.

He was rewarded by hearing Courtenay continue, after a pause. 'You have been a most effective Lord Mayor, my friend. The measure you instituted curtailing usury, for example, this alone is a great step forward. Quite different from the days when the henchmen of John of Gaunt spoiled the city with their brigandry. But of course, the King's uncle is in Scotland now. . . .'

He stopped speaking, as if he were waiting, and Walworth said, 'Let us hope he stays there.' If what Courtenay wanted to hear was assurance of his opposition to John of Gaunt, he would voice it. But that was well enough known; there must be something else.

If there was, Courtenay did not intend to reveal all of it now. He merely urged his horse closer to Walworth, placed a hand on his shoulder and rode along so in silence, until the falcon screamed, causing the Bishop to pull his hand back hastily.

Margaret, who had stopped singing when the carts passed them, began again.

Courtenay touched his arm once more and pointed. Far along the Cheapside Walworth could make out the slight figure of Salisbury, accompanied by his squire, disappearing into Ironmonger's Lane. He made a grimace of distaste, never having been able to abide even the sight of the greying noble with his carefully modulated voice and his elegant, studied gestures. It was said that Salisbury had fought valiantly in France. Walworth had his doubts; the man had not even been able to fight for the woman he wanted. He grimaced again and saw Courtenay's covert smile.

Just before they turned off Poultry Street toward the Moorgate, Walworth recognized a pie baker recently convicted for baking entrails and rotten meat in his pies. The man had been subjected to the usual penalty: imprisonment in the stocks while his wares were burned under his nose. He scowled up at Walworth now until the Lord Mayor shouted jocularly, 'Ha, Ralph, I see you've survived, you and your nose alike,' at which the baker essayed a twisted smile and called back, 'No, Lord Mayor, this is a new nose. I've put the old one in a pie and had it sent round for your supper.'

Walworth laughed, and Courtenay said softly, 'You love your city, do you not, Lord Mayor?'

Just as softly, Walworth answered, 'With my life, Your Grace.'

'And if your city were in danger, what would you do?'

'Fight to protect it, naturally.'

'There could be an occasion when it would be wiser to avoid that extreme.'

'Defending my city is no extreme for me.'

And as he spoke, an uneasiness was stirring in him, aggravated by the memory of Agnes's warning over two months ago and the attack on his life the same night.

'Nevertheless,' Courtenay was saying, 'there might be circumstances under which those who love the city would do best to retire . . .'

'Desert London?'

'Briefly, of course. Only in order to be able to heal matters more effectively upon returning.' Then he added, so quietly that Walworth was not certain he actually said it, 'Not to mention the new and exalted positions that might be waiting for the discreet and the clever.'

Walworth asked guardedly, 'Your Grace is speaking of something specific. . . .'

Courtenay turned an urbane smile on him and said nothing.

They had been on the moor for only a few moments when Walworth saw the wood-lark. He turned to Margaret, pointed, and said, 'Now!'

He could see the scar clearly on the back of her hand as she raised it to slip the lunes from the merlin. At the same moment the lark left its tree and soared at the sun in steep, ever-widening circles. They could hear it singing, a burst of sound calling up a vision of joy refined to its purest, of happiness redistilled. Walworth knew, however, that this was the tiny bird's hymn to fear, that it sang now only in expectation of death.

Which came quickly enough. The lark was facile of wing beyond belief, but the merlin was more powerful and equally quick. No matter which way the quarry darted, the hawk was there, rising or swooping into its line of flight. Finally, the merlin manœuvred above the songbird and in arrow-swift descent made its capture. The lark's song was cut off in mid-note.

Margaret released her breath in a long sigh, which might have been either of pleasure or of regret: Walworth could derive no indication from her expression.

After a helper had retrieved the merlin, Walworth and Courtenay unleashed their birds. The tiercel climbed sluggishly, but the falcon was aloft in a matter of moments, circling easily high above their heads, waiting on the prey they would flush.

It turned out to be a grouse, skittering out of the bushes and making off in a short, powerful spurt of flight.

The tiercel did not even see it, but the falcon was already on her unerring way, accelerating straight downward until she was no more than a blur against the bright sky. She thudded onto the back of the grouse with such force that, although they were some distance away, the sound of impact reached their ears clearly. Then, recovering with breathtaking grace, she floated to the ground, talons sunk deep in the limp body of her victim.

Walworth galloped his horse toward her. As he approached, the falcon opened a beak stained with blood and screamed her defiance and triumph. 'Come, my sweet,' said Walworth happily, dismounting and holding out the gloved hand in which he had placed a chicken head. 'Come. . . .'

Reluctantly, the falcon came, lighting and immediately attacking the lure. Walworth picked up the grouse, put it in his saddlebag, laughing and crooning to the falcon the while. 'You're my sweet one, aren't you? Take no quarter, give none. That's the way it will always be. Always.' The bird looked up, then dug her curved beak into the chicken head.

Walworth was still chuckling with pleasure as he rode back to join the others. He saw Courtenay looking at him, fleshy face pale, eyes disquieted.

Out of courtesy, he kept the falcon leashed so that the Bishop's tiercel could have some sport. It made two kills, neither as spectacular as the single flashing performance of his falcon.

By the time they started back toward the city walls, Courtenay had recovered both his colour and his calm. He rode up alongside Walworth, put his hand on the Lord Mayor's arm and said, 'I hope you will remember and consider what I said earlier. The time for decision may not be far off.'

2

TRY as he might, Salisbury was unable to rid himself of his presentiment.

That afternoon it had become so oppressive that he had sought out Thomas and asked him to take his sword to an ironmonger and have a good edge put on it. Then he decided they should go together and have new weapons fashioned for them both. His squire had been ecstatic, and the young man's show of good spirits lifted some of the gloom from Salisbury. He knew that Thomas, despite his flippancy, was devoted to him and took special delight in being seen with him in the streets of London. Moreover, he could see that the squire thought this expedition a mission of some importance, and the sight of him puffing out his chest like a pit-cock almost always afforded Salisbury some affectionate amusement.

The weather had been brilliant; St. Paul's square grey tower was traced with startling clarity against a blue-green sky. Yet Salisbury's morbidity had returned rapidly, and almost as soon as they started out he wished he had not come. Of what use would a new sword be against . . . against what? He did not know, but the impression of imminent danger had given him the feeling he was smothering under a great dark cloak.

Now it was early evening, and he stood before a window of his house, watching the changing colours of sunset on the waters of the Thames. To his left, rising above the wood wharf, was the home of Sir Simon Burley. The knight was absent now on one of his frequent trips out of London. He was a trusted servant of Joan and did the business of her estate throughout Kent.

The thought of Joan depressed him even more. He let his gaze wander past Burley's house, down-river toward the bridge, but this did not help now. It only recalled numerous trips abroad, and one in particular. Twenty-one years ago this same month he had been at Bretigny, near Chartres, preparing to depart for England on a double note of triumph. He had just concluded negotiations for a treaty with France which would bring his country considerable territory and money, including the incredible sum of three million gold crowns as ransom for the captured French king. Also, by the last courier had come news of the death of Thomas Holland, whose marriage to Joan had been upheld by Papal sanction eleven years before. Now at last Salisbury could reclaim her. His elation had very nearly unbalanced him.

Then, the very day of his departure, another courier had arrived. Among the diplomatic papers was a proclamation from King Edward. His son the Black Prince was to marry Joan. . . .

The Thames was shedding its colours, darkening about the barges moored at Paul's Wharf.

Salisbury turned from the window. Inside the house it was already night. He called for a servant and obtained a candle from him, made his way toward the solar he and Elizabeth shared as sleeping quarters.

She was speaking when he entered the room, and for a moment he thought someone was with her. Then he saw she was holding her Maltese spaniel on her lap, fondling the animal and touching her tongue to its lips.

She got up when she saw him, gently placed the dog on the rushes (where it at once messed), and advanced on him with her little sidewise step of adoration.

He embraced her with a strange mixture of feeling: warmly, because he had surprised her in an act displaying her naked deprivation, a deprivation of his making; and yet with a small cold twinge of revulsion.

'William,' she said, 'don't you think we could go soon to Canterbury? I mean, don't you truly? You did promise, you know. I've been thinking about it, and the weather has been so warm here, and it would be a pleasant trip through Kent. I mean, we could travel early in the day and again for a while in the afternoon. To avoid the heat, you know. You do know, don't you, William? My skin suffers so from the heat . . .'

She rattled on in her quick nervous fashion, he replying in monosyllables at the appropriate pauses. And all the while her eyes were on him, possessive, watchful, but also containing a deep calm sadness contrasting vividly with her fluttering manner and the swift shallow stream of her words.

She stopped in mid-sentence now, squinting a little, her face taking on something of the wizened look of spinsterhood it had held when he first knew her. 'William,' she said, 'you're feeling ill again. I know you're feeling ill. Truly I know. I can see it in your face. Your colour is bad. William, please don't be ill.'

'I'm not, my dear. It's only a small chill. . . .'

'I knew it. I was absolutely sure of it. You've not properly rid yourself of the chill you had early in the spring. I mean, ever since you returned from that journey to the north. . . . The King should be ashamed for sending a man of your age off on . . . That wanton boy. . . .'

'Elizabeth!'

'I don't care. I truly do not care. You're going to bed at once, with some seed of white henbane to make you sleep. . . .' She paused, then said slowly, with an air of infinite tenderness, 'My darling, do you truly feel dreadful?'

He replied, suddenly deeply moved by the love in her voice, but keeping his own dry and casual, 'It's nothing, my dear, nothing at all.'

She was silent then, looking at him, and he realized how faded and worn she had become in the thirteen years of their marriage. It was not through lack of trying to be attractive. Her dress was impeccable. She had plaited her brown hair and gathered it beneath a caul of gold mesh. Her gown was rose, exquisitely fashioned. But there was no more beauty or delicacy in the overall effect than in a bundle of straw draped out in rich materials. The cruelty of the metaphor, even as a thought, made him remorseful. He touched her hand with genuine affection. She smiled, and he saw how she might have been had he not inflicted his own deficiencies on her. What slaves we are to each other: Elizabeth to me, I to Joan....

A servant shuffled his feet loudly in the doorway, muttering and clearing his throat.

'What is it?' Salisbury asked.

'A messenger, my lord. He says he must speak with you at once.'

Salisbury took up a candle and went toward the entrance hall, his hand shaking so that the hot tallow spilled over his thumb. He scarcely noticed it, did not feel it.

When he returned from speaking with the messenger, Elizabeth, who was standing just as he had left her, gasped and said, 'William, you're truly pale now. You must go to bed at once. At once, William. . . .'

'I'm afraid that's not possible,' he said, striving to keep his voice steady. 'I must go to a special meeting of the Council. There's been a disturbance at Brentwood.'

He leaned over to kiss her. She drew away abruptly. 'I know!' she said, her tone spiteful, venomous. 'I know very well why you're going to the Tower!'

Salisbury stared at her, his fear over receipt of the message struggling with the guilt and compassion he felt toward her. For an instant he considered asking her to prepare to leave with him at once: for Canterbury, for France, for the heart of Spain.

But only for an instant. He knew how impossible this would be for him, from every point of view.

He ran from the solar, calling for a servant to bring him a cloak.

'I do not honestly believe,' Courtenay was saying smoothly, 'that the incident merits more than our passing attention.'

'How can we be sure?' asked Salisbury. 'How can we know that this disturbance does not represent the vanguard of something more . . .'

'In my opinion . . .' interrupted Hales, his jowls flapping, and as usual everyone looked toward him expectantly. He giggled and said, 'Shoeless ruffians.'

'I think,' said Courtenay, 'that if you question Bampton carefully, you will find that there were very few peasants, badly armed, if in fact they were armed at all. Naturally, Bampton would try to exaggerate to some extent. He would hardly admit to a cowardice occasioned by the shouts of a handful of . . .'

'Shoeless ruffians,' said Hales.

106

'Shoeless ruffians,' repeated Courtenay, sweeping all of them with an amused glance.

'Has anyone questioned the soldiers and clerks who accompanied Bampton?' asked Salisbury.

'Totally unnecessary,' countered the Bishop. 'It was a local disturbance. We've had them before. After all, no one was slain. In these villages, as you probably know, my lord,' he said, turning to Salisbury and edging his words with sarcasm, 'they regularly vent their feelings by pummelling each other. Far from discouraging such activity, we should look with favour on it, since in the end it makes them more tractable. Though, of course, it was unfortunate that Bampton happened to be in the process of collecting taxes at the precise moment.'

'We should send out a force large enough to teach the scum a lesson,' said Walworth. 'No matter how we look at it, this was a blow against authority, and something we cannot tolerate. I would not brook it in my own city.'

Salisbury thought he saw Courtenay flash an annoyed glance in Walworth's direction, but he had no time to reflect on its meaning. The King was beginning to grumble. He had been roused from his bed for the meeting and had never thoroughly awakened. Now the debate and the bad air in the chamber were making him sleepier, but the room was too damp and his chair too uncomfortable for a proper nap.

'Will you squabble all night, my uncles?' he asked irritably. 'Surely you know you've taken me from my rest.'

Salisbury's own irritation was growing. He thought: if a boy of fourteen needs more rest than I do at the age of fifty-three . . . But he said, 'We shall dispose of the matter soon, Your Majesty. It would be unthinkable if we made any important decisions without the benefit of Your Majesty's sage consideration.'

'The decision is not so important, after all, is it, my lord Salisbury?' asked Courtenay.

'There is something,' said Hales, and again all eyes rested on him. He looked around weightily and said, 'We should get the tax. Yes, we should get the tax.'

'We shall get the tax,' snapped Courtenay, angry at having been taken in once more. Yet, Salisbury knew, the next time Hales demanded attention, he would receive it immediately; he could never understand what gave the fat priest this power.

Sudbury rubbed his pate and said, speaking for the first time since he had opened the deliberations, 'I agree with His Grace, the Bishop of London. The peasants are good people and mean us no harm. There was once one of them who met a pardoner and a summoner on the road from Canterbury . . .'

'If it please my lord Chancellor,' said Courtenay, his voice like rippling velvet, 'we would be delighted to hear his story later, over a cup or two of wine. For now . . .'

'We should send an army to crush them,' said Walworth. 'Now. Before they begin to feel they can flout authority.'

This time there was no mistaking the glance Courtenay flung at Walworth. It was one of unequivocal contempt: of only an instant's duration, so that Salisbury was sure the Lord Mayor had not even noticed it. But Salisbury had. He was aware of his own vanities; his gift of intuition was not one of them. There was no undue pride in his knowledge that he possessed sensitivity and understanding to a degree far beyond the ordinary. In his relationship with Joan this had not worked to his advantage. Sensitivity had paralysed his firmness, and his understanding had seemed weakness. However, in dealing with other diplomats, he had found intuition his chief asset. The barely perceptible movement of a nostril or the curl of a lip or a wavering glance spoke to him in a special language, mostly unintelligible to others.

He was fairly sure now there was something between Courtenay and Walworth. In time, perhaps, he would learn what it was.

Courtenay said, 'It is my opinion that if we send too large a force we should be advising these villagers that we are overly troubled by their insolence. I would suggest we dispatch a small detachment of soldiers and clerks to Brentwood, preferably under the charge of a jurist, who can both command respect and sentence a few of them to be hanged as an example.'

The Council, including Walworth, voted in favour of the Bishop's plan. Salisbury hesitated before casting his own vote, then concurred with the others.

It was decided that Sir Robert Belknap, Chief Justice of Common Pleas, should be instructed to start for Brentwood at dawn.

3

JACK STRAW said mass that Sunday morning in Brentwood. When he entered the church and stomped up the nave toward the chancel, the parish priest opened his mouth in angry protest. Whatever he intended to say, however, was reconsidered. Straw raised his arms and stood facing the altar like a malevolent raven with half-spread wings. The parish priest, already uneasy over the developments of the past few days, drew his vestments about him like shreds of dignity and began a sedate retreat from the church. Before he reached the transept his pace had quickened to a brisk walk. By the time he passed Tyler, who was standing just inside the door, he was running.

They crowded in then, almost the entire population of Brentwood, their numbers so augmented by the influx from Fobbing and the other marsh villages that most of them were unable to get past the porch.

Straw recited the Latin words as if he were importuning God. At the end of the service he paused, then said, his angry voice carrying out into the churchyard, 'They will come today. They will come and we will teach them. They will learn that we are not dogs, nor are we slaves. We are free men, and we will resist them with the strength of free men.' He added, growling out the words, 'Let God be with us!'

They poured out of the church, milled about the churchyard, sat on gravestones, appearing aimless and a little disconsolate. Tyler walked among them, saying quietly, 'To the market-place. All gather in the market-place.' They trooped after him, a few carrying longbows, the rest trailing axes, scythes, sticks.

Straw hurried up alongside Tyler. 'What's the matter with them?' he demanded. 'Slinking about like Noah's children, acting as if they were frightened every time the wind passes through the trees. What's the matter with them?'

'They are frightened.'

'Why? No blood in them, that's why. Their moment has come, and they've no blood in them.' He turned and shouted at the men drifting along behind them. 'Ho there, alive, alive, you're men, not trash. Alive there!' He cuffed the man nearest him, a hard-handed fisherman from Corringham. 'Alive there!' The man stared at him, large eyes baffled and almost frightened.

As unobtrusively as he could, Tyler grasped Straw's arm, forced the priest to walk beside him. 'You'll not strike one more of them,' he said in a low voice.

'They're mine. I know what's best for them. I'll do as I like with them.'

'Are you a lord?'

Straw's face turned a mottled red. His breath began to rattle in his throat. Then suddenly tears sprang to his eyes, and his arm went limp in Tyler's grip. 'So long,' he said, 'I've waited so long. My whole life, it's been my life. Waiting, scheming. . . . We mustn't fail now, we can't . . .'

'We won't,' said Tyler grimly.

Straw raised his fist at the sky. 'God, give them strength. Give them strength!'

When they reached the market-place, Tyler made a final rough count, estimated their numbers at slightly over five hundred. He ranged them in ranks on either side of the square. Except for several who had seen military service, the men allowed themselves to be moved about and placed with the mute submissiveness of bullocks.

'I don't understand, not at all,' said Straw. 'Many of these helped drive Bampton from the town . . .'

'Today is different,' said Tyler. 'Everything is different today.'

The sun was well above the trees now, and the air was beginning to throb with heat. An hour went by, part of another. Some of the women of Brentwood collected at the edges of the square, talking in low voices, looking toward their men.

A farmer from Brentwood started an argument with the fisherman from Corringham whom Straw had cuffed on the way to the square. The fisherman leaped on the farmer, bit his ear. Tyler ran across the square and separated them, held them apart by the scruffs of their necks. He surveyed them, let them go, slapped them on their backs and laughed. 'Not long now, lads. Soon you'll have enough to do.'

He remembered the tension before some of the skirmishes in France: the nimble French crossbowmen advancing with their unwieldy equipment across the rolling hills, the gut-tightening moment when you could see the plumes on the knights' helmets, the sun on the blades of the pikemen. And the fray itself, when much was forgotten in the dissolving warmth of violence. Except that later one always remembered, and memory was bitter, for the mangled and the dying were almost inevitably the foot-soldiers, the farmers and artisans who found in France only mutilation or death, while the knights took other knights captive and reaped rich ransoms.

A woman shouted, 'They're coming . . .' and a cry rolled round the square, both mournful and angry, to die in a silence so complete that Tyler could hear a bird singing in the churchyard.

'No,' called another woman. 'She's wrong, it's no one.'

Then there was laughter, and men began to embrace one another as if they had already won a victory. Only Jack Straw, his face dark and tormented, remained unsmiling.

Over the laughter Tyler heard the distant sound of hoofbeats. 'Now . . .' he said to Straw, and the glow in the priest's eyes leaped into flame. 'Now!' Tyler called out to the ranks of peasants, and once more the silence in the square was complete, as all of them listened to the drumming of horses' hooves racing toward them down the long incline of the London Road.

The horsemen slackened pace as they reached the square, entered it in impressive double file. There were twenty-four of them: a score of soldiers, helmeted and lightly armoured, three clerks in priests' habit, and one man wearing a red velvet cloak.

'The clerks are the same,' Tyler heard a man behind him whisper. 'The very same as came here last Thursday.'

One of these clerks, after a glance at the man in red velvet, unrolled a parchment and began to read in a nasal sing-song. 'In the name of His Lordship Simon of Sudbury, Archbishop of Canterbury and Chancellor of the Realm, and in the name of Sir Robert Hales, Treasurer of the Realm, it is hereby commanded that all present freemen and serfs of the town of Brentwood, together with the villages of Fobbing, Corringham, Stanford-le-hope, Bulphon, Herongate . . .'

'By cock, he can read, so he can,' cried a peasant in one of the forward ranks. The laughter that followed was like a single thunderclap, and was as abruptly gone. The soldiers reined in horses grown restive and looked at the man in red velvet. He sat impassively, as if nothing had occurred.

'All are commanded,' continued the clerk nervously, 'to submit to a true enumeration and to pay the poll tax enacted by His Majesty in Parliament. The enumeration and collection will take place under the supervision of the representative of His Majesty, Sir Robert Belknap, Chief Justice of Common Pleas . . .'

'We'll not pay one farthing!' shouted Straw. 'Not one farthing more!'

A neatly trimmed beard decorated Belknap's long jaw. He touched it now and turned to his soldiers. 'Arrest that man,' he said.

'If you try,' called Tyler, 'your heads will line the London Road.'

Belknap stared coldly at him, let his glance slide about the square. Tyler could see that he was taking note of the ragtag mob, their lack of proper arms. He took a step forward. 'You may kill ten, or fifty, or even a hundred of us. But in the end . . .'

'We are here to collect taxes,' said Belknap, 'and collect taxes we shall.'

His voice was as cold as his eyes. Tyler could feel the cry of rage gathering inside him, starting up his throat. He leaped at Belknap, seized the Justice's leg and with one clean smart motion unseated him from the saddle and dumped him on the ground.

The soldiers tried to go to Belknap's assistance, but it was too late. Already the people were swarming over them, and in a few moments the detachment was disarmed. Once more the square grew silent. The only noise was made by the Corringham fisherman. He was sitting astride a soldier, rapping his knuckles against the man's helmet as if he were pounding at a door. His concentration was so intense that Tyler had to call out to him three times before he would desist.

Tyler pulled Belknap to his feet and said, 'You deserve nothing but the most severe punishment. For your actions here today, the commons have every right to lop off your head and the heads of all those with you.'

Belknap touched his beard, which was now streaked with dust, but he made no reply.

'However,' Tyler went on, 'since you have come to the commons as a representative of King Richard, with whom we have no quarrel, in fact whose loyal subjects we are and will remain, you will merely be required to swear that you will never again, so long as you live, attempt to collect taxes from the commons. After you have done this, you and your men will be allowed to return to London.'

'But not the clerks!' cried Straw.

'Swear,' Tyler said to Belknap. When the Justice failed to speak, Tyler shook him violently. 'Swear!'

Belknap said in a flat voice, 'I swear.'

Tyler released him. 'You and your men are free to go.'

'Not the clerks!' Straw cried again. 'Twice they came here, twice! They must die!'

Tyler studied Belknap, the soldiers and the clerks in turn. Then he looked slowly around the square. The assemblage bore little resemblance to the uncertain, fumbling crowd of a few hours before. Their expressions were set and savage. They had to be satisfied.

'The clerks will die,' said Tyler.

'Now!" shouted Straw.

'Now,' said Tyler.

The three priests commenced babbling, each in a different key, begging for mercy. The one who had read from the parchment suddenly ceased pleading, leaned over and retched.

'Now,' said Tyler again. 'In the name of the true commons, for crimes committed against the people. As a warning and an example. Now.'

The executions were carried out by three farmers with axes. Several of the soldiers turned away, but Belknap watched stonily.

Tyler ordered the Justice and the soldiers to remount. They did so hastily and galloped weaponless, in groups of three or four, out of the town.

The people stood silently, gazing at the bodies of the three clerks.

From the churchyard the bird's song rose again, clear and untroubled.

The village of Fobbing clung to the top of the highest hill in the district.

In the hours of late afternoon Tyler, Straw and some two hundred of those who had been with them at Brentwood earlier in the day climbed the steep rise dominated by the church. Each man carried an armful of wood.

Straw ordered the bell to be rung, and its frenetic tolling continued while they piled the wood in a small field not far from the church.

Tyler looked out across the marshland. To the south, a broad ribbon of light in the waning day, was the Thames. North and east lay the numerous villages of Essex.

Straw joined them. A woman brought them bowls of salt fish and chunks of bread. Straw waved his away, but Tyler ate hungrily and asked the woman for ale.

The events of the day had left him with the sense of fulfilment he had expected, but there was something else: an odd poignancy which seemed to be probing for his heart, robbing him of the will to act.

He shook his head vigorously, downed his ale.

At dusk the church bell stopped ringing.

Tyler walked over to where the people were congregated about the great heap of wood. There was not much talk.

It grew dark.

'The torch,' said Tyler.

A man brought it, touched it to the wood in several places. The flames mounted.

Straw joined him. 'There's no turning back now,' said Tyler.

'Why should we turn back?'

A voice from the other side of the fire began to chant:

> *When Adam delved and Eve span,*
> *Who was then the gentleman?*

The others took it up, drowning the crackling of the flames.

'They'll see this,' said Tyler, his spirits suddenly rising. 'They'll see it and pass it on. They'll know we've begun.'

Straw did not seem to have heard him. His head was thrown back and he was smiling. It was not a pleasant smile.

4

FOR days the rumours had been growing.
('Like cherries on a tree,' observed Abel. 'Let's pick them,' said Roger excitedly. 'They'll fall, they'll fall,' counselled Abel.)

But they did not. Each peddler who came through the village told a different tale. And each successive version of what was happening drove Roger to greater frenzy. 'We're going to be free!' he would exult one moment. And the next, 'There'll be nothing for us, ever.'

'You'll neither be free nor unfree,' Abel told him. 'You'll be mad, and they'll kill a black cock and tie it about your head, and the whip against your buttocks will make your tongue rattle like a leper's clapper.'

In the end, though, Roger persuaded Abel to come with him to Gravesend. 'They'll know there,' he said. 'They'll be able to tell us what's happening.'

Abel said with heavy sarcasm, 'Gravesend is the fount of all wisdom. In Gravesend they know everything.'

The truth was that he was not uneager to go. Though the town was seven miles from their village, he had only visited it three times during his life, and the last occasion was eight years ago, when he had disembarked on his return from France. It would make a pleasant expedition. The fields could do without his presence for a day or two. And, despite his reluctance to admit it, he was also curious about the rumours.

They took their longbows. If they were stopped, no one would question their carrying the bows. Archery was an accepted peasant sport, encouraged above the rowdy kickball contests which too often ended in mayhem.

They avoided the main footpath and found their way among oak and chestnut trees. The only serious obstacle to such roundabout travel was the profusion of holly.

'Catches at your breeches like money to Elias's fingers,' said Roger.

114

'Elias, Elias,' Abel sang, 'wishes he could buy us. But his greedy heart isn't worth a fart, and that's the truth, so cry us.'

'Sing about Barbara,' said Roger.

Abel was pleased to oblige. 'Barbara, Barbara, pretty bitch, gives a man a craven itch. But if you pine for a well-turned leg, your itch will switch to a wench called Peg.'

Roger shied a stick at him, and ahead of them a deer darted out of a thicket, stopped dead and stared at them, quivering. They looked at each other questioningly, and Roger's hand stole toward his bow. 'Not now,' cautioned Abel finally. 'Maybe on the way back.'

They came in sight of Gravesend shortly before noon. The town lay atop a gentle marshy incline sloping down to the bank of the Thames. After a few moments of discussion, Abel and Roger decided it might be wiser to cache their bows in some bushes outside the town. 'We'll look strangers enough,' said Abel, 'without drawing more attention.'

They need not have troubled. The town was in turmoil, the streets clogged with people. No stitch of work was being done, and everyone was anxious to tell them why.

'I saw fires last night,' said a pewterer. 'Across the river in Essex.' He bent close to them and whispered like a conspirator. 'Signal fires, I'd say, John of Gaunt back from the north, and he means to overthrow the King.'

A woodmonger said, 'All serfs are free now.'

'The top of your head is loose,' a tanner told him, snickering. 'They're going to gather up all peasants and woodmongers and send them to France to fight.'

'I've heard they're marching,' said the woodmonger.

'Who's marching?' asked the tanner. 'Robert Hales' tax collectors?'

'Never mind talk of Hob the Robber,' said a butcher, shaking an admonishing bloodstained finger. 'He's taken all the taxes he'll get here.'

'Bold talk,' replied the tanner. 'After he's sent collectors here twice, each time taking away money, and nobody . . .'

'All serfs are free now,' said the woodmonger.

'The bear, the bear, see the bear dance!' cried a voice behind them. They turned to watch the motley-cloaked bear-driver prodding his charge with a goad. The bear was performing a clumsy dance on its hind feet. Its left eye was closed and bloody, and the driver was using the goad on the other.

'Looks like a drunken friar, he does,' said the tanner, and retreated as the bear dropped onto all fours and ambled toward him.

'Don't fret,' cried the driver. 'No fear, no fear at all, he's had all his teeth and claws drawn. See?' He prodded the bear up onto its hind feet again and forced its mouth open to display a double row of lacerated gums.

A knight and five soldiers galloped past them. Seated on one of the horses in front of a soldier was a man in tattered hood and tunic.

'That's Sir Simon Burley, the knight there,' said the pewterer to Abel and Roger. 'In the service of the King's mother, he is.'

'And up to somewhat, from the look of him,' observed the tanner.

'Likely,' said the pewterer, 'he's out looking for any of John of Gaunt's men he can find.'

'He'll find none here,' said the butcher.

The mounted company halted abruptly at the end of the street, and the tradesmen raced toward them, Abel and Roger following along behind.

Two of the soldiers swung off their horses and dashed into a narrow alleyway, returned shortly dragging a stocky young man in a leather apron. The tanner gasped. 'It's my prentice, John Belling.'

'Pick his feet up,' called the knight jovially. 'Wouldn't want them to get dirty, would we now?'

'My prentice,' said the tanner again.

A crowd was beginning to collect.

'Look lively,' said the knight to the man in tattered clothes who had come with them. 'Look lively and well and speak your piece.'

'It's him, Sir Simon,' breathed the man. 'It's John Belling.'

'Well spoken,' said Sir Simon. 'You're lively and you've said a good mouthful. You'll have your penny for this and a drink of wine besides.' He looked at Belling. 'Thought you could run away, did you. Well, my pretty aproned fellow, you'll have a long run to Rochester Dungeon, you will. Bind him,' he said to the soldiers. 'Bind him and put him on a lead from my saddle.'

'He's my prentice!' cried the tanner.

'Is he indeed?' asked Burley. 'He may be your prentice now, but he was my serf before that.'

'It's him, Sir Simon,' said the tattered man again. 'It's John Belling.'

'Yes, yes,' replied the knight. 'We've all agreed to that.'

The butcher blew his nose between his fingers, cleared his throat and said, 'He's lived in the town for over two years. The law . . .'

'The law,' said Burley, 'is what one makes of it. And I make this man to be a runaway serf, subject to punishment for what he's

116

done.' His tone was still affable, but there was an undernote of irritation that made the crowd stir and mumble uncomfortably.

'He's a good prentice,' said the tanner. 'I'll buy him. I'll pay the fine and buy him back.'

Sir Simon smiled. 'Now there's a proposition that interests me. Money. The shine of silver, the glint of gold. Though I'll warrant if Sir Robert Hales could hear you boasting of your wealth, he'd be here with his hand stretched out for another few groats.' He laughed.

'How much?' asked the tanner. 'How much to get my prentice back?'

Burley appeared to be thinking deeply. He rubbed his pink cheeks, stuck his thumb in his mouth and popped it out. 'I'll name it fair,' he said finally. 'Neither too hard on you nor too easy on me.' He looked skyward and said slowly, 'Three hundred pounds will buy him, free, sold, and delivered over your threshold.'

The tanner stared at the knight. 'Three . . .' he began, and swallowed.

Burley laughed uproariously.

'Three hundred . . .' the tanner managed this time.

'Tie him,' said Burley to the soldiers. 'Tie him and we'll be away. It's a weary ride to Rochester.'

Belling began to struggle, kicking out at his captors. One soldier pinioned his arms while the other proceeded to smash his fists into the prentice's face. Blood gushed out of Belling's nose and mouth. His knees sagged.

Abel saw Roger start toward the soldiers. He pulled the younger man back, but then was amazed to find himself lunging forward, cursing through clenched teeth. The soldier who was holding Belling shouted a warning, and the other spun about, drawing a poinard with savage swiftness. The first slashing stroke laid open a gash across the back of Abel's right hand.

'Take him as well,' called Burley.

Abel fled down the passageway from which Belling had been taken, and in a few moments saw why the prentice had been unable to escape. The alley ended in a cul-de-sac heaped with garbage and excrement. He crouched as close to the wall as he could, resigned to capture. Blood was dripping from his injured hand.

There was a great deal of noise coming from the street. They would be following him now, and shortly he would be trussed up like Belling.

Steps sounded along the passageway. Abel got to his feet. He supposed he had better fight, though he knew he was too frightened

117

and confused to put up much resistance. Even in his fear his mind shaped the question: should a fighting fool make a foolish fight? It was not quite apt; he would have to rearrange the words before anyone would laugh.

He braced himself and raised his hands. His pursuer was almost upon him, a menacing silhouette against dim light from the street.

'They've gone, Abel.'

He lowered his hands and blinked at Roger.

'Why did I do it?' he asked disgustedly. Then, 'Gone?'

'The townspeople were beginning to turn ugly. They decided they'd better just take Belling and leave.'

'Why did I do it? Interfering in something that was none of my affair. . . .'

He shook his head and followed Roger out of the passageway.

When they emerged onto the street, Abel was greeted with approving shouts. He shook his head again, still angry with himself. His hand was beginning to pain.

The pewterer brought him ale in one of his metal cups. It was good ale, Abel noted appreciatively.

He looked around at the admiring expressions of the townspeople. How often, he wondered, can a man play the idiot and be regarded as a hero?

However, he was not such an idiot as to refuse the offer of a woman to dress his wound. She was a widow, not young, but still short enough of tooth to make a bite from her enjoyable. And when she insisted on his remaining in her house for the night so she could better observe the wound and keep it from festering, he agreed. To be a fool once was perhaps understandable. To compound foolishness in the same day was unforgivable.

The sound of excitement continued in the streets of Gravesend far into the night, but after an hour or so Abel heard little of it.

5

EACH morning, just as dawn lent the circular window a sickly light, the rats and mice disappeared. During the hours of darkness they swarmed over the cell, squeaking, scratching and gnawing at whatever they could find: straw, filth, any scrap of food Ball and Simon might have left. One night Ball awakened to find a rat sitting on his chest, nibbling at his lips. Usually they

118

were not so bold, though the jailer had been right about one thing: surely, as far as size went, they were the most impressive in all England.

Where they went during the day Ball could not discover; he was merely thankful that they departed. The lice were not so considerate. They were in his hair, his beard, and the private places of his body. First there had been only the itching, then the burning, now the raw open sores he scraped (his nails were useless for scratching) and even bit on himself.

Despite the rodents and vermin, he found he could sleep at least a few hours each night. But always he was awake in time to watch light growing in the window.

This morning a letter was taking shape in his mind. It had been a long while since he had written one. The letters had never come to him in the same manner as his speeches. Words he directed to people in market-places and churchyards bore the mark of necessity; their fibre was tough, their meaning sure. The letters had only been written on those rare occasions when hope was so strong in him that it could not be contained and had to be shared. He could hardly say he felt hope now, but there were times when despair plumbed so deep that its extremes bore some resemblance to hope, as intense pain sometimes resembles pleasure.

He never felt that he actually wrote the letters. They seemed to come to him whole, a fabric woven without discernible warp and woof. The one that was coming clear in his mind now seemed to be materializing in the usual fashion. One instant there was nothing, a void; and then the letter was there, complete.

'But I shall never be able to write it,' he said, unaware that he had spoken aloud until Simon asked, yawning, 'Be able to write what?'

'A letter,' Ball replied absently.

'To another priest?'

'Some who would read it are priests, most not.'

Simon got up off the straw, scratching himself in a desultory way: the lice did not seem to trouble him as they did Ball. 'I should not feel easy about helping you send a letter to priests. I hate them, you see.'

After a moment Ball said, 'How do you mean, helping?'

The little man emitted a dry chuckle of self-satisfaction. 'The jailer,' he said. 'The jailer will bring you writing materials. He'll also take your letter to where you wish it sent.'

'Yes,' said Ball, sighing.

'Oh, I don't mean he'll do it as a favour. But for money . . .'

'I have no money.'

'I have.'

'Yes,' said Ball again, remembering his first day of internment, when Simon's malice had tricked him into a delusion of escape.

Simon rushed over to him, trembling with indignation. 'You don't believe me! Why don't you believe me?'

'Is there any reason why I should?' Ball asked wearily.

'Listen.' Simon's expression grew crafty. 'If I give you money to bribe the jailer, will you do what I ask of you when we're free?'

'What?' asked Ball, his attention beginning to stray.

'If I give you money, will you go with me into a church and defile it?'

Ball looked steadily at him, too despondent to reply. The sly expression dissolved from Simon's face. 'Forgive me,' he mumbled.

'It doesn't matter.'

'It matters. You trust me, and I've come to trust you.' He continued hesitantly. 'I even think . . . perhaps when I'm free again, I might not . . . who knows? It's a difficult thing to say.'

'One can never say what he'll do. I once thought a man should be able to live by set principles. This and this I will do in this and this situation. I've learned: no man can ever allow himself the luxury of such vanity . . .' He stopped, surprised that he had spoken so freely.

Simon's eyes grew moist. 'This is why I've come to trust you. Not once have you laughed at me or called me mad. I want to help you.'

Ball thought of his own madness, when he had exhausted himself pounding at the door of the cell, and of the comfort Simon had given him. 'You have helped me,' he said.

'This letter . . . is it very important to you that it be written and dispatched?'

'Please . . .'

'Is it important?'

'I don't know.'

'It is. I can feel that it is.'

Ball watched disinterestedly, then in disbelief, as Simon's fingers fumbled beneath the hem of the crusty tunic he was wearing, ripped the lining and brought forth two gold nobles. He handed them to Ball, who turned them over in his hands, staring stupidly at the designs of the ships cut clear on the faces of the coins.

'You can give him one when he brings the writing materials . . . and a lamp, he must bring a lamp. The other he can have when he brings proof he's delivered the letter.'

Ball struggled to speak.

'Don't tell me you can't,' said Simon. 'The day you came in here, I tricked you. Because you're a priest and I hate . . . I haven't lied to you since. Don't lie to me. Don't say you can't take the money.'

'You'll need it when you're free.'

'When I'm free,' mused Simon, his voice becoming soft with longing. He looked at Ball. 'It's my money,' he said firmly. 'Is it not then for me to decide how it should be spent? Even,' he added with a touch of bitterness, 'if some who read your letter will be priests.'

The wick burned brightly in the bowl of fish oil, and the lamplight together with the bench the jailer had brought gave the cell an atmosphere of cosiness that made Ball oddly uncomfortable. No matter, he thought ironically, soon enough we'll be restored to more acceptable austerity.

He read over what he had written. He had set the words down exactly as they had come to him that morning; once a letter assumed its shape, he seldom changed it.

Simon was watching him. 'He'll return soon.'

Ball nodded.

'I was looking at your face while you were writing. . . . Why is it so important to you?'

'I hope . . .' said Ball, and stopped.

'Hope what?'

'The words I write . . . the words I speak . . . spoke,' he amended, then went on, 'I hope they will help people to set themselves free.'

'And you've wanted this a long time.'

'A long time,' repeated Ball.

Longer, perhaps, than even I myself know. The restlessness while I served in the Abbey, the fervour (and the feelings of futility) during the first years of my wandering when I tried to convince myself that my sermons on the morality of wedlock were my true mission. For so long I sought to escape the burden I knew I would eventually have to shoulder. And even when I did begin to preach what I thought was truth, it was not enough, for there was substance without a core of meaning. I felt I understood the misery I saw, and I spoke out against it. My words moved others without moving me. Until the dreary winter morning when I happened on the leper sitting on a rock outside a Sussex town: starving and exhausted, the flesh of his face eaten away, the wooden clapper proclaiming him a pariah clutched to his chest. And when I brought him food and drink and a cloak to wrap about his wasted body, he accepted them and looked up at me without expression. Then he spat in my face. And for the first time my eyes were opened, as if I had been blind before and the leper's spittle was the healing touch of Christ. Never afterward could I see without feeling, and never again could I feel without suffering the same pain that had caused the leper to fling his anguish at me.

Simon was asking, 'And what do you want for yourself, John Ball?'

'Nothing.'

'That cannot be. Every man wants something for himself.'

'I want nothing.'

'You told me they put you in prison twice before.'

'Yes.'

'And you have known fear and hunger and weariness and loneliness.'

'These things I did not tell you.'

'These things you did not have to tell me. Nor do you have to tell me how you long for peace, and the simple pleasures of living. . . . Why then, John Ball? Why?'

Ball said, groping for words, 'There comes a time in a man's life . . . in his understanding of his own heart . . . when he can no longer turn away from the cruelty and injustice he sees . . . when he must say: if this goes on, if some few men can enslave and oppress many others . . . and if I stand by and do nothing to stop this . . . of what value is my own life to me?' He stopped speaking, his heart pounding heavily. The words had cost him a great effort.

Simon was silent for a moment. Then he said slowly, 'To be free. . . .'

A key turned in the lock, and the door swung open. The jailer shuffled in, carrying two bowls of grey-looking mush. He set them down, began scratching himself vigorously. 'A bleedin' lord's castle in here, it is.' He plucked the letter from the bench. 'This what I'm meant to see gets somewhere?'

'To the baker in Aylesford,' said Ball. 'And you're to ask him to see it reaches Wat Tyler in Colchester.'

The jailer belched and stared at the parchment. He read aloud haltingly, 'John Ball greets you all well and gives you to know he has rung your bell.' He laughed and said, 'Whose bell can a priest ring when his own gives off no sound?' He looked down at the letter again. 'With might and right, with skill and with will, let might keep right, and skill go before will and right before might.

And if might go before right, and will before skill, then is our mill in sorry plight.' He came close to Ball. 'Mill? What mill, Sir Priest?'

'You'll deliver the letter?'

'Give me the gold.'

'After you've brought proof . . .'

'The gold.'

Ball looked at Simon, who shrugged. He handed the coin to the jailer, who examined it, then pouched it. He laughed and gripped the letter in both hands, preparing to tear it. Ball did not move. Twice the jailer's hands tightened convulsively on the parchment, twice he let them go limp without tearing it. Finally he said, 'I'll see it on its way.'

'Will you not take it yourself?'

'No!' cried the jailer. Alarm spread across his face. He began trembling. 'I can't leave here, don't you know I can't leave here?' Gradually he grew calmer. 'You're mad, Sir Priest.' He scratched himself in silence for a few moments. Then he said quietly, 'And if the mad speak to the mad . . .'

He put the letter in his pouch and left the cell.

6

VERY early in the morning Tyler and the others had stormed one of the manors belonging to John of Gaunt. 'Storm' was in itself a misuse of the word: Straw insisted on so calling what they did. In fact, they had climbed the hill and walked into the manor house; it was that simple.

There were more than three thousand of them. The signal fires two days ago had brought reinforcements from all over Essex, and every hour more were flocking into the camp they had set up in the meadows between Fobbing and Brentwood.

In the dawn foray they had encountered no opposition. As they proceeded from the great hall to the solars, and from there to the kitchens and storerooms, they had seen everywhere evidence of hasty departure by the occupants. In all the enormous reach of rooms they had discovered only one person: a drunken, half-witted groom who could tell them nothing.

Tyler had ordered some of the men to search out all documents in the manor house and bring them to the courtyard. There he had burned them, thus keeping faith with one of John Ball's primary tenets of action.

('First burn the records,' Ball had said. 'Then, if we fail later, at least that will be done, and the manors will have no legal rolls by which they can hold their serfs.'

'We shall not fail,' Tyler had replied.

'In any event, we must first destroy the records. We might be slaves to the lords, but they in turn are slaves to parchment.' He had smiled his gentle, ironic smile. 'So, you see, it is really the lords we shall be liberating.')

Tyler had continued to think of Ball as he watched the smoke rising from the heap of parchment scrolls. He had wondered how his friend's face would appear when he was finally able to look on their triumph.

Later in the day, when the sun was at its height, they climbed another hill, this one leading to a manor house owned by Robert Hales. Like the one they had entered in the morning, this was unprotected by a moat, and as they toiled up the hill, the peasants laughed and called out to each other, expecting to find another set of deserted rooms and halls.

The first shower of arrows killed five of them.

They stopped short, gaping at the bodies of their fallen comrades. Tyler, cursing himself for not having insisted on a more cautious advance, shouted at them to spread out. They appeared not to have heard. Another half dozen were felled by arrows apparently loosed from behind the parapet atop the house. Still the others would not move.

Tyler rushed among them, ordering, cajoling, exhorting until his voice cracked. He might as well have been running through a forest: the peasants remained immovable as oaks.

Suddenly the whole mass of men trembled as if swept by a strong wind. Heedless of the arrows flying among them with lethal effect, they continued up the hill, purposefully, not speaking.

The manor house gate delayed them for only a moment. They surged into the entrance hall, leaving the heavy timbers smashed in their wake.

Tyler, following as quickly as he was able, forced a passage for himself up the spiral stone staircase to the rooftop, and was greeted by a desperate sight. Some two hundred of the invaders had overpowered the dozen or so henchmen who had been defending the manor house. The corpses of the archers were being savagely torn apart.

The carnage was being carried out in almost complete silence.

Only the laboured breathing of the peasants at their brutal task marred the stillness.

Tyler beat his way back down the staircase and hurried along the corridors of the lower floor. The men there, unable to reach the rooftop and so far uninfected by what was taking place above, were drifting about, fingering tapestries and velvet drapes, caressing intricately carved chairs, tables and chests. Tyler moved among them, opening doors and peering into chambers.

As he was about to enter one solar, the door swung open, and a man stepped out to face Tyler. He had a small beard, oiled and pointed; his tunic and hose were dark blue, spangled with tiny silver stars.

'Exactly what,' he demanded imperiously, 'is the meaning of all this?'

Tyler was struck momentarily speechless by what could only be incredible courage or insane effrontery. Then, recovering himself, he inquired, 'Are you the steward of the manor?'

The other looked at Tyler with disdain. 'I see no reason,' he began, 'why I should . . .'

He got no farther. Tyler strode up to him, cuffed him twice, smartly. 'Answer!'

The man nodded. 'I'm the steward.'

'Show me where you keep your records.'

Tyler had some of the peasants carry the chests of documents out of the manor house. Straw was waiting in the bright sunlight of the courtyard. The steward said, 'If you do not tell these people to go home at once, they will all answer to Sir Robert when he comes.'

'Hob the Robber,' snarled Straw. 'We'll see him before you. And when we do, he'll do the answering, not us. That is, if his head can speak from the end of a pike.'

The steward gagged suddenly and turned away.

Tyler ordered the records to be burned. As the flames began licking around the cross-piled chests, there was a scream from the gateway.

Three peasants were dragging a young girl out of the manor house. They threw her onto the ground, and one of them held her down.

The steward started toward them, eyes gone wild, shrieking, 'Edith, Edith!'

Tyler caught him, sent him sprawling into a rose bush. Then he charged at the peasants, scattered two of them with a pair of blows, picked up the one who was holding the girl and shook him until the man's mouth flew open and his eyes bugged. Tyler dropped him like a discarded garment and walked back to Straw.

The priest was so furious he could barely speak. 'You protect these swine . . .'

'Our quarrel is with their masters, not them.'

'You protect them, and you strike . . .' He gasped. 'You strike your own people . . .'

'I'll do the same again, if ever I catch them at looting or raping . . .'

'Your own people!'

The girl was getting to her feet, looking around her bewilderedly. Her eyes lighted as she saw the steward. He was picking himself out of the rose bush where Tyler had thrown him. The thorns had scratched his face, and enmeshed in the hairs of his beard were two pink rose petals.

He started toward the girl, arms stretched out to her. When he had taken two or three steps, Straw suddenly drew a knife from beneath his habit, dashed at the steward and stabbed him viciously. The steward eased slowly to the ground, as if he were looking for a comfortable spot to lie down. The girl ran to him, knelt beside him. She put out her hand hesitantly, took one of the rose petals from his beard, crushed it wonderingly between her fingers.

Tyler walked over to the steward, saw that he was dead, turned to look at Straw, who stared back defiantly, then wiped the knife on the hem of his cassock.

After a moment Tyler called out to the peasants gawking at the body, 'Go and tell all inside to come out. Then burn the house.'

The girl was weeping. Something in the strangled sound of her grief made Tyler think of Isabella. He wanted her near him now with a longing that almost made him cry out with its sharpness.

The invaders poured out of the manor house, some with evidence on their hands of the gruesome massacre on the rooftop.

Tyler put the girl in charge of one of the men he knew and trusted, instructed him to take her to Brentwood and find a family to care for her.

A dozen torches were lighted from the still-burning heap of records. Soon the manor house was blazing.

Straw was beside Tyler as they retreated from the heat of the fire. 'They're enemies,' he said, 'enemies of our people.' When Tyler only nodded agreement, Straw said insistently, 'They are!'

The priest's words afforded Tyler an odd sense of relief. He glanced sharply at Straw, for the first time saw uncertainty in the other's eyes, knew that even his fanaticism was susceptible to doubts.

126

The awareness of this made Tyler feel easier about leaving him in complete charge of the Essex contingent.

For soon, he knew, very soon, he would have to cross the Thames and make his way to Maidstone.

7

WHEN Abel came out of the widow's house, his only concern was how quickly he could find Roger and begin the seven-mile walk back to their village.

Both Abel and the morning were miserable. A heavy, chilling fog shrouded Gravesend. Despite the widow's frequent ministrations, his hand was throbbing, and he had both a headache and an unstable stomach from the quantities of good ale he had drunk. He neither understood nor cared why there was still so much excited activity in the streets.

A pardoner passing by nudged his injured hand, and Abel swore at him. The pardoner turned pale and said, 'Good sir, you seem in need of a relic of Our Lord.'

'I seem in need of some ale.'

'Ale is not my province. I deal in solace for your soul. This scrap of wood, observe it carefully, for it's no ordinary bit. Mark you, it was taken and preserved from the original crucifix to which they nailed Our Lord. For thruppence . . .'

Abel turned away and saw Roger, carrying their bows and arrows, dodging nimbly through the knots of tradesmen and peasants gathered the length of the street.

'They're marching,' he called, too excited to wait until he reached Abel. 'They're marching in less than an hour.'

'We're marching,' said Abel sourly, 'back to our own village. Now.'

'They'll ring the church bell,' said Roger. 'When the bell rings, it's the signal to be off.'

'Tuppence ha'penny,' said the pardoner. 'For tuppence ha'-penny you can possess an indulgence from His Holiness the Pope for all the sins you committed last night.'

'How do you know whether I sinned last night or not?'

'Everyone did,' replied the pardoner piously, waving a document under Abel's nose. He did not know if it was the parchment or the pardoner, but something smelled of leeks, garlic and stale urine. His stomach roiled, and he calmed it with difficulty.

127

'I told them we'd go,' said Roger.

The energy of his wide-eyed enthusiasm turned Abel's innards over once more. 'Go where?' he asked irritably.

'Look here,' said the pardoner. 'You don't know how painful the fires of purgatory can be . . .'

'I'd welcome them,' retorted Abel, and again to Roger, 'Go where?'

'Three hundred have just arrived from Dartford under a man named Robert Cave. A hundred more from Erith . . .'

'Burning,' said the pardoner. 'Fire, brimstone, the torture of the rack . . .'

'They say all Essex has risen,' Roger went on. He threw back his hood. His cheeks were flushed with excitement, his eyes disgustingly clear. 'There are two hundred ready from Gravesend . . .'

'Go where?' shouted Abel.

'For only tuppence,' said the pardoner.

'From here to Rochester Castle. It's been agreed we should take it first and free John Belling . . .'

'Take a castle? What in the name of madness . . .'

'There are also,' said the pardoner, 'indulgences for future sins . . .' He broke off and watched apprehensively as Abel took his longbow from Roger and carefully fitted an arrow to it. 'What are you going to do, good sir?'

'I am going,' Abel said distinctly, 'to shoot this arrow into one of your holes and out the other and hang you up over one of your own purgatorial fires.'

'Then you'll certainly need an indulgence.' He began his retreat, calling back over his shoulder, 'Don't delay, good sir. Tuppence, the price of half a roast hen . . .'

He collided with the pewterer, who was conversing with the butcher, and at once began to harangue them, earnestly extolling the virtues of the wooden relic.

'Abel,' said Roger, 'we'll go, won't we?'

The church bell began to ring. Far down the street someone shouted. Abel looked at the wound on the back of his hand. A powerful desire to see his fields and his hut was at work in him.

'Abel?'

'Yes, by cock! Of course we'll go!'

He stood with his mouth open, stunned by what he had said, not truly certain he had said it. Then he followed Roger toward the band of men forming in the market-place.

The drizzle which had begun when they left Gravesend grew steadier and stronger halfway to Rochester.

Despite the discomfort of the march, feverish talk flew back and forth among the men. Some of those from Erith had actually been across the Thames. They had not seen the Essex men who were supposed to have risen, but they had heard first-hand from villagers all that had happened, including the fact that Sir Robert Belknap and eight hundred soldiers had been slaughtered by peasants when they tried to collect taxes at Brentwood. There was much discussion of what they would do after they had captured Rochester Castle, but no one came forth with a plan. Robert Cave, the baker from Dartford who had assumed command of the group, walked at their head without saying anything.

All during the march Abel kept thinking he was mad to be where he was. When he caught his first glimpse of Rochester Castle on a hilltop overlooking the town, he was convinced of it.

The walls were enormous, easily three times a man's height. Above them rose the keep, a massive structure of grey stone topped by battlements and a fighting platform.

Abel's longing for his village revived with sudden intensity.

The town seemed deserted when they entered it, the streets so quiet that the sound of six hundred pairs of feet sloshing through the mud was a weird and frightening complement to the drumming of rain against thatch roofs and the gurgle of water flowing in the ditches.

'Where is everyone?' asked Roger.

'Dead,' replied Abel. 'Just as we'll be if we're fools enough to attack that castle.'

Robert Cave marched them three-quarters of the way up the hill before he halted them, too close to the walls for Abel's liking. The moat was visible now, broad and filled with muddy water. Off to their right, the fortifications overlooked a steep drop to the River Medway.

Cave was walking up the hill. 'The idiot,' Abel whispered to Roger. 'We're already so close that an arrow well-aimed . . .'

He stopped speaking, fascinated by the baker's foolhardiness. He was standing now at the edge of the ditch, contemplating the water. For a time he remained in deep thought. Then he beckoned the others to join him.

Abel, watching the walls nervously, approached close enough to Cave to hear what he was saying. The baker spoke as slowly as he moved. 'The bridge across the ditch,' he said, 'we'll take that.' He massaged his chin with pudgy fingers. 'Aye, that's what we'll do.'

A quartet of soldiers appeared on platforms flanking the far end of the drawbridge, and stood regarding them curiously. 'We'll have to kill them first, I believe,' said Cave, nodding sagely.

The soldiers were not difficult targets. Abel could have sent a shaft through each of them in quick succession. But I have nothing against them, he thought. To take the life of a man standing before me more innocent than a doe . . . Even as this was running through his mind, the soldiers deployed to cover and began to send arrows across the water. A Gravesend man a few feet from Abel gasped and collapsed in the mud, a shaft through his neck.

Abel fitted an arrow and sent it winging toward one of the soldiers momentarily exposed. The man spun about and fell. His foot caught in a crevice, and he hung head downward over the water. After a moment he stopped thrashing.

Two of the other soldiers were killed almost simultaneously. The fourth received an arrow in his back as he turned and ran toward the keep.

Roger and a farmer from Erith swam to the far side of the arched span, hoisted themselves onto it and lowered the drawbridge. Cave led the triumphant invaders across and through the gateway, where their cheers faded abruptly as they looked at the keep. It towered above them, vast and brooding. There appeared to be no entrance except across another, smaller, drawbridge, which was raised. As far as anyone could see, the fortress was impregnable, and their position at the foot of the walls was extremely vulnerable. Abel knew they should retreat, but everyone seemed strangely powerless, hypnotized by the sound of rain beating against the stones above their heads.

'Now . . .' said Cave thoughtfully, then stopped and turned toward them with a sheepish and indecisive smile.

The drawbridge chain rattled, and they started back in terror as the platform descended and thudded into place. Abel watched, incredulous, as the portcullis groaned upward, and almost immediately three soldiers emerged, weaponless, holding their hands high in the air.

No one spoke. Even after the soldiers reached them, each man only looked stupidly at his neighbour.

One of the soldiers with a mountainous wart on his nose said, 'We've come to surrender.'

Still no one replied.

'Can we put our hands down now?' asked another, a seamy-faced ancient with a cast in one eye.

'Where are the rest?' Cave was finally able to stammer.

'There are no more of us,' said the wart-nosed soldier. 'We've never had more than a dozen here for the past two years.'

'But we thought . . .' said Cave, and stopped, shaking his head.

'Can we put our hands down now?' asked the ancient.

'There are no more of you?' asked Cave, his head still wagging from side to side.

'Only the Constable, Sir John Newton, and his wife and two children. There were some servants, but they went away yesterday. . . .'

Something occurred to Abel. 'Where are the townspeople?' he called out.

The third soldier, who had not spoken before, stared unbelievingly at Abel. 'I thought you knew,' he said. 'The men of Rochester marched yesterday morning to Maidstone.' He turned to his comrades, blinking rapidly. 'I thought they knew.'

'The women and children, where are they?'

Wart-nose said, 'They ran away to villages outside the town early this morning.' He tittered. 'It's said they heard an army was on its way to Rochester to slaughter them . . .' His voice died away.

The ancient, his eyes rolling wildly, lowered his hands, a few inches at a time, until they reached shoulder level. Then, satisfied that he would not be butchered for his boldness, he allowed them to flap down against his sides. The others followed suit.

'Is John Belling here?' asked the Gravesend tanner.

The soldiers looked at each other, suddenly frightened. 'He's here,' said the ancient. 'We had orders to keep him in the dungeon . . . we had to . . .'

'What about Sir Simon Burley?'

'Oh, him, he's not here. He and his men came and went last evening. They only brought . . .'

He was interrupted by a horrible scream from one of the men nearest the wall. They turned to see him and two others lying on the ground, writhing and groaning. Their heads and shoulders were liberally spattered with a thick black liquid.

Abel had seen this happen before, in Spain. 'Get back!' he cried. 'It's pitch, boiling pitch! Get back from the wall!'

As everyone retreated, the ancient shrieked, 'It's not our doing. It's him, him!'

They looked up and spied a tiny figure on the fighting platform, brandishing a bucket.

'Sir John,' said Wart-nose, 'it's Sir John Newton. . . .'

Cave's indecisiveness burned away. 'Go and get him,' he snapped. A dozen men dashed across the drawbridge and disappeared into the keep. 'You,' said Cave, beckoning to Abel. 'Take one of these fellows and free Belling.'

The ancient accompanied Abel. As they passed under the portcullis, three pigeons shot off a ledge and flapped about their faces with frightened cries before soaring out across the castle grounds. The soldier directed Abel down a flight of stone stairs. 'Here,' he said, taking a ring of keys off the wall and unlocking a door.

The stench hit Abel's nostrils. His stomach, which had begun to behave fairly well, revolted again. He had to lean against the dank wall for a moment before he could control it.

The dungeon was a pit falling away precipitously below three stone steps. What little light and ventilation there was came from a tiny opening in the wall. The ancient brought a torch, and he and Abel lowered a ladder into the pit.

Three men emerged, all of them covered with filth. Belling merely squinted about him, but the others bore the unmistakable look of madness in their eyes. They tottered a few steps, then sat down on the stone floor. Nothing he could do would persuade them to move. He finally left them and went out of the keep with Belling and the soldier.

Standing in the rain before Cave and the others were a woman and two children, their clothes bedraggled and sodden. Held by two peasants was a very small man with great glossy moustaches, wearing armour far too big for him. A sword almost as long as he was tall lay at his feet. Abel assumed this was Sir John Newton.

'Cowards!' he was shouting at the soldiers. 'Bloody swine and cowards!"' Then, all at once confused, he said, 'What? What is it?' He glanced at the woman and children and began shouting again, struggling to be free. 'If you so much as put a hand on them . . .' And once more pathetically confused, 'I don't understand . . .'

His wife ran to him and said, 'We'll do well, John. They'll not harm us.'

Newton shook his head. 'I don't understand,' he repeated.

The woman put her hands on his shoulders, and the constable suddenly smiled. They looked into each other's eyes, seemingly unaware of the band of men around them. Abel watched, torn between a desire to weep and a swift, unreasoning jealousy.

'We'll take them along,' said Cave. 'Yes, we'll take them all along to Maidstone.' He looked around, scratching his head. 'I suppose that's where we'd better be going. . . .' His voice trailed off. Then, as unpredictably as before, his manner became decisive. 'We'll sleep here tonight. Tomorrow we go to Maidstone.'

Abel helped care for the men who had been burned by the boiling pitch. One was worse off than the others; almost all the skin had been eaten off his face. He died as they were carrying him into the keep.

Just before dusk, the rain stopped. The failing sunlight did little to relieve the grim appearance of the castle. Abel walked out across the drawbridge, resolved to find himself a place to sleep in the town. A cloud of gnats swooped down on him, flurried briefly about his face and hands, then circled out across the moat.

The soldier he had killed still hung head downward over the water. Abel turned away from him. He had a premonition that it would be a long time before he would see his village again.

8

THE high street of Maidstone inclined gently toward the river for part of its length, then took a final steep plunge to the bank of the Medway. When they arrived from Rochester, it was mid-morning, and the street held more people than Abel had ever seen in one place outside the army.

They had made the march in good time, which would have been better had they not been slowed by the presence of Lady Newton and her children. She walked by her husband's side, her expression strained, except when Sir John happened to glance at her. Then she managed a smile.

Early in the journey Abel had picked up the smaller of the two children with the intention of carrying him on his shoulder. Lady Newton, not understanding, had cried out, and Newton emerged momentarily from the lethargy into which he had sunk the night before. 'What?' he asked. 'What . . .'

'Nothing, John,' she replied, touching him while turning an anxious gaze toward Abel.

'He'll be safe with me,' Abel had said, and when she essayed her small, tremulous smile, he had wanted to add, 'You're a woman of courage. I respect you for it,' but he had said nothing more and had only looked at her, attempting to convey the message with his eyes.

In Maidstone, Cave ordered three men to remain with the Newton family at all times, until it was decided what should be done with them.

Abel had been noticing the change in Cave. He still displayed a certain indecisiveness, but he had already learned not to speak until he had made up his mind, and when he gave instruction it was in a clear, firm voice. The men responded by obeying at once. There was every difference between the band that had made its straggling entry into Rochester and the company that marched into Maidstone.

But it would have taken a commander stronger and more experienced than the Black Prince himself to hold a troop together in the face of the chaos they encountered. Minstrels were playing along the street and in the glutted square, men were dancing and shouting, tipplers were adding to the general confusion. The Maidstone women were more glad of the influx than their men; they were chattering animatedly, each woman with a score of swains clustered about her. Roger said that marchers from all over Kent had converged on the town, and Abel could well believe it.

While Roger was babbling excitedly in his ear, Abel saw something which made him stare in disbelief. Talking to one of the Dartford men, hands resting comfortably on his paunch, white teeth gleaming in an occasional fitful smile, was Old Elias. Abel and Roger pushed through the crowd to his side. Elias threw back his head and bellowed, and for an instant they were alarmed. Then they understood that he was overjoyed to see them. He embraced them as if they were his brothers, told them Nicholas and Robert had also come from the village. 'It was no good trying to work anyhow,' he said. 'The peddlers with their rumours were like crows. They made so much noise you could hear nothing but their screeching.' He smiled, but his eyes were hard, not with greed now, rather with another, indefinable, light. Abel, looking at the man he had known all his life, saw a purposeful stranger.

However, he could not resist nudging Roger and whispering, 'Your chance, lad. If you rush home . . .'

'There's no going home now,' said Roger.

Abel looked sharply at him. Roger's eyes were still wide and innocent-appearing, his expression cherubic, but he also had changed. Abel had seen this kind of change take place in men before, seldom so quickly. Yesterday at Gravesend Roger had still been a boy. The incident at Rochester Castle had been hardly more than a skirmish, but men had been killed. It was the knowledge of violent death that he saw now in Roger's face.

Abel's attention was caught by the sight of a man making his way through the crowd. He was tall, with heavy, stooped shoulders. He wore no hood; his curly brown hair was sparse, receding deeply from the temples. His eyes were dark and restless, his mouth full and mobile, but also, Abel surmised, capable of cruelty. He did not know why he continued to look at the man, nor why the other, after glancing impatiently about, made straight for Abel.

'Who's in command?' he asked at once.

Abel would have resented the brusqueness of the question, except for the warmth he saw flickering for an instant in the man's eyes.

'Command is a large word,' he replied. 'Some of us have marched under Robert Cave of Dartford.'

'Take me to him.'

Abel gave the man a cool, appraising glance. 'Take?' he inquired. 'Shall I carry you in my arms or drag you?'

The other laughed heartily, rubbed the stubble on his cheeks and said, 'I suppose it would be easier to break out of purgatory than to get a cup of ale in this bedlam.'

'I've broken out of drier purgatories,' said Abel.

'We'll test the bonds together if you like,' said the man, and added, 'Later.'

Abel smiled and looked around for Cave, saw him leaning against a cart, talking with the tanner from Gravesend.

The man was as peremptory with the pudgy baker as he had been with Abel. 'How many men do you lead?' he asked.

Cave replied guardedly, after a pause, 'Why do you ask?'

'How many?'

'Six hundred,' said Cave, stammering, then recovering and growing truculent. 'Who are you to come . . .?'

The other cut him off. 'Go among the people and find the leaders from each town and village. Tell them I want to meet with all of them in front of the church at noon.'

'Who are you?'

'Wat Tyler of Colchester,' replied the man. He looked around the crowded street. 'We have a great deal to do.'

Cave planted himself squarely before Tyler. 'I've led my men for almost a week,' he began, 'and no . . .'

Tyler took his arm. 'You'll lead them still,' he said gently. 'You'll be at their head when we stand before the King.'

Abel saw Cave beginning to succumb to the man's magnetism, just as he had done. Tyler smiled, and the baker shuffled his feet, then grinned back. 'At noon,' he said.

'Now,' said Tyler, 'I must find John Ball. Was he ill when he was released? Is he resting comfortably?'

Cave looked blank. 'Ball?' he asked. 'I've heard of him, but . . .'

Tyler's face darkened. Abel had been right; the mouth could

135

be cruel. 'Has no one freed . . .' He clenched his fists. 'Bring me someone from Maidstone.'

The tanner, who had been listening to the exchange, scurried away at a glance from Cave and returned in a few moments with a thin, pockmarked man. 'A tanner like myself,' he mumbled, then fell silent before the expression on Tyler's face.

'Is it not enough,' said Tyler to the Maidstone man, 'that you allowed John Ball to languish in that stinking hole . . .' He brooded for an instant, then shouted, 'Why have you not freed him?'

The pockmarked man struggled to find words, gave up and shrugged. Tyler made a movement toward him, checked himself, slammed his fist into his palm. He asked, very quietly, 'Is the prison well guarded?'

The tanner shook his head uncertainly. Tyler turned to Cave and said, 'Fifty men should be more than enough. Get them.'

Tyler's hands were trembling. Abel had the feeling that anger was not the only cause.

Ball had awakened as usual at dawn. The window was beginning to admit light, itself like an eye slowly opening.

To him the start of the day seemed no different from any other. It was Simon who thought that something extraordinary would happen. The little man was brushing back his unkempt hair with a series of awkward, angular gestures when he suddenly said, 'They're coming. You'll be free before sunset.'

Ball asked, 'What makes you think that?'

'I feel it,' Simon replied calmly, as if this made it an accomplished fact.

The jailer entered the cell with their food. Normally he was loquacious, abusive in a good-natured way. This morning, after he had set the bowls on the floor, he stood scrutinizing Ball gloomily. When he finally broke the silence, it was with a flat and lifeless voice, 'Speak to me, Sir Priest.'

'Good morning,' replied Ball.

The worn little catechism, having long since outlived its initial touch of ironic humour, would still never fail to arouse some response in the jailer: usually a sharp bark of laughter, followed by some colourfully varied obscenities. Today he merely said glumly, 'Good morning, Sir Priest,' and left the cell at once.

Ball heard the noise before Simon. At first he did not know what it was. He crossed the cell, took a stand directly under the window and waited. One moment it sounded like the hum of a multitude of insects, the next like the rush of a river swollen by spring floods.

136

It was only when he heard the high shrill note, distinct as birdsong at dawn, and recognized it as laughter, that he understood.

He turned to Simon, feeling excitement take hold of him. 'You're right,' he said. 'They've come.'

'I told you they would. You'll be free.'

'You as well,' said Ball.

He was not prepared for what happened then. Simon stared at him, the muscles of his face twitching furiously in a way that was both ludicrous and frightening. Suddenly he began to run about the cell, blindly, in horrible random spurts, bumping into the walls. Ball tried to catch him, and several times almost succeeded, but just as he would lay hands on him Simon would elude him in another mad gyration. Ball tripped, fell heavily, got halfway to his feet, slipped on the straw and went headlong again.

Simon stopped abruptly in mid-dash and sat down. Blood was flowing from two cuts on his cheek, staining his beard. He was weeping bitterly. 'I have never,' he said between laboured sobs, 'felt happiness like this.'

'I should think,' said Ball, still gasping for breath after his own exertions, 'it's just as well.'

They were silent for a time, listening to the undulant sounds of the crowd reaching them through the window. Then Simon said haltingly, 'I believe now . . . if it's true what you say, and I shall also be free. . . .'

'It's true,' said Ball.

'Then I do not think I shall find it necessary to . . .' He paused, thinking. 'But how can I be sure . . . will I ever be?'

Ball crawled on his hands and knees across the matted straw to where Simon was sitting. He meant to touch his cellmate's shoulder reassuringly. Instead he found himself placing his hand on Simon's head in a gesture of blessing.

The morning wore on. It was very difficult to wait now. And as time passed, Ball's earlier apprehensions returned. Perhaps they did not intend to release him after all.

Simon said in the stillness, 'They will,' and Ball was reminded of Christiana's ability to read his thoughts. Perhaps only those who have suffered together, in one form or another, have the key to each other's minds.

He was actually visualizing the word 'key' when the lock grated, the door swung open and Tyler stepped into the cell, holding a torch high above his head.

For a moment Ball could not bear to look at his friend's face, and so found himself peering past him. In the corridor stood a pudgy, middle-aged man and another, carrying a longbow across his shoulder, with a craggy face and eyes that held both humour and deep sadness.

When at last Ball felt he could bring his glance back to Tyler, he had to blink away tears in order to see him at all.

'The scum,' said Tyler in a low, harsh voice. 'I promised if they mistreated you . . .'

'No, Wat.' He felt a surge of panic. 'The jailer . . . you've not . . .'

'Not yet.'

'He was kind to us. He . . .' His words dropped away.

'Essex has risen, John. Kent and Sussex . . .'

He had never heard Tyler speak so softly, nor seen such an expression of gentleness on his face. Perhaps then . . . 'Wat,' he said hopefully, 'there's been no killing . . .'

'Did you truly believe there would not be?' Tyler's features contracted in a brutal spasm. The gentleness returned to his voice before the savagery left his eyes. 'We've needed you, John. We need you now.'

Tyler turned to leave the cell, and Ball heard a voice wail from the far corner, 'You're free . . .'

He had for the moment forgotten Simon, who was crouching abjectly in the straw, lips drawn back from his teeth in an expression of terror. Ball hurried to him, helped him rise. Simon's breath whistled from him in a shuddering sigh of relief.

They walked along the corridor, entered the room where Ball had been brought the first morning of his imprisonment. The jailer was sitting on a bench, greedily chewing at a shank of mutton. He got up, swallowed noisily and said, 'You told me twenty thousand would come, Sir Priest. You did tell me. Twenty thousand men will come here to free me. Your words, Sir Priest. . . .'

'We need as many men as we can find. Will you march with us?' The jailer's eyes grew round. He bit off a great greasy chunk of mutton and chewed frantically.

Tyler shuffled his feet impatiently. Ball asked again, 'Will you come with us?'

'Me come with you? Me?' Alarm quivered in the jailer's voice, died to despondency as he said, 'Don't you know I can't leave here? Ever. Don't you know? I wish I could, oh, how I wish I could . . .'

He backed away from them, staring, never taking his eyes off them as he sank his teeth once more into the meat and chewed, his jaws working exaggeratedly.

Tyler took Ball by the arm. As they left the room, the craggy-faced man who had come with Tyler swung around for a last look

at the jailer. Ball saw his eyes when he turned back. They were
filled with compassion. As they descended the stone stairs leading
out of the prison, the man sang in a soft voice, 'I prayed to my lord
for a coat of mail. He said, dear lad, it's yours without fail. But
first we must set you free from jail. I said, my liege, if you can't
give me mail, I'll stay in jail for a bucket of ale. . . .'

A company of forty or fifty men was waiting outside. Ball turned
his face up to the sunlight, savouring it. He looked at the river
flowing quietly past the willows bowing toward it from either bank.
He turned and scanned the prison wall, searching for the circular
window. There was nothing but an unbroken expanse of stone.
Terror struck at him until he realized the cell was on the other
side of the building.

They walked toward the high street, following the river. Simon
trotted along at Ball's side, bright eyes desperately trying to look
everywhere at once. Ball had known Simon was small, but in the cell
he had not been aware how impossibly frail he was. Nor how filthy.
Then he looked down at his own garments. He found himself thinking with ironic amusement how shocked Christiana would be if she
could see him. Irony failed him and the thought of her was painful.

He turned to Tyler. 'Christiana . . .'

'Isabella said she would go to her.'

Ball nodded. He touched the crusty, tattered cloth of his cassock.
'I must . . .'

'We'll see you get one. The priests have left Maidstone. I doubt if
they took everything with them.' Tyler looked searchingly at Ball.
'Do you want to rest?'

'Rest now?' His voice was so incredulous that Tyler laughed.

Even before they reached the high street, they could see people
spilling out along the lanes and down to the river bank. Ball's heart
began to pound, with pride, but also with some return of the
anxiety he had experienced while addressing the crowd in the
market-place at Chartham.

The mob pressed about them so closely that Tyler called out to
the pudgy man, 'Cave, have your men clear a passage for us.' And
to Ball he said, 'We'll be meeting with the leaders at the church.'

Simon's head turned quickly, and he stared at Ball and Tyler
for a moment, then resumed his avid survey of his surroundings.

After his prolonged inactivity, Ball was feeling the strain of
climbing the hill. To keep his mind off his fatigue, he peered at the
faces of people they were passing, recognized some he had seen in
widely scattered towns and villages.

He said to Tyler, 'There are only Kentishmen.'

Tyler nodded.

'They would hardly have even heard of you here. Yet you've been able . . .' Ball stopped speaking as Tyler grinned engagingly. He remembered how rapidly the carpenter had risen to command in Essex, which was already far better organized than the territory south of the Thames.

'I did not mind that they knew nothing of me here,' said Tyler. 'They will now. What I do mind,' he went on, and bitterness edged into his voice, 'is that they did know you, and that you were in prison, and they did nothing . . .'

'I'm free now,' said Ball.

Tyler grunted.

As they reached the churchyard, Ball saw the baker from Aylesford seated on the ground with his back against a tombstone. He wondered if Tyler had received the letter he wrote from prison and was about to ask him when he noticed Simon staring fixedly at the church. The little man's face was pale beneath its coat of grime. He took a few tottering steps toward the church, stopped, turned and came slowly back. He was trying to say something to Ball; his lips moved soundlessly. He began to sway. As Ball reached out to steady him, Simon crumpled to the grass and lay still.

Tyler knelt beside him, put his ear to Simon's chest, slowly looked up at Ball.

A spindly bare shank was protruding from the bundle of rags Simon wore. Ball made a futile effort to cover it, began to whisper the words of the rites for the dead. When he had finished, he felt a hand on his shoulder. The craggy-faced man was bending over them. 'I'll take him,' he said.

He lifted the tiny body with infinite care, bore it to the far end of the churchyard, toward a space where there were no tombstones.

Ball remained on his knees for a time. Then he sighed, got up and said to Tyler, 'There'll be much to do. We'd better begin.'

9

WHEN Ball came to tell him she was there, Tyler was first confused by the priest's words. When he finally understood them, his immediate reaction was one of irritation.

In the two days since his arrival in Maidstone he had seldom been idle. The Kentishmen were quarrelsome. Tyler had been forced to spend more time than he wished settling petty squabbles.

It annoyed him, but he had tried to be patient. For he had come as an outsider to this Kentish town and imposed his will on them. This had required skill and more than a little bravado. He had won quick acceptance from them, but it was a motley throng collecting here; as readily as they had tendered him respect they could turn against him. So he had judged their disputes as tactfully and with as little resentment as he could.

He had managed to control his temper all the first day. In addition to dealing with wrangles, he had seen to the setting up of a camp outside the town (there were already ten thousand or more men gathered, and some of the Maidstone houses had been badly damaged by the milling mob). He had begun to deal with the problem of food; he had issued and enforced stern instructions against looting. And whenever there were a few moments to spare, he had conferred with Ball, planning tactics for what lay ahead.

By noon of the second day his temper had swollen, and the patience covering it had become thin. He had listened to the two contenders who had sought him out then: a Maidstone mason accusing a smith from Tenterden of trying to steal his wife. Each man possessed a loud voice, and each was shouting at the top of it, paying no attention to the other. Tyler had suddenly seized them and knocked their heads together. When they came to, they had agreed that perhaps their quarrel was not nearly so urgent as they had originally thought.

Thereafter, the number of squabbles dropped off appreciably, but there was more than enough work to occupy him.

Now Ball was telling him that Isabella was here in Maidstone. Tyler choked down an impulse to shout at the priest; her presence here was not Ball's fault.

She was sitting under an oak tree at the edge of the camp, huddled in her cloak, looking even more delicate than he remembered. She did not see him approaching through the twilight, and when she raised her head and saw him standing over her, she leaped up, her expression first startled, then defiant.

'How did you get here?'

'I walked,' she replied. 'I rode in carts when I could. A peddler I met had two horses.'

'You might have been murdered.'

'I wasn't.'

Fires were beginning to glow around the camp. A minstrel wandered toward them in the dusk, idly strumming a zither, halted close by. Men drifted away from the fires and began to gather around the musician. Several were peering curiously at Isabella. Tyler seized her arm roughly and hurried her away from the camp, down the slope toward the river.

'You'll go back to Colchester,' he said bluntly.

'I'll go. Tomorrow.' She paused, then said in an oddly musing voice, 'The house was empty. I wanted . . .' She let the word hang between them, tentative, poised for instant retraction.

'How did you know I was in Maidstone?'

'I thought you were still in Essex, somewhere, I didn't know. . . . When I found Jack Straw . . .'

'Straw told you . . .'

'He didn't want to.' She added, almost primly, 'I persuaded him he should.'

The idea of anyone, particularly a woman, persuading Straw to do anything tickled his imagination, and also made him somewhat proud of her. He grinned. She turned her face up to his. He had seldom seen her laugh. It transformed her features, let mischief out through her eyes. He was not sure he liked it.

'Have you eaten?'

'I've eaten,' she replied, the laughter dying.

Darkness was settling about them. There seemed nothing else to say.

'I've work to do.'

'Yes.'

For some reason he could not understand the image of the dead steward at Hales' manor house seeped into his mind, shadowy and elusive, then vividly clear. The throbbing noonday warmth, the spangled blue of the man's tunic, the girl weeping . . . Before he realized he had done it, he had taken Isabella's hands in his. She drew in her breath, moved closer to him.

He said, 'I wanted you then.'

'When?'

'The man was dead. . . .' He knew it made no sense to her.

'And now?' she asked.

'Now?'

Her voice was indistinct. 'Now do you . . .'

He tried to unravel the hard knot of his confusion. 'The man was dead . . . and the others . . . it was all wiped away. . . .'

She was waiting, her hands warm in his. He drew her to him, slowly, fearing that if he made too sudden a movement something would be shattered, something he did not understand but treasured desperately. His lips brushed hers, lost them, found them again. He folded the softness of her into his arms. Her breath against his

142

cheek was as soothing as sleep, her body the quickening fire of dawn, and there was something he almost understood. . . .

Then the violence was in his blood, mounting, fiercer than ever before. He wanted to shout against it, for it was not of his heart. His heart lay baffled, trampled by his anger. But his limbs had the violence in them, a violence beyond passion, and they used it on her, so that she cried out in pain, and his body was goaded to deeper violence.

And then, when they lay apart, the aloneness was in him again, sharper now, for he knew he had lost whatever it was he was treasuring and longing for, and he felt as if his heart had died and his body lived on, grieving. There was nothing he could do. The distance between them was a great moat, forever unbridgeable.

Yet he found himself reaching out for her in his anguish, finally touching her gently. She came to his arms at once, and for a few moments she wept quietly. Her sobbing stopped, but he could feel her tears against his own cheek.

'When they died,' she said, 'each time I wanted to weep. Their little bodies . . . and you and I . . . I wish I could have wept then.'

The broad expanse of St. Mary's Field, the Roman wall beyond the church, and the sun shining brightly each time they buried one of their sons, when the sky should have been ghostly grey. . . .

He held her closer and without knowing why began to speak to her as he never had before: of his hopes for what they were doing, of the thirst for freedom John Ball had set burning in his spirit, of what it would mean when they had won. Then, suddenly ashamed of how much he had talked and the extent to which he had revealed himself, he stopped abruptly, and was grateful when she did not question him.

After a while she said, 'I wish . . .' and put her hand over his mouth when he started to reply, saying, 'I know. I shall go back to Colchester tomorrow.'

'I'll send someone with you.'

'I came alone.'

The old brusqueness had come back into their talk, but it was different now, bled of its acerbity. 'The man can take messages to Straw on the same journey,' he said.

They were quiet for a time. A breeze whispered through the trees. She said, 'I was afraid . . .' and a while later, 'Wat . . .'

He did not learn what she was going to say, for at that instant a tumult arose in the camp: the bellowing of men's voices roused to fury.

143

Tyler got up quickly. He leaned over Isabella, touched her hand, then turned to climb the slope.

It was another altercation. A heavy-set fellow with a sizeable paunch was tussling with a man from southern Kent, both being urged on by their respective friends. Tyler managed to pull the two opponents apart.

'He said we wouldn't march to the King,' grumbled the fat fellow. 'He said we'd never march anywhere.'

'We'll march to the King,' said Tyler.

'You see?' gloated the first man, pushing out his paunch. He showed surprisingly white and perfect teeth in a vicious grin at his foe. 'You can't trust foreigners. You can't trust them at all.'

At which it all started again, with two peasants, one pale and fish-faced, the other massive and hairy-armed, backing up the fat fellow and threatening to murder everyone who hailed from south of Maidstone. Again Tyler managed to silence them without losing his own temper. The man named Abel said they were from his village and he would see they kept the peace.

When Tyler returned to Isabella, she was asleep. He lay down beside her quietly, and in a few moments he also slept.

I O

'WHAT you need . . .' Agnes was saying.

Walworth, a little drunk, cut her off. 'What I need is what I need, and I need no one to tell me.'

She stopped walking and made a deep, mocking curtsey 'As my Lord Mayor wishes.'

The fine line of her thighs strained at the material of her gown. He admired the slender ankles encased in elaborately laced shoes, and, as she straightened up again, the curve of her hips and bosom. Then, inevitably, his gaze was drawn to her ravaged face. She winced and turned a little away; the wrinkles around her mouth deepened as her lips twisted into a sardonic smile.

They had just entered what was known as the Main House. It was still early in the evening: a dozen or so girls lounged on the benches, preening, murmuring, a covey of doves with the predatory eyes of ravens.

Two of them got up suddenly and began clawing at each other, squawking and screeching so loudly that the low-raftered room was

144

hideous with noise. They were the brothel's most recent acquisitions: the young Flemish girl, and the one from Coventry, whose upper lip had been cut off.

Agnes crossed the room swiftly and cuffed them both. Her hands were small and dainty, but there could be no doubt of their strength, or of the authority they exercised. In an instant the girls lay whimpering on the rushes. 'Save your energy for the customers,' said Agnes harshly.

The Flemish girl crawled across the floor and wrapped her arms about Walworth's knees. She looked up at him piteously, her striped hood awry. 'Oh, Lord Mayor,' she moaned, her words so heavily accented he had difficulty in understanding them. 'They don't pay me proper respect here. I'm not a trollop, like the rest of these.' The Coventry wench snarled, and the Flemish girl pressed closer to Walworth, her fingers beginning a slow dalliance with the backs of his legs. 'My father was a prosperous man, a wool merchant, who had all his earthly possessions stolen from him in Flanders. He came here to seek a new fortune . . .'

'They find fortunes right enough, these Flemings,' said the whore from Coventry. 'Banding together, cheating honest Londoners . . .'

'My father was a man of good birth, and clever, too. He worked hard, and in a matter of months he had a fine house and servants and gold to spare.'

The Coventry wench asked snidely, 'Why aren't you across the river now, living in that fine house?'

'My father died,' said the other in a low, sorrowful voice.

'Of a pox he caught from you, no doubt.'

The Flemish girl swung round and spat at her adversary, then resumed her attentions to Walworth. 'Oh, Lord Mayor, it's such a terrible thing for a young girl like me . . .'

Agnes laughed coarsely. 'Was there ever a whore who couldn't spin out the saddest tale this side of the grave?' She nudged the girl with her foot. 'Get up and straighten your gown, slut. And sew a new foxtail to it. Your goldsmith is coming tonight, and you know what he . . .'

'I don't like what he does,' whined the girl, clinging to Walworth.

'He likes what you do,' said Agnes. 'And he pays well for it.' She gave the girl a sharp kick which broke her hold on Walworth's legs and sent her sprawling. She lay looking venomously up at Agnes while the others laughed.

Agnes took Walworth's arm and led him into her private room.

The wine was buzzing in his head. 'You didn't answer the question I asked you before,' he said.

'Rumours,' she said shortly. 'Months ago when I spoke to you about rumours, you weren't interested.'

He drained his cup, refilled it. 'I'm interested now.'

She put her hands up to her face, thoughtfully smoothed her sagging jowls, the pouches under her eyes. 'There's trouble in Kent, trouble in Essex.'

'How much trouble?'

'Wouldn't your King's Council know that better than I?'

'They know nothing.'

'I'll warrant one or two of them knows more than he tells,' she said. 'If they were to pay me a visit now and then, I'd soon enough know all they knew.'

He found the thought of some of his fellow advisers spending a night in his brothels excruciatingly funny. 'Sudbury,' he sputtered, choking on a mouthful of wine, 'I can see the Chancellor sidling in here . . .' He imitated Sudbury's crablike walk. 'And the girl with no upper lip coming to him. . . .'

She was in the spirit of it. 'Or my good Earl of Salisbury,' she said, also mimicking.

He reeled with mirth as she travestied Salisbury's elegant, studied gestures. 'No,' he said finally, reining in his laughter. 'No . . . my lord Salisbury only has eyes for the Princess Joan.'

'Now there's competition I'd fear,' said Agnes.

'She's fat now,' said Walworth. 'Fat and bloated.'

'And I'm wrinkled. But we each know the way of a man.'

'She was never much, I'll warrant. Look at her eyes. And her mouth. Even when she was young . . .'

'She was a beauty,' said Agnes.

'All wiles and a pretty face. The eyes and the mouth, you can see everything there. Never a thought of pleasing a man. Pleasing herself was all that mattered, and I doubt if she ever did even that.'

'The Black Prince . . .'

'The Black Prince was a soldier and away much of the time. When he returned home he was sick. The Princess was a bargainer. She used what she had like a moneylender uses a bag of gold. Only when the candles were out and the coverlet drawn you'd soon enough know that the gold was only brass.'

'She has style, Lord Mayor. Even now she has style. She was born a lady . . .'

'What does birth matter?' he asked, suddenly angry.

Agnes shrugged. 'I didn't mean . . .'

'All of them,' he said savagely. 'Their titles and their airs. I was born poor. I didn't have it all served up to me on downy pillows and . . .' He lost the thread of what he was saying. 'Perfumed gold hair . . .' he said, then, 'I have a hawk . . .'

'You have a wife,' Agnes said, smiling.

He ignored her and took a gulp of wine. 'A peregrine falcon. From the day I found her as a haggard . . . took her home and sewed her eyes shut to tame her in training . . .' He laughed. 'Never tamed. Obeys and never tamed. Takes no quarter, gives none. I can depend on her. Never betray me.'

'Nor will I, Lord Mayor.'

'They'll not hound me out . . .'

'Who, Lord Mayor?'

He was not sure. There were the troubles in the shires, at least rumours of them. The Council had not met since its decision to send Belknap to Brentwood. It was as though by not facing one another, they could deny Belknap's failure and the implications of it. A week had passed, and no one seemed to know more than one simple fact: the Chief Justice of Common Pleas had been dispatched to punish an unruly mob and had barely escaped with his life. He gritted his teeth. If they had listened to him and sent enough soldiers . . . But Courtenay's will had prevailed. He thought again, for at least the thousandth time, of his conversation with the Bishop during the afternoon of hawking.

'The people of London will stop them,' he growled. 'They'll drive them down to the sea.'

Agnes poured him more wine.

'You're not drinking tonight,' he said.

'Tonight you need me.'

'The people of London . . .'

'I'll be at your side,' she said calmly, as if he had not spoken.

'He wants me to leave. He says if we leave and return after . . .' Walworth stopped, watching Agnes moodily.

'After what, Lord Mayor?'

He struck her. She staggered back a few steps, recovered her balance, came at him and slapped his face several times before he was able to catch her wrists. They both laughed, and Walworth began to feel better.

'You're twice the woman the Princess Joan is,' he said, rubbing his cheek.

'And you're twice the man the Earl of Salisbury is,' she said tauntingly.

'My wife says you cheat me out of receipts.'

'Only because you let her keep the accounts. If I kept . . .'

He raised his hand, brushing at her words. It was not what he wanted to talk about. He drank some wine. 'The City . . .' he said, but he had drunk too much; he could not bring his words and thoughts together. 'No need to make a decision yet, is there?'

'You'll decide wisely when you must, Lord Mayor.' Her voice was low, her manner deadly earnest.

He put his hand to her face, let his forefinger gently follow the deep crease running from her nose to her mouth, shaking his head confusedly when he saw pain spring into her eyes. 'I love the City,' he said, his tongue stumbling over the words. 'The falcon . . .'

'What you need,' she said slowly, 'is some more wine. Then we'll go and have a look at the Flemish girl. Her goldsmith should be here by now, and from behind the curtain . . .'

'If Margaret . . .'

Agnes interrupted, screaming, 'A pox on Margaret! A bloody pox on that prissy . . .' She stopped abruptly, her wrecked face working in torment.

'If Lovekyn were only . . .' He finished the wine in his cup and stared at Agnes. She was standing slim and straight, holding out her arms to him.

His feet would not obey. When he tried to walk toward her, the extended toes of his shoes snarled in each other, and he sank to his knees.

She was beside him, pressing his head to her. He could feel the firmness of her breast against his cheek.

I I

'IF MY father the Black Prince were alive,' said Richard angrily, 'none of this trouble would be taking place.'

Salisbury looked down at the council table, struggling with his annoyance. The boy never referred simply to his father, or to the Black Prince. It was always 'my father the Black Prince', spoken as if it were one word, in that irritating reedy voice. Still, it was only then, or when he mentioned his mother, that the lines of his face grew less spiteful, and the sly eyes took on some warmth and softness. 'We shall attempt, sire, to deal with the situation as best we can,' Salisbury said, omitting for once the flattery he knew would soothe Richard.

The oval face crinkled up in its colicky expression. The King looked around the table, his pointed chin directed accusingly at each of them in turn. 'You've not properly told me what the situation is, my uncles. You're keeping things from me.'

'My liege . . .' Salisbury began, and was interrupted by Hales, who said, 'The situation is this,' and when everyone looked at him, stuck out his fat lower lip and mumbled petulantly, 'They burned my favourite manor house in Essex. They killed my steward.'

'I don't understand,' put in Sudbury. 'Two months ago . . . or was it three . . . no, it was two, in April . . . I was travelling for several days in Essex. To confer with one of my bishops on a matter of the liturgy, that was the purpose of my journey. . . .' He plucked at his fringe of hair. 'The villages I passed through were the soul of peace, and when my company and I stopped to speak to some of the peasants, on my order, you understand, for I like the people . . .'

Courtenay interjected suavely, 'If my lord Chancellor . . .'

'It seems to me, my son,' said Sudbury, suddenly testy, 'that you are forever interrupting my stories. If you would show me the courtesy of hearing me out, perhaps you would see they are not merely the ramblings of an old man.'

The Bishop was taken aback. 'My lord Chancellor,' he murmured. 'Please forgive me, and pray continue.'

'No, my son,' replied Sudbury. 'I shall save it for another time. After all, you understand the peasants so much better than I. And understanding is what is required now, is it not?'

Again Courtenay was disconcerted. Salisbury smiled behind his hand, partly with pleasure at seeing the Bishop's blatant manipulation of the Chancellor rebuked for once, but also because this reconfirmed one of his basic beliefs: that each person is multifaceted and a mass of contradictions.

Courtenay waited a moment, then said a trifle hesitantly, 'My knowledge of the situation is not as clear as I might wish. . . .'

Was it, Salisbury wondered, only Sudbury's reprimand which was making Courtenay unsure of himself? He doubted it; the Bishop possessed far too tough a core to be overly concerned at the momentary tartness of an old man. There was some other cause. Courtenay's fleshy face had been paler than usual, Salisbury realized now, ever since he entered the council chamber. The smile was not quite so oily or so frequent, the voice a little less smooth. Salisbury had seen this kind of faintly troubled expression before. When diplomats with whom he was negotiating were playing for exceptionally large stakes, and when they were not quite certain of all the elements involved. . . .

'In Essex,' Courtenay continued, interrupting Salisbury's thoughts, 'several manors have been burned, and my informants . . .' He paused, pursing his lips as if angry at himself, then amended his words. 'It has been reported that some eight to ten thousand peasants have left their villages and are wandering the countryside in open rebellion.'

Salisbury could feel the sense of shock vibrating in the air.

Richard broke the silence. 'If my father the Black Prince . . .' He let his hand fall onto the table. Everyone looked at the hand as though they had never seen it before: the fingers, still more those of a child than of a man, ring-bedecked, vulnerable-looking.

'The scum!' said Walworth. It was the first time he had spoken since the meeting began. In fact, he had said nothing to anyone since entering the chamber, had sat scowling blackly, toying with the embroidered sleeve of his tunic.

'Shoeless ruffians,' said Hales, and giggled, a sinister, mirthless little laugh.

'The situation in Essex is far from bright,' said Courtenay. 'But in Kent . . .'

The King's heavy chair rasped on the stone floor. Richard's face was grey. He was striving unsuccessfully to rise.

'My liege . . .' said Salisbury, getting up and going to the boy. Richard pushed him aside. 'Where in Kent?' he asked. 'Where?'

'It has been reported,' Courtenay replied carefully, 'that at least nine or ten thousand of these peasant bandits are collected at Maidstone.'

'Are you certain?'

'Sire, if you believe I would alarm you and your advisers unnecessarily . . .'

'Maidstone . . .' said Richard. 'She will have to pass through . . .'

'Who will, Your Majesty?'

'My mother,' said the boy, gasping a little. 'For two weeks she has been at one of her estates near Ashford. She will be starting for London . . .'

Salisbury's head began to swim. He broke in on Richard. 'You did not tell me . . . she said nothing about . . .'

The King turned on him viciously. 'I did not know it was necessary for either the Princess Joan or myself to report her activities to you . . .'

'No, my liege, of course not.' Salisbury swallowed to subdue a mounting nausea and groped his way back to his chair.

'Surely,' said Courtenay, 'the Princess will hear of the disturbances and wait at Ashford until they have subsided.'

'Surely she will do nothing of the kind!' Salisbury knew his voice was climbing toward hysteria, but he could not control it. 'She will return to London because she will fear for her son's life.'

He was never more certain of anything. Joan cared little for the two sons she had borne Thomas Holland. They were a bad lot in any event and she knew it. But for Richard . . .

'Now, now,' said Sudbury. 'I am sure the reports are greatly exaggerated. And even if they are not, the peasants would never harm the King's mother. . . .'

Salisbury could see her, forced out of her carriage by the mob, their sweaty bodies all around her, filthy hands reaching out for her. And when she looked at them with those eyes that even in fear would have the power to inflame the most unreceptive man to . . .

'They will!' he shouted. 'They will harm her!'

And Richard's voice, pitched in the same near-hysterical tones as his own, 'Send an army! Send an army at once!'

Suddenly Salisbury felt himself becoming icy calm. The council table, the advisers, the tapestry on the stone wall behind the King's chair, all took on a startling clarity of line. This then was what he had been fearing all these months without knowing it, and now that it had come, had taken tangible form, he found himself more resigned than afraid. If nothing else, he had always been a realist. 'Sire,' he said, 'there is no army.'

'We have fighting men!' shrilled Richard. 'We have loyal soldiers who will go out and teach the bandits . . .'

'We have, Your Majesty,' said Salisbury, 'exactly six hundred fighting men. Mercenaries under the command of Sir Robert Knolles. Quartered here in the Tower. Six hundred.'

'Then recruit more!' cried Richard.

'In London . . .' began Walworth, and lapsed into silence when Courtenay looked at him.

'Ruffians,' said Hales. 'Dirty shoeless ruffians.'

Courtenay began drumming his fingers on the table.

'Sire,' said Salisbury, 'it would be folly to send our only protective force away from London. And it would be impossible to recruit soldiers, train them, and send them out to quell disturbances at such short notice.'

'Not to mention the fact,' said Courtenay, 'that many of those we would recruit are among the outlaws.'

'His Majesty's uncle, John of Gaunt, has soldiers with him in Scotland,' ventured Sudbury. 'Perhaps if we send word to him by the fastest courier . . .'

Courtenay gave him a withering, incredulous glance, and the Chancellor stopped speaking.

'The only thing we can do,' said Salisbury, 'is wait. It is possible that these peasants will soon grow tired of being away from their homes. Once they disperse . . .'

'And if they do not?' asked Courtenay.

'Then,' said Salisbury, 'we must be prepared to lay down our lives for England.' He knew his words and manner were pompous, but he could never help this when he was under stress. Any more than he could help saying again, 'Our lives for England.'

12

As THE sun began to rise, Ball looked back from his position near the head of the column.

What he saw stirred him strongly. Six thousand were marching on the highroad to Canterbury, more than half of them those who had gathered at Maidstone. It mattered little that the clothes of many of them were ragged, that their weapons were makeshift, that they marched in untidy formation or none at all. This was the army of the people, making its first organized move in the quest for freedom.

They had set out before dawn. The decision to send a force to Canterbury had been made the night before. The cathedral town was too important from every point of view for them to ignore. If Canterbury belonged to the people, it would strengthen their position when they reached London. On the other hand, an unsecured Canterbury might leave a harassing force of indeterminate power at their rear. This had been Tyler's reasoning, and none of the other leaders had offered opposition.

Ball had known of Tyler's natural talents for leadership. But even he was surprised to see them emerging so forcefully and fully developed. One would think Tyler had been accustomed all his life to commanding vast forces. He was in control of every detail, from deciding how many should march and how many remain, to providing for the comfort, under strong guard, of Sir John Newton and his family (Tyler planned to take Newton with them to London as a hostage).

At Tyler's suggestion, the people had adopted a simple programme to govern their actions until they reached London. They professed their loyalty to King Richard and their unalterable opposition to

John of Gaunt. They would molest no citizen who swore allegiance to Richard and the true commons. Under no circumstances would they engage in any kind of thievery, even if the property belonged to an acknowledged enemy of the commons.

There was no question in Ball's mind now as to Tyler's genius for leadership. His doubts lay in a different direction. There had already been killing. How far would Tyler permit the violence to go? Or, to put it more disturbingly, how far would he actually encourage it to go?

The sun was climbing high above them now. Ball's throat was dry. The weeks in prison had hardly equipped him for such a long march. Once or twice his steps faltered, but he pressed on resolutely, resisting the temptation to drop out of the march, to lie down by the side of the road and rest.

He stumbled and almost fell. A moment later Tyler was beside him, looking into his face. Ball managed a smile.

'Can you carry on?'

'Of course,' said Ball.

'We can find you a horse.'

'No one else is riding.'

'You're a stubborn priest.'

'May God be thanked for that.'

Tyler grinned. There was gentleness in his eyes, an openness and sensitivity Ball had never seen there before. 'May God be thanked for you, John Ball,' he said. 'You've brought us far. We'll go farther yet.' He put his arm round Ball's shoulder and continued with something akin to shyness, 'I'm proud to have you as my friend.' He gripped Ball's shoulder and then was gone, back to his place at the head of the column.

Ball was deeply moved. He was also relieved. The commons might be engaged in battle, perhaps at Canterbury, perhaps later. This he would have to accept, much as he regretted it. To be forced to fight was one thing; to wallow in wanton carnage was another. What he had feared was unchecked violence, the people's cruel and brutal revenge against those who had oppressed them. There had been some of this; Ball felt now that Tyler would countenance no more of it. They would achieve their goal without senseless slaughter, by peaceful, orderly means.

The assurance gave him new strength. He raised his head and quickened his stride.

They began chanting the couplet as they passed Chartham. Ball had never heard it voiced by more than a few hundred. Now

153

it was shouted in cadence by thousands, rolling like thunder across the quiet hills:

> *When Adam delved and Eve span,*
> *Who was then the gentleman?*

The bell began to ring in the Chartham church where he had met the Abbot weeks before. Women came running from the village to the highroad, calling and waving. The chant fell away as the marchers shouted bawdy remarks and got back better than they gave. Then, out of the laughter, the couplet emerged again, and they left Chartham behind.

Less than an hour later they came over the crest of a hill and saw the walls of Canterbury. The town gate was closed.

Abruptly the marchers fell silent, and silently they advanced toward the gate. Those who carried longbows unslung them. The others gripped their staves and scythes, unsheathed their knives. Some picked up large rocks from the roadside. Tyler raised his hand, ordering a halt. The gate opened slowly.

Through the gateway came a score of men. At their head was a man cloaked in forest-green velvet. He led his group up to Tyler and said, 'The aldermen of Canterbury welcome you in peace.'

Tyler accepted the greeting with no show of surprise. He asked, 'Do you and the people of Canterbury swear allegiance to King Richard and the true commons?'

The alderman hesitated just an instant before replying, 'We do.' He added, 'Most of us. . . .'

Tyler ignored the qualifying remark and said, 'If the people of Canterbury wish to march with us to London . . .'

The alderman interrupted him. 'We've already discussed this among ourselves. Many of us will march. If you had not come to us, we would have found you.'

Tyler said, 'There are matters we must dispose of at the Cathedral and the Archbishop's Palace.'

'We shall take you there.' The man paused, studying Tyler. 'The Archbishop is not there, you know. As Chancellor, he is in London most of . . .'

Tyler grunted, cutting him off. He called his leaders around him, told them he would take five hundred men into the town. The rest would wait outside the walls.

Tyler entered the Cathedral ahead of him. A mass was in progress. Ball heard the antiphonal singing. Then, as he came into the nave, he saw the monks, more than two hundred of them, far ahead in the choir.

Ball saw Tyler stop walking, wait for a few moments, then stride up the nave.

Brilliant light flooded through the stained-glass windows, touching the worn stone floor with glory. The voices of the monks swelled, reverberating among the pillars, dropped to a rustling whisper, grew again and rolled upward to the vaulting. Ball peered through the haloing radiance of sunlight, past the choir, toward the high altar and the shrine of martyred Thomas Becket.

The magnificence of man's tribute to his Maker overwhelmed him, filled his spirit with reverence. But there was another more disquieting emotion stirring within him. The people of England were beginning their journey toward freedom. When it was concluded, when victory was in their hands, would matters not be different from what they were now, different from what they had ever been? His own role . . .

Simon had asked him what he wanted for himself. Nothing, he had replied, and nothing was the true answer in a prison cell when hope alone was a rare and sufficient boon.

Now. . . . He had always striven to be honest with himself, though he understood that such striving is a delusion and the first victim of man's frailty. He asked himself, standing among the hallowed stones, if his ambitions all these years had been as selfless as he professed. He could not answer with any certainty. . . .

The singing halted abruptly in mid-response. Plucked out of his untranquil reverie by the sudden hush, Ball advanced bewilderedly toward the choir.

Tyler was standing in the centre, surveying the silent monks with a slow sweeping gaze.

After a terrible moment which contained overtones of death, one of them called out, 'How dare you enter God's house and disrupt divine service?'

Tyler replied, his voice echoing oddly down the nave and off into the transepts, 'Only for the most urgent purpose.'

'What can be more urgent than the worship of God?' asked the monk.

'That He be truly worshipped in the freedom He decreed for men.'

'And you are the saviour who brings this freedom?' The monk was sneering now.

Ball saw Tyler clench his fists, held his breath until the hands relaxed and Tyler spoke again. 'I have come to tell you that you will soon have an Archbishop who will truly serve the people of England.'

The monks murmured. Ball's heart leaped wildly, and he thought: if it were offered me . . .

The spokesman coughed drily and said, 'We have an Archbishop.'

Tyler said calmly, 'The Archbishop you now serve is also Chancellor of England. He has persecuted the commons and has thus become their enemy. In due course this traitor will be executed by the people.'

The monks stared at Tyler. He waited a moment, then walked along the choir toward the nave, his footsteps echoing from the stone floor like the steady beating of a drum.

Flames rose from the last batch of records and court rolls taken from the Archbishop's Palace.

Ball said waspishly to Tyler, 'Why do you not burn the furniture and tapestries as well? The whole building . . .'

Tyler regarded Ball with faintly troubled eyes. 'If you are soon to be Archbishop . . .'

'Who gave you the right . . .' Ball began angrily, then turned away from Tyler.

He kept his face averted during the strained silence that followed, still refused to turn back when Tyler said casually, 'I think it would be well to issue orders that no one living within twelve miles of the coast marches with us to London. The French would be happy to take advantage of towns and villages left undefended.'

'Your solicitude for the country,' Ball said icily, 'is touching '

'Why are you angry with me, John?'

Ball swung around to face Tyler. 'You do not know?'

'Since we came from the Cathedral . . .'

'Yes. Since we came from the Cathedral. Think about what you said to the monks there. Think about it.'

Tyler made no reply to Ball. He kicked at the glowing ashes, all that remained of the mass of documents which had filled three rooms of the Palace. Then he called to one of his leaders, who was gaping up at an immense stained-glass window, 'Gather the men and take them outside the walls to join the others. We shall be returning to Maidstone shortly.'

Tyler walked off without looking at Ball, who followed at a little distance.

The streets of Canterbury had gone festive since their entry into the town. Men and women passed them, singing and laughing. A procession of young boys circled the market-place, chanting the Adam and Eve couplet. The inevitable peddlers, pardoners and herbalists scurried about, offering wares in loud voices.

In one of the narrow lanes just north of the gate the way was blocked by a crowd of men: prentices and perhaps a few journeymen, Ball decided. There was a great deal of shouting and confusion, and at first Ball could not make out what was the centre of their attention. Then the crowd parted momentarily, and he saw three men kneeling on the ground, their hands tied behind them.

Tyler seized one of the prentices by the arm and asked him what was happening.

The prentice's face was flushed. He smiled broadly as he replied, 'Three traitors. We're going to execute them.'

'Traitors?'

'Against the people. They're the local tax collectors.' His eyes blinked rapidly. He was so excited it was an effort for him to get the words out properly. 'They beat us . . . put some of our guild members in prison. We've released the prisoners. Now the traitors must die.'

Tyler thanked the prentice and stepped back. Ball accosted him. 'Will you not stop them?'

'Will you?' asked Tyler, regarding him steadily.

Ball took a couple of steps toward the shouting, milling men. His legs began to tremble. He felt that if he tried to advance another step he would collapse. He watched, sick with horror and with anger at himself, as three prentices with axes did their bloody work. One of the victims wept piteously until the instant of his death.

When the triumphant mob had left, bearing the relics of their violence, Ball turned to Tyler. He could feel tears starting in his eyes. 'I have no courage,' he said.

'It's not a matter of courage,' said Tyler. 'You did the right thing. The people here know better than we who has betrayed them.'

'Out of what great knowledge and sense of justice do they pass sentence?'

Anger flickered in Tyler's eyes, was gone. 'Out of the knowledge of slavery and oppression,' he said. 'As for justice, they've received less at the hands of those they killed.'

'They're still alive,' said Ball softly. Then, deliberately, 'There are times when I feel the people we have spent these many years working to free are less worthy of freedom than the oxen with which they plough their fields.'

'There's a proverb,' said Tyler with sudden asperity. 'He who would live a day in delight, let him cook a hen, for two days a goose, for a week a pig. If he would be happy a whole year, let him take a wife. But if he would live in pleasure his whole life long, let him take to the priesthood.'

Ball stood with bowed head, letting Tyler's scorn pour out over him. They began walking toward the gate. After a time Ball said, 'When will it stop, Wat? When will we have done with killing?'

'When we've won.'

'That may be too late. By then we may have become as brutal as the masters we've overthrown.'

'First,' said Tyler, 'we have to overthrow them.'

13

THE whole of the Kentish commons which had gathered in Maidstone were marching together toward London. Tyler found it difficult to determine precisely how many there were. On his return from Canterbury, he had learned that at least another thousand, chiefly from southern Kent and Sussex, had joined the ranks. This brought the total number of marchers, as nearly as he could estimate, to around thirteen thousand. In all probability a multitude of equal size would be following Straw on the north side of the Thames.

Tyler was pleased with the way matters were going. On the second day of June a band of timorous peasants in Brentwood had defied the Chief Justice of Common Pleas and sent him scuttling away in shame. Only nine days had passed, and two great armies of the commons were advancing toward London, where, Tyler was confident, the King would grant their demands.

The Kentishmen under his command were still quarrelsome; he doubted if anything could ever be done to remedy that. But their discipline in action was excellent. That morning he had led parties against two manor houses: one belonging to John of Gaunt, the other the personal holding of Sudbury. They had encountered no resistance; the stewards and bailiffs had fled, and the serfs attached to the houses had joined the commons. The invaders had found the records and burned them, then stripped the buildings of everything

158

they contained and added these to the flames. There had been no looting, though Tyler knew his ragged army had been greatly tempted by some of the richly-worked garments.

Now, with the afternoon sun in their eyes, London and their audience with the young King were closer than a day's march.

Tyler was uneasy about only one thing. Whenever he glanced over his left shoulder, he could see Ball, plodding along with his head down. Now and then the priest would raise his hand to his mouth in an absent gesture, indicating more clearly than any words the extent of his unhappiness.

He wished he could make Ball understand and accept what was and what had to be. The time of freedom would come only after a moment of violence. There was no alternative. The lords who ruled them had grown fat on the blood of the people. That blood must be avenged. It was inevitable that some who were less guilty would die along with those whose brutality and viciousness were undoubted; that could not be helped.

Ball had awakened the people. He had shown them a vision; he had given them the strength to overthrow tyranny and become their own masters. He should know that men cannot cast off their chains in sweetness and reason.

Tyler himself, whenever he thought of Hales or Sudbury, which was often, knew he could kill them with his bare hands and not be troubled by an instant's regret.

He was roused from his uneasy contemplation by a sudden sense of something amiss. It swept over him so strongly that he stopped walking and gave the signal to halt. The long, unkempt procession slowed and came to a standstill.

At first Tyler thought they might be marching into an ambush. They were passing through thickly-forested land; soldiers might be concealed in dangerous numbers among the trees ahead of them. Somehow, though, he felt this was not the case.

Then he heard it: the faint din of men's voices rising from the rear of his own ranks. He swung about, narrowing his eyes, looked far back along the highroad. Ball had raised his head and was watching Tyler. The hostage, Newton, shuffled his feet.

The clamour was increasing. Tyler grew impatient. He was just about to start toward the rear to discover the cause of the disturbance when he saw it. The ranks of men were separating, peeling away to either side. Along the centre of the road, surrounded by peasants, drove a large, beautifully-fashioned carriage. Besides the coachman, there was an escort of four armed horsemen, all apparently terrified by the multitude they had encountered.

Tyler's men conducted the carriage and retinue close to him, then, seizing the reins of the horses, brought them all to a stop.

Newton uttered a low groan. His face was pale, and his long moustaches quivered. 'The Princess,' he said. 'It's the Princess Joan's carriage.'

Tyler told the soldiers to get off their horses. He was taking no chance of their making the beasts rear and so attempting a plunging, trampling escape. He called out to the men nearest the carriage, 'Tell whoever's inside to come out.'

One of the peasants flung open the carved door. Four women, three of them fairly young and all of them frightened, stepped out, holding their silken skirts up from the dusty road. For a moment Tyler could not understand why their appearance struck him as odd, until he realised that their hairlines had been plucked clean far back from their foreheads, and they had practically no eyebrows.

The men looking at them began to roar with laughter. Abel Threder inspected each woman in turn. He said to his fellows, 'If the chickens in my village looked like this, I'd fear they'd take cold. I might even have to take them to bed of nights to keep them warm.'

The women shrank from the burst of derisive laughter, but Tyler noticed that all of them kept casting apprehensive glances toward the carriage. He said to Abel, 'See if there's anyone else inside.'

Two of the women began to whimper and clutch at each other. Abel put his head through the door and called back to Tyler, 'The fattest hen of all. No longer a pullet, I'd say, and sitting on a pile of cushions like she means to hatch them.'

Tyler made a gesture, and Abel reached into the carriage. A woman's imperious voice cried out, 'Take your grimy hands off me,' and Abel backed out hurriedly, saying, 'My eyesight's gone bad. That hen is a hawk.' Then, leaning into the carriage again, 'Come, dear. Let's all see you.'

The woman who emerged was indeed fat, but she carried herself well, with the air of one who believes herself beautiful. So she must have been once, thought Tyler. The cool grey eyes, the elegant nose, the perfectly shaped lips were remnants of comeliness in a face gone sallow and puffy.

She surveyed the assemblage with a shrewd, rapid glance and at once addressed Tyler. 'You there,' she said. 'Why have you allowed your ruffians to stop my carriage?'

'Our reasons,' said Tyler, 'are our concern, not yours.'

The woman turned on the four cowering soldiers. 'Is there none of you with courage enough to instruct this oaf how to address the King's mother?'

'If I were in their shoes,' remarked Tyler mildly, 'I'd do exactly as they're doing.'

'What you would do is of no interest to me,' snapped the Princess. 'Tell your thieving rogues to withdraw, and we'll be on our way.'

Tyler, who had been about to tell the party it could leave, said evenly, 'You'll be on your way when I give the word.' He stepped close to her. 'If I give the word.'

'Your Highness . . .' cried Newton.

She looked at the little knight, her nostrils flaring with contempt. 'Who is this fellow?'

'Sir John Newton, madam,' said the Constable. 'I had the ill fortune to be captured by these outlaws . . .'

'That will do!' shouted Tyler, and Newton fell silent.

Tyler turned back to the Princess and saw that his outburst had had an unintended effect. Her grey eyes held fear now. 'What will you do with us?' she asked breathlessly.

Tyler looked at her without replying, and the two women whimpered loudly.

'Do you mean to keep us with you?' asked the Princess. 'If it's a matter of ransom . . .' She glanced at the sun. 'It will soon be night. I can send one of my soldiers to London, and by morning he can . . .' She shivered. Tyler could see her struggling to maintain her composure. 'You must provide for our proper comfort while we await ransom. If you do not . . .'

'They'll kill us, madam!' cried one of the women. 'Surely they mean to kill us!'

'Do you mean to kill us?' asked the Princess slowly.

Tyler was about to reply that neither he nor those with him had any intention of harming the mother of the King, to whom all of them had sworn allegiance. He hesitated, searching for the right words.

The Princess must have misinterpreted his hesitation. Her eyes were still fearful, but now Tyler saw something else in them which for a moment he did not understand. Then he saw her lips curving in an almost imperceptible smile, one shoulder moving ever so slightly. Skilfully, unmistakably, but so covertly that he doubted if anyone else had perceived it, she was making him a promise.

'It will be worth your while,' she said, 'if you keep us from harm.'

The tone contained some of its former imperiousness, but her eyes were still directing their secretive message at him.

Tyler stared at the fat, ageing woman. Seldom had he felt such sadness as was sweeping over him now. 'You may go on your way,' he said brusquely.

'You mean we are free to leave . . . now?'

'Now,' said Tyler. 'We are loyal subjects of your son.'

For an instant the Princess's expression was baffled. Then her face went blank. 'Come,' she said to the women.

They climbed into the carriage. The soldiers remounted, and the entourage moved off.

Abel turned from looking after them. From his wry smile Tyler knew that he had also seen, and understood.

'Small wonder the Black Prince died young,' said Abel softly.

14

UNTIL now Walworth had never noticed the narrow streak of grey in her golden hair.

She was bending over the table, engrossed in his accounts. Her power of concentration was amazing; when she was working, hardly anything could distract her. He knew the figures would be absolutely accurate, each notation set down in surprisingly square and heavy writing. Other men he knew set their wives to the task of keeping accounts, but often he had heard them complain about slovenly pages and unbalanced totals. Margaret's work was always precise, perhaps too precise. If he had been able to find an error . . . but he never did.

The grey hair disturbed him, not by its presence (after all, she was in her thirties, and some women went grey at twenty-five or earlier), but because It must have been there for some time without his remarking it.

Walworth had always thought he knew every detail of his wife's appearance. He could recall the silken gown in which she had been married, the turquoise velvet in which she had attended the coronation of the boy-King (the fountains on the palace grounds had been flowing with wine that day, and some lout had spilled a whole flagon over her dress; he had been preparing to thrash the offender with the flat of his sword, but she had restrained him, accepting the man's clumsiness as she did everything, with maddening calm).

He was late for a meeting: the mid-morning bell had long since

162

rung from St. Michael of Crooked Lane. But (perhaps because of the grey hair . . . a hint of vulnerability?) he suddenly felt a desire to talk with her.

Her eyes when she finally raised them from the papers were still filled with dark abstraction. Only gradually did the hazel absorb light, in a way that reminded him of shadowed crannies of the Thames picking up bits of sunrise.

'There are troubles,' she said.

He was accustomed to directness from her. She was not talkative, and when she did speak, her words were so forthright they often bore the stamp of irrelevance.

'In the accounts?' he asked.

Margaret shook her head. 'I've heard people talking in the market-places . . .'

'I've told you,' he said angrily, 'not to go into the markets. There are servants to do . . .'

'There is talk,' she said, interrupting him imperturbably, 'of trouble . . .'

'In the shires,' he said. 'The scum have turned outlaw in the shires.'

She touched the scar on the back of her right hand, seemed to be studying it. 'What do they want?' she asked.

'Want?' His ire rose, choking him. 'They want thrashing. They want a taste of chains and dungeons. And those who have stirred them up . . .'

But she had withdrawn. Her eyes held no more light, and he saw only the cold perfection of her features turned up to him in obedient politeness.

He wheeled about to leave, frustration pricking at him like hedge-nettles. He glanced over his shoulder, hoping she would not have gone back to the accounts.

She had.

A servant entered, telling him that the Bishop of London was waiting and urgently requested his presence. He had shown His Grace, the servant said, into one of the larger solars.

Courtenay was pacing restlessly. As Walworth entered the solar, he noticed that the Bishop was wearing a drab green cassock and heavy boots in place of his customary rich and exquisitely coloured robes. Courtenay faced him and said, 'It's time.'

'Time for what?' asked Walworth.

The Bishop made an exasperated sound in his throat and said, 'Rebel armies are marching toward London. They will reach the city by nightfall. Unless we leave now . . .'

Walworth knew he should be thinking quickly, shrewdly, but his mind felt like some stagnant backwater. 'And if we leave . . .'

'As I told you. It's the only way. We'll return when they've gone. London will need strong leaders. England . . .'

'We're needed here now.'

Courtenay looked at him with an expression of pity. 'Did you know Sudbury tried to resign earlier this morning?' He came close to Walworth and let his hand rest on the Lord Mayor's sleeve. The suave smile crept across his features. 'The King wouldn't let the old man go. He was really quite stubborn about it, and when that young idiot gets stubborn . . . Now do you understand?'

Walworth nodded. 'Where . . .'

'To the west. It's the only quiet section of the country within easy reach of London. I've arranged for reports to come to us twice daily. We'll know precisely when the rebels have dispersed . . .'

'And if they do not?'

'They will. No band of peasants can maintain any serious purpose for long. If in fact they have a serious purpose. Unfortunately, they can do a great deal of damage while they're running wild. A great deal of damage.'

'They'll not get into London,' said Walworth.

Courtenay stared at him and withdrew his hand from Walworth's sleeve. He pursed his lips and said, 'If they are even more successful than I believe they will be, no one will condemn us for fleeing the country. I have good friends in the Papal court at Avignon. They'll see we're well and gainfully employed until such time as . . . Oh yes! I've arranged for your wife to be taken to France while we're in the west.'

'You've planned well, Your Grace.'

Courtenay shrugged. 'You may pay me compliments later. I shall be hungry for them during those boring weeks while we're away.'

Walworth asked slowly, 'When do you propose to leave?'

'As quickly as possible. You must join me outside Aldersgate by noon. Your wife will be escorted to the Thames by two of my servants. She will know them by the paper they bear with my seal. . . .'

'The scum will never get into my city,' Walworth said calmly.

'Aldersgate at noon,' said Courtenay.

'My people will drive these peasants back to their hovels. My people will bury them in holes so deep . . .'

Courtenay again put his hand on Walworth's arm. 'Now, at once, Lord Mayor. If we delay much past noon . . .'

164

'I shall remain in my city, Your Grace.'

'Walworth . . .' Courtenay's tone was close to anguish. He turned and left the room without another word.

When Walworth passed through the common room, Margaret was still bent over the table, his accounts spread out before her.

15

SALISBURY made two trips to the Tower before noon.

He paid his first visit early in the morning, as he had been doing for several days, to inquire if there had been any word of the Princess Joan. Today the news was good. He learned from Sir Robert Knolles, the mild-mannered captain of the Tower mercenaries, that Joan had returned the night before, after having been detained briefly by the peasant army on the Kentish highroad.

Aware of Knolles watching him curiously, he tried to check the trembling brought on by sudden relief, and said casually, 'I'm glad Her Highness came to no harm.' To himself he said: why do I try to deceive him? He knows as well as anyone else how I feel; why do I not simply give way to the tears of joy that are struggling to be out? Instead he repeated, 'I'm glad,' in a voice he made deliberately gruff, and strode off to Joan's apartment.

Her ladies could speak of nothing else but their miraculous deliverance from the bandits. However, they were so frenetically voluble that he could obtain no coherent account of the episode from them. He did manage to learn that Joan was up and about, but she sent out word that she was still much too upset to receive Salisbury. He did not mind. It was enough that she was safe.

His sense of joy and relief stayed with him most of the morning. Then suddenly his anxiety returned, no longer for Joan now of course, but perhaps stronger because he could once more think objectively.

He returned to the Tower. The streets through which he rode en route seemed the same as always; cluttered with refuse and dung-heaps, obstructed by all sorts of litter from building materials to dyers' frames. The people, too, seemed the same; strident, quarrelsome, but also displaying a rough and bawdy good humour. Yet Salisbury found something disturbing in the atmosphere, some undercurrent whose nature he could not determine, but which served to intensify his apprehension.

He tried to convince himself that his feelings were groundless, but he could not dismiss them. Instead, they strengthened his resolution that something should be done quickly.

It was his intention to urge the immediate convening of the Council, but he found it impossible to locate the other advisers. So he took it upon himself to speak to Richard. The boy had been napping and was surly at having been disturbed, so Salisbury had to spend the greater part of an hour plying him with flattery before he could come to the purpose of the conference. And even then he was not certain what action should be taken. He did obtain agreement from the King to send a messenger across the Thames to seek the outlaw band and determine what they wanted (and, incidentally, their strength).

'I shall dispatch him at once,' said Salisbury.

'Do not trouble yourself, my lord Salisbury,' Richard said languidly. 'In a little while I shall dispatch him.'

'It would be preferable, sire, if it were done now.'

Richard stopped yawning. 'Perhaps,' he said bitingly, 'my lord Salisbury fancies he has ascended the throne of England.' He waited, a sly smile hovering about his lips, then said, 'The messenger will be sent forth in a little while. . . .'

At mid-afternoon the commons reached the great flat open space called Blackheath. Here Tyler gave the order to make camp.

Between them and London now lay only a few miles of low, wooded hills rolling down to the Thames.

Ball stretched out on the ground. The day's march had exhausted him, though only a few months before he had often walked twice the distance in the time between dawn and dark.

He heard a movement beside him and opened his eyes to see Tyler sitting a few feet away. For a time neither of them spoke. Then Tyler said quietly, 'Soon, John. It will not be long now.'

There had been violence, with a prospect of greater violence still ahead. Yet Tyler seemed to become more gentle and even vulnerable with each passing moment. Before Canterbury this had given Ball hope. Now it confused him.

He struggled up onto one elbow. 'Wat . . .'

'You'll rest,' said Tyler. 'There'll be enough for you to do later.'

Ball's glance went to the sword lying on the ground at Tyler's feet. It was one of the weapons taken the day before at the sacking of John of Gaunt's manor house. Tyler stood up and thrust the sword through his belt, alongside the dagger. In answer to Ball's unspoken question he said only, 'I'll be taking some of the men a little closer to the city, so we'll know better what we're facing.'

Ball did not reply, and Tyler went away. Ball watched him selecting a company from around the campfires which had already begun to sprout across the heath.

When Tyler had gone, taking about five hundred men with him, the encampment grew quiet. There was little of the quarrelling and roistering which had marked the approach of each evening until now.

Ball crossed the heath in a different direction from the one Tyler had taken. A dip in the terrain and a small copse hid him from the army of the commons.

He fell to his knees in an attitude of prayer, but after his lips had formed the words 'almighty God' several times, there seemed nothing more to say.

'I've heard,' said Walworth, 'that the clods are approaching London from the south. You will find them wherever they are and tell them that if they try to enter the city, they will discover it stoutly defended against them.'

Afternoon sunlight streamed through the window of the solar onto the faces of the three aldermen he had selected to bear his message to the rebels. Two of them blinked and nodded assent as he was speaking.

John Horne asked in his confidential whisper of a voice, 'And if, Lord Mayor, they do not listen to us?'

'You will tell them,' said Walworth, 'that if they do not quickly disperse and return to whatever hovels they call home, the people of London will massacre them and leave their bodies for carrion.'

He wished he could face the scum and tell them himself. But he understood the value of sending a delegation first. Later, perhaps tomorrow, if it became necessary, he could ride out to meet them himself and deliver a last warning. Besides, this evening it would be wiser for him to see that all was well with Agnes and her charges, and to consider with her the advisability of a temporary removal to other quarters.

He had selected the three aldermen carefully, mindful of the special qualities each possessed. Carlyll and Fresh were phlegmatic and unimaginative, without brilliance, but also not likely to be stricken with fright when they faced the rebels. Horne, despite his annoying whispering voice, was an eminently sensible man who could be depended on to bring back an accurate report of whatever ensued.

Horne was pondering something now. His angular face bore an

earnest expression, intensifying the habitual droop at one corner of his mouth. He leaned forward confidentially. 'Lord Mayor,' he said, 'perhaps if we . . .' He stopped.

'What is it?' asked Walworth impatiently.

Horne inclined his head apologetically. 'Nothing, Lord Mayor,' he whispered. 'A passing thought of no account.'

Walworth rose and made a gesture of dismissal. 'You have your instructions,' he said. 'I have no idea where the louts will be sleeping for the night. Wherever it is, find them.'

When the aldermen had gone, Walworth looked for Margaret. He found her in the solar directly above the great hall. As often when she was not working, she was sitting with her hands in her lap, staring absently out the window.

He watched her for a time, then said thoughtfully, 'It might be wise for you to take up quarters in the Tower for a few days.'

Terror coursed into her eyes. One moment they had been blank; the next, filled with panic.

'For a few days,' he repeated.

'You said they would not come into London.' Her voice was surprisingly even, reflecting only a little of the fear in her eyes.

'Nor will they,' he replied emphatically. 'You need have no fear of them.'

'I'm not afraid of them.'

'What are you afraid of?' he asked bluntly.

'The Tower.'

He laughed. 'You've been there before. It's not a prison. That is, not the White Tower, where your quarters would be.'

'It has walls.'

'So has London.'

'Yes,' she said. Then she repeated, 'You said they wouldn't come into London.'

'They won't,' he said angrily.

'I'll not go,' she said.

'You'll go if I order you.'

'No,' she said calmly.

He shrugged. It had only been a random idea, a precaution against the remote and unthinkable possibility that the rabble would gain entrance into London. He had made a point of saying they would not. Her refusal was, after all, an acceptance of his judgment.

Walworth left Margaret and went to the falcon shed.

When Tyler saw the Marshalsea, he felt for a moment that his decision to storm the prison at this time had been unwise.

The walls were ten or twelve feet high and appeared to be several feet thick. A heavy-timbered gate had slammed shut when the guards spotted the band of men approaching.

Tyler wished he had kept his full company with him, instead of sending almost half farther up the river to burn the Archbishop's Palace. At least he should have had the foresight to fell some trees to be used as battering rams.

He considered retiring until dark, then rejected this alternative. Their presence was known, and the few hours before nightfall would only give the prison guards respite to prepare a better defence.

He studied the walls for a few more moments, then called the men around him and outlined his plan, pausing between each several sentences to allow time for his words to be passed on to the outer edges of the troop.

The tactics were simple. They were to split up into small groups, deploying at close intervals around the wall. One man in each group was to act as a human ladder for the others. They would climb onto his shoulders and vault from there over the wall. If it were done quickly and well, they should be able to put two hundred men into the prison courtyard before the defenders were fully aware of what was happening.

Tyler would lead one party himself. His ladderman was to be the heavy-set fellow from Abel Threder's village, who was now grumbling and cursing. 'All the way from home I've come,' he was saying, 'then all the way from camp where I could have been eating supper, just to let a bunch of fools walk on me. I'm reeve of my village, and I've been hayward, too.' He showed his white teeth. 'Let one oaf set foot on my head instead of my shoulders, and his wife will have little use of him when he gets home.'

The men who had farthest to travel around the walls left first. When Tyler felt enough time had elapsed, he gave the signal for the rest to move forward.

He climbed over the bulwark and leaped into the enclosure. All around him his men were dropping off the wall. The guards, about fifty of them, were waiting with drawn swords.

Some of the peasants forgot their newly acquired weapons and used either their heads or their bellies to butt their opponents. These tactics, which might have been suicidal, so amazed the guards that many of them did not even try to defend themselves.

However, some did, and a number of Tyler's men fell. Tyler himself had used a pike, in France, but never a sword. He learned its use quickly enough now. His hands and tunic were soon spattered with the blood of Marshalsea guards.

169

The battle was fierce but brief. Only a few moments after they had clambered over the walls, the invaders were in control. About fifteen guards lay dead or dying; the rest were disarmed. Victors and defeated wandered about the prison courtyard in little aimless circles, or simply sat down on the ground, all their faces wearing the same vapid expression.

Tyler sent some men to open the doors of the cells and dungeons. Several hundred prisoners came out, some crawling or tottering, many with iron shackles still around their arms and legs, all filthy and unkempt.

The surviving guards bleated with fright and huddled together near the wall. But the prisoners stared at them with more curiosity than hostility. A few ventured forward and touched the guards, drew their hands back quickly. Then, sensing that nothing would happen to them, they touched their jailers again. Others pressed in to join them, reaching out with soft childlike cries. The guards were nearly smothered by the prisoners seeking to lay gentle hands on them.

Suddenly one of the liberated men, less emaciated-looking than the rest, called out, 'Where's Imworth?'

As if the name were a signal, the others looked around and took up the cry. 'Imworth!' Their grating voices were like the chorusing of a forest of screech owls. 'Imworth . . . where's Imworth?'

Tyler went to the man who had first called out and asked him who Imworth was. 'The chief jailer,' replied the man, shouting to be heard above the din. He ripped open his ragged tunic, revealing a cruelly lacerated chest. 'Imworth did that,' he cried. 'Chained my arms behind me . . . used his dagger . . .' He pointed to an old man with mangled hands. 'Imworth!' He led Tyler to another, who had raw sockets where his eyes had been. 'Imworth!'

Tyler shouldered through the crush of prisoners around the guards and asked where the chief jailer was. Those who heard his question shrank closer to the wall. 'Fled,' said one. 'Fled when first you approached,' said another. And a third, 'He said if we dared follow, he'd have us put to death.' He laughed suddenly, a breathless squeal. 'Put to death, that's what he said.'

The prisoners' clamour began again. 'Imworth!' they shouted, waving their arms in random fluttering movements, a strange parody of rage. 'Imworth . . . kill him . . . kill . . .'

The servant from the Archbishop's Palace in Lambeth pointed out the brothels.

'We'll burn them,' said Cave. 'Bring the torches.'

'Fitting enough,' said Abel to Roger. 'If we burn Archbishops' Palaces, it's only fair to burn whorehouses.'

Roger's face was still flushed with the excitement of watching the fire they had started in Lambeth. 'The glass,' he said. 'Did you see the glass melt? Just like water it ran down the wall. I never knew glass would melt.'

'What a learned fellow you're becoming,' said Abel. 'A fortnight ago you didn't even know what glass was. Now you know it melts.'

Someone put a torch in Abel's hand, and he walked with a dozen others toward the row of houses on the riverbank. At their approach the doors flew open and a bevy of girls rushed out. They wore multi-coloured striped hoods and flimsy gowns with bushy fox-tails attached behind. The men halted their advance and stood open-mouthed, gawking at the girls, who stared back at them in frightened silence.

Into the space between the two groups strode a woman dressed in a flowing light-green gown. Her body was slim and shapely, her hands and feet beautifully formed, but her face was shockingly at variance with them, wrinkled and debauched.

She smiled and said in a rich warm voice, 'What's it about, lads?'

'We're burning these places,' replied Cave. 'They belong to John of Gaunt.'

'Ah,' said the woman, 'you're mistaken about that.'

'We were told they belong to John of Gaunt,' said Cave, less certainly.

'Now, lads, there's no cause to burn them. The man who owns these houses would never cause you harm.'

'Anything owned by John . . .'

'John of Gaunt has nothing to do with any of us.'

'Then who . . .'

'Maybe,' said the woman, smiling again, 'my girls can convince you you're making a mistake.'

Two or three of the whores tittered and started toward the men. In a moment others followed and began twining themselves about those who carried the torches. 'We can't invite all of you in at once,' said the woman, still smiling, 'but there's time for everyone. Isn't there, girls?'

The ranks behind the torchbearers wavered and broke as the men pushed forward to cluster about the girls. Laughter rippled from group to group. Torches fell to the ground and lay forgotten. 'Wine,' called the woman. 'There'll be wine and ale for everyone.' The men cheered and the girls laughed.

Suddenly Cave tore himself from the embrace of a tall whore who was running her hands beneath his tunic. He snatched up the torch he had dropped and cried, 'John of Gaunt's brothels must be burned!'

He ran to the nearest house, reached up to the thatch roof and touched fire to it as the woman shrieked, 'No, you're wrong! You're wrong!' She started after Cave. Two of the men seized her and held her arms. The flames shot skyward and began to crackle viciously. The woman kicked and struggled as Cave went on to the next building. She was weeping, and the tears coursed down her ruined face. 'No!' she screamed. 'Don't burn his houses! Don't burn his houses!'

One of the girls, younger than the others, was standing beside Abel. He saw her reach beneath her gown and bring out a small, shiny-bladed knife. Before he could understand what she intended, she rushed at the woman. The knife flashed, and the woman went limp in the grasp of the men holding her. Their mouths opened in amazement and they let her slide to the ground, where she lay still, a dark stain growing like an evil flower beneath her breast. Her eyes were wide, unblinking, but from one of them welled a single tear which rolled down her cheek.

A dark girl with no upper lip made an abrupt threatening gesture at the one who had killed the woman. 'Flemish pig!' she cried. The girl backed away from her, toward Abel. Now the others began to shriek and wail. 'Flemish pig!' they echoed. 'Foreign bitch!' They closed in on her.

The girl threw herself into Abel's arms. 'Help me,' she said in a heavy accent. 'Please help me. That woman kept me as a slave.' She pressed against Abel, her body writhing in a frantic travesty of seduction. 'My father was a poor man, a labourer. She killed him and stole me from my mother. Please help me!'

Abel managed to get his hands on her shoulders and hold her far enough from him so he could look at her face. What he saw there made him push her away roughly.

As he did, the whores sprang at her. The girl disappeared in their midst. Her screams were cut off sharply, and the only sounds that remained were the snarling of the pack of females and the crackle of flames from the burning houses.

The men stood dumbly watching the women who, a short while before, had been caressing them. Then they turned and slunk away.

16

AFTER leaving the King, Salisbury had returned to his house and lain down to rest, but sleep had not come. He rose late in the afternoon and went to a window overlooking the river. Across the water smoke and flames were pouring out of the Archbishop's Palace.

At once he went to his wife and told her what she must do.

Elizabeth proved stubborn. 'Truly, William,' she said, 'to ask me to go to the Tower is impossible, absolutely impossible. I mean, I shouldn't be able to have proper clothes ready before next week, at the very earliest. And you know how I dislike, truly despise, sleeping in strange rooms. For you it's different.' She flashed him a spiteful glance. 'Men don't mind where they sleep, in the Tower, or the brothels across the river, it's all the same. Truly it is. I . . .' She broke off and gave him a shy, remorseful smile. 'William, you look ill. Truly you do. You must rest more.' She patted the caul covering her hair, searching for any loose strands that might have escaped. 'No, I simply cannot go to stay in the Tower. It's not necessary, not necessary at all.'

Salisbury watched her glumly. He could smell the faint, acrid odour of smoke from the burning palace.

Elizabeth took his arm and looked at him imploringly. 'William, you simply must rest more. I mean, you've been up since long before dawn, I heard you moving about . . . William, oh, William . . .'

He was miserable at the extent of her distress, but there was no alternative, and she knew it as well as he. She began to weep. 'My dear . . .' he began, and stopped as he saw the despair deepening in her eyes. 'You will have your own chambers,' he said delicately, 'and need meet no one else. . . .'

'Truly, William?' she asked through her tears. 'I mean . . . no one . . .?'

'No one,' he assured her firmly.

Unfortunately, matters did not work out that way at all.

Just as Salisbury and Elizabeth were about to enter the White Tower, he saw Joan and her ladies approaching from the opposite direction. It was obvious that an encounter could not be avoided.

Elizabeth did not see her at first. She was clinging to Salisbury's arm, keeping pace with him in a little sidewise adoring skip, gazing at him yearningly. 'William,' she was saying, 'oh, William, I wish we could have gone to Canterbury. I mean, you did promise me . . .'

Her words trailed away as Salisbury stopped walking, and her face went chalky. Salisbury put his arm beneath hers for support. She brushed it away with an angry, surreptitious gesture and curtsied as Joan came toward them.

Salisbury bowed. 'My lady Joan . . .'

'My good Lord Salisbury.' She flicked her glance over Elizabeth. 'And how pleasant to see your charming wife. It's so seldom we're able to enjoy her company here at the Tower. You must not keep her so much to yourself.'

'Your Highness,' murmured Elizabeth, looking at the ground.

'I heard some account,' said Salisbury, 'of my lady Joan's terrible experience yesterday with the outlaws in Kent. . . .'

'It was dreadful,' said Joan, 'simply dreadful. There were thousands of them.' She paused to recover from a fit of breathlessness. 'They're animals, wild beasts. The stench from them, and their filthy paws, and the way they looked at me . . .'

She shuddered, and before he could stop himself, Salisbury made a solicitous movement toward her.

'You have no idea how fortunate I was to escape with my life.' She looked at Salisbury in the way she had once looked at him only when they were alone. 'I've been so shaken since it happened, my Lord Salisbury. I was hoping you would have come to visit me before now. . . .'

'I did not wish to disturb Your Highness,' said Salisbury stiffly.

Elizabeth looked up and said in a clear voice, 'I'm truly grateful to hear of Your Highness's deliverance.' She let her gaze rest briefly on the bloated, sallow face, then travel over the corpulent lines of Joan's body. 'However, I'm sure that as soon as the rabble saw who stood before them, they abandoned whatever fearsome designs they might have had. I mean . . .'

'If my lady Joan will permit us to withdraw,' said Salisbury hastily.

'Only if my Lord Salisbury promises to visit me at the earliest opportunity,' replied Joan, smiling at him.

Later, when Elizabeth and Salisbury were alone in her bedchamber, she said tearfully, 'I wish I were dead.'

That, he thought as he went through the motions of comforting her, is something we all may be soon enough, whether we wish it or not.

For a long time Walworth remained in the falcon shed watching the peregrine, which looked balefully back at him. These past few days he had been too busy to exercise her. Tomorrow he would rise before dawn and take her out to the moor. Prolonged inactivity was not good for her.

While he was crossing the courtyard between the shed and the house he happened to glance at the sky. A thick curtain of smoke was rising from the south.

He rushed out onto Thames Street, sprinted down Ebb Gate Lane and came out onto the bank of the river just above the gate. People were standing at the water's edge several rows deep. He pushed them aside and plunged forward, ignoring the thick mud which sucked at his feet.

Upriver, across from John of Gaunt's Savoy Palace, clouds of smoke were billowing out of the shell of the Archbishop's mansion. And almost directly opposite the point where he was standing, his own property was ablaze.

He did not realize what he was doing until he found himself struggling against restraining hands. Four members of his fish-mongers' guild were striving to hold him.

The water of the Thames was up to his waist.

Only then did he become aware that he was howling with rage.

When Tyler returned to camp after his capture of the Marshalsea, Ball met him with the news that a messenger had come from King Richard, inquiring after the intent of those gathered at Blackheath.

'I told him,' said the priest, 'that it was our desire to meet with the King and present our grievances. He promised that he would take the message back. . . .'

Ball stopped and stared moodily at the bloodstains on Tyler's hands and tunic.

'Tomorrow is Corpus Christi,' he said finally. 'We shall need no wine to celebrate it.'

17

TYLER washed in a stream at the edge of the heath. He honed his dagger on a stone and scraped the stubble from his face. As he walked back through the slow June twilight he saw Ball approaching him. He braced himself for another admonitory sermon, but Ball said simply, 'We must talk once more about what we shall say to the King.'

They sat beside one of the fires and went over the points they had discussed together many times in Colchester.

The sky was still light overhead, but darkness was gathering at the edges of the heath when Tyler heard the hoofbeats. He glanced up and saw a solitary dark-cloaked rider moving toward them from the east. He stopped and spoke to some men, then dismounted and came on, leading his horse. Not until he was quite close to them did Tyler realize he was a priest.

They got to their feet as the man stopped in front of them. 'Tyler?' he asked; then, 'You must be John Ball.' He smiled wearily and let the reins fall to the ground. The horse's head was lather-flecked, its coat mottled with dust and dried sweat; it stood without moving. 'I've ridden from Suffolk since yesterday morning,' said the priest. 'By way of Maidstone, since I heard you were there.' He smiled again. 'John Wrawe,' he said.

Tyler studied the man with whom he had exchanged messages for three years but had never met. Wrawe's manner was easy, his smile quick and warm.

'I've come to tell you,' said Wrawe, 'that the peasants of Suffolk are ready to rise.'

'You've had a long journey,' said Ball. 'If you care to rest for the night, and then in the morning . . .'

'There's no time for rest,' said Wrawe.

He spoke offhandedly, but somehow his words contained a remonstrance. Tyler felt an odd, small-boy sense of guilt, as though he had been caught taking his ease when he should have been bustling through the camp, engaged in frantic activity.

'I shall hear your plans,' Wrawe went on, 'and receive instruction, then return to Suffolk.'

'Tonight?' asked Tyler.

'Of course, tonight There's no time for rest. Listen . . .' He leaned toward them, his eyes lighting up. 'The people of Suffolk are ready. You should see them. Fifteen thousand of them are ready to rise from slavery. I've never seen anything so inspiring.'

'Ours aren't always so inspiring,' said Ball drily, 'but we're also ready.'

Wrawe said, 'We're going to right the wrongs of generations, of centuries.' He looked around the camp, his gaze probing far across the heath. 'Why,' he asked puzzledly, 'are your people so quiet?'

'Quiet?' asked Tyler.

'Quiet,' repeated Wrawe. 'So close to their goal and there's no singing or shouting. . . .'

'Which pleases me more than I can tell you,' said Tyler. 'I've had enough of their squabbling these past few days.'

Wrawe looked pained. 'Squabbling? The people. . . . Why have you allowed . . .' He smiled. 'Ah well. You're doubtless tired, and one can't attend to everything. But peasants should know that their only enemies are the lords, the tyrants who have kept them in subjection. . . .' Suddenly he grew pale. His knees began to buckle, and if Tyler had not put out a hand to steady him he would have fallen.

'You must rest,' said Ball firmly.

'There's no time,' said Wrawe, giving them a wan smile. 'I apologize for . . . but no matter.' His voice became stronger. 'I'll hear your plans and take my instructions and be off.' He leaned toward them again, eagerly. 'There's a group of men in Stowmarket. I've watched their understanding growing for years. My friends, you've never seen such fire and nobility as I've seen in the faces of these men . . .' Wrawe swayed again and almost fell. For a moment or two he was actually asleep. He opened his eyes and said, 'There's no time for rest. If I sleep . . .'

'If you don't sleep,' said Tyler, 'you'll never get back to Suffolk.'

'I'll get back,' replied Wrawe grimly, and Tyler had a brief glimpse of the force which had made this man the unchallenged leader of those in his shire.

'We hope to see the King tomorrow,' said Ball. His words seemed mild and prosaic to Tyler after Wrawe's glowing enthusiasm.

'Now that we're so close to freedom,' said Wrawe, 'I find I can scarcely wait.' His eyes lighted up again. 'To see the day when a man can till his fields and keep the harvest he has sweated to grow. When mothers can look at their children without despair, knowing they will grow up free. . . .'

Tyler shuffled his feet. He was tired, and he wanted to sit down, but he felt that Wrawe would disapprove, and, strangely, he found himself caring about this.

'For a man to be able to grind his own corn and brew his own beer without being taxed for it,' Wrawe continued. 'For people to be able to hold up their heads proudly and walk freely through the realm. . . .' Once again he fell asleep, and Tyler had to support him. He awoke and smiled. 'No time,' he said. 'Give me my instructions.'

When Wrawe was about to leave, he looked at them both and said in a low, thrilling voice, 'For freedom . . .' Then he swung onto his horse and was gone.

Tyler saw Ball start to sit down, then glance uneasily after Wrawe.

177

'I think,' said Tyler, 'it's all right now.'

But he also looked guiltily across the heath before he sank down beside the fire.

The three aldermen sat in a straight line, facing Ball and Tyler. 'Come to the point,' said Tyler angrily.

They had arrived shortly after Wrawe's departure, and aside from telling their names and saying that they represented the Lord Mayor of London, they had so far failed to mention the purpose of their visit.

The man called Horne seemed to be the only one who possessed a tongue. When Tyler interrupted him, he was in the midst of a rambling discourse explaining how they would have reached Blackheath earlier had it not been for one of their horses going lame, necessitating a return to London for a fresh mount. 'Not to our liking to be abroad so late,' he was saying now, disregarding Tyler's admonition. He spoke in a whispering, confidential voice which made Tyler's back prickle. 'We should long since have been home in our beds. . . .'

'Tell us why you've come then, and go,' said Tyler.

Carlyll stirred and spat into the fire. He had a large, flat face with heavy features. 'The Lord Mayor said to tell you clods . . .'

Tyler reached out and seized him by the tunic. Carlyll looked at him impassively. 'The Lord Mayor's words, not mine.' Tyler released him. 'You should not attempt to enter London,' Carlyll continued.

'You will discover it stoutly defended,' said Fresh in a pure, high-pitched voice.

'What my colleagues mean . . .' put in Horne.

'They've said what they mean.'

'The Lord Mayor said further . . .' Carlyll went on in a monotone.

Horne interrupted in a paroxysm of anxiety. 'Perhaps we should . . .'

Carlyll had scarcely paused. '. . . that if you do not disperse to your homes . . .'

'Not homes, Carlyll,' said Fresh. 'The Lord Mayor said if they do not disperse and return to whatever hovels they call home . . .'

Tyler half-rose, then reluctantly sat down as Ball put a restraining hand on his shoulder.

'That's right.' Carlyll nodded gravely. 'If you do not disperse . . .'

'Quickly disperse,' corrected Fresh.

'If you do not quickly disperse and return to whatever hovels you call home . . .'

Horne leaned forward. One corner of his mouth drooped pathetically as he whispered, 'What the Lord Mayor meant . . .'

Carlyll plunged ahead. 'The people of London will . . .' He stopped and turned to Horne, his heavy features baffled. 'I forget the rest.'

Horne said eagerly, 'The Lord Mayor hopes you will understand . . .'

'No no,' piped Fresh querulously. 'Didn't you listen to him? He said the people of London would massacre them and leave their bodies for carrion.' He glanced at his companions in breathless triumph.

Tyler got to his feet, aware of Ball watching him apprehensively. 'You tell your Lord Mayor . . .' he began quietly. Then he shouted, 'He'll not insult the commons!'

Some Kentishmen at a neighbouring fire turned sharply, then resumed their low-voiced conversation.

Horne looked up at Tyler. His voice was like the rustling of dry leaves. 'Now we've come to the point. Now you have the message of the Lord Mayor.'

Tyler, glowering down at the earnest face turned up to his, was about to reply when Horne winked. Tyler stared at him, and Horne said, 'If you're wise, you'll heed the Lord Mayor's warning.' He winked with the other eye.

Tyler sat down heavily, suddenly sure he had gone mad.

And Horne got up. 'We've said what we came to say,' he murmured. 'We'll go now.'

Ball and the other two men rose. Tyler picked himself up slowly. As he did, Horne nudged him. Tyler clenched his fist and the alderman stepped nimbly away. He told his companions that he had to relieve himself, that they should go ahead and he would overtake them. As he walked out of the circle of firelight, he beckoned to Tyler.

After a moment Tyler followed him. Horne was waiting in a patch of darkness between two oak trees. Tyler approached cautiously and heard him say, 'The people of London . . .' and then something unintelligible.

'What?' asked Tyler.

Horne's mumbling reply was almost inaudible.

'Speak up,' said Tyler.

Horne said in a loud clear voice, 'The people of London will welcome you.'

He gasped and put his hand over his mouth, looking around wildly. Then he said, whispering now, 'The people are your friends, ready to act with you and show you obedience.'

Tyler asked slowly, 'How do I know you're telling the truth?'

The corner of Horne's mouth drooped lower. He looked like a child who has been beaten. Suddenly he leaned forward and said, 'Farringdon sends greetings.'

Tyler recalled the narrow-faced man who had visited him in Colchester and had sat nervously pushing the floor-rushes back and forth between his feet as he grumbled about the tenements he said had been stolen from him. 'Farringdon . . .' he said.

'Even now he's on his way to meet Jack Straw and the Essex-men.'

Tyler's eagerness overcame caution. 'They're near London?'

'This afternoon they were at Barking, not ten miles from the walls.' Horne waited for Tyler to digest this, then said, 'You see, we've kept good note of your progress. And I can tell you, many thousands in the city will welcome you and join your cause. Artisans, prentices, members of all guilds . . . we've waited a long time for your coming.'

'Why?' asked Tyler.

Horne's lips twisted. 'Do you think injustice is confined to the countryside?' He leaned forward and whispered, 'We'll win.' Then he gripped Tyler's arm and said in a clear, firm voice, 'We must win.'

18

THEY dispatched Newton on his mission before mass on Corpus Christi morning.

The sun was coming up over the heath. Tyler was occupied for the moment . . . a provision shortage was developing, and he was working out a ration system with the leaders . . . so Ball was left alone with the diminutive knight.

Newton looked altogether a pitiful and bedraggled figure. He had refused to remove the outsize armour in which he had been captured. The breastplate had rubbed his neck raw, and the sores were beginning to suppurate. Before the meeting with Princess Joan on the highroad he had spoken little, since then not at all. Now, suddenly, he turned to Ball, his eyes alive and angry. 'If harm comes to my wife and children . . .'

'None will,' said Ball.

'If they suffer one moment of discomfort . . .'

'Your family will be safe,' Ball again assured him.

'They'll be safe,' said Tyler, coming up to them, 'as long as you follow instructions.'

The knight wheeled and glared up at Tyler, who went on calmly, 'You will tell the King that we wish to meet him today.'

'You will also tell him,' said Ball, 'that we are acting only in his interests.'

Newton laughed in a high, cracked voice. Tyler's lips went white with anger, and Ball stepped between the two men. 'Tell the King,' he said, 'that England has been ruled dishonourably for too long. Men like John of Gaunt and Hales and the corrupt clergy have oppressed the people and made it necessary for us to seek redress for wrongs against us. Tell the King we have no quarrel with him and mean to remain his loyal subjects.'

'But tell him,' said Tyler grimly, 'that we will not be put off. Can you remember all we have said?'

Newton stroked his moustaches and replied with dignity, 'My family's safety will keep my memory sharp.'

Tyler looked at him for a moment, then said quietly, 'We have no salves or potions here. Take time to have your sores dressed before you come back to us.'

Shortly after Newton departed, Ball said mass. When he had completed the office, he mounted the pulpit which Tyler had ordered some men to erect in the centre of the heath. He placed his hands on the rough log railing and felt his breath catch as he gazed around him.

The sun was well up, its rays touching the dew on the trees fringing the vast flatland, making them blaze like torches. Within the great flaming circle, looking up at him in silent expectation, stood thousands of men, the commons of Kent and Sussex.

When Ball had spoken in their villages, more often than not fear had touched his heart and choked off his voice. Now it was awe that nearly overwhelmed him, so that for some moments he was unable to begin.

His first words came out in such a hoarse and grating jumble that he had to start again. And suddenly he felt power flowing through him, heard his voice become strong and sonorous.

'When Adam delved and Eve span, who was then the gentleman?'

He hoped they would not take up the chant, for he had much to say to them, and for his purpose there could be no clearer text than the couplet.

They remained silent, and he went on. 'The opportunity is before us now, waiting in radiance. Its name is freedom. We have only to reach out and grasp it.'

He could barely make out the figures at the edges of the multitude. Even the faces nearer him were featureless. But he knew their hearts.

'The yoke you have borne, the slavery you have endured, is at an end. Let us take courage and behave like the wise husbandman of scripture who uprooted the weeds which choked his grain.'

The image was developing in his mind. He pursued it avidly.

'The weeds of England are those who rule by oppression, and the time of harvest has come. When the great ones have been dealt with, all will enjoy equal freedom, all will have common nobility, rank and power. It is our task to pluck out the weeds which plague us: the evil lords, the corrupt clergy, the unjust judges, the lawyers, every man indeed who threatens the common good. . . .'

He was not prepared for the uproar which interrupted him. The pulpit trembled with it. He looked around, bewildered. So far he had said nothing to provoke such a response. The meaning of his message still remained to be spoken. Then he caught sight of Tyler at the foot of the pulpit, smiling ironically. He began to distinguish individual words in the holocaust of sound. 'Kill Hales! Kill Hob the Robber! Death to Sudbury!'

Horrified, he tried to make himself heard. 'No!' he cried. 'That's not what I meant . . . not to kill . . . justice, not slaughter . . .'

But the clamour did not abate. And now he could hear them shouting his name, and coupled with it the word Archbishop.

The pillared nave of Canterbury swam up grandly before his inner vision, sank drowning in a sea of remorse and horror.

He raised his hands to quiet them, to make them understand, but he might as well have tried to silence the wind.

The Tower grounds were beginning to swarm with those seeking refuge: all members of the aristocracy who had decided that their houses would be frail havens if the peasants entered the city.

As he crossed the green in the early morning sunlight, Salisbury saw a doddering admiral, Sir Thomas Percy, conversing with Thomas of Woodstock, John of Gaunt's brother. Joan's two sons by Holland, ferret-faced idlers in their late twenties, were shying stones at the ravens, to the displeasure of the warder charged with protecting the scavengers. John of Gaunt's son Henry, about the same age as Richard, skulked near the Beauchamp Tower, maintaining a studied aloofness from the others.

Joan came toward him as he gained the entrance hall of the White Tower. Her ladies were not with her. 'My good Lord Salisbury,' she said, then had to pause while she gasped for breath.

Salisbury, moved by her discomforts, forgot his customary propriety and took both her hands in his. They were deathly cold.

Her lips trembled as she attempted a smile intended to be coquettish, but which only lingered against her pallor like an unwelcome guest. Yet, listening to her rapid and uneven breathing, watching the rise and fall of shoulders and bosom gone gross, Salisbury could, as always, remember the Joan of passion-fire and insouciant promise.

He saw the grey eyes accepting his regard, not with gratitude, but as her due. She regained some of her composure, and, removing her hands from his, said, 'You promised me no harm would come to him.'

'You may be sure, madam,' he replied, falling into the stilted phrasing which plagued his moments of agitation, 'that we shall do all within our power to protect the King, with our hearts, our spirits, and our blood.'

She nodded absently and said, 'They'll invade London, I know they'll invade London,' in a bleak and inconsolable voice.

'Perhaps not,' he replied, unable to muster much assurance.

She turned away, and he thought she was about to depart, but suddenly she was facing him again. 'Oh, my dear,' she cried, 'how empty . . .' And this time she was gone, leaving her sentence unfinished and Salisbury with his heart beating erratically.

By the time he reached the council chamber his mouth had the bitter taste which heralded one of his intense digestive upsets. He found it somewhat amusing that the sight of the knight with the great moustaches, whose message they were gathering to hear, and whose presence signified only danger, actually soothed him. Is love then, he wondered, a greater menace to life than death, and smiled sourly at his desperate sophistry.

'I am delighted to see,' said Sudbury gloomily, 'that my Lord Salisbury is able to discover some source of comedy in our present situation.'

The Chancellor had aged alarmingly in the past few days. His complexion was grey, and the flesh about his mouth seemed to have collapsed, giving his features a striking resemblance to those of Elizabeth's Maltese spaniel (which Salisbury had returned to their house to fetch for her the night before, and which had become so panic-stricken the moment they entered the Tower that it had at once messed over his tunic).

He did not reply to the Chancellor, and Sudbury seemed to have forgotten he had spoken. He stared fixedly at the tapestry behind the King's chair.

The knight (Salisbury believed his name was Newton) fidgeted at the end of the chamber, touching his moustaches now and then, keeping his eyes averted from the Chancellor and Salisbury.

Hales entered, whinnying as usual, casting a quick shrewd glance about the room, scowling at the knight. 'I would hang them,' he said to no one in particular. 'I would hang them all.'

Walworth stomped in, obviously in a vile mood. His eyes were bloodshot, and his mouth was working furiously. When Hales said again, 'I would hang them,' Walworth spat viciously in the Treasurer's direction. Hales avoided the spittle with amazing nimbleness and chuckled mirthlessly.

They were all watching this bit of byplay and so did not notice that the King had come in until a petulant voice said, 'My uncles . . .'

Richard was wearing a cream-coloured tunic embroidered with gold. He smoothed it as he stood looking around, nostrils flaring with anger. 'My uncles . . .' he said again, the skin of his face beginning to crinkle.

Sudbury bowed rapidly several times, his joints cracking as he bobbed up and down. Hales inclined his corpulent torso briefly. The knight went down on one knee. Salisbury was just beginning his elaborate courtier's obeisance when Walworth said gruffly, 'Sit down, Your Majesty.'

'Mercy!' gasped Sudbury, looking sidewise at the King.

Richard, however, hesitated only an instant before scurrying to his seat.

'The Bishop of London . . .' began Sudbury, moving to his own chair.

'His Grace will not be present,' snapped Walworth. They all looked at him, waiting for further explanation, but the Lord Mayor merely sat down and said shortly, 'Let's hear what this fellow has to say.'

The knight came forward falteringly, his gaze downcast. He was wearing an ill-fitting armoured breastplate, which had rubbed sores on his neck, and he stank abominably. 'They're keeping my wife and children prisoner,' he said in a forlorn voice. 'Otherwise . . .'

Salisbury cut him off. 'Tell us what they have charged you to tell. We hold you excused.'

Newton brightened a little. He told them how he had been captured at Rochester, and what he had seen at Maidstone. When he began to describe how the peasants had stopped Joan's carriage, Salisbury's innards contracted, and he said abruptly, 'Their strength . . . tell us how many there are.'

'Fifteen thousand or more at Blackheath.'

Richard snorted. 'The messenger I sent out yesterday told me there were no more than six or seven thousand.'

'Fifteen, sire, at least,' Newton insisted politely. 'And I've heard there are as many again in Essex.'

In the despairing silence that followed, Newton bowed to Richard, then said, 'Sire, they wish to have no one but yourself, and they say you need have no fear of them, as they will do you no harm. They have always respected you as their King, and will continue to do so. But they desire to meet with you and tell you many things they say it is necessary for you to hear.'

Richard smiled. 'Is this not fine news, my uncles? They have respect for me.'

Sudbury sighed noisily. 'You see? Always I have said they were good people. . . .'

'My lord Chancellor,' said Newton mournfully, 'they do not include you and the Treasurer in their loyalty. I feel I must tell you . . .'

'I don't want to hear,' said Sudbury shrilly. Perspiration broke out on his forehead in little oily droplets. He said pitifully, 'Why? Have I ever harmed . . .' He stopped, shaking his head, and a drop of sweat flew onto Richard's tunic.

'Animals,' grumbled Hales. 'Beasts.'

'The swine . . .' said Walworth.

'Yes, Lord Mayor,' Hales agreed eagerly. 'Yes, you're right.'

'My lords,' said Newton, 'I do not believe we should under-estimate . . .'

'Animals,' said Hales. 'Shoeless ruffians.'

'Ruffians they may be,' Newton persisted, 'and shoeless many of them are. But they are not stupid. There is a man called Tyler, and a priest with the name of Ball. . . .'

Sudbury moaned loudly.

'But they mean me no harm,' said Richard, looking pleased.

'Sire,' said Salisbury, glancing quickly around at the others, 'will you agree to meet with them?'

'If my uncles will come with me,' replied Richard. He clapped his hands delightedly. 'I shall ask them to kiss the hem of my robe. Yes, I shall wear my coronation robes and ask . . .'

'Perhaps, Your Majesty,' said Salisbury drily, 'it would be just as well if you appeared in garments a little less ornate.'

Richard pouted, crestfallen. Then he brightened. 'They will swear allegiance in concerted voice. That will have a beautiful sound. My father the Black Prince . . .'

'Sire,' said Salisbury, 'I must warn you. This meeting could place you in a certain amount of danger. . . .'

'You heard what he said,' cried Richard, gesturing at Newton. 'They know who their King is.'

Salisbury stifled his impatience and turned to Newton. 'Tell them the King will come to them at Rotherhithe.'

'Will we go on the barge then?' asked Richard. 'It will be cool on the river. Perhaps my mother would enjoy . . .'

'Sire!' shouted Salisbury. He bit his lip, then said very quietly, 'Perhaps Your Majesty would care to withdraw and prepare himself. We shall await Your Majesty with the barge beneath St. Thomas' Tower at noon.'

When the King had left the room, Salisbury said to Newton, 'Go, and God be with you,' adding in a low voice, 'And with us.'

As they were leaving the council chamber, Walworth motioned Salisbury to remain behind. He waited, curious, but even after the room was empty, Walworth only stared at him in silence, his eyes rolling. For a moment Salisbury thought the Lord Mayor had lost his senses. Finally Walworth said, 'We'll keep them out of London. We'll fight.'

'We'll do what we can.'

'We'll fight!' Walworth's lips twisted, then suddenly relaxed. There was an expression on his face which puzzled Salisbury, until he realized with great surprise that it was a look of grudging respect.

'You didn't leave,' said Walworth. 'You could have run away just as he did, but you stayed.'

He turned and strode out of the council chamber.

Now Salisbury understood why Courtenay had not been present. And he could conjecture with considerable confidence what had passed between the Bishop and the Lord Mayor.

The barge slipped smoothly downstream, guided by the ten oarsmen. They had no escort. Salisbury had argued successfully with Walworth that the meagre guard they could muster would provide scant protection from the rebel force and might only inflame them.

Richard preened delightedly in the bow; Sudbury brooded in the stern, and Hales sat next to Salisbury, muttering over and over, 'They need another tax. That's what the beasts need, another tax.' On Salisbury's other side Walworth kept his hand on his sword, clutching it so tightly at times that his knuckles turned white.

They rounded the slight bend to the north, then entered the great crescent which swept down to Rotherhithe.

186

In a few moments they saw them, clustered so thickly on the southern shore that they blotted out the bank.

Sudbury cried out sharply, and Walworth growled, 'They'll pay. They'll pay with their stinking blood for what they've done.'

There was no sound from the rebels until the barge drifted directly abreast of their centre. Then they burst into thunderous cheering. Richard beamed.

But as the oarsmen began manœuvring the craft closer to shore, the cheering ceased abruptly. Salisbury heard a few isolated cries, rising like a complaint of gulls into the still air. He made out the names of Sudbury and Hales, and immediately the shouting began anew, but this time it was angry, menacing. Some of the peasants began to shake their fists, others made lewd gestures.

A priest standing at the edge of the water raised his hands and called out something to the mob. Gradually the din subsided. The priest hunched over and put his hand to his mouth. It appeared to Salisbury that he was chewing his fingernails, but it seemed such an incongruous gesture he was sure he was wrong.

A huge, heavy-shouldered man next to the priest called out, 'Put the King ashore in our midst, so we can discuss our grievances with him.'

And the multitude began to roar again. Most of them seemed to be cheering, but there was enough of an ominous note in the clamour to cause Salisbury uneasiness.

He gave a quick order to the oarsmen, who began to back water, holding the barge in its position, less than a hundred feet from the shore.

'The King!' shouted the rebels. 'The King!'

In a momentary lull Salisbury could hear the big man's voice booming out, 'Put Richard ashore among his commons!'

He could see there were archers among them, and he knew well enough they were within easy range. Beside him, Walworth was pale with anger. Fear stabbed at Salisbury. He rose, held up his hands to the mob.

Miraculously, there was silence. Salisbury called across the water in precise accents, 'Gentlemen, you are not properly dressed, nor are you in fit condition to talk with the King.'

The silence continued. Salisbury could see the men on shore gaping at the barge. 'For the love of God, row!' he cried out to the oarsmen.

Their blades roiled the water. With painful slowness the barge began to move away from the bank.

Salisbury watched the rebels apprehensively, knowing that a first arrow would be followed by many others, and in a matter of moments they would all be corpses.

No one on the bank moved. There was not a sound.

Finally, when they were well out of arrowshot, the uproar did begin again: a lamenting, baffled wail.

Salisbury said, in self-mockery of his pompous utterance to the peasants, 'Gentlemen, you are not properly dressed, nor are you in fit condition to talk with the King.

'Gentlemen . . .' he began again, but a bitter mirth suddenly caught his words and turned them back into his throat.

There seemed no alternative now to entering the city.

As if in response to his thoughts, Ball heard Tyler say, 'We'll try the Bridge. Our food supply is low. We'd not have enough for another night at Blackheath.'

Tyler spoke quietly, and though he gave a tactical reason for their next move, Ball knew the encounter with the King and his advisers was rankling in him powerfully. An hour had passed since the arrogant repudiation had been flung at them across the water, and Tyler's hands were still bunched into fists. Ball himself had experienced first disbelief, then anger at the sight of the elegant nobleman making a languid, disparaging gesture in their direction and following it with the studied, contemptuous insult. Not properly dressed, indeed. And what was a fit condition in which to talk with the King to whom they had sworn allegiance?

Ball knew that if anger was still glowing in him, Tyler must be close to white heat.

And what of the commons?

After the fiasco of his misinterpreted sermon that morning, Ball hardly dared consider the temper of the people.

Since the one prolonged, agonized cry of frustration when they saw the barge pulling away and finally realized there would be no conference with the King, they had been strangely quiet. Tyler had spoken to them at once, assuring them that this had been the work of Sudbury and Hales, and that they would soon be able to separate Richard from his perfidious advisers and present their grievances. They had listened in silence and had fallen into ranks, following Tyler and Ball westward away from Rotherhithe.

Ball did not trust their apparent docility. As they marched toward Southwark and the gate to London Bridge, he prayed they would meet no resistance to their attempt to enter the city.

If they did, there would be bloodshed beyond the most terrible limits of his nightmares.

188

The sun was hot. A foul odour was rising from the river. Few people were abroad in the narrow streets of Southwark. Those who watched them pass made the sign of the cross and shrank back into alleyways. It was not the way he had envisioned their triumphal entry into the chief city of England.

The Bridge Gate was open and deserted, and Ball began to believe that perhaps the alderman had told Tyler the truth, until he remembered that the drawbridge still lay ahead of them.

As they approached the gate and looked up at the heads of criminals mounted on pikes above the archway, Tyler said, 'Soon there'll be other heads stuck there. The sooner the better.'

Ball did not think it would be prudent to remonstrate with him at the moment.

They passed through the gate, followed by the first orderly ranks of the commons.

The drawbridge was raised, with armed men massed on the far side.

Tyler did not give the order to halt until they were almost at the edge of the stone-paved way.

Then, just as he lifted his hand, signalling those behind him, there was a rumbling as from the bowels of the earth. The great wooden platform swung through the air, crashed into place.

Before the drawbridge had fully descended, a man began running across toward them.

He was thin, intense-looking, and he stuttered. 'Alderman Sibley,' he cried while he was still approaching, 'alderman of the Bridge Ward, alderman to welcome you. . . .' He grasped Tyler's hand, dropped it, took up Ball's hand, dropped it as well. 'Welcome . . . welcome . . . the people of London . . .' He did an excited little dance and motioned them to follow him.

They started across the drawbridge. Ball saw now that the armed men awaiting them were dressed in rough clothes no better than those of the commons. They were raising swords and pikes, and cheering. Sibley continued to dance ebulliently about Ball and Tyler.

Suddenly the hubbub ceased, so suddenly that for just an instant Ball wondered if he had gone deaf. Then he heard the sound of horse's hooves and looked along the bridge to see a stocky, richly garbed man riding recklessly toward them.

Sibley jumped out of his path with a sharp cry. Ball followed him. Though Tyler turned pale, he stood without moving until it seemed certain he would be trampled. A few paces away from Tyler, the rider reined in the horse and dismounted in a series of swift, angry movements.

He was one of the men who had been on the barge with the King.

He strode at once to Sibley, seized his arm in a powerful grip and bellowed, 'Will you let the scum in without a fight?'

'Lord Mayor,' stammered Sibley, 'they must come in. Horne told me . . .'

'Horne's a fool. It's what I deserve for trusting fools . . .'

'They mean no harm, these people . . .'

'No harm?' The Lord Mayor released Sibley and struck his own forehead with the flat of his hand. 'No harm! Burn my property and kill . . .' His face twisted, and Ball had a sudden peculiar notion that the Lord Mayor might weep. But his eyes went opaque, and he shouted, 'They'll not enter my city!'

He drew his sword, wheeled about and faced Tyler, who unsheathed his dagger and braced himself.

Just as the Lord Mayor took a step toward Tyler, a shout came from one of the men crowded along the stone railing of the bridge. 'Don't do it, Will!'

And another cried, 'Go after him and we'll have to kill you!'

The Lord Mayor's mouth sagged open. He turned his head slowly to look at the men. Tyler remained motionless, dagger outthrust, watching his opponent.

'My city . . . to let these . . .'

'It's our city, too, Will. We want them in,' said the first man. 'Put up your sword. We've had no quarrel with you. We want none now.'

'You . . . members of my own guild . . .'

'Put up your sword, Will.'

It seemed to Ball that the Lord Mayor's glance slid past the bridge and over to a point on the Southwark shore before returning to fasten itself on Tyler and the throng of men following him.

He rammed his sword into the sheath, turned his back on Tyler, remounted his horse and galloped off furiously.

The forward ranks of the army of the commons gave an exuberant shout and poured across the bridge.

He had run away.

With all his talk of defending his city, of never allowing the peasant pigs to set foot across London Bridge, he had not had the courage to strike a single blow.

It was the treachery of his own fishmongers which had unnerved him. Of all Londoners, these were the last he had expected would ever side against him. Walworth was still trembling from the surprise and confusion their words had set off in him, though he was thankful he had been able to ride away quickly enough to avoid showing them his consternation.

And now they were in his city. He could hear them whooping behind him as he turned his horse onto Thames Street.

It was his own fault. Not that he could have stopped them at the Bridge. Even if his fishmongers had not meant what they said about killing him, the rebels would have seen to it soon enough. If he had acted the night before, instead of brooding over the loss of his brothels and the death of Agnes . . . he gritted his teeth, thinking of her: they would pay yet for having murdered her . . . if he had been able to rouse himself to action then, the clods might never even have approached the Bridge Gate.

He should have understood when Horne returned from meeting with them. Horne, usually so sensible, so cool-headed, had told Walworth he did not think the rebels should be opposed if they tried to enter London. There were too many of them, Horne had said, and besides, he was convinced they meant no harm. He had heard his alderman's words, but he had been so disturbed by the other matters that their full import had eluded him. And instead of lashing out at Horne for his soft-headedness, he had listened in silence to the whispering voice and had even bidden the man a civil goodnight.

If he had possessed half the wit on which he prided himself, he would have gone at once to the leaders of the various victuallers' guilds on whom he could rely, and to the fifty or so great merchants who controlled London commerce. Together they could have worked out a plan for defence, a plan which might have provided them with five, six, perhaps seven thousand armed men.

Even now it could be done. He was certain, despite the defection of some members of his own guild, that most of his Londoners would rally behind him to drive the rabble out.

But now that they were in the city, there was something he had to do first, quickly, before he set about organizing the resistance.

He galloped the horse into his courtyard, dismounted, raced into the house and called out to Margaret.

There was no answering sound except his own breathing. He called again, and a third time, then ran from room to room. If she were working on the accounts, or dreaming beside a window, she had probably not heard.

She was not in any of the rooms.

In the whole enormous house he could find no one, not even a servant.

For the first time in his life, Walworth knew the taste of terror.

He shouted Margaret's name once more. Now that he knew the house was empty, he heard his voice come back to him with an oddly plaintive reverberation.

He ran outside. His horse nickered and shied as Walworth rushed by and plunged into the falcon shed. For a frantic instant he thought the peregrine was gone. Then the bird screamed at him, and he found himself laughing aloud: a grim sound, but nonetheless a laugh.

Walworth gathered up some chicken heads, stuffed them in his pouch, then put on a gauntlet. 'Come, my sweet,' he called to the falcon, unleashing her from the perch. 'Come . . . they'll not take you. . . .'

The peregrine hopped onto the glove and opened her beak defiantly. Walworth set the jesses, then, unthinking for a moment, he brought his right hand up, intending to stroke her head. The falcon struck, and blood welled from a jagged wound in Walworth's finger. He laughed loudly, and as he fumbled in his pouch for a kerchief, he said to her, 'Well done, sweet. You'll never betray me, will you?'

And he felt a surge of grief as he remembered Agnes saying: nor will I . . . and a return of panic as he wondered where Margaret could be.

But there was little time for indulging emotions. For days he had been squandering time. He must seize it now and hold back its spendthrift flight. Later he would return for Margaret.

The first mercantile establishment he visited was closed and shuttered, as was the second, and the five others he tried while his anxiety mounted. Neither were the merchants in their homes, and in only one of the houses did he discover even a servant. The man stared at him and backed away. Suddenly Walworth realized how he must appear: carrying a falcon on one gauntleted hand, a bloody rag wrapped around the other, and no doubt wild-eyed. . . . He laughed, the peregrine screamed, and the servant fled yelping into the house and slammed the door.

He was not able to find any of the officials of the victuallers' guilds. The panic marched back heavy-booted through his belly. He leaned against a wall in Poultry Street, struggling to oust it.

Incredibly, much of the city's ordinary activity seemed to be going on as usual. Small shops and stalls were doing their customary noisy business. True, the rabble were everywhere, gawking about the streets, poking their heads into windows, hallooing to one another, pressing in around the vendors' stalls. But some of them were making purchases, actually paying for fowls and pies and ale.

And the ones who seemed to have no money simply stood and looked sadly and enviously at the goods displayed, making no move to thieve.

He gave up trying to understand, got on his horse and rode off to see if he could find the head of the bakers' guild. He had not been at his establishment in Bread Street; perhaps he could be found at his home, in the wall near Aldgate.

As he rode along the Cornhill and passed into Lime Street, he wondered how Lovekyn would have reacted to this situation. But you, old man, he thought bitterly, addressing his mentor's ghost, you never had to deal with anything like this. And that's exactly what you'd tell me. You'd stare at me with those wise, hooded old eyes and say: When I have to look it in the face, boy, then I'll tell you what I'd do.

He was drawing near the gate now. If he could not find the man he was seeking, he would go back to fetch Margaret, take her with him to the Tower, then see if the Council were contemplating any action. He had no more liking now than formerly for Salisbury: the voice and the elaborate gestures still maddened him. But he had to admit that the fellow . . .

The peregrine screamed and the horse reared, almost throwing Walworth. When he had succeeded in calming the animal, he looked ahead down Leadenhall Street, and felt himself gaping as open-mouthed as any peasant.

Streaming through the Aldgate was a ragged horde, unkempt rows of them stretching as far back beyond the opening as he could see. At their head was a priest, cowl thrown back, face streaked with dust, teeth bared in an exultant grimace. The marchers were chanting the same words over and over again, but Walworth could only make out something about Adam and Eve.

Standing beside the gate was a man called Farringdon, whom Walworth had always despised as a troublemaker. Next to him, smiling and calling out to those entering the city, were Alderman Tonge and Alderman Horne.

Walworth turned his horse sharply and set off at full speed for the Tower.

Tyler entered the broad expanse of the Corn Market. He heard the familiar accents of Essex all about him, responded warmly to the greetings shouted at him. He was so overjoyed that when Straw came to meet him, he very nearly embraced him.

He was spared the display of emotion. The priest, eyes glowing more hotly than ever, said at once, 'My men are hungry. Tell me where the bakeries and butchers' stalls are located. We'll go there and take what we need before we go on with our work.'

'I've issued orders,' Tyler said calmly, 'that any looting will be punished immediately by death.'

'Looting?' cried Straw. Saliva appeared at the corners of his mouth. 'My Essexmen need food!'

'The men of Essex are under my command.' Tyler laboured to keep his voice even. There had been enough already that day without having to contend with Straw. 'Those who can pay may buy what they wish. We shall obtain food for the others before nightfall.'

He hoped what he said was true, though at the moment he had no idea where they would obtain it.

Straw grumbled, 'There must be more than enough provisions in the shops and stalls . . .'

'The people of London have opened their gates to us,' said Tyler. 'Shall we repay them with thievery?'

'The lords . . .'

'The lords will reap all they have sown.'

'Now? Today?' Straw's voice was at once eager and pleading as a small boy's.

'I shall take one band to the Savoy Palace and the Temple. You'll take another with you. There are two prisons . . .'

'The Fleet and Newgate,' Straw said impatiently. 'No need to tell me more about them. I've heard what foul, stinking holes they are. . . .'

'So John Ball states,' Tyler could not resist saying. 'He was imprisoned in one of them.' But the point was lost on Straw, who only nodded absently. And Tyler realized this was as it should be. Injustice, past and present, cries out for action, not pity. 'Release the prisoners you find there,' he said to Straw 'Then burn the buildings. You'll wait here until Ball brings the Kentishmen who will help you . . .'

'Kentishmen!' Straw burst out contemptuously. 'My Essexmen . . .'

'From this moment on,' said Tyler, 'there is neither Kent nor Essex, Sussex nor Surrey. We have come from our shires, and we shall return to them. But while we remain in London, we are the commons of England.'

'Then,' said Straw waspishly, as Tyler was already beginning to turn away, 'you will not be interested in what I have to say of Colchester. . . .'

Tyler swung around. Straw waited briefly before he said, 'Nine-tenths of them came to march with us. In no other town have such numbers risen.'

The priest's lips struggled with a smile. 'I would not have said it before, Wat Tyler, and even before dusk we may quarrel again. But I shall tell you . . .' The smile triumphed, rested uncertainly on the cadaverous face. 'I am grateful to see you here.'

Abel had looked on stately buildings before: the rambling stone manor houses of Normandy, the dazzling white walls and filigree gates of Castile. But never, he decided as he made his way toward the entrance with an armful of robes fashioned from beaten gold, had he seen anything to rival the Savoy.

It was not alone the evidence of wealth; here luxury was compounded. Not only were the floors laid with delicate-hued marble; they also contained designs worked into the stone in heavy silver. Every piece of furniture was so finely carved that a man would have to spend hours gazing at it before his senses took full note of the craftsmanship. Gold glinted from corners and niches: it gilded the balustrades sweeping around graceful staircases; it gleamed from the borders of rich tapestries.

Knowing that all this would be destroyed hurt him. Not, of course, out of any pity for John of Gaunt. But men had wrought the loveliness of this palace, at great effort, over a long period of time. And now he, Abel Threder, was helping to obliterate their work, and soon it would vanish as if it had never existed.

He longed to talk with someone about this, but he knew if he tried, he would only provoke laughter. Abel the clown, spinning another jest. Moreover, the laughter would be merited. For by the time whatever was in his heart mounted to his lips, it would have donned motley and come cavorting forth seeking its reward of snigger and guffaw.

One of the Gravesend men brushed past him, so reeling drunk it was a marvel he still stayed upright. 'Down here . . .' he called past Abel. 'Down here . . . wine . . . barrels . . . wine and wine. . . .' He tripped, fell headlong down a flight of stone steps. Abel waited a moment, walked on when he heard the man's voice emerging from the depths, blurred, but raised in obscene song. As Abel turned a corner in the corridor, he glimpsed three men crossing the polished marble, scrabbling in their haste to reach the cellar.

Outside the palace, in the gardens, the work Tyler had ordered was proceeding energetically. Some of the men were casting gold and silver plate, goblets and ornaments into the river. Others were pounding precious stones to powder in mortars taken from the kitchen. Abel threw the robes he carried onto a great heap containing similar exquisite apparel. He squatted beside Roger and some others already engaged in tearing the glittering garments to shreds.

Tyler walked among the men, surveying their activity in sombre silence. How remarkable, Abel thought, looking at him, that his face does not seem to change. Neither weariness nor triumph were reflected in it. It seemed to Abel that Tyler was feeling nothing, and the notion made him uneasy.

Suddenly Tyler called out, 'Bring that man to me!'

He pointed to a one-armed peasant in a greasy tunic and torn hose. The man screeched with terror and began to run. Half a dozen pairs of hands seized him, and his captors bore him, squirming and blubbering, before Tyler. His mouth flew open, and Abel could see he had no teeth.

Tyler ripped apart the front of the man's tunic. A silver plate fell to the ground. 'You heard,' said Tyler sternly, 'the same as everyone else. You heard. . . .' He looked around, nodded curtly to Abel, then at an axe leaning against a tree.

When Abel brought it, the one-armed man snuffled loudly, looking at Tyler with unbelieving horror. 'You won't . . . no . . .'

Tyler's voice was flat. 'You knew the penalty.'

The garden grew quiet as everyone stopped what they were doing to draw near the little group.

Suddenly the man wrenched himself free. Abel thought he would try to escape, but instead he fumbled frantically in his pouch and brought out a grimy scrap of parchment. 'Poitiers!' he screamed. 'I was at Poitiers! It's all written here . . .' He thrust the parchment at Tyler. 'The Frenchman's mace . . . nickety-nick, our arrows . . .' He threw back his head and shrieked at the sky. 'Nickety-nick . . . Poitiers , , '

The men seized him again and forced him to his knees. He looked up at Tyler and said in a low, mourning voice, 'I know John Ball.'

Tyler's face twitched. His lips parted, but he said nothing.

Nor did the man speak again.

After it was done, Tyler cleansed the axe in the river. He glanced at the sun and called out, 'Finish up quickly. We must fire it and move on. There's more to do.'

The palace was stripped, the destruction of jewels and finery completed. Tyler motioned to those who held the torches. They moved to their task, bending and swaying, reapers with blazing sickles.

The flames moaned and sighed as they were sucked inward through doors and windows, crackled as they sprang out again from the floor above.

Then there was another sound: men's voices screaming from inside the palace.

Abel sickened, recalling the Gravesend men he had encountered. 'The wine cellar!' he cried. 'They're in the wine cellar!'

He leaped forward, looking for an opening in the sheet of flame. Powerful arms encircled him from behind. He twisted around and saw that it was Tyler holding him. He stopped struggling and closed his eyes.

What's come over me, he wondered. Am I so anxious to die in the newness of summer that I must keep offering my life, meddling in business that is not my own? He opened his eyes and looked down at the wound on the back of his hand, scabbed over now and healing. I'm as big a fool in London as I was in Gravesend. He listened to the roar of the flames vying with the agony of the men trapped inside.

The screams mounted to a crescendo and stopped. Tyler released him. Abel turned, and their glances met. Tyler's eyes were tormented; tears glistened in them. They continued to gaze at each other. For a moment Abel had the mad feeling that they were one person, each regarding the other half of himself. Tyler's lips moved, and Abel's moved in response, but neither of them uttered a sound.

Finally Tyler said hoarsely, 'The Temple. We still have to burn the law records there.'

Abel walked back to where Roger was standing. 'We do well,' he said. 'Today we've defeated John of Gaunt. We've defeated him so roundly that he drinks ale and chases wenches in Scotland while his palace continues to murder for him.'

But Roger was not listening. His eyes were narrowed, watching the fire. His lips were pressed tightly together, and his customarily innocent expression held an odd, bitter exultancy.

19

HORNE walked between them, leading the way to Farringdon's. His head nodded left and right, his finger stabbed
toward darkening lanes, his whispering voice instructed
them as to the landmarks they were passing. 'The Lord Mayor's
house,' he said, not long after they had crossed the street leading
from the Bridge.

Tyler glanced dutifully up at the vacant faces of the windows
brooding above them. Ball, watching the slow, almost indolent,
movement of his friend's head, then the slight slumping of the
massive shoulders, concluded that Tyler at last knew weariness.
It would be harder for him to bear, for he had so little knowledge
of it. Ball had come to accept weariness as an old and honourable
enemy; they lived together, first one triumphing, then the other,
each satisfied to take his turn at victory. Tyler would strive against
it, as he fought any intrusion on his purpose, and weariness would
gloat, for struggle was the meat on which it fed.

Smoke from the fires they had lighted that day still hung heavy
over the city. Tyler had been reticent in telling of the burning of
the Savoy Palace. Whatever had occurred, Ball did not wish to
hear of it now. The freeing of prisoners from the Fleet and Newgate
had proceeded without incident. True, he had recoiled from the
vindictiveness on Straw's face when the torches were set, but his
fellow priest had contained his choler. The guards had surrendered
meekly, and there had been no need to use weapons. Now the
commons were encamped about the King's fortress, some on Tower
Hill, the rest on St. Catherine's Wharf. Tyler had intercepted food
supplies bound for the Tower and had set up a strict system for
distributing them. The people had eaten, and they were remaining
orderly. Whatever had happened at the Savoy already belonged to
the past. Perhaps, after all, there would be little more violence.

They turned north toward St. Paul's. 'The London home of
the Abbot of St. Mary's at York,' murmured Horne, nudging Ball,
who looked at him sharply. No, he decided, the alderman could not
know; his elbow prodding my arm was an accident. He gazed
curiously at the Abbot's house, wondering if his old friend were
there. Friend, for even after the meeting at Chartham, he still
regarded him as such: when once a man has lighted the inner

darkness of another's life, his spirit can never be dismissed. The dwelling appeared as deserted as the Lord Mayor's.

A group of men and women passed them, carrying a standard on which was painted a mermaid and merman, tails entwined. 'Fishmongers,' said Horne, then chuckled. 'I hear they took the edge off the Lord Mayor's sword this morning.'

Tyler grunted, looked suddenly at Horne and asked, 'How much farther?'

'Not far, not far,' replied Horne, inclining his head toward him.

They passed several more bands of Londoners, some singing, all seemingly in a holiday mood. Before St. Paul's a gaunt pardoner was haranguing a flock of leather-aproned men. 'Tanners,' Horne informed Ball and Tyler. 'In London we've lived too long in layers. Guild by guild, merchant by merchant . . .' He glanced at them both, beckoning them closer. '. . . lord by lord. All that will change now.'

As they came round St. Paul's and again walked north, a bell set up a measured clangour from somwhere directly ahead of them. Horne stopped walking abruptly. 'Curfew,' he said. 'It's always rung from St. Martin's-le-Grand.' The corner of his mouth drooped. 'Even tonight.' He smiled sardonically. 'Tonight for once it carries no threat.' He looked from one of them to the other with appealing wistfulness. 'How long we've waited for your coming.'

Probably true, thought Ball, but that will not prevent jealousy and perhaps even distrust from developing now that we have arrived. He and Tyler had discussed this for a few moments before Horne came for them, and had agreed that the possibility existed.

Farringdon welcomed them into his house with a nervous grin which flickered on and off his narrow face. The common room they entered was large and comfortably appointed. Farringdon saw Tyler looking at some drinking vessels near the hearth. 'Gold,' he said, his smile disappearing, then returning with excessive brightness. 'My family were once goldsmiths. Myself, I own tenements.'

Ball thought suddenly of Christiana, savouring the memory of her presence in the Colchester house. Soon, he thought, and the prospect of peace made him a little dizzy. The burden finally carried to its destination and unshouldered, a grail sought and acquired. The end of fear and care, the death of loneliness . . .

'Tenements,' Farringdon said again.

'You told us,' said Tyler.

There was a knock on the door, and Farringdon crossed the room

199

hurriedly, the flames of the beeswax candles bending and sputtering in his wake.

Alderman Sibley entered with a man he introduced as Alderman Tonge. 'He welcomed your friends at Aldgate as I did . . .' He began to stammer so badly that he could not finish, and contented himself with shaking hands with Ball and Tyler, each twice, and performing the same little rejoicing dance he had executed that afternoon. 'We've been waiting,' he said, this time without faltering over a syllable.

'We're still waiting,' said Tonge. He was a young man with clear-cut, regular features, who would have been strikingly handsome had his face not been marked with deeply indented pocks.

Farringdon motioned them nervously to chairs. 'Now,' he said, 'let it be understood . . .' His feet toyed with the rushes on the floor, bunching and scattering them by turns. 'We are chiefly interested in London, of course. What takes place here is our concern.'

'And ours,' said Tyler.

He spoke in a placid tone, but Ball saw his fingers curving slowly inward to meet his palms.

'And yours, of course.' Farringdon favoured them with his fleeting smile. 'What I intended . . . the matters pertaining to the serfs . . . they are your domain . . .'

'We shall settle those with the King,' said Tyler.

'Naturally,' agreed Farringdon. A rush crackled under his foot. He glanced down, quickly looked up again at Tyler and Ball. 'But London matters . . .'

'The Flemings,' said Tonge, his tone suddenly malevolent. 'The foreigners are our affair.'

Sibley gasped and tried to say something, but his tongue tangled around the first word. He grew pale with trying, finally gave up and subsided, staring glumly ahead.

'What Alderman Tonge means . . .' began Horne.

'I mean we have a score to settle,' Tonge said. 'The foreign pigs . . . coming here, living off our city, sending wealth out of England . . .'

'My tenements . . .' said Farringdon.

Tyler got to his feet, stood towering above them. The Londoners looked up at him apprehensively. Ball knew what was coming, but even he, who had seen Tyler perform a few times before, under somewhat similar circumstances, could not help being impressed by the power radiating from him, filling the room.

Farringdon's feet worried the rushes. Tonge's hand crept up to his face; his fingers explored the pits on his cheek.

Tyler surveyed them all in silence. He would do so, Ball knew, until he felt their balance wavering, their wills beginning to flounder. Then he would speak. And then, if he did not lose his temper, he would have them.

'London,' Tyler said finally, 'is your city.'

He had only stated the simplest truth, one which, in fact, they had been voicing in more contentious terms. Yet such was the magnetism Tyler exerted at these times that he could even endow redundancy with a quality of revelation.

Farringdon and the aldermen were nodding in vigorous agreement. From their expressions Ball could tell they were anxious to please Tyler, ready to follow where he led.

'We have entered the gates with your assistance. We are in your debt.'

Again they nodded. Sibley seemed about to burst with joy.

'But,' continued Tyler, 'we have come to your city with one purpose in mind: to see the King and demand that he remedy injustices the commons have suffered for too many years.'

'We too . . .' whispered Horne.

'Exactly,' said Tyler. 'And as we win our battle, you will win yours.' He was speaking rapidly, confidently now. 'That is why it will be necessary for all who strive toward the same goal to submit to one command.'

He paused, and Horne leaned forward. 'Last night,' he said, 'I told you last night we were ready to act with you and show you obedience.'

'Good,' replied Tyler, offhandedly, as though Horne's words were only what he had expected. But Ball knew he was still tense, probing for the feeling of the others, ready to exert more pressure if necessary.

'For years,' said Sibley, 'the poor of London have suffered. They've laboured for trifling wages. They've been at the mercy . . .' He stumbled, managed to go on. 'At the mercy of the lords and lawyers. They're called free, but they live in worse slavery . . .' He tried to continue, but this time he foundered.

'They will have their freedom,' said Tyler 'When we leave London, all Englishmen will be free.'

Tonge and Farringdon looked at each other. Farringdon's vacillating smile came on and off, a torch lighted and snuffed. 'The Flemings,' said Tonge.

'Will be dealt with in due course by all of us,' Tyler said. 'Those who have oppressed the poor or committed other crimes against the people will be punished.'

Tonge muttered to himself, then shrugged.

Now, thought Ball, it's done. Farringdon will offer no opposition, the Londoners will accept our authority, and matters will proceed peacefully. We shall accomplish what we came to do in orderly fashion . . .

'There are some measures,' Farringdon said, 'originating with Sir Robert Hales. Excessive taxes against the people of London. Those who cannot pay . . .' He kicked angrily at the rushes. 'Hales must be punished!'

'He will be,' said Tyler firmly.

Farringdon nodded, and in the silence that followed, Ball spoke for the first time. 'Then if we're all agreed, perhaps it would be well to discuss the demands we intend to place before the King . . .'

'He stole tenements from me,' Farringdon suddenly wailed. 'Hales stole my tenements . . .'

Tyler's face darkened. He clenched his fists. 'We didn't come to London to get back your tenements!' he shouted. 'You . . .'

He broke off abruptly, biting his lip. When he spoke again, his tone was conciliatory. 'All grievances will be considered and acted on. Yours will have equal importance with ours.'

His recovery had come too late. Farringdon's feet were once more busy with the rushes. Tonge shifted restlessly in his chair, resentment surging across his face. Even Sibley appeared distressed, and Horne leaned forward, drumming his fingers on his knees, a faraway look in his eyes.

'Our demands to the King cover four points,' said Ball. His voice sounded dead in the silence of the room. He could not bring himself to look at Tyler.

20

IT was almost dark. Salisbury could hear the distant babble of voices rising from the two rebel camps outside the Tower walls. A while before, he had climbed to the top of the Devereux Tower and surveyed the ragged multitude squatting on the hill. Then he had traversed the grounds and completed his reconnaissance from the parapet of the Develin Tower. He had learned two things: Newton's estimate of a force totalling thirty thousand had been substantially correct; and the greater concentration was on the east side of the Tower wall, crowding the wharf and extending far back toward the Abbey of St. Mary Graces and Hog Street. There was a third piece of intelligence: both encampments seemed orderly and not disposed to launch an attack that evening. But this, of course, could change at any moment.

His squire had accompanied him as he made his survey. Thomas' face had paled as he peered from the Devereux Tower. By the time they had finished assessing the situation, the lad had gone quite pasty. Salisbury had told him to go and have a goblet or two of wine, then, when he was sure he had recovered from his queasiness, to inquire after Elizabeth's comfort.

Salisbury was a little surprised by his own composure. He was, on the one hand, more shaken and fearful than he had ever been. Yet now, with the possibility of death no longer merely a conjectural matter, he found a certain elation in the very completeness of his resignation. He had heard that this could sometimes happen: a man of limited courage, as he knew himself to be, feeling death at his shoulder, would turn calm and brave. However, he also understood the fallacies inherent in all such glib axioms explaining human behaviour. At any moment his knees could give way and he would sink cowering to the earth.

At the base of the fat round Lanthorn Tower he almost collided with the leathery soldier who had served under him in France. The mercenary kept his eyes averted, and when Salisbury greeted him, he mumbled, 'Good evening, my lord,' and hurried on. No talk of Poitiers tonight, thought Salisbury, drawing some grim amusement from the fact that one of the many predictable conversational exchanges of his life had now vanished forever. But, he reflected, crisis rarely changes men's basic natures; it only muddles them for a time. If he and the mercenary both lived through this extremity, they would doubtless develop another pattern of talk, just as predictable and unvarying.

If they lived.

On the green he encountered Sir Robert Knolles. The commander of the mercenaries appeared to have no other concern than savouring the last bit of daylight in the sky. It was difficult to remember that this slight, mild man, with all his air of dreamy vagueness, had not long ago led a savage band of marauders and had captured more than thirty castles along the Loire.

Knolles cocked his head to one side, birdlike, as Salisbury said to him, 'The spirit of the men, Sir Robert, I fear is . . .'

'Uncomfortable, my lord, distinctly uncomfortable.'

They stood facing each other, two smallish, greying men, quietly distilling the essence of danger from the diffuse spate in the air about them.

'Will they fight?'

'And if they do?'

They had asked and answered. There remained only the grave and formal bows. Knolles resumed his stroll; Salisbury turned toward the council chamber.

It was an ordered, inevitable progression toward death, and he felt it as such.

But it was interrupted.

Round the corner from the north end of the White Tower came an excited little procession led by Richard. Salisbury had never seen the boy show so much energy and purpose. Just behind the King came Hales and Sudbury. Walworth, gloomy and distraught, followed, two or three paces ahead of servants with torches.

The Chancellor detached himself from the group and sidled across to Salisbury. 'The King is going to speak to them!' he burbled. 'He'll address them, and they'll disperse. I knew my prayers on this Corpus Christi day would be answered . . .'

He skipped along crablike beside Salisbury, who was hurrying to overtake Richard. The King had almost reached the gate beside the Wakefield Tower when Salisbury caught up with him.

'Sire . . .' he said breathlessly.

'I shall speak to them,' said Richard grandly. 'My father the Black Prince would have done no less.' He passed through the gate, turned left and hastened along the broad passage between the two walls, toward the Develin Tower.

'What will Your Majesty say?' asked Salisbury.

The boy threw him a sly glance. 'I shall know what to say. They respect me as their King. If you had let me speak to them this morning, they would be on their way to their homes by now.'

Salisbury knew there was no point in trying to dissuade him. He dropped back beside Walworth and said, 'If this is to work at all, we should keep Sudbury and Hales out of sight.'

The Lord Mayor made an ugly sound in his throat. 'There's only one thing will work now,' he said savagely. 'Fight the swine. Drive them into the river . . .'

Salisbury peered closely at him. Walworth was even more wild-eyed than he had been that morning. The Lord Mayor hawked and spat copiously onto the ground ahead of them. Salisbury felt his nose wrinkling with distaste. He made a detour around the place where the spittle had fallen and came back to Walworth's side in time to hear him say, 'No need to trouble yourself about Sudbury and Hales. They'll never mount that tower.'

He was right. At the entrance to the Develin Tower, Hales waddled to a stop, and Sudbury looked around uncertainly, as though wondering how he happened to be there. 'I remember,' he said, 'how in the early days of the realm, a bishop . . .' He shook his head in a confused manner. Hales chuckled and sat down on the ground.

Richard mounted the staircase resolutely, Salisbury and Walworth following, carrying torches they had taken from the servants. Salisbury's mouth was dry. He wondered why he was allowing the boy to attempt such a foolhardy act. If something were to happen to him, Joan . . .

Joan? . . . All of them . . .

They gazed down from the parapet. Salisbury, having been there only a short while before, was able to look out calmly over the vista of smoking torches and the massed figures of men on the other side of the moat, stretching from the river's edge up onto the east end of Tower Hill.

Richard sucked in his breath and turned a frightened face to the two men as Walworth exclaimed violently and obscenely.

The rebels had not yet seen them. 'Sire,' said Salisbury rapidly, 'if you wish . . .'

Then it was too late. One or two voices were crying out, 'The King . . .' and another shouted, 'Long live Richard and the true commons!'

Richard's fearful expression changed swiftly, moving toward a kind of dreamy ecstasy. He bowed and postured, and at one point nearly fell over the parapet. This seemed to please the mob mightily.

After some moments they grew quiet.

Richard began speaking in his reedy, imperious voice. 'My people,' he cried, 'your numbers impress me . . .'

His words touched off some more vociferous approval, mingled with good-natured laughter. It was an encouraging beginning. Perhaps it would go well, after all. Salisbury felt relief plucking at him in the guise of sudden fatigue.

'My people,' Richard repeated when they were quiet again, 'you will all be forgiven.'

This time there was silence.

'You will all be forgiven,' the King continued uncertainly, 'if you disperse peacefully and return to your homes.'

For one tense instant they remained silent. Then there was an

outburst of rage and derision which made the clamour at Rotherhithe seem gentle by comparison.

Richard's face was beginning to crinkle. 'What have I done, my
uncles?' he asked pathetically. 'Why are they angry with me?'

The protesting din began to die. Salisbury heard a single deep
voice, which he remembered from Rotherhithe. 'We did not come
to London to be told we must return home. Meet us, and draw up
charters granting our demands!'

Through the shouting which followed, Salisbury heard Richard
asking, 'What shall I say, my uncles?'

Salisbury replied urgently, 'Tell them you'll send them a charter
within the hour.'

Richard followed Salisbury's instruction. The only response was
a sprinkling of grumbles and curses. Salisbury was waiting for some
comment by the deep, insolent voice of their spokesman. When,
after some moments, it did not come, he said to Richard, 'We shall
leave. Now.'

Walworth was growling to himself as they descended the steps.
Richard said anxiously, 'My uncles . . .'

At least now there was something to be done. Salisbury still felt
a sense of hopelessness, but he found he was no longer resigned. He
was not sure this pleased him.

The commons were crowded together much too closely for any
kind of comfort, and the arrogant performance of the King had
not sweetened their dispositions. Still, he had promised to send
them a charter, and the animosity which had been flickering among
them because of the cramped quarters ebbed.

But, as time passed and the charter did not arrive, their restlessness began to return. Groups formed, dissolved, reformed, eddied
up the hill and drifted slowly back to the wharf.

Abel was sitting with the other four from his village. They
occupied a spot on the wharf not far from the moat. Elias got up
quietly and went away, returned with two huge jugs of ale, which
he handed around. When he saw Abel looking at him quizzically,
he grinned and said in an uncharacteristically warm voice, 'The
reeve of a village can't let his men go thirsty.'

'See you remember that when we get home,' said Abel.

'When we get home is a different matter,' snapped Elias.

Robert and Nicholas were bickering over the question of how
many men had been with the King when he addressed them from
the tower. 'Four,' said Robert.

Nicholas plucked something from the forest of hair on his arm, held it up critically to the torchlight and murmured, 'Larger in the city . . .' Then he said, 'There were three with the King. I saw them clearly.'

Robert's mouth opened and closed several times before he was able to reply. 'Four,' he said with finality.

Roger leaped up, swearing softly. 'They've put us off again. They don't mean to make us free.'

He walked away, picking a path through the swirling mass of men. Abel set down the jug of ale reluctantly and rose to follow him.

He lost Roger in the crowd, found him again at the edge of the wharf. Close by, Tyler and Ball were discussing something in low, vehement voices with the priest from Essex.

For a time Roger was silent. Then he said angrily, 'If they don't make us free, I'm not going back to the village. I'll find a town . . .' He stared out across the black river. Harsh lines were forming on his forehead and around his mouth.

Some men from Canterbury stopped near them. 'She wanted to get rid of him,' one of them was saying, 'and she knew his temper. It was in her mind to prod him to violence against someone, so he'd be hanged, or at least sent out of the realm.' He laughed suddenly. 'She never took into account that the violence might come out against her . . .' The laughter died away as the Canterbury group moved away and was swallowed up in the crowd.

'I swear I saw it,' someone else said. 'A horse eating another horse. Mark my word, bad days are ahead . . .'

'There might still be some ale,' Abel said to Roger, who smiled grudgingly and turned to go with him. Their way was barred momentarily by two men carefully dividing a chunk of cheese between them. 'She caught me on Hock-Monday,' one of them was saying. 'Put a rope round me and said, custom demands you pay me a forfeit, where's my forfeit? Forfeit, I said, with a face like yours . . .'

Roger caught Abel's arm and pointed along the wharf. Cave was bringing two soldiers toward Tyler and Ball. As more of the commons caught sight of them, a circle of silence formed, elongated and spread slowly upward through the encampment.

When the soldiers reached Tyler, one of them took a scroll from beneath his tunic and held it out.

'Read it,' said Tyler. 'Loud, so all can hear.'

The soldier sneered. 'Are you not able to make out the words?'

Tyler made a movement toward him. The second soldier cuffed his companion, snatched the scroll from him, unrolled it. 'The

King thanks his good commons for their loyalty,' he read rapidly
in a high, braying voice, 'and pardons all their illegal offences.'
He paused, gasping for breath, then continued with greater speed.
'But he wishes everyone to return home and set down his grievances
and send them to him. By the advice of his lords he will then
provide such remedy as will be profitable to himself, his commons,
and the whole realm.'

Before the soldier had finished reading, the Essex priest was stomping about frenziedly, his lips drawn back from his teeth. When the
soldier looked up from the charter, the priest croaked, 'You see,
you see, I told you it would be this way. You see . . .'

Tyler put a hand on the shoulder of the priest, who twisted away
furiously. 'Tell the King,' said Tyler in a voice that carried clearly
and reverberated from the walls across the moat, 'that our patience
has run out. If he does not grant us a proper audience at once, we
will storm the Tower. Not only will we execute Sudbury and
Hales . . .' Abel saw John Ball make an abortive movement of
protest. '. . . but we will also execute the others on the Council and
the King himself. Tell him what I have said, and tell him we have
no wish to do this, but his actions so far leave us little choice. We
cannot wait longer. Nor will we!'

The soldiers backed away from Tyler, then turned and ran down
the wharf toward one of the Tower gates.

Strangely, the incident did not stir the commons to active anger.
However, as he walked through the crowd with Roger, Abel
noticed that the men they passed seemed preoccupied and moody,
disinclined to talk.

Perhaps this was why he heard Elias' voice so clearly, some
moments before they reached him. As they drew near, Abel saw
the reeve facing another man, shaking a fist under his nose. Robert
was standing by, slowly opening and closing his mouth, and
Nicholas was scratching his head, looking embarrassed.

When he and Roger came up to the group, the stranger was
saying something which Abel could not hear. He had thick, loose
lips, and a smirk sat fatly on them. Elias slapped him, the leer
vanished, and Abel grabbed the reeve just as he was balling his
fist for a more solid blow. Elias wailed, 'Do you know what this . . .
a foreigner he is, Sussex, that's where he says he's from. Says he's
heard of our village and of me.' He struggled to free himself.
'Says a peddler was talking about my wife, spreading stories about
her . . .'

'True as scripture, they are,' said the man, licking his lips. 'The
peddler's no liar. He says the woman's a saucy one, and she . . .'

'She did no such thing!' roared Elias, breaking away from Abel and lunging at the Sussex man, who dodged him and said, 'Not only with that peddler . . .' Then, as Elias wheeled for another charge, the man clipped him on the jaw, neatly, expertly. Elias smiled beautifully and slid to the ground. The Sussex man watched him, fascinated, then looked frightened and started to run away. He had waited too long, however. Nicholas stepped up to him, lifted him in the air with a single spectacular punch. The man descended and lay beside Elias. Robert cheered shrilly.

A crowd was beginning to thicken about them. Abel, fearing that Elias would be trampled, bent over and took one of his shoulders. Roger lifted the other, and together they dragged him across the wharf to a spot less heavily trafficked.

They looked at each other across Elias. The fierceness had vanished from Roger's face. He was smiling, faintly, a little sadly.

They were waiting for the message to be delivered and an answer returned. Hales suddenly suggested they should all go to pray.

Walworth rumbled incredulously, but Sudbury said, 'Oh yes,' and at once started for the winding stone stairs leading to St. John's Chapel. The others followed.

Despite the habit Hales wore, one often tended to forget that his career had begun in the Church. Now, as he watched the Treasurer kneeling before the altar, the grossness of his face tempered by candlelight, Salisbury had a sense of the quiet power buried in all that corpulence. And now at last he could understand more fully Hales' capacity for gaining attention whenever he spoke, and the paradox of his then having nothing to say grew even more grotesquely ironic. Once there must have been intellect, earnestness, ambition. Somewhere these qualities had run off course, had foundered, and now lay rotting on shoals of indulgence and indifference. Could this derelict, Salisbury wondered, ever be resurrected and turned to use again?

One of the soldiers they had dispatched appeared at the north door of the Chapel. Salisbury went to him, and when he heard the man's message, glanced again at Hales. The question he had asked himself a moment before would probably never be answered now. The plan that was forming in Salisbury's mind was cruel and desperate.

In the council chamber, Walworth spoke first and offered a plan of his own. 'We'll go out now,' he said. 'We'll take the Tower soldiers and attack the rabble, wipe them out before they know what's at them.' He ground his teeth. 'We'll drive them out of the city. We'll turn the river red with their blood.'

Salisbury, replying, made no mention of the fact that they could not rely on the mercenaries to fight. He emphasized instead that there were only six hundred of them, and while they might be able to inflict considerable damage on the rebel force, they could not be expected to conquer thirty thousand or more. He added to that the point that there was no guarantee that many Londoners would not come to the assistance of the rebels.

'I can raise a force of seven thousand Londoners,' Walworth said fiercely.

Salisbury waited an instant, then asked, 'How soon?'

The Lord Mayor smashed both fists down on the council table. Richard and Sudbury cried out fearfully, in concert.

'If we begin what we cannot carry through,' Salisbury said calmly, injecting all the persuasiveness he could muster into his voice, 'we should never be able to repair matters. It will be all over with us and those who come after us, and England will be a desert.'

Hales giggled.

'I still say we should fight,' grumbled Walworth, and without a pause asked, 'What then?'

'Our whole strategy must centre about making them return to their homes.'

'I told them that,' said Richard. 'They wouldn't listen.'

'I know, sire,' Salisbury said patiently. 'Now I fear we must grant them certain concessions, or at least appear to do so.' He looked around the table. The sight of Sudbury rubbing his pate with a trembling hand made him falter, but he knew he had to go on. 'We must send word that we shall meet them tomorrow, outside the walls . . .' He hesitated, thinking. 'At Mile End.'

'We shall not be able to go, Hales and I,' blurted Sudbury. 'They say they mean to kill us.'

'My lord Chancellor,' said Salisbury, 'there will be no need for you to go. You and the Treasurer will do better to remain in the Tower.'

And now Walworth understood. Salisbury could see it in the glance he bestowed on the Chancellor and the Treasurer before looking down and beginning to study a wound on one of the fingers of his right hand.

Sudbury also understood. 'They'll come after us!' he cried. 'They'll drag us out and kill us!'

'Oh no, my uncles,' said Richard. 'They would not dare lay hands on two ministers of the King.'

Salisbury swallowed hard and said, 'The soldiers will remain here, and the Tower itself is virtually impregnable. The rebels will be with us, three miles or more outside London. If we are skilful enough, they will disperse without ever returning to the city.'

In this last, he knew, lay the only hope for Sudbury and Hales He also knew how much depended on chance. But unless the plan was carried out, the King, and England with him, might well be no more before morning.

Often, in his career as a diplomat, he had bargained with the lives of men. On these occasions, however, the talk had been of armies or of ransom. There had been an impersonality about such negotiations which had permitted him to maintain a distance, to avoid becoming involved.

He had no such protection now.

21

A dozen or more men came running down the wharf, calling Tyler's name. Ball, who had been sleeping a few feet away, sat up, digging his knuckles into his eyes.

Thick ropes of mist were uncoiling from the surface of the river. The sun was coming up. For years, Ball reflected with a mixture of amusement and concern, he had awakened each morning before dawn. On this, the day which could mark the culmination of a quarter-century's labours, he had slept into sunrise.

He began listening, idly at first, to the words of the men clustered about Tyler. Then the last vestiges of sleep dropped away, for they were speaking of Sudbury.

The Chancellor, it seemed, had only a short while before tried to escape from the Tower. Just as dawn was streaking the sky he had descended the stairs of the King's Gate, had been about to step into a small boat moored there. But a woman, the wife of one of the London fishmongers, had seen him and cried out, raising the alarm. Sudbury had retreated.

Ball could picture him, scuttling back up the stairs in that peculiar crablike sidle made more ludicrous by fear. He could hear the ragged expulsion of breath, could smell the sweat of terror which must have soaked the underside of the Archbishop's brocade robe. Sweat or more, for Sudbury's body was no less subject than any other to weaknesses of the flesh.

Yet it was the same body before which Ball had once stood, watching the lips beneath the splendid mitre moving, pronouncing the round syllables of excommunication. The same body, its skin perhaps a little less grey and shrunken, but even then the voice performing its office of denunciation must have possessed the capacity for crying out in mortal terror.

And now that body would be recovering, the sweat drying, the blood moving again to cheeks gone ashen, the robe with its shameful evidence cast off and a fresh one donned.

So Sudbury had greeted the day. How would he bid it farewell?

Walworth waited while the Tower drawbridge was lowered, glaring back at the rebels who were staring at him curiously but without hostility. When the bridge was down, the mercenaries saluted, and he rode across the causeway.

The rabble had not attempted to halt him, either at dawn when he started out for his house, or on the return trip. They had, in fact, paid him practically no attention.

This made him feel somewhat easier about Margaret's absence. Once again he had gone from room to room without finding anyone. The solar she used as her bedchamber had a feel of continuing vacancy.

She had no family to whom she could have gone; the last of them had died the year before they were married. Nor had she friends. There were the families of the merchants she had met through him, but he doubted whether she would knock on any of their doors to ask for refuge. For that matter, who knew where the merchants themselves were?

Concerned as he was, somehow he did not fear for her safety.

As he approached the Wakefield Tower, he saw Sudbury standing near the gate, motionless as a piece of statuary, staring up at the heights of the outer wall. Though Walworth rode within a few feet of him, the Chancellor showed no sign of recognition.

Walworth felt a strong urge to see his falcon, but he had entrusted her to one of the warders, instructing him to protect the peregrine with his life. There was no time now to go and seek the man.

The occupants of the Tower were assembling on the green. It had been decided that the women and younger children would proceed to the Queen's Wardrobe, a house with ample accommodation in Carter Lane across from St. Paul's. The men would accompany Richard to Mile End.

Walworth, dismounting, saw Salisbury engaged in close conversation with Princess Joan. The Earl's face was radiant. He looked like a lovelost adolescent, and the fat wench was playing up to him, rolling her eyes and making little coy flirtatious gestures, though they appeared to be arguing about something.

Suddenly Walworth realized he was standing next to Salisbury's wife. She had not noticed him, for her gaze was fixed with terrible intensity on her husband and Joan.

Then she turned, and when she saw Walworth her face worked frantically, trying to rearrange itself into a smile. 'Lord Mayor,' she said brightly. 'I mean, it's the finest morning, Lord Mayor. Truly . . .'

Walworth muttered something and swung away from her abruptly, shutting his eyes against what he had seen in hers.

The first procession, bound for Carter Lane, moved off. Then their own began to form, consisting with one exception of men on horseback.

The exception was Joan's whirlicote. Salisbury had not been able to dissuade her from travelling to Mile End. She had argued with him, then said simply, 'My son is going. I shall go, too.'

She might have said her sons were going, for the two Hollands were included in the entourage. They were standing beside her now, repulsive fellows in costly, untidy finery. He wondered if he would dislike their appearance so strongly if they bore less resemblance to Thomas Holland. She was treating them as she always did, with amiable contempt, her glance probing past them for a sight of Richard. One of them, the older he believed it was, had his hand on her shoulder. She turned quickly, and his hand slid down, brushing against her breast. Holland guffawed, and Salisbury felt a wave of nausea, intensified when he saw the shadow of a reflexive smile cross Joan's face.

Richard appeared, wearing a sky-blue tunic beneath his scarlet robe. He urged his dappled charger toward the head of the column, stopping en route to greet his mother. How alike they look, Salisbury observed, their expression softened by affection, oblivious for the moment to all others. Joan called out something to her son, then climbed into her carriage, followed by two of her ladies.

It was only then, as he rode forward to take his place behind Richard, that Salisbury realized he had forgotten to bid Elizabeth farewell.

Remorse for this omission was still nagging at him when the procession drew near the Wakefield Tower, and he saw Sudbury gazing up at the ramparts. Just as Salisbury passed by, the Chancellor turned and saw him. The old man's expression filled with such disconsolate reproach that Salisbury could not bear to look at him. He was glad that Hales seemed to be nowhere about.

Tower Hill was clear of rebels, except for a few hundred who had evidently been left behind to keep the exits from the fortress under surveillance. Perhaps, thought Salisbury, if the Chancellor had not made his foolhardy attempt to escape, the rebels would have taken even these men with them to Mile End, and Sudbury and Hales might truly have had an opportunity to flee. At once he chided himself sadly, thinking: you'll not be allowed off the rack that easily.

At the top of the hill he turned in his saddle to look back at the Tower. The entire procession had cleared the gate several moments before, yet the drawbridge remained down. Salisbury sighed.

They rode past the Convent of the Crutched Friars, and on to Aldgate. The streets within the walls were empty, but shortly after they had passed under the great portcullis he saw the rebels waiting, lining both sides of the Mile End Road.

He saw them close at hand now for the first time: the ragged, stained and greasy garments; the stubbled faces, the insolent eyes, the rotten teeth visible between slack lips. He saw also the weapons they carried: the lethal longbows, the axes, scythes and pikes. And he could smell the odour of them as they crowded forward, shouting rudely, to touch the legs of the King's party.

Salisbury shrank from the contact but bore it in silence. Walworth, however, was kicking out at them, cursing them with a continuous flow of vileness. They did not seem to take it amiss, laughing uproariously at the Lord Mayor's gamy oaths.

At Whitechapel a narrow-faced man, much better dressed than the others, broke through the line of rebels and seized the King's bridle, bringing his charger to a halt. Salisbury was about to ride forward, then hesitated, for the man did not seem to mean Richard any harm. A vague and uncertain smile kept flitting on and off his face. 'Your Majesty,' Salisbury could hear him saying, 'a word in the name of justice.'

'Your name?' inquired Richard, looking very frightened but somehow most regal.

'Thomas Farringdon, sire. Some of my tenements were stolen from me by Sir Robert Hales. I demand to have them back.'

Richard gulped, but his thin voice was steady as he replied, 'Justice will be done for all.' Salisbury was quite proud of the boy. He was beginning well what promised to be an extremely exacting day.

His answer, however, did not satisfy Farringdon, who tightened

214

his grip on the bridle and said menacingly, 'I shall have my tenements back?' And now some of the peasants began to press closer. 'Give him what he asks for,' one of them bawled. And another cried, 'When Adam delved and Eve span, who was then the gentleman?'

This last somewhat mystified Salisbury, but it had an odd and immediate effect on the rebels. They began screeching and braying, crowding around the King's horse. None of them did anything more threatening than shaking his fist, but there was an undertone which made Salisbury apprehensive.

Behind him he heard the sudden sound of hoofbeats and half-turned to see the two Hollands, whey-faced, galloping their horses out of the procession. They streaked across the Whitechapel fields, never once looking back.

Their flight diverted the crowd's attention, and in the lull Walworth shouted, 'Back, all of you! The King rides to Mile End!'

Farringdon released the King's bridle, the rebels fell back, and Richard rode on at once. As he was passing Farringdon, Walworth aimed a vicious kick at him, narrowly missing the man's head. Farringdon's smile went on and off with frightening rapidity. He screamed, 'I'll get my tenements! Hales will die!'

The Tower lay behind them, but it was still a long way to Mile End. The road ahead quivered before Salisbury's eyes.

Tyler watched for the arrival of the royal party, squinting through brilliant sunlight toward the little rise over which they had to come.

Most of the commons, all those who had not been left on guard at the Tower, or who were not lining the road all the way back to London, were here, massed about him on the great open fields of Mile End. He was pleased to see that the men from the shires were mingling in free and friendly fashion with the Londoners. He would have been better pleased if he had been able to attain the same relationship with their leaders, but what he had done he had done, and regrets were useless now.

Perhaps his sending Straw with Farringdon on the special mission to Hales' manor house at Highbury would help to restore harmony, though he was not sure he cared for the potential of that combination. However, they had gone now, and he had to admit to feeling considerable relief over not having to endure Straw's intensity for an hour or two.

The pony whinnied softly beside him, and he patted its muzzle. Some Surrey farmers had brought it to him just before he gave the order to march out of London. The King would be on horseback, they had said, and the leader of the commons should also have a steed. Ball had agreed with the Surrey men at once, and Tyler had been pleased with the idea. But perhaps because he liked it so well, a strange perversity had come over him, and he had refused to ride to Mile End, trudging along the road instead, the pony between him and Ball.

It would not be long now. He could feel excitement coursing in him. Excitement, and a small twist of doubt, snaking through his confidence, undermining his eagerness to face them. To be a leader of men was one matter: to knit their purposes together, direct them in the name of action, exert his will over their energy. But to deal with words, ideas, demands . . . He turned to Ball and said, 'Perhaps it would be better if you . . .' Ball smiled and answered, 'You're the leader of the commons, and their spokesman. But I shall be here beside you.' He smiled again.

Tyler heard the sound of a horse approaching, not from the direction of London but from the north. The ranks of the commons were parting to let the rider through.

When he reached them, he reined in and leaped lightly to the ground, a sinewy, heavy-browed, fresh-faced man. 'The people of St. Albans marched on the Abbey this morning at dawn,' he said without preamble. 'We told the Abbot all the things we wanted, and after a while he agreed we should have them.'

This could only be the man called Grindcobbe, and the Abbot of whom he spoke the brutal de la Mare, whose reputation for tyranny and savagery had spread far beyond St. Albans. Yet Grindcobbe spoke of the rising against him as casually as if it occurred each morning.

'We told the old gentleman that we wanted our handmills back . . . he stole them from us and paved a floor in the Abbey with them, made it a hanging crime for us to grind our own corn . . . and that we wanted serfs freed and hunting and fishing rights for all, and ever so many other things. He listened and said yes.'

'And insisted, no doubt,' Ball said gravely, 'on giving you his blessing before you rode down here to tell us.'

Grindcobbe's bushy brows lowered, screening his eyes. His face twitched. Then he opened his mouth and released a great gust of laughter. He sat down on the ground and laughed until he wept.

'Almighty God,' he said finally, getting up. 'Almighty God, it was a sight. Every word he spoke, he swelled up beforehand like a toad. I thought he would burst. I'm glad he didn't. Think of the corruption he'd have spattered over us! And he said yes to all we asked. Much as we trust his word, though, we thought it would be wiser to have it confirmed by the King. So I borrowed a horse from the Abbot . . .' He swung his head in a slow, sweeping survey of the assemblage. 'Almighty God,' he said in muted awe, 'so many in one place . . .' Then, 'It is to meet the King you've gathered? We heard, but one hears so much . . .'

Tyler nodded, and Grindcobbe's laughter boomed out again. 'The Abbot's face when it swelled up . . .' And in a bantering tone, 'A little thing you might hold, grinding our own corn, not having to bring it to the Abbey mill. A small matter, but . . ."

'It's no small matter,' said a grating voice behind them.

They turned to see Straw, hands, face and habit smeared with ashes, scowling at them.

'I was about to ask after you, Jack Straw,' said Grindcobbe. 'A long time now since I visited Fobbing . . .'

'It's no small matter,' repeated Straw. 'They've crushed us and oppressed us, ground us under their feet and . . .'

Grindcobbe gave Straw a great wallop on the back, cutting off his diatribe. 'Trouble with you, friend,' he said, 'you've too much black bile in your blood. Must be what you eat, or a lack of ale in your diet.' He whacked Straw again, more vigorously.

Tyler watched, fascinated, as Straw staggered and almost fell, sputtering angrily, then suddenly began to laugh. He clapped Grindcobbe on the shoulder with a stiff, angular gesture, croaking mirth spilling out of his thin lips. He doubled over, smacking his thighs. 'Black bile in the blood,' said Grindcobbe, and the words sent Straw into a new convulsion. 'We burned Hales' house in Highbury,' he said, wheezing with laughter. He wiped away his tears. 'We burned it to the ground . . . down to the very ground . . .' Now his eyes began to glow again, relighted with sombre hatred. 'They'll pay for what they've done to the people.'

'You're right, old black bile,' said Grindcobbe easily, and once more Straw began to cackle.

Tyler felt a twinge of jealousy, bordering on resentment, that Grindcobbe, with no apparent effort, could turn Straw malleable, while he . . .

Ball said, 'Wat . . .' and at the same instant the commons began to cheer excitedly.

The royal procession was cresting the rise. Behind the King rode the arrogant little grey-haired noble who had thwarted them at Rotherhithe, and the hulking Lord Mayor. Following them came a carriage which Tyler recognized as the one they had stopped on the highroad in Kent. The rest of the cavalcade was an assorted lot:

some more noblemen, a few soldiers and servants, and a number of black-habited clerks.

Tyler started, a little self-consciously, to mount the pony, then decided against it. He made no move to advance, and when the King stopped a short distance away, he continued to wait. Richard glanced back at his two advisers. Then the three of them rode slowly forward, halted when they reached Tyler's group, and sat looking down at them.

He sensed their uncertainty, and his own confidence began to flood back, but he said nothing.

'Do you not kneel before your King?' the Lord Mayor demanded angrily.

'Before my King, yes,' said Tyler. 'But not before his horse.'

His reply provoked the laughter he had been hoping for from the men standing nearby. He could hear his words being repeated and passed outward into the massed commons, until all around them was the sound of sniggers.

The Lord Mayor's face was darkening, but the grey-haired man said something to him, then nodded to Richard, and all dismounted.

At once Tyler dropped to his knees. 'Wat Tyler brings you the allegiance of your commons,' he said. He got to his feet and cried out loudly, 'Long live King Richard and the true commons!'

The echo from the people was deafening. Richard looked around, smiling expansively. The door of the carriage opened and Princess Joan emerged, blinking at the sunlight. She negotiated the two steps with difficulty, looked anxiously at Richard, then around at the commons. A smile, much like the King's, began to grow on her face. She saw Tyler watching her; the smile faltered and grew distressed; her eyes glittered dangerously before she turned away.

When the commons were quiet at last, Richard said to Tyler, 'The King thanks his people and inquires what they wish of him.'

'We have four general demands. First: that no man who has journeyed to meet with the King be prosecuted for his action.'

'Granted,' said Richard.

Tyler drew a deep breath. The grey-haired man and the Lord Mayor were staring at him, one speculatively, the other with blatant contempt. He returned their gaze, took another breath and said, 'All serfs are to be freed from their lords and all services to these lords cancelled.'

Richard hesitated, very briefly, then said in a low voice, 'Granted.'

Tyler had to make a great effort not to let his breath out in explosive relief. They had won! He managed to keep the exultancy out of his voice as he stated the other two demands: freedom to buy and sell goods and produce wherever they wished, and the fixing of rents for all lands at fourpence per acre per year.

The King spoke his assent to each of the two points, then said, 'If that is all . . .'

Tyler decided to postpone for a few moments mention of the one matter still outstanding. He said, 'All that you have granted here we wish to have written down in charters, so that each town and village represented will have proof of the King's word.'

'It will be done,' said the grey-haired man.

'Now,' said Tyler.

The nobleman made a languid gesture toward the rear of the royal procession. 'We have brought clerks. The charters will be drawn up here, and the people may take them at once to their villages.'

Ball, stirring restlessly at Tyler's side, whispered, 'Tell him the people will return to their homes only when we direct them to do so.'

He stared at Ball. The priest's expression was morose. 'What's the matter?' asked Tyler in a low voice.

'Tell them,' urged Ball.

Tyler was annoyed. Victory was theirs, and Ball was concerning himself with trifles. However, he repeated Ball's words to the King and his advisers.

The grey-haired man shrugged elegantly, carelessly. The gesture nettled Tyler but also reassured him. 'Draw up the charters,' he said.

While the clerks were being summoned, word of the successful negotiation was working its way through the ranks of the people. There was no outburst of cheering, but Tyler could feel the joy in the powerful and excited throb of voices.

He called out, asking if anyone had brought ale with him. A dozen jugs were proffered. He took two, drank deeply from one, then the other, raised them above his head and basked in the immediate sunburst of laughter. 'It went well,' he said to Ball.

'Too well.'

'They granted everything we asked.'

The priest nodded moodily. 'If they had not agreed so readily . . . if they had not brought clerks . . .'

Tyler did not want to be angry. He wanted to savour this moment, to revel in the knowledge that they had won. He wanted to walk among the people, receiving their admiration, celebrating with them the concessions they had wrested from the lords. Ball was spoiling the taste of freedom.

'Are you never satisfied?'

'If they do not really intend . . .'

'They've given us what we asked. What more . . .'

'The people must not leave London,' Ball said doggedly, 'until we're certain we've won. Will you tell them?'

The anger he had been damming up broke through. 'Tell them yourself,' he snapped. 'I have more important business.'

He strode back to the King and his advisers. 'There is another matter,' he said.

'You made four demands,' said Richard, growing petulant. 'I granted them.'

'Four items for the charters. We also demand punishment for Sudbury and Hales. It is the will of the people that they be executed as traitors.'

Richard's eyes widened. He looked around distractedly at his advisers, who stared back, their faces impassive. 'Justice will be done for all,' said the King in a high, faltering voice.

'Your commons will see that justice is done,' said Tyler, turning away.

He passed Ball without speaking, ignoring the priest's stricken expression.

Tyler waited in the centre of the drawbridge. A knight in battle armour, carrying his helmet, stepped out of the gateway and came toward him. He was a small man, and he walked with an air of vagueness, as if he were not quite sure where he was. 'I am Sir Robert Knolles,' he said when he reached Tyler. 'Commander of His Majesty's forces in the Tower.'

Tyler glanced past him. Ranks of soldiers were arrayed in the gateway, watching curiously and whispering among themselves. There were not many of them, but they were well armed. He saw Knolles looking over at the men he had brought with him, a force of several thousand.

'We've come,' said Tyler, 'to deal with the Chancellor and the Treasurer.'

Knolles did not reply.

Tyler fingered the charter he carried, the first of the documents drawn up at Mile End and sealed by Richard. He unrolled it and showed it to the knight, who inspected it without interest and shrugged.

'Will you allow us to enter and take the traitors, or must we fight our way in?'

Knolles twisted his head and regarded Tyler for a long moment. Then he said suddenly, sharply, 'If I had one thousand of those who fought under my command in France . . .' He broke off with a little moan, looked up at the sky, and when his gaze returned to Tyler, it was no longer vague. 'Why,' he inquired bitterly, 'do we not die when we should?'

He turned and strode back across the drawbridge. The soldiers moved out of the gateway to let him pass. When the knight disappeared, they did not return to their former positions.

Tyler signalled, and the foremost third of his force followed him into the fortress. They proceeded cautiously at first, but it was quickly evident that they would not encounter even token resistance. The commons, overjoyed at the easy entry, and still jubilant over the victory at Mile End, shook the soldiers by the hands and patted their heads and beards in rough gestures of friendship.

One of the men-at-arms said he thought they would find those they were seeking in the White Tower. He led Tyler and a company of several hundred to an inner gate, pointed out the imposing cream-coloured structure whose battlements they had been able to see from outside the walls.

They searched methodically, spreading out over the ground floor first, proceeding from one chamber to another. The corridors began to echo with cries: 'Where are the traitors? . . . Where are the spoilers . . .'

Tyler and a few other men entered one apartment more luxurious than the rest, and further distinguished by a faint, provocative, musky perfume emanating from the satin hangings. Open cupboards and chests gaped like maws; filmy gowns and silken robes were draped carelessly over chairs and tables. On the headboard of the great curtained bed was carved the same crest Tyler had seen on the door of Princess Joan's carriage. He felt a sudden hunger for Isabella, fierce as fever, and in the bereft, unthinking instant he picked up a gown and ripped it savagely.

The others, taking his action as an example, began to tear up robes and smash furniture. A bat-eared man from Brentwood set about chopping up the bed with his axe; a Fobbing fisherman heaved one of the chests through a stained-glass window. They destroyed with eager fury, until Tyler, emerging from a reverie compounded of desire and fatigue, reprimanded them more angrily than he had intended.

He led them into the corridor, resumed the search through dank halls and labyrinthine turnings. Near the end of one passage he saw a staircase spiralling toward light above and, followed by his men, ascended the stone steps. The questing cries continued to float eerily about them, now muffled, now distinct and pulsing with anger: '. . . traitors . . . spoilers . . .'

They reached a level landing. The staircase did not end here, but through an arched opening he saw candles lighting a small chapel, and before the altar, kneeling with their backs to him, three men. He heard the soft purring of Latin words.

As he entered, there was a shout from another doorway: 'There they are! There are the traitors!'

One of the kneeling men rose and turned toward them. Tyler and his followers stopped short, as did those plunging in from the other side of the chapel.

He recognized Sudbury. When Ball had pointed out the Chancellor sitting in the royal barge the day before, Tyler had not realized how old he was, nor how frail. The arch enemy of the commons was wearing a gold-encrusted mitre and a flowing scarlet robe. His eyes were gentle, and fear kept rising in them, like blood to the surface of a wound. 'You have come right, my sons,' he said in a quiet voice. 'Here am I, your Archbishop, neither a traitor nor a spoiler.'

How long they stood there, motionless, Tyler never knew. Perhaps they would have remained even longer had not the second of the three men, a great mountain of flesh clothed in a green habit, tumbled over onto the stone floor in a dead faint. He lay on his back, fat jowls turned up to the candlelight. 'Hales . . .' someone said venomously. 'Hob the Robber . . .'

They left the third man, a friar, kneeling where he was, head twisted back over his shoulder regarding them in a grotesquerie of horror.

Sudbury came along willingly, but Hales gave them difficulty. He recovered from his swoon, glanced around, and at once fainted again. In the end they had to half-drag, half-carry him down the stairs and out of the White Tower. As they passed through the doorway, Tyler saw a cask of water against the wall. He commanded the men to put Hales down, then emptied the contents of the cask over the Treasurer's head. Hales sat up, gasping, a pendant of green slime swinging from one ear. 'Walk,' said Tyler. Hales struggled to his feet and retched. 'My son,' murmured Sudbury, going to the fat Treasurer. Hales said in a loud, clear voice, 'I think . . .' and everyone turned, waiting expectantly. The Treasurer regarded them blankly, then retched. He nearly fell over again, but managed somehow to remain upright.

As they crossed the drawbridge, Sudbury came close to Tyler and said, 'When I was a young man studying at the University in Paris, I met a man one day on the bank of the river. It was just at noon, and the bells of the great Cathedral on the island . . .'

He looked at Tyler, childlike surprise dawning on his features. 'I shall never see it again, shall I?' He scuttled along at Tyler's side, taking little crablike steps, his mitre askew. 'Never . . .'

Tyler watched them abstractedly: the old man, and the great mound of fat which had to stop every few stumbling paces to vomit. He wished he had never seen them.

They were climbing Tower Hill. The commons watched silently as they passed. In a few more moments this would be over. Then, soon, all the charters would be drawn up, Richard's seal set upon each, and the people could disperse, begin their journeys home, secure in the knowledge that they had won their freedom.

Ball's anxiety, he felt certain, was unfounded. Ball had lived too long with fear and doubt and all manner of inner torment. It would take time before he could believe in their success. But could he not have kept his niggling qualms to himself at the very instant of triumph?

Tyler's ire was rekindled, and its flame burned away the irresolution which was beginning to descend on him.

He was walking so quickly that Sudbury had to run to keep up with him. 'Wait, my son,' the Chancellor cried.

But now there was no need to wait, for there was no need to go farther. The spot for execution had been selected beforehand, and they had reached it. The executioner had also been chosen, had in fact never been more than a few steps away from Tyler since they had entered the Tower. He came forward now: the man from Brentwood, bright eyes and pointed bat's ears giving him an impish, and at the same time sinister, demeanour.

Hales stared with sick fascination at the great log beside which they had halted. A sudden spasm shook Sudbury's frail body. His mitre fell to the ground.

Tyler nodded to the executioner, who stepped up to Sudbury. 'What is your name, my son?' the Chancellor asked him.

'John Starling,' replied the man, then added, 'my lord.'

'*Ego te absolvo*,' said Sudbury, making the sign of the cross and continuing with the Latin in a calm, unhurried voice.

Starling's eyes darted about; his pointed ears twitched desperately. The Chancellor concluded his prayer, said, 'May God forgive us all,' and knelt beside the log.

The executioner was horribly clumsy in carrying out his first task.

Six men had to seize Hales and force him down. The Treasurer bellowed and thrashed about with unbelievable strength. Then all at once he became quiet. As Starling raised the axe, Hales said,

'If you . . .' and stopped. The executioner lowered the axe, and everyone waited for Hales to speak. He uttered a long-drawn-out neigh and was silent.

The axe went up again. Hales screamed suddenly, 'You fools! You think you've won! They want you to think that! Wait till you leave here, you shoeless . . .'

The instant the torrent of words began, Tyler made a move to check Starling, but he was too late. And this time the executioner did his work with singular efficiency.

The shrill syllables of Hales' broken speech were tumbling about in Tyler's brain, taunting him. He took the charter out of his tunic, stared first at the scrawled black inkmarks and the seal of red wax, then at the gory spectacle on the ground.

He was so stunned by what he had heard that for some time he did not notice that he was standing alone at the top of the hill. Then he became aware of the sustained roaring of the commons from far below. He saw a group of men dragging someone in a black cassock across the Tower drawbridge.

He ran toward them and was able to get close enough to see that the captive was the friar who had been in the chapel with Sudbury and Hales. But before Tyler could make his way through the howling crowd, Starling had performed his third execution.

'John of Gaunt's chaplain,' a man said to him. 'We've just settled with John of Gaunt's chaplain.' He put his lips close to Tyler's ear and shouted, 'Long live King Richard and the true commons!'

'I could not hold them,' said Ball despairingly. 'I tried to reason with them, but they only waved the charters and shouted. I don't know how many left for their homes. Half, three-quarters . . . I don't really know . . .'

Tyler stared at Ball without replying, then walked away from him, down the nearly deserted Tower Hill.

By mid-afternoon he had reasserted his control over the commons.

A number had indeed left for their homes after the charters were sealed at Mile End: about five or six thousand, as nearly as Tyler could reckon. It was a serious blow, but it could have been much worse. Twenty thousand or more had returned to the city.

As soon as he had assimilated the import of Hales' last words and understood that they would have to take further and more decisive action, he had set about reorganizing his forces. Using the pony given him by the Surrey farmers, he had travelled back and forth along streets thronged with celebrants, seeking the leaders of the Essex and Kent contingents, instructing them to gather their men and set up camp once more about the Tower.

Then he and Straw led a large group on a grim but significant expedition across London Bridge. There they set the heads of Sudbury, Hales and the friar on pikes over the arch of the Bridge Gate.

The commons responded quickly enough to his leadership, but the Londoners were a different matter.

At first he was even optimistic about them. Returning over the Bridge, he encountered Alderman Sibley, who greeted him warmly and said, 'We must soon meet, all of us, and decide on a course of action. New measures, laws . . . there is much to be done. . . .' He clapped Tyler on the shoulder, struggling to go on, and was finally able to say, 'Soon . . . soon . . .'

But only moments later Tyler saw Horne riding up and down outside the Lord Mayor's house, a flock of Londoners running behind his horse. 'Justice!' the alderman was crying, in no whispering voice now. 'Justice for all!'

Tyler saw him dismount from his horse as a group of people approached him, pushing a foppishly dressed man ahead of them. There was some talk Tyler could not hear. Then Horne shouted, 'Robert Morton, merchant, you have directed insulting words to John Pecke, fishmonger. Therefore you will pay ten pounds to John Pecke. I order you to do so at once, on pain of death!' And again he called out, 'Justice, justice for all . . .'

He saw Tyler and came to him swiftly, the corner of his mouth drooping, eyes glazed as those of a drunkard. 'Justice,' he said. 'We have our justice now.'

'Whose justice?' asked Tyler.

Horne leaned forward confidentially. 'Mine.' Then, throwing back his head, he bellowed, 'Let all who have suffered injury come forward. . . .'

Tyler could hear his voice long after he lost sight of him, calling out with the shrill stridency of a peddler, 'Justice . . . draw near and receive justice. . . .'

Tyler repaired to St. Catherine's Wharf, hoping to find Ball and begin planning what they should do next. He could not locate the priest, but while he was seeking him, he learned an important piece of news from one of the Tower soldiers.

Instead of returning to the fortress after leaving Mile End, Richard and his company had gone to a mansion in Carter Lane.

From the same soldier he heard that the friar who was executed by the commons had been the personal confessor of the King.

It was then that Robert Cave came to Tyler. The baker was distressed; the story he told was confused, and it was only with difficulty that Tyler made sense of it.

Cave had suddenly remembered that he had left two of his men in a dwelling not far from the Tower, charged with guarding Sir John Newton. He had hurried there to make sure all was in order. It was, but as he was returning he had come across some Londoners engaged in a peculiar activity. Led by a man whose name he had learned was Farringdon, they had formed a cordon across the intersection of two large streets and were stopping everyone who wished to pass. 'Say bread and cheese,' Farringdon instructed them, and he had waited with an odd smile for them to repeat the words. Those who did to his satisfaction were allowed to pass. Cave heard some, however, speaking with a strange accent. 'Bread and cheese' came out as 'brod and case'. Whenever he found someone who spoke like this, Farringdon had beaten the man and flung him to others, who had bound his hands behind him.

Curious, Cave had approached Farringdon and inquired if the men he was capturing were lords or lawyers. Farringdon had sneered. 'They're Flemings, you stupid peasant,' he had said.

'When they had stopped and bound about thirty of these people,' Cave went on, 'they took them . . . I followed . . .' He shook his head. 'If you will go to the street they call the Cheapside . . .'

Fairly sure what he would see there, Tyler went at once. In the centre of the broad thoroughfare an improvised scaffold and block had been set up. Under the direction of Alderman Tonge, and cheered on by a hooting London mob, three executioners were at work.

Tyler watched helplessly, knowing that if he were to interfere, he would only succeed in setting the Londoners against his own people, and the precarious advantage still held by the commons against the lords would be lost.

He was on the point of mounting his pony and leaving the Cheapside when his attention was caught by a spare figure running wildly toward the Londoners. The cassock he wore was flapping out at his sides like a pair of great wings, and he was shouting, 'Stop! Stop this slaughter!'

The mob grew quiet, too quiet, as they turned toward the priest. Ball's voice, hoarse and cracked, was still crying, 'Stop . . . no more killing! No more killing!'

Tyler reached him just as the crowd was beginning to growl ominously. He saw Tonge staring down hostilely from the scaffold.

Ball was trembling as Tyler seized him. His eyes were wide and

226

furious, containing no recognition. 'Killing!' he shrieked. 'Stop the killing. . . .'

He stiffened, then went limp. Tyler kept him from falling, picked him up and bore him carefully to the pony, laid him across its back.

Before they turned off the Cheapside, Tonge had already resumed his systematic massacre of the Flemings.

22

A HUNDRED torches on the wharf lighted the faces of the elated commons. Talk spun in crazy circles festooned with mirth. Men embraced one another and cried out, 'Freedom . . . freedom!'

Elias swigged his ale and said excitedly, 'Now I can buy a cow or a pig wherever the bargain is best. I can sell them when and where I wish without being fined. Why . . .' His eyes widened, then slitted cunningly. 'I can even buy and sell in Gravesend or Rochester.' He grinned and clapped his hands. 'If I want, I can come back here to London, and no one will stop me. Not the lord, not his bailiff. No one. Money will drop into my hands like rain.'

Abel checked the comment poised tart and delicious on the tip of his tongue. Old Elias was just recovering from the moroseness which had followed his encounter the evening before with the malicious tale-bearer from Sussex. The horns of a cuckold grow green with dawning knowledge, too tender for tweaking.

'Ah,' said Nicholas, 'when we . . .' His words were swallowed up briefly by the raucous horseplay of some passing revellers, came clear again. '. . . the best ale in my inn.'

'I shall buy my wife a gown,' said Robert, 'like one I saw in John of Gaunt's palace. Our daughters will marry . . .' He turned to Abel. 'What will you do?'

'I shall buy myself a surgeon and keep him near me always.'

Robert's pale face grew solicitous. 'A surgeon?'

'To fashion the new stomachs I'll need to deal with Nicholas' best ale.'

Someone shouted, 'Freedom . . .' and Roger, who had been sitting in silence, repeated the word softly, his glance darting restlessly about the wharf.

Abel got up and was at once surrounded by a band of dancing men. 'With whom do you hold?' one of them asked him.

He sprang onto his hands and walked about, kicking his heels at the torches. 'With King Richard and the true commons. . . .' He made one foot bow to the other, then involved them in a furious struggle, in which the left foot was finally defeated and retired sullenly. He let himself collapse in a heap, and the dancers fell down all around him, helpless with laughter.

His head was swimming from his antic exertion and the ale he had drunk. He was assailed by a sudden melancholy. Quietly, without anyone noticing, he rose and slipped away from the others, strolled aimlessly along the wharf.

Around him fluttered the banners bearing crudely-drawn emblems of their patron St. George, fashioned by the commons in imitation of the Londoners' guild banners. A man held a torch too close to one. It flared up brilliantly for a moment, then smouldered, smoke rising from it into the still, warm air.

A girl in a striped hood accosted him at the end of a street's deep gloom. She carried herself with peculiar stiffness, and when she came close to him, he realized she was sodden with drink. She leaned against him and a tremor of lust fluttered through his loins.

A shaft of light touched the wall of a house and split the darkness into wavering shadows. He could see her face now: the mouth had no upper lip. He recalled at once where he had seen her before and tried to move away, but she clung to him. She was trying to say something to him. Her lower lip flapped grotesquely, her teeth clicked. A rush of sour breath enveloped him. 'Bread and cheese,' she groaned, 'bread and cheese.'

He tore himself out of her grasp and ran. Her footsteps pursued him, and the tremulous, agonized voice. 'Bread and cheese . . . bread and cheese . . .'

He made a sharp turn, and another, down a fetid alleyway, splashing through puddles of water, tripping over something wooden which splintered against his shin. And always behind him he could hear the drunken, erratic steps, the blurred, insistent syllables. Until breathlessness blunted the edge of his panic, and he turned to face her, a little ashamed of having fled so ignominiously from a whore. 'My reputation will suffer for this,' he said. His words fell on silence. There was no one there.

He drifted through the streets, neither knowing nor caring where he went. In the distance he could hear vagrant sounds of revelry. A church loomed up in passing torchlight, vanished quickly. Once a cart clattered by. Somewhere in the depths of a lane shutters grated open, and an old man's quavery voice said, 'Night's not long . . .' A church bell pealed wildly for a moment, then was still.

The street he had been following ended in a high wall, with lanes branching out along it in either direction. As he hesitated, he heard a burst of gay laughter and a flurry of singing, shouting men brandishing torches swirled about him, and he was suddenly the centre of their mad cavorting. They seized his hands, spun him, flung him from one of them to the other, but always with such riotous good humour that he could not begin to take offence. In fact, after a few moments, their high spirits began to break through the shell of his melancholy, and he found himself laughing and prancing with them. But then, as quickly as they had come, they were gone, leaving him standing bewildered in a deep throbbing silence. He was not even sure they had been there. Yet they must have been, for they had left one of their torches behind, stuck into a crevice in the stone wall.

It was then that he saw her. She was wearing a cloak of soft, rich material and was standing with her back to him, next to one of the houses. He knew she had not been with the men, and he supposed she had come along one of the lanes bordering the wall.

When she turned into the light, he saw that her face was lovely, the features almost flawless, but troubled by a strange air of distraction.

Abel raised his hand to wipe the perspiration off his forehead and heard her gasp. She was staring at him so intently and in such an odd manner that he thought she was ill and started toward her. She turned at once and began to walk away. He stopped. So did she, looking back over her shoulder, and he understood that she wanted him to follow. He did, and shortly he saw her turn through a great arched gateway. He realized now that the wall was the one which encircled London, and that this was one of the exits from the city.

The gates stood open, and though smoking torches flanked either side, he could see no one about.

The woman was well ahead of him now, walking quickly. He had to hurry to narrow the distance between them.

There was a church on his left. When he had passed it, he could see the beginnings of an open field, and a few trees ghostly and indistinct in the starglow.

He slowed down, unwilling to venture too far into the darkness. Witches under oaks . . . the woman herself. . . .

She had stopped and was waiting for him. When he reached her they stood facing each other, saying nothing. The silence was making him uneasy, but he had a feeling that if he spoke she would disappear.

An owl hooted close by, and they both jumped. Then she laughed, and abruptly his uneasiness was dispelled.

She took his hand, gazed at it for a moment with peculiar concentration, then led him off the path.

She turned and came into his arms. Her body was slender and pliant, her ardour such as he had never known in any woman.

The sounds of jubilation were beginning to abate. Men lay sprawled on the wharf in exhausted sleep, and only from the city itself rose an occasional roistering clamour.

Ball was glad. The celebration had sickened him, based as it was on the commons' false assumption that they had already won a complete and sweeping victory. He had wanted to explain to them, tell them the truth of why it was necessary for them to remain in London. 'We have no right,' he had said to Tyler, 'to do otherwise.'

Tyler had disagreed emphatically. 'Will we be able to make them understand what we ourselves don't clearly understand? If we confuse them now, we can be sure many more will leave for their homes. Or,' he added, regarding Ball sombrely, 'they could turn against us, claiming we have misled them.'

'They could be right.'

'Have we failed?'

Ball shook his head.

'Well then.' Tyler had reflected a moment. 'It's enough that they know our business in London is not finished. That's as much as we know.'

In the end Ball had given in, respecting Tyler's tough realism. Once Tyler had accepted the possibility that there might have been trickery, he took it as an accomplished fact that there was, and asked only what could be done to counter it.

Ball's attempts to order his thoughts early in the evening had been unsuccessful. He was too shaken by his experience on the Cheapside, the sight of the executioners' axes and the terror in the victims' eyes, though he could only recall in fragmented moments what had actually happened.

Now, with the night half gone, he was beginning to feel clearheaded again, but physical weariness was threatening. Tyler was waiting patiently, and this gave Ball strength. If Tyler could tame his impatience, Ball could stave off exhaustion a little longer.

A church bell in the bowels of the city set up an urgent cacophony, ceased suddenly, and the night returned to stillness.

'They were killing,' said Ball. 'Killing the innocent . . .'

230

'We could not have stopped them.'

'Violence will defeat us.'

'Then,' said Tyler evenly, 'the defeat would be partly my fault. Sudbury and Hales . . .'

Ball could feel his voice filling with dejection. 'There seems no end. . . .'

Tyler smiled at him. 'You have taught me what I know. Often I've differed from you, sometimes in anger. But if it had not been for your teaching . . .'

'My teaching,' said Ball bitterly. 'To have spent twenty-five years planning what should be done, only to learn in the space of a few hours how naïve and foolish . . .'

'We've not lost.'

'Nor have we won.'

Tyler leaned forward. 'We're in London. We have an army with us. If we've made mistakes, we have the power to remedy them. The advantage is still ours.'

Ball sighed. 'It's easy to understand now why they agreed so readily to what we asked. It was not only that we possessed strength of numbers. But they knew that once we were persuaded to leave London . . . I suspected it at Mile End . . . what you heard from Hales would seem to confirm . . .' He chewed at a thumbnail. 'There was one thing . . . if we had . . .' He lapsed into silence, pondering it.

'Our main mistake,' Tyler said slowly, 'was that we were trusting them to carry out the concessions we wrung out of them.'

Ball laughed loudly, triumphantly. A peasant sleeping nearby moaned and rolled over on his back. 'You don't need me to teach you any longer.'

An odd expression crept onto Tyler's face, rested there for an instant, far too briefly for Ball to fathom it. 'Without you . . .' Tyler said reflectively, then with sudden energy, 'You've decided what must be done.'

'We've both decided. The charters as they stand are worthless. But if the people in each town and village had the legal right to bear arms and enforce what's in the charters . . .'

'We'll send Newton to them, tell them we want a meeting to-morrow . . .' He glanced at the sky. 'Today.'

'With God's help . . .' said Ball.

Tyler, who had been getting to his feet, sat down again. 'It's been troubling me,' he said. 'We pray to God. And in Carter Lane the King and his Council pray to God. What . . .' He broke off perplexedly.

Ball fought his desire for sleep and said, 'In the monastery when I was young, I tried to understand God. Now I know better. I act as I believe He would wish. That's all I can do.'

Tyler was looking down at his hands. 'I've begun to believe,' he said thickly, 'the way you believe about killing . . .'

Ball stared at him incredulously.

'It was easier,' said Tyler, 'when I didn't know. Now . . .' He shrugged. 'I'll send someone for Newton.'

They lay with their heads resting against a grass-covered hummock and looked up at the sky whitening through the branches of a tree. She shivered, and Abel pulled her close to him. Her cheek was wet with tears.

'I'm a clown, my lady,' he said. 'Your permission, and I'll make those tears vanish.'

'That would be wicked of you. I'm weeping for joy.'

'Women,' he said. 'They weep for joy, and clowns laugh out of sadness. There. I've told you my deepest secret. Tell me one of yours.'

'The joy of being free,' she said quietly.

'You were free before.'

'I am now.'

He clucked his tongue. 'I know a woman can get many things from a man, and the other way round. But I never knew freedom could be passed on that way.'

She laughed and said, 'You are wicked. And you've made me laugh when I asked you not to.'

'There's a rule,' he said. 'If a woman asks you not to do something, it's nearly always exactly what she wants you to do.'

She laughed again, and he drew her to him. 'Those two crossed branches,' she said dreamily, 'and the whole sky beyond . . .'

'In my village at this very moment the sky will be turning rose, and a breeze will be beginning to stir the grain. . . .' He stroked her hair, which was wonderfully soft, and golden as a harvest day. He wished the night were not fleeing. 'The sun will soon be up.'

'There was a shed where I came to sleep,' she said. 'Hawks are kept there. They were hungry and there was no food. I tried to set them free. I opened the door, and they flew out, but then they flew back in and wouldn't leave.'

'In my village . . .' he began, then said angrily, 'I'm tedious with this talk of my village.' He thought of the lord's forest. 'There's a pool, and a big trout I've been trying to catch for years, but I've really hoped I never would. To know he's there . . .' He looked at her. 'If we had not found each other last night . . .'

'We had to,' she said soberly. 'There was a sign.' She smiled, and smoothed the furrows from his forehead. She took his right hand and traced the healing wound on the back of it with her forefinger. Then she turned her own hand over, placed it beside his, and Abel saw the scar puckering the soft skin. 'You see? We had to . . .'

'If you . . .' Then he forgot what he intended to say, for her lips were on his.

When he became aware once more of the growing day, the trunk of the tree under which they lay was black against the red rising sun.

'I must go back,' he said.

'No,' she said disconsolately.

But she walked along beside him. 'The Bishopsgate,' she said, 'and St. Botolph-by-the-Stone. How many times I've prayed passing on the way out and despaired going back in.' She put her hand on his arm. 'Don't leave me.'

He smiled. 'The lady and the peasant buffoon. It's enough to make God laugh.'

'I'll go with you,' she said. 'Wherever . . .'

Hope beat its wings against his heart like the foolish bird he knew it was. But it would not be still. 'Perhaps . . .' he said.

'Oh yes. Yes,' she said. 'I'll wait here.'

'You're not coming into the . . .'

'I'll wait,' she said quietly.

They embraced, and he walked away. When he turned just before passing through the gate, he saw her standing beside a giant chestnut tree.

It was shortly past sun-up when Salisbury's squire came to tell him about Imworth, but in the Carter Lane wardrobe, shadowed as it was between St. Paul's and the Convent of the Black Friars, darkness still ruled.

Salisbury had spent the night pacing the dreary corridors. From time to time Elizabeth had sent word by one of the servants, asking him to come to her, and he had intended to do so, but each time the intention had got lost in the maze of gloomy reflection on other matters. Toward dawn she had sought him out herself. She had stood before him, a cloak over her nightdress, cradling the spaniel against her meagre breast. 'Truly, William,' she had said, her glance darting into every recessed doorway, 'truly, there's no

233

reason . . .' She had uttered a little cry as a woman's figure approached them from the other end of the corridor, had squeezed the spaniel so hard that it also cried out, then had watched with trembling lips as the woman, who turned out to be one of Joan's ladies, passed them without stopping.

He had wanted to tell his wife that he had not seen Joan since his return from Mile End, which was the truth, and that the Princess was far from his mind at the moment, which was a half-truth. But to tell Elizabeth anything of this sort would have been foolish, and he had committed enough state stupidities in the past day without compounding them by personal folly.

He had spoken gently to Elizabeth and told her he would join her soon, and when she left him after one of her nervous, rambling speeches about his health, he had resumed his lonely, restless pacing of the corridors.

Then Thomas found him, and before he spoke handed Salisbury the cup of wine he had brought. Salisbury drank it thirstily and spoke a word of gratitude to the squire, who flushed, the first colour Salisbury had seen on the lad's face in two days.

Imworth, Thomas told him then, was dead.

After the fall of the Marshalsea, the chief jailer had sought refuge in Westminster Abbey, where he should have been perfectly safe. But the rebels had not respected the right of sanctuary. At dawn they had entered the Abbey, two score or so of them, and had discovered Imworth clinging to the shrine of the Confessor. When the jailer refused to relinquish his hold on the sacred stones, one of the rebels, a priest according to the story Thomas had heard, had simply hacked off his hands. Then they had dragged him from the Abbey and beheaded him.

All this had happened within the past hour.

Salisbury was sure then that the situation could only grow increasingly desperate. The rebels had killed Sudbury and Hales (he felt a return of his remorse, dismissed it quickly and brutally), as he had been certain they would once the plan of persuading them to return to their homes had failed. Even poor harmless Appleton, the King's confessor, had fallen prey to their savagery. All the rest of the day there had been butchery of small citizens, mostly foreigners. Now they were once more turning their wrath against officials, men of position. They had professed allegiance to Richard, and in truth not one rebel had tried to enter the Wardrobe, but who knew when this tenuous loyalty might crumble? And if it did . . .

He himself had committed the cardinal error against which he had schooled himself through all the years of his career: underestimation of one's opponents. He had realized the magnitude of his mistake while Tyler was presenting the rebel demands. The points had been concise and well-ordered, and though they were somewhat naïve, they were not the work of ignorant or bumbling men.

Ball, he surmised, had been the author of the programme. Even in his consternation, Salisbury had had to admire the priest as he watched him moving among the rebel ranks, exhorting them not to depart for their homes. Ball was a man of ability and great intuitive intelligence, but Salisbury sensed that he could not operate effectively without Tyler.

Salisbury had felt the presence of animal force in Tyler's massive physique, in his direct, fearless manner, but it was not this alone that made him dangerous. Tyler possessed cleverness and warmth, two qualities which, together with energy, marked the born leader. He had organized the rebels well, and they obviously adored him. They would follow wherever he led. The question was, where did he intend to lead them? Certainly not out of London. There was no point now in hoping the insurrection would die by attrition, that with the passage of a little more time the rebels would weary of being away from their homes and return to them. They would remain as long as Tyler told them to do so.

He remembered the anger which had blazed up in Tyler's eyes as he made his peremptory demand for the lives of Sudbury and Hales. Under this man's leadership, lawlessness and violence could only spread, until it overwhelmed all of them. Imworth's murder was proof enough of this.

Salisbury began to search for Walworth. As he walked through the corridors, the nobility who had taken refuge in the Tower and then come to the Wardrobe importuned him in droves. Their quarters were cramped and uncomfortable, they whined; they had been promised that after they left the Tower it would be safe for them to return to their homes. Why did Salisbury and the Lord Mayor not deal decisively with these ruffians and restore order? Salisbury replied quietly and courteously to their questions and complaints, until finally he could bear it no longer. 'Miserable idiots!' he shouted. 'England is dying, and you can only snivel about the comforts of your worthless bodies. . . .'

They backed away from him, astounded into silence. Salisbury was so upset by the fury which had come boiling out of him that he only half-noticed Joan standing among her ladies, watching him with widened eyes. He heard her voice summon him falteringly,

'My Lord Salisbury . . .' but for the first time in his life he paid no attention to it.

The Lord Mayor, a servant told him, had been in and out of the Wardrobe at various times during the night. He did not know if the Lord Mayor was presently in the mansion.

Salisbury continued to look for Walworth, but his search was interrupted by the arrival of Sir John Newton bearing a communication from the rebels.

The knight's moustaches, in which he must once have taken great pride, were scraggly and crusted with bits of dried food. He stank so horribly it required all Salisbury's self-control to remain near him while Newton delivered the message, which mercifully was brief and straightforward.

Ball and Tyler demanded another audience with the King, at the earliest possible moment.

Salisbury told Newton to wait.

He resumed his circuit of the corridors, still on the lookout for Walworth, at the same time turning over in his mind the new development, which was hardly unexpected, but now that it had taken place seemed to portend only trouble.

Suddenly he stopped walking and said, 'Guillaume Cale . . .' in a voice so loud and harsh that John of Gaunt's son, who had been loitering by a window, turned and cried, 'My lord . . .' and fled before the intensity of Salisbury's gaze.

When Walworth entered the mansion, Salisbury met him, seething with an excitement which was sharply vitiated by the Lord Mayor's appearance. Walworth's face was haggard. His usually over-impeccable costume was dirty and dishevelled. On his gloved left hand he carried a hooded falcon, which was digging its talons viciously into the leather.

Walworth did not seem to hear Salisbury's greeting. He asked a passing servant for water, and when it was brought he rinsed his mouth several times, spitting the water onto the floor.

Salisbury wanted to inquire the reason for his distress, to help if possible, but the barrier of dislike, though mitigated, still remained between them. Better, he thought, to plunge straight away into the details of the plan he had been formulating.

'Three days ago,' he began crisply, 'you said you could muster six or seven thousand armed men.'

Walworth's expression was blank. 'Not there,' he said. 'She's still not there . . .'

'You said . . .' Salisbury shook Walworth's shoulder gently, pulled his hand back when the falcon emitted a muffled shriek.

'Six — seven thousand,' said Walworth dully.

'Do you think you can still find that many Londoners who will oppose . . .'

Intelligence started returning to Walworth's eyes. 'I can get them,' he said; then, in a burst of vehemence, 'We'll kill them!'

'Softly,' said Salisbury. 'To tell the truth, I now find myself frightened of dying, which we shall all surely do unless we plan carefully.'

'We'll wipe them out,' said Walworth, his voice rising. 'We'll slaughter every last one of them. We'll free the city . . .'

'Not just yet,' said Salisbury, cutting him off. 'If you'll see to the raising of a force we can depend on, I'll be responsible for the rest.'

Something in Salisbury's tone must have steadied Walworth. His voice was calm and cold. 'What have you in mind?'

'I'll tell you,' said Salisbury.

He turned and walked toward the room they had designated as a council chamber.

Straw came stomping along the wharf carrying a blood-stained sword.

'We've killed the traitor Imworth,' he exulted. 'Never again will he torture others, never again lock innocent citizens in foul dungeons. . . .' He threw back his head and screamed, 'We've killed another traitor!'

Ball waited, hardly daring to breathe, to see what Tyler would do.

Straw began to wave the sword. 'There are others who will soon taste the justice of this blade. There are others who deserve . . .'

His words died in a surprised gurgle as Tyler seized his arm and pried the sword from his hand.

'No one else will be executed,' said Tyler, 'without a trial.'

Straw's face went white. 'The people . . .' he sputtered. 'The vengeance of the people demands . . .'

'The people will be properly avenged,' said Tyler firmly.

There was no doubt that Straw intended to voice extensive objections, but just as he drew himself up to begin, Sir John Newton approached them. Straw wavered between indignation and curiosity, the latter triumphing. He pulled his cassock tight about his shoulders and came closer to Ball and Tyler.

The knight halted before them and said flatly, 'The King has consented to grant you an audience. One hour before Vespers, at

Smithfield, just outside Aldersgate. The King will await you in front of the Hospital of St. Bartholomew.'

Tyler turned to Ball. 'Now,' he said in a low voice. 'It will go well this time. I feel sure of it.'

23

ON HIS way to the King's chamber, the words Salisbury had spoken earlier to Walworth kept recurring to bemuse him: To tell the truth, I now find myself frightened of dying. There seemed to be no correlation in his spirit between hope, hopelessness, fear of death and resignation to it. The past few days he had experienced each of these, singly and together, sometimes in outlandish and illogical combinations.

The only thing he knew with certainty was that they must carry out what he had planned. If the realm, and they along with it, had been in danger before, it was nothing compared with the present peril. The plan was desperate. It could succeed brilliantly, but there were numerous possibilities for failure. If it failed, they would die.

He stated it as baldly and simply as that in presenting it to Richard.

The King dipped a sop of bread into one of the sauce-bowls before him (the concoction was one toward which Salisbury felt a particular aversion: red wine and spiced almond milk, sweetened with sugar and flavoured with saffron which lent the whole mess a nauseating orange hue).

'I shall think it over, my uncle,' said Richard.

'You will think nothing over, sire,' Salisbury replied. 'If we begin to consider too carefully what we must do, with all the implications, none of us will have the courage to attempt it.'

He heard a gasp, half-angry, half-frightened, and turned from the King to see Joan standing in the doorway, her bosom heaving in that alarming prelude to one of her fits of breathlessness. Yet somehow she managed to control it as she said, 'My son will have no part in this wild and irresponsible scheme.'

Salisbury said coldly, 'If your son refuses to do what I have proposed, that is his royal right and privilege. He can make his choice: to chance saving his kingdom and perhaps die doing so, or to die in a day or a week or a month along with England.'

The King chewed meditatively, watching Salisbury and his mother. Joan toyed with one of her rings, said finally, 'Then I shall accompany the King.'

'No, madam, you will not.'

She started forward in anger, checked herself, came to him with her lips curving in the smile of cajolery, grey eyes pleading, hand extended in the soft, conciliatory, promising gesture he knew so well. 'My Lord Salisbury would hardly refuse a mother the right to be at her son's side. . . .' She touched his cheek, let her fingers rest there a moment. 'Salisbury . . .'

He felt the familiar churning in his stomach. Some men, he reflected grimly, at least feel the effects of such thraldom in their loins.

'Salisbury . . .' she said again, her voice low, caressing each syllable of his name. She moved her head enticingly, and the miracle repeated itself: the re-emergence through the layers of fat and the creased, lifeless skin of the young and irresistible, the willowy and ardent. . . . Watching his eyes, she laughed huskily. 'Then it's settled.'

'Yes, madam,' he said, his throat constricting. 'It's settled. You will remain here in Carter Lane.'

She threw herself at him in a fury. If he had not stepped aside and caught her arm, her bulk would have bowled him over. 'I refuse to listen to this nonsense any longer,' she stormed. 'I have said I will go, and this is my . . .'

'Enough, Joan.'

He spoke quietly, but the anger in his tone stopped her. She began to breathe loudly, hoarsely.

'In an hour, sire,' he said to Richard, 'I shall meet with you and go over the details once more.'

'Salisbury . . .'

Her voice was very small. He glanced at her quickly. There was an expression on her face he had never seen before.

'Stay with me for a while.'

'There's too much to do, madam.'

He left the room without looking back, but he was aware that she had followed him almost to the door.

The ride to Westminster was a sombre affair. Only three others besides himself were making the trip to the Abbey: Richard, Walworth, and the squire Thomas. The rest, servants and a few of the nobles, would meet them later at Smithfield. There would be no soldiers in the company, now or later: this was an integral part of the plan.

Richard was pale. Apprehension had drained slyness from his face along with colour, and he looked pitifully young. May God not judge me too harshly, thought Salisbury, if we fail.

He felt sorriest for Thomas. At last his squire was participating in something he had always longed for: a mission of great importance and urgency, and he was striving manfully to conceal his fear. Salisbury rode close to him. The lad gathered the flowing robe he wore closer about him and managed a smile. 'It will go well,' said Salisbury. Thomas swallowed hard.

Walworth's expression was set in sour lines of hatred. As they passed the blackened stone shell of the Savoy Palace, he began to laugh hollowly. Salisbury observed him with some concern. So much depended on all of them keeping cool heads. If Walworth were to act impulsively . . .

When they arrived at the Abbey, Salisbury's first task was to arrange for someone to serve as Richard's confessor. This was not a simple matter. The monks were still in a turmoil brought on by the forcible extraction of Imworth from the sanctuary they had considered inviolable. None of them seemed capable of even the simplest activity, but Salisbury was able to gather several from whom Richard could choose.

Then the King turned stubborn, refusing four candidates in succession, saying petulantly, 'None of them is like Appleton.'

'Appleton's dead, sire,' said Salisbury, pitting a calculated cruelty against the shortage of time.

Richard declined three more confessors before accepting one who, Salisbury noticed, bore a slight resemblance to the Black Prince. Soon the King was in earnest conversation with the friar.

Thomas was kneeling at the shrine of Edward, motionless, his gaze fixed on the floor. Salisbury thought his squire was praying with particular fervour until he looked down, saw the great reddish-brown stain and realized what it was. Thomas turned to him. Salisbury could feel the nausea in the lad's voice as he asked, 'Will our blood look like that, my lord?'

Walworth was leaning against a pillar, observing the monks with an expression of bitter disdain. 'There's not much time,' Salisbury reminded him.

'No,' said Walworth, looking back at him steadily.

Salisbury went to make his own confession.

Horne came riding to meet Ball and Tyler on the Cheapside, as they were leading the commons toward Smithfield.

The alderman's face, Ball noticed, bore the ravages of exhaustion,

240

and the look peculiar to those who have indulged in wild and prolonged debauchery.

'The people of London,' Horne whispered to them, 'are with you. I wanted you to know this before you met with the King.'

'And you?' inquired Tyler.

'I . . .' Horne's expression grew anguished. 'For so long we waited, and when it happened . . .'

Tyler put his hand on the alderman's shoulder. 'We shall need the people of London. Tonight we'll meet again . . . you, Sibley . . .' He looked questioningly at Horne.

'Tonge and Farringdon,' said Horne, then added, 'I believe . . .'

'No matter,' said Tyler. 'After we've finished our business with the King, I'll seek them out, and we'll talk.'

Ball saw Horne gazing with admiration at the throng behind them, stretching as far as one could see along the broad Cheapside and Poultry Street, the crudely-fashioned St. George banners fluttering jauntily above the ranks in the late afternoon sun. 'The people of London . . .' said Horne again.

'We've noticed,' said Tyler pointedly, 'that the streets are somewhat deserted.'

Horne bent forward, a twisted rueful smile on his lips. 'After yesterday . . .' His eyes remained downcast. 'Londoners are strange. . . . They'll be out again, soon enough. But after yesterday . . .' He looked up at Tyler and Ball, pleadingly. 'We waited so long. . . .'

'Yes,' said Tyler softly. Then, 'We must go.'

'We'll be watching, Sibley and I, from the wall,' whispered Horne. His head inclined once more, came up slowly, and he said in a clear, firm voice, 'May God be with you.'

Walworth sat on his horse among the others, waiting for the rebel forces to arrive, sick with a kind of anger he had never known before this past week: a demon that sat in his belly, goading him to fury and at the same time robbing him of the will to act.

Yet, being at Smithfield stirred memories which in part revived his spirits. It was not exactly a place of garden beauty, this vast flat cattle market, where over the years such quantities of livestock had been slaughtered that the earth itself gave off a reek no rains could ever dispel.

In his youth, though, on some long summer days like this, Smithfield had been transformed. Because of its size, it had been the site of the lavish tournaments beloved of King Edward. The day before a jousting, the animals would be removed, the ground swept, and

241

laved with flower-essence poured out of the great jugs captured in France.

He remembered the first tourney he had attended as a guest, a raw stripling at Lovekyn's side, so fresh from being a fisherman's helper that the scale-cuts had not yet healed from his hands. On this day Alice Perrers, the King's mistress, had made her own spectacular entrance into Smithfield, paling even the splendid procession of the combatants. Dressed as the Lady of the Sun, in clinging cloth of beaten gold, she had ridden at the head of sixty of her ladies, who were garbed in parti-coloured breeches and tunics moulded to their bodies. The ladies were leading sixty knights by golden chains and carrying on such lustful pantomime with them that Lovekyn had said, 'There'll be furious bedding tonight, if they can still their itch that long.'

Alice Perrers had passed close to them. He had wondered how this slightly dumpy woman with a face that looked as if a scow might have collided with it could maintain such power over the King. Then she had turned directly toward him, and he had felt the force of the blatant carnal light filling her huge brown eyes. Lovekyn must have sensed what was going on in Walworth's mind, for he laughed and said, 'Not yet, boy, there's many a man ahead of you, though no doubt she'll run out of provender soon enough . . .'

Richard, beside him, shifted in his saddle. It was difficult to accept the fact that this mawkish brat, ready to puke with fear, was the grandson of the man who had conquered France and in his prime had ruled England with such rugged virility.

The sun was beginning to set. Its slanting rays touched the slimy surface of the Horse Pool far across the market, turned it to brief, gem-like brilliance before losing it to encroaching shadow. Twilight would soon be upon them. Walworth had to admit that Salisbury had chosen both the place and time for this encounter with consummate skill.

He turned to look at the Earl, who was sitting on the other side of Richard and peering toward St. Sepulchre's for a first glimpse of the rebels. There was no doubt that the man was afraid. He had admitted it openly, and the hand shielding his eyes from the sun was trembling. But he was here, in the forefront, ready to act.

Since Courtenay's flight, Walworth had developed a certain respect for Salisbury. For the handful of nobles the Earl had forced to join them, however, he could feel only contempt. Whining, womanly scabs, all of them, squeaking about like mice, turning up their pimply noses at anyone without a title. And as for their females, he'd trade a score of them for one of Agnes or Margaret.

. . . He drew in his breath sharply, and anger thickened again in his throat. He hawked and spat past Richard's horse, which shied nervously. The King bit his lip as he calmed the animal, then glared at Walworth.

When Salisbury heard Walworth gasp, he turned abruptly to observe him, first troubled by his bereft expression, then disgusted by his unnecessary display of vulgarity.

Yet, Salisbury knew, with all his boorishness, Walworth was both bitterly honest and courageous. His courage would be needed now.

He reviewed the details of what they were about to do. The plan should work. Certainly the precedent on which he had based it was sound enough. Over twenty years ago in France, Charles of Navarre had been faced with a similar situation. A man named Guillaume Cale had led an insurrection against him. Charles, intimating that he was prepared to grant the rebels what they asked, manœuvred Cale into appearing alone before him and his advisers. Then he had given the order for Cale to be slain, and the rebel forces, left leaderless, had disintegrated.

Salisbury's plan had a single focal point: the death of Tyler. But this had to be accomplished efficiently, at exactly the proper instant, and in such a manner that the rebels would be unaware of what had happened until it was too late.

He was sure he had laid the groundwork well. Smithfield was a perfect locale. With the royal party ensconced before St. Bartholomew's, the rebels would be forced to assemble in the only area capacious enough to accommodate them: the far end of the market, some two hundred yards away. The time of the meeting was propitious. Daylight would soon begin to fail. Any actions viewed from a distance of more than a few yards would take on a deceptive ambiguity.

Whether Tyler would agree to meet them alone was perhaps questionable. But Salisbury was relying on the streak of vanity he thought he had detected in the man at Mile End. If Tyler felt that victory was certain, he would be anxious to pursue negotiations alone, so that the final glory would belong to him and no one else. However, there was still a question as to whether he would come unaccompanied. Salisbury wondered if he had judged wisely in deciding to send Walworth to summon Tyler. Perhaps it would be better if he went himself, or at least rode along with Walworth, to rescue the situation if it began to get out of hand. Once again he rejected this idea. He had sensed at Mile End that Tyler disliked him, and his presence before the rebel leader at such a delicate moment might ruin everything. He would have to trust Walworth to curb his anger, and he had stressed to the Lord Mayor the importance of doing so. Walworth was crude, but not a fool, and Tyler would suspect bluntness less than polished niceties.

If Tyler came to them, the rest should go fairly easily. They would have to tempt Tyler into their midst completely divested of caution, so they could then surround him in a concealing circle and overpower him. The luring would be Thomas's task, and Salisbury had faith in his squire's ability to carry it out.

Once Tyler's death was a fact, the royal party would be able to retreat quickly. Their avenue of escape was Duck Lane, a narrow passage running between St. Bartholomew's hospital and convent, and leading directly to Aldersgate. In the city, the armed force Walworth had been able to recruit would protect them and bring the leaderless rebels under control.

He had worried about that armed force until well past noon. Without it the plan was worthless. But then Walworth had returned to Carter Lane. When he had recovered from the combination of surliness and vagueness which seemed to attack him each time he went forth in the city, he had told Salisbury that he had been able to locate most of the merchants and guild leaders who had disappeared during the early hours of London's invasion. Now, disgusted by the murders which had taken place, and fearful of what would happen if the mob went unchecked any longer, they were ready to act. They and their retainers, Walworth assured him, formed a troop of several thousand, and were concealed even now, waiting, within the walls of the city.

All was as ready as it could be. Much could still go wrong, but if it did, he would not want to live in the England that would survive. This, he felt sure, was their last chance to save the realm for sanity, justice and order.

The sound of a cadenced chant came rumbling up from the direction of Newgate. Long before he saw the rebel force, Salisbury could make out the words they were intoning: 'When Adam delved and Eve span, who was then the gentleman?' Their meaning was clear enough now. Salisbury shuddered.

The insurgent host came into sight, Tyler and Ball walking at their head, a pony ambling along between the two men. Salisbury saw Tyler look round, then, as he had anticipated, lead his men into the wide area at the other end of Smithfield.

Now they were quiet, waiting. It was time.

Salisbury nodded curtly to Walworth, watched the Lord Mayor make sure his robe was securely fastened before he nudged his horse with his knees and started across the market through the slowly deepening twilight.

The Lord Mayor, wearing a long, resplendent silken robe, had almost reached them. His features were stiff with anger, but as he came closer Tyler noticed that his eyes belied the harsh rigidity of the rest of his face. His eyes contained a soft, almost grieving, quality. The King's advisers, then, knew they had lost. It was just as well. The task of the commons would now be that much simpler.

'His Majesty the King,' said the Lord Mayor without any word of greeting, 'wishes to speak with Tyler.' The speech came out with a peculiar guttural force which Tyler had no difficulty in recognizing: he understood the nature of the rage and frustration striving beneath the apparently calm demeanour. 'His Majesty,' the Lord Mayor continued, 'is prepared to conclude matters with Tyler to the satisfaction of all.' He paused, looked away, his profile revealing even more clearly the odd compounding of vagueness and resentment. He turned his head back slowly, until his gaze was fixed directly on Tyler. 'Will you come with me now?'

Tyler hesitated, and Ball whispered to him, 'If we go together ...'

He hesitated again, looking at the priest, then said, 'Better you stay here, John. I'll know what to say. We've rehearsed it well enough. If I forget anything, I'll call.'

He turned away quickly, swung onto the pony and followed Walworth toward St. Bartholomew's.

Perhaps, he reflected in an instant of compunction, he should have taken Ball with him. But he had done the talking before, and they had agreed that he should be the one to continue negotiations. He would be able to manage quite well alone.

It occurred to him as the Lord Mayor led him across the market that perhaps they intended to separate him from the others in order to do him harm. However, he had noticed that the Lord Mayor was unarmed, and as he drew closer to the royal party, he could see there were no soldiers among the two or three score men drawn up awaiting him. Even if they were plotting some bit of treachery, did he not have his entire commons with him? If matters went wrong, the whole of the royal group could be surrounded, and destroyed or captured as he saw fit. They were in the power of the commons, and they knew it.

He laughed aloud at himself for having entertained even an instant's misgiving, and the Lord Mayor turned to look at him.

He wished he had thought of asking someone for ale before leaving his own ranks. The trip from St. Catherine's Wharf had been dusty, but he had not realized until just now how dry his mouth was.

The King and all his entourage dismounted as they rode up. Tyler had to make a considerable effort not to smile. Their attitude had altered somewhat since the meeting the day before. He was sure now that he had been right when he had told Ball that it would go well this time.

Tyler sprang from the pony, knelt before the King. Then, observing the boy's pale face, he rose and took his hand, saying, 'Brother, don't look so glum. Within a fortnight you'll have more thanks from the commons than you ever had before. You and I will be good friends.'

He dropped Richard's hand, which was too smooth and clammy for his liking. The King said, 'I granted all you asked yesterday. Why have you and the others not returned to your homes?'

'Because,' said Tyler, allowing himself to smile now, 'the charters you gave us are incomplete.'

'Incomplete,' repeated Richard, looking around at the grey-haired man.

Tyler stopped smiling. It was time to get on with it. 'We want,' he said, 'no law except that of Winchester.' He paused, and when the King did not reply, he went on. 'In other words, we demand the right to bear arms in our villages and towns to enforce the terms of the charters granted by the King.'

'We are aware,' the grey-haired man said with some acerbity, 'of the implications of the Law of Winchester.'

'Then you understand well enough,' said Tyler evenly, 'that the charters given by the King are worthless unless it is applied.'

'You dare insinuate,' said the Lord Mayor sharply, 'that the King . . .'

He stopped speaking and stared past Tyler toward the commons. Tyler waited a moment, then said, 'People are no longer to be outlawed and punished at the whim of the lords. All men in the realm are to have the same status, free and equal before the law. They are to have the right, for example, to hunt in the forests and fish in the streams, freely and without fear.' He looked at Richard. 'We shall want these points, and others to be discussed between us in detail, added to the charters before we leave London.'

Behind the King, the stained-glass windows of St. Bartholomew's glowed vividly for an instant under the last rays of sunlight. Then Smithfield lay shadowed.

Richard shook himself like a small dog. 'My Lord Salisbury . . .' he said uncertainly to the grey-haired man, who nodded, at which

246

the King rattled out a speech in a rapid monotone. 'All that you have asked for I promise readily if only it be consistent with the regality of my crown. And now let the commons return home, since their requests have been granted.'

'Not,' said Tyler firmly, 'until we are certain they have been granted.'

'We shall meet again tomorrow,' said Salisbury with sudden meekness. He glanced at the sky. 'By the time the sun sets again, I hope we may find all matters satisfactorily concluded.'

'To that I say amen.' Now, truly, they had won. Tyler was glad he had been able to bring it off alone. 'Tomorrow then. At an early hour, directly after Morrow Mass. Here?'

'Here,' said Salisbury, and the King nodded his head in emphatic agreement.

'Then I will leave you.' He moved toward his pony.

'Wait!' called Salisbury. 'Shall we not mark our agreement with a bowl of wine or ale?'

Tyler smiled. His thirst had been growing unbearable. 'Ale,' he said. 'But first some water.'

'You shall have both.' Salisbury spoke a few words over his shoulder to a young man, who hurried away toward St. Bartholomew's.

When he returned, Tyler accepted the two bowls, rinsed his mouth with the water, spat it onto the ground, took a long draught of the ale. Over the rim of the bowl he caught sight of the commons, waiting silently and patiently for him and at once felt a twinge of shame. His celebration should be with them, not with these . . .

And then he noticed that no one else was drinking.

At the same moment, the youth who had brought him the ale, having retired to his position near Salisbury, cried out, 'I know that man Tyler. I recognize him now. He's the greatest thief in all Kent.'

Tyler laughed. The lad was swaying back and forth, staring, his hair straggling down over his forehead. Probably when he had gone for ale, he had gulped a copious quantity himself, and now that it was working back out through his skin, he thought to show himself courageous before his masters. 'You've a ready tongue, boy,' Tyler called to him. 'But take care, if you don't want me to twist it for you.'

'Your mother plied a whore's trade in the streets before you were born!'

Tyler smothered his irritation. Surely they would put a stop to

247

this rogue's impertinence. But no one spoke a word of reprimand. The King and all those with him were watching Tyler, as if they thought it was up to him to reply to the insults.

'Come here,' he said to the young man, who made no move to do so, but cried out in a louder, shriller voice, 'Your father was your mother's pimp!'

'Look now . . .' Tyler began angrily, then shrugged. He would not mar the sweet perfection of victory by brawling with a drunken snotnose. He took a few steps toward his pony, turned and called out, 'See you're not in this company tomorrow. Otherwise . . .' He drew his dagger and pointed it in the lad's direction with a jocose flourish.

He saw the Lord Mayor suddenly moving toward him with a sword in his hand, snarling, 'You dare draw a weapon in the presence of the King. . . .'

Now Tyler perceived how he had been their fool.

He had almost reached his pony when he heard the sword whistle close to his ear and realized he would have to fight. He wheeled, ducked under the Lord Mayor's upraised arm and struck hard at his breast with the dagger. The point was deflected, Tyler's wrist spun, and the knife flew from his hand.

Beneath his silken robe the Lord Mayor was wearing armour.

Tyler could see the dark cavity of his assailant's mouth, opened wide with effort. He felt the first sword-stroke graze his forehead, was scarcely aware of the second cutting into his neck. In a burst of rage and chagrin he flailed at the Lord Mayor with both fists, staggered him with a blow which sent him reeling back into the path of those rushing to his assistance.

He managed to get to the pony and climb onto it, smacked the animal hard on the rump and started it toward the commons. He saw them ahead of him, still in their ranks, and tried to call out, but he could not force the sound from his throat. And now blood was streaming into his eyes, blotting out vision, but he feared if he let go the reins he would slip off the pony.

Then, incredulously, he realized he had let go the reins. His hands were dangling at his sides, and he could not control them.

He struggled to keep his balance, knowing that only the pressure of his knees against the pony was keeping him upright. He held on savagely with all his failing force.

For an instant Salisbury did not comprehend that Tyler was getting away. The rebel leader's head was so bloody it was almost impossible to make out his features, and the left side of his tunic was already sodden with blood pouring from the wound in his neck.

But with the first sound of hoofbeats it was apparent that Tyler was indeed escaping. Salisbury cried out to his companions to stop him, and himself tried to run after Tyler. The royal party, however, was stricken by such confusion, stomping and staggering about like drunkards, that Salisbury could not clear a way through them. Someone shoved him; his feet became entangled in the hem of his long robe; he went down and had difficulty in rising.

His head remained clear, and he knew their only safety lay in fleeing now, before Tyler reached the rebel ranks and informed them what had happened.

Already some of the nobles and servants had mounted their horses and, bawling with panic, were urging the animals toward the predetermined avenue of flight along Duck Lane.

Salisbury peered across the market, and his heart leaped. Tyler's pony was just now nearing the rebels' front lines, riderless.

He could not see Tyler anywhere, but this made little difference. The important thing now was that they would have the few extra moments they needed to make good their escape.

Salisbury ran for his horse, mounted, and had actually turned toward St. Bartholomew's before he remembered to look around for Richard.

When he finally saw him, fear and nausea strove together, became one in his innards.

The boy was galloping his charger with frantic speed, straight toward the solidly massed rebels.

Salisbury's body remained incapable of action. No matter how he willed it, response failed. He could only manage to sit on his horse, staring with terrible fascination, as Richard reined in before the insurgents.

He waited for what he knew must follow: the human tide surging forward to inundate the King in wrath, the last despairing note of that reedy voice drifting back through the twilight.

The mob was surging forward now. Salisbury's stomach convulsed, and bitterness shot up into his mouth. His ears roared . . . or was it the concerted fury of thousands of voices he heard? . . . he did not know. Only his vision remained startlingly, mercilessly clear.

And he did not believe what he saw. For Richard had turned and was cantering sedately to the north, toward Clerkenwell Fields.

Following him eagerly, and with no apparent hostility, was the whole great mass of rebels.

Salisbury did not know how much longer he sat without being

able to act. He did know that when he eventually recovered enough strength, it was the unearthly sound of his voice more than any physical initiative that catapulted his horse forward, in the direction of Clerkenwell.

It was by no means dark, but dusk had settled a haze over Smithfield, so that even nearby objects were a trifle distorted, creating a troubling illusion of unreality.

When Ball had seen the gleam of metal across the market, he thought it was a sword, but there was the peculiar light, and in any event his sight was so short he could not be sure. The idea that it might be a sword puzzled him and made him mildly apprehensive.

Then a voice behind him said, 'By cock, they're making our Wat a knight, they are,' and Ball's confusion increased.

He was able to discern a flurry of activity among the royal entourage, but there was obviously nothing to be disturbed about, for the commons were watching as closely as he, and he could sense no alarm from them.

Perhaps the King was indeed knighting Tyler. He thought it unlikely, but possibly Richard's advisers believed they could bribe Tyler into moderating his demands. Once more, Ball regretted not having gone along. It was not that he lacked confidence in Tyler, but the men around the King were wily, and a second person might discern a falsity which could deceive a lone negotiator.

He distinguished the form of pony and rider approaching, and the commons, who had remained remarkably silent, began to hum with excitement. Ball sighed with relief; he gnawed at a fingernail. His anxiety, this time at any rate, had been without reason.

Then he strained forward. Tyler had slipped off his pony and lay on the ground, very still, as if he were wounded. Or dead.

Surely, Ball thought, he must be mistaken. His faulty vision must have played him another trick, for instead of crying out, the men around him were snickering.

'They've made our Wat drunk, they have,' said the voice that had spoken before. 'Knighted him and made him so drunk on the King's ale he can't even sit astride a pony. . . .'

Thoroughly unsettled now, he was about to cross the field to Tyler when someone seized him by the arm and said, 'Eh, John Ball? Will we have some of that good ale by nightfall? The drink of freedom. . . .'

He wrenched himself free, took a step or two and was brought up short by the sight of the King practically upon them, his horse rearing as he tugged at the reins. 'Come with me!' Richard's thin voice cried. 'Come with me to Clerkenwell!'

And at once the commons began to move off after him. Ball could hear the King's words being repeated, passed back from man to man, until the message was lost in a welter of babbling voices.

He very nearly followed Richard himself, so compelling was the temptation, so reassuring the knowledge that the King had come to them, alone and unarmed.

But he had to know what had happened to Tyler. The notion that he was drunk was ridiculous. Perhaps the strain . . . the cumulative exhaustion . . . a moment of dizziness. . . .

It could be no more than that, for there was the King, riding in all vulnerability at the head of the cheering commons.

Ball would revive Tyler, and together they would go to Clerkenwell, where they would stand with the King, celebrating their triumph, for now they must truly have won.

When he reached Tyler, he thought he had completely lost his reason. Nothing made sense now. He was being driven through some weird and unbelievable dream which shortly had to end. But the wounds he saw were real enough. He knelt beside the body.

Tyler's eyes were closed, but he was breathing.

Ball called after the departing commons. No one replied.

He peered with longing and desperation at the gloomy shape of St. Bartholomew's far across the deserted market.

Salisbury could see Richard sitting on his horse, and even at a distance it was evident that the boy was terrified.

The rebels did not seem to know this, nor did they appear to have learned what had happened to Tyler, for they were ranged about the King in a vast, irregular semicircle, cheering lustily.

When Salisbury rode up beside Richard, his first impulse was to box his ears, but the boy was so pathetically relieved to see him that his anger melted, leaving a strange and distrait affection to mingle with fear over their predicament.

'Uncle, uncle, what have I done?'

'That,' replied Salisbury as drily as apprehension would allow, 'is something of a question.'

'I saw that fellow running away, and I remembered all you had said and I tried to think of what my father the Black Prince would have done, and before I thought further I was galloping toward them and then . . .' He stopped, breathless. Tears came into his eyes. 'And then it was too late to turn back.'

251

'Yes,' said Salisbury absently. The cheering was moderating as more and more faces turned up to them inquiringly. 'Tell them,' he said with sudden urgency, 'that they must be patient, that you'll have a most important proclamation to make to them shortly.'

Richard spoke to the people. It's fortunate, thought Salisbury, that his voice is so miserably thin under the best of circumstances; now terror and haughtiness rode the same tremulous inflection.

'And now?' asked Richard when the cheering began again.

'And now,' said Salisbury, 'we should breathe deeply of this lovely evening air for as long as their patience lasts.'

He saw Richard blanch, and regretted what he had said, for his annoyance was with himself rather than the boy. Somehow he had botched matters. The plan, which had seemed to be succeeding so brilliantly, had suddenly come apart in their hands.

When a diplomat, he reflected wryly, ventures into the alien area of physical action, he is inclined to neglect certain fundamental and laboriously-learned principles.

The flaw, he knew now, lay in his having misjudged Tyler. Salisbury thought he had gauged Tyler's temperament precisely: the impulsiveness, the volatile temper, the affinity for violence which should have drawn him into their midst after Thomas's first slanderous words. How had he managed to miscalculate so badly?

By accepting the provocation mildly, even goodnaturedly, Tyler had remained aloof, in a position where it had been virtually impossible for them to carry out their assault as planned. And Salisbury had certainly not anticipated that the plan, salvageable by hasty retreat even after Tyler's escape, would have been wrecked so irrevocably by Richard's momentary fit of bravery.

The cheering of the rebels was beginning to go sour again. He saw one reason for this. A priest in a filthy cassock was circulating through the ranks, gesturing angrily, expostulating, provoking an undercurrent of dissension wherever he walked. Eyes which had been regarding Richard with enthusiastic approval were starting to fill with doubt. Now and then Salisbury could hear an expression of derision, a sprinkling of jocular but pointed invective, a restless drumming of feet on the Clerkenwell turf.

He began to wonder if there was any purpose in putting off longer the inevitable moment of catastrophe.

As soon as Walworth recovered from Tyler's counter-assault, and saw the rebel leader rushing away on the pony, he realized that it would be foolish to pursue him. Even if he were able to overtake

Tyler and finish the job he had begun, his actions would be clearly visible from the other side of the market. He would be at the mercy of the swine, and he had no illusions about what would then ensue.

Clearly there was only one thing to do, and it had to be done quickly. He must reach St. Martin's-le-Grand, lead the force concealed there back to Smithfield and strike at the rabble while confusion was still upon them.

He had to fight free of the clutching hands of the idiots who had come along with the King and Salisbury and were now blind with terror. He rapped two or three of them sharply with his fists, and the others fell back, allowing him to reach his horse.

As he galloped along Duck Lane and swung left onto Brettone Street, he could hear the squealing voices of the nobles and the pounding of hoofbeats not far behind him and knew they had at least regained enough wit to flee.

But then there was another sound, seeming to rise from a distance, puzzling him. He swerved his horse aside just before Aldersgate in order to listen.

The nobles swarmed past, and for a few moments he could hear nothing but their shrieking and the thunder of the horses' hooves. He cursed them ferociously, but they did not even notice him. Finally they vanished through the gateway.

He had not been mistaken in what he thought he had heard: the din of a cheering multitude. Only now it seemed to be coming from even further north, toward the Priory of St. John.

Walworth considered for a moment, then decided it would be wise to investigate. He turned north on Aldersgate Street, skirted St. Bartholomew's and the raw new buildings of the Charterhouse. Then, as he was veering west along Pardon Churchyard, he pulled his horse up abruptly.

Richard, alone and apparently in no danger, was riding ahead of the mass of exuberant rebels, leading them toward Clerkenwell.

Walworth did not understand exactly what was happening, but one thing was evident. Since the rebels were following Richard with such compliant fervour, they could not yet know of the attack on Tyler.

If Tyler was still alive, he must be sought and killed. If he was dead, Walworth had to find his body.

He turned back toward Smithfield.

The two friars who had helped Ball bring the wounded man into the hospital withdrew, and a few moments later Tyler opened his eyes.

First there was fear in them, then a fierce striving anger, and he tried to get up. Ball restrained him easily, despairing as he felt how little strength was left in the massive body.

Tyler stopped struggling. Into his eyes now welled a calm acceptance, and this Ball found hardest to bear.

'Wat,' he said, 'we'll . . .'

But he did not really know what he had intended to say, and Tyler smiled sadly. 'I wanted to do it alone,' he said. 'The power . . .' He gasped. A line of fresh blood sprang out along the wound on his neck. Ball dipped a cloth into the earthen basin beside the pallet, wrung the water out of it and applied it to the wound. 'I didn't know, John. Even when I rode to meet . . . I do now . . . when we had won, I wanted to be . . .' He smiled again, painfully. 'Once you've led people this way . . . swayed them, controlled them . . . the King's right hand . . .' His smile was a grimace now. 'Forgive me, John.'

'I, too,' whispered Ball. 'In Canterbury . . .'

But Tyler's eyes were closed again.

If this man dies, thought Ball, my own life will be at an end.

Tyler, without opening his eyes, said, 'How does it happen . . . the more violence . . . killing . . . the closer I felt to her . . . in Maidstone . . . to know her as I did then . . . I want her . . .' He opened his eyes. 'Tell her. Tell her, John.'

'Rest now.'

'We could have won. You could still . . .'

'Rest.'

'Priests,' said Tyler, his voice growing stronger. 'It takes them so long to understand anything. I'm going to die, John. Hurry and do whatever it is priests have to do, before I . . .' His breath rattled. Ball's heart faltered, but after a moment Tyler began breathing more easily.

'Wat   '

'Now, John!'

His eyes grew wild, gyrating out of kilter. Ball said quietly, 'Repeat after me . . . My God, my God, my mercy and my refuge . . .'

'My God, my God, my mercy and my refuge . . .'

'Thee I desire, to Thee I flee, to Thee I hasten to come . . .' He heard himself tracing the words of the prayer, marvelling at the calmness of his voice, pausing at intervals so that Tyler could say the words after him. 'Despise me not, placed in this tremendous crisis, be merciful to me in these my great necessities. I cannot redeem myself by my own works . . .'

Tyler's voice was growing fainter. 'I trust more in thy mercies than I distrust my evil deeds. My faults, my great faults . . .' His eyes closed, flickered open, and slowly closed again, as if an enormous weight were forcing them shut. He lay still.

'My brother . . .' said Ball. And then his old enemy, weariness, pressing close in comradeship now, would not allow him to say more. He took Tyler's limp hand in his.

He might even have slept, he did not know, but the voices echoing from somewhere along the hospital's stone corridors startled him, and he blinked around the bare room in which he sat. He recognised the tones of one of the friars who had helped him carry Tyler, shrill and womanish, crying, 'Shame, shame for speaking . . .' And another voice, gruff, peremptory, which Ball suddenly realized belonged to the Lord Mayor. 'The master's chamber . . . where?' And the friar again, angrily, 'Shame come to you for speaking . . .'

The sounds were drawing closer: the shuffling footsteps, the mingling confusion of disjointed words.

Ball had thought he did not care about living. Now he found he still did. And Tyler was past help or harm.

He got to his feet, stumbled, saved himself from falling only with tremendous exertion, recalled with a queer desperate kind of humour that Tyler had once said to him, 'With all your clumsiness, John, I'll die before you.' And now he turned to Tyler's body and blurted angrily, 'You did, why did you . . .'

He ran from the chamber, darted around a corner in the passage, catching a glimpse as he did of the two friars, and the Lord Mayor carrying an unsheathed sword, just entering the other end of the corridor.

Then he stopped, horrified. For Tyler's voice had rung out, crying fearfully, 'Isabella!'

Even now, he thought, even now I've failed you.

But he lurched ahead, peering down the murky passage for a way out.

Walworth left St. Bartholomew's, having accomplished what he came to do, carrying the grisly proof under his robe. Behind him he could still hear the one friar crying, 'Shame, shame,' to the other who would still be smiling as he had been when Walworth first addressed him, a scabby grin reflecting both fear and self-righteousness.

It had not taken him long to locate Tyler. The trail of blood led along the dusty earth from the centre of the market to the hospital steps, and the friars had been hovering near the entrance.

Walworth made his way at once to St. Martin's, where a restless troop of merchants, guild leaders, retainers and assorted mercenaries were roaming the enclosed grounds of the college and the church. Sir Robert Knolles, in whose charge he had left them, had been having some difficulty keeping them under control. They had heard the jubilant shouts of the rebels, and some of the nobles who had been at Smithfield had brought back weird and frightening accounts of what took place there. 'I had to threaten,' said Knolles in his mild, casual tone, 'that I would kill the first man who attempted to leave.' He cocked his head to one side and added drily, 'It was not necessary. There is no one here that brave.'

Walworth sent him through the darkening churchyard to collect the force. Two aldermen greeted Walworth, then also stood by their horses, waiting.

'I told you the Lord Mayor would return before nightfall,' said Carlyll. 'He said he would be back to get us and we would destroy . . .'

'Wipe out,' corrected Fresh in a clear, piping voice.

'Wipe out the rabble . . .'

'Scum. It was scum he said this time. "I'll be back, and we'll march together and wipe out the scum." That's what he said.'

'You're exactly right,' agreed Carlyll. 'I'd forgotten. That's just what he said.'

The sky was assuming the blue-grey presaging darkness when they rode out of St. Martin's and turned toward Aldersgate. Two men rushed forward to intercept them. Walworth first recognized Sibley, then heard Horne crying, 'Lock the gates! Lock the gates and stay inside! The King has been killed . . .'

Sibley, looking up at Walworth, seized Horne's shoulder The two alderman shrank away when they became aware of what the Lord Mayor was carrying. Walworth regarded them contemptuously as he passed, wondering, however, if they might not be telling the truth about the King. Some time had passed since he had seen Richard with the rebels, and though they had been cheering then . . .

He exchanged a glance with Knolles and galloped his horse ahead. The walls of St. Bartholomew's first and then the Charterhouse reverberated with the sound of hoofbeats. They crossed No Man's Land, and as they topped a small rise near the Priory of St. John Walworth saw the rebels spread out before them, forming an enormous semi-circle.

In the centre were Richard and Salisbury.

256

Walworth gritted his teeth and rode forward. Only when he was well under way did he experience a small, niggling doubt over what they were doing.

Swine the rebels were, and leaderless now. But there were archers among them, and pikemen. And they outnumbered Walworth's untested troops by at least three to one.

Straw was so angry he could not remain still.

Abel had watched the priest as they all grew more and more restless, and Richard, prompted by the nobleman at his side, had spoken from time to time, telling them to be patient. Straw had first paced back and forth irritably, then had begun waving his arms about and shouting. When, at one point, the King and his companion had seemed about to ride away, Straw's temper had risen to frenzy. Now, a little calmer, he was still stomping his feet and shrilling imprecations, not at the King, but up at the grey-haired man, who was keeping his head carefully averted from Straw.

'Can't blame him,' Abel said to Roger. 'Even high up on a horse's back he's bound to catch some spray from Straw. Hardly the kind of cooling off I'd enjoy, even at the end of a long hot day.'

'Must you make a jest about everything?' Roger asked coldly.

'Only,' replied Abel, hurt, 'about the most serious things.'

He was relieved when he saw the band of horsemen approaching. Ball and Tyler would be among them. Straw's grating harangue would cease. The celebration would begin, and by dark they'd all be gloriously mellow with a jug of brown ale apiece. By tomorrow, or the next day at the latest, he'd be back in the village.

Tonight, he decided, he'd go to the Bishopsgate. It was mad to think she'd be willing as she had said she'd be, even more mad to think of her coming with him, but still he'd go to Bishopsgate. Most of the day he'd managed to relegate her to the fringes of his mind, but now he could think of her again: of the golden hair with the lovely narrow streak of grey and the slender body and the wonderfully untrammelled laughter and her desire calling out to his. Perhaps, if not for always, at least for tonight. . . .

The leading horseman was the Lord Mayor. He galloped up beside Richard, and the others coming behind him spread out in long sinuous ranks to either side.

Abel wondered at the sudden silence which fell over those nearest the King. He saw the reason as the Lord Mayor held the pike high in the air.

He thought the great grieving cry that rose at once had come from other throats and that his own anguish was soundless. Then, as the lament began to die away, he could hear his voice wailing like that of a wounded animal, and the pain inside him grew unbearable.

All around him, in that vast multitude, men were dropping to their knees. Roger on the ground beside him was weeping like a small child. His own legs gave way.

Only Jack Straw, raging and exhorting, still remained standing. He did not even seem to be aware that two men in armour had seized him, bound his hands behind his back, and were now leading him away.

Richard said at once, waspishly, his face crinkling, 'Kill them, kill them all!'

And Walworth, still holding the gory symbol of victory aloft, grumbled some words of agreement.

But Sir Robert Knolles said mildly, 'No, Your Majesty. Most of the wretches do not even know why they're here. Besides . . .' He glanced around, his eyes gleaming briefly, alertly, before dimming to their customary vague and weary indifference. 'There's no fight in them now, but if we rouse them to desperation . . .' He looked at Salisbury. 'My lord?'

'Tell them,' Salisbury said to Richard, 'to disperse at once and return to their homes.' And when the King continued to look at him, Salisbury murmured, 'Sire . . .'

He was now certain the rebels would obey the King's order, and they did, rising from their knees and departing, first only a few at a time, then in rapidly increasing numbers. Since the first agonised shriek when they had seen Tyler's head, the only sounds of resistance had come from the filthy-cassocked priest, who had now been pounded insensible a little distance away from the royal group.

Salisbury should have felt elated. Instead he found himself struggling against a terrible, devouring emptiness. He was sure he was about to come down with a chill.

'Walworth,' Richard said suddenly, 'dismount.'

'Sire?'

The King unhooked his robe, drew his sword, touched it to Walworth's shoulder as he gave him the accolade of knighthood.

Walworth flushed with pleasure. When Richard pronounced the words, 'Sir William,' the Lord Mayor kissed the King's hand, hawked, spat, mounted again and retrieved the pike bearing Tyler's head from Salisbury.

Less than a quarter of the rebels were left when they decided it was safe to depart from Clerkenwell. Safe, but also necessary, for darkness was almost upon them.

Richard chattered blithely on the ride back to Carter Lane. They would have a feast that evening, he decided. He would command the cooks to concoct a special subtlety, with lettering in pink sugar, commemorating his deliverance. 'And I shall wear my coronation robes. Shall I not, my uncle?' He pointed his chin defiantly at Salisbury, who forced himself to smile and replied, 'Of course, sire, if you wish.'

Joan was waiting in the entrance hall of the wardrobe. She and Richard exchanged a long, meltingly affectionate look, oblivious of the nobles who stood near, simpering and bowing. 'My son,' she said, 'I've been in pain and anguish for you all this day.'

'I know, madam,' replied Richard, taking her hand. 'I know it well. But now rejoice and praise God, for today I have recovered my heritage that was lost, and the realm of England also.'

'My good Lord Salisbury,' said Joan, turning to him, 'how pleasant to see you.'

'Madam . . .' he began, then, before he could stop himself, 'Perhaps later . . . when I have made myself more presentable, the Princess Joan would receive . . .'

Her grey eyes flicked over him. She still held Richard's hand as she said, 'Not tonight, my lord, I'm far too weary. Perhaps to-morrow, or the next day. One of my ladies will inform you . . .'

His stomach began to roil.

He turned and saw Elizabeth among the courtiers, watching him, a tight smile on her lips.

24

WHEN Knolles called Salisbury away from the King's festive table that night, the Earl was more than willing to leave.

He had eaten a little of the crab poached in ale and wanted no more, but good manners required that he should submit to having each successive dish placed before him and endure its presence while the others ate. When Knolles appeared beside him, Salisbury was trying not to gag at the sight of a mound of boiled pork swimming in a fatty sauce of red wine, garlic, cinnamon and raisins. And Elizabeth was whispering maliciously in his ear, 'Truly, William, you do look ill. I mean, you'll perish if you don't eat more. This pork . . .'

He fled gratefully in Knolles' company.

Together, escorted by a score of the mercenaries with torches, they rode up round St. Paul's and along the Cheapside. There was considerable brawling, most of it between Londoners. They broke up a dozen bloody conflicts by the simple method of riding their horses through the vortex of a disturbance, then passing on, pursued each time by a flood of rich London obscenities.

There did not seem to be many of the rebels from the shires about. Most of those they saw looked at them with cowed and baffled expressions, pressing close to the walls of buildings to let them pass. Yet in the eyes of some lay such virulent hatred that Salisbury felt himself growing uneasy again.

He said to Knolles, 'Don't molest them unless they cause trouble. Complete success depends on their leaving London peacefully. But watch them well.'

'That's why I called you away, my lord,' said Knolles quietly. 'I felt you should see what I have seen. They seem peaceful enough now, but . . .' He shrugged, and bitterness edged his gentle voice. 'I'm an old man and live too much with old men's fears. There was a time when I would have paid little heed to a few surly looks or gestures.' He twisted his head to one side and spoke more mildly. 'But then I would not have noticed the wretches' despair, either. Everything has its price, does it not, my lord? From the castles I once won in France to the victory we claimed today. And sometimes we do not know the price until much too late.'

Salisbury was in no mood for philosophy. 'You'll watch them well and report any change in their present temper?'

'I'll watch them.'

'I had thought,' mused Salisbury, 'that when we disposed of Tyler . . . Now . . .'

'I had nearly forgotten, my lord. The priest fellow, the noisy one who sprayed and foamed, we've locked him in the Wardrobe dungeon. Jack Straw, he calls himself. What names the beggars have!'

Salisbury sighed. 'We'll have to behead him, of course. Perhaps tomorrow. And knowing he's to die, perhaps he'll talk. If we

260

know whatever he knows, it may help us to prevent further trouble.' He sighed again. 'Somewhere there must be a land without strife and bloodshed.'

'I've heard, my lord, that there's a part of Ireland where no one ever dies.'

'That wasn't what I meant,' said Salisbury.

When they returned to the Wardrobe, Walworth was just entering the courtyard, and Salisbury realized he had not seen him since their return from Clerkenwell. The Lord Mayor had turned distrait again, and this time, knowing he was risking a rebuff, Salisbury took him aside to ask quietly, 'Can I help?'

Walworth regarded him blankly for a moment, then said in a listless voice, 'My wife . . . she's not in my house . . . she's not been there since . . .' He stopped, shaking his head.

'My dear fellow,' said Salisbury. 'I had no idea. I assumed she was safely lodged with one of your merchant associates. My dear fellow . . .' Then he too stopped speaking, distressed by his own sterile, stilted phrases.

Walworth spat morosely. Salisbury told him about Straw, and ended by saying, 'We should question him, Sir William.' The Lord Mayor revived a little. They procured torches and the keys to the dungeon from Knolles and walked together through the narrow musty passageways beneath the Wardrobe until they reached the cell in which the priest was confined.

Straw growled and threw up his hands against the sudden intrusion of light. When he lowered them, Salisbury saw that his face was blotched and swollen from the blows he had received.

'You're going to die,' said Walworth.

'*You're* going to die,' croaked Straw.

Walworth lunged at him, flinging the priest back against the wall. Straw glared at them, eyes gleaming in the torchlight.

Salisbury took a step forward, a question on his lips, but Straw spoke first, in a low, even, matter-of-fact voice. 'We'll capture the King,' he said, 'and all of you who advise and serve him. We'll take the King and force him to pass sentence of death on all the lords. He'll also give his seal to government of the commons in each district. Then, when he's served our purpose, we'll kill him and all of you.'

'You see?' said Walworth, turning to Salisbury. 'You see what they intended? We should have slaughtered every one of them while we had the chance.'

Salisbury was unable to reply.

'Then,' said Straw, continuing in the same discursive tone, 'we'll kill all the clergy: bishops, abbots, rectors. Everyone but the wandering friars, who will be the voice of God in England.'

Walworth's voice rose. 'You see?'

'Then,' said Straw, 'we shall . . .' He broke off, looking at them with a strange brooding smile.

Salisbury's heart was thudding heavily.

Suddenly Straw was shaking with laughter. His knees buckled, and he slid down the damp, crusty wall onto the floor. He struggled to speak, 'Black bile,' he gasped. 'Black bile . . .' Then he was convulsed once more, rolling about on the floor. His wild, choked mirth filled the cell.

'He's mad,' breathed Walworth. 'The fellow's mad.'

'Yes,' said Salisbury, immeasurably relieved.

But after they had left Straw, the priest's words continued to haunt him, and the relief he had felt gave way to troubled reflection.

Abel was not accustomed to being stunned, incapable of feeling. To him it seemed a condition worse than death, a half-death in which life lay somewhere out of reach, elusive and frightening. But now his stupefaction, which had lain around him with the dull oppressiveness of thunderheads, was beginning to break up. Abel was heartened, and found himself welcoming the pain of returning awareness.

They were walking purposelessly through the dark streets of London, he and his fellow-villagers, now and then encountering others of the commons and passing them by without a greeting.

Once the grey-haired noble who had been with the King at Clerkenwell rode by in the company of a band of soldiers. Abel watched their passage indifferently, but when he glanced at Roger's face he was horrified by the expression of hatred he saw there. At the same time he was envious, for Roger had at least recovered the power to feel, if in fact he had ever lost it.

Perhaps, he thought, if Tyler had not rescued him at the burning Savoy Palace, he would not have been so shocked by his death. But there was more than that: the moment when he and Tyler had reached their wordless understanding had sealed a bond of brotherhood between them, and though it had neither been defined nor pursued, Abel knew it was the deprivation of this he was suffering from.

'If we leave now,' said Nicholas, 'we'll be there this time tomorrow.'

Robert's mouth opened and closed. 'We'll be fined,' he said.

'The bailiff will fine us for running away. If he doesn't kill us . . .'

'They won't kill us,' said Nicholas. 'Someone has to work their land and brew their beer and pay them tallage.'

'But they will fine us,' wailed Robert. 'They'll take away all our crops for years and years . . .'

'Why go back at all?' snapped Roger.

Nicholas rubbed his arms. 'What else?'

'We can still fight,' replied Roger in a low, angry voice.

Robert moved away from him with a small terrified cry.

'Fight,' said Abel softly. 'The little pisser with a pike of words. They'll hoist your head soon enough on a real pike.'

Roger stared at him. 'You're going back? I'll never set foot in that village again. Not as a serf.'

Abel shrugged, and Old Elias, who had been excessively quiet, said unctuously, 'Some of us have families to support.'

The words and tone, conjuring up familiar images, set Abel's heart beating with an absurd, perverse joy. Could it be the same, then, as it had been before? Not good, but not bad, either. The sweat of a day's work in fields where his father and grandfather had sweated, the inn in the evening, Peg's favours lightly given and lightly received, the unchanging rhythm of season in season out, the sadness of passing time breeding buffoonery . . .

'Yes,' he said, addressing his words to all, but meaning them for Roger, 'I'm going home.'

More soldiers passed, eyeing them suspiciously, and they walked faster, seeking the street which led to London Bridge and the Kentish highroad.

Roger, hard-faced, dropped away from them without saying farewell. Abel forced himself not to look back.

Then he heard Roger's voice far behind them, calling his name. He smiled with relief for until now he had been sure his friend had meant what he said, and they would not be seeing each other again. Now Roger had relented. Abel would go back to him, and after a suitably stubborn argument Roger would allow himself to be persuaded. Life would indeed be the same: not good, not bad, but the same as before.

He told the others to go ahead and retraced his steps. Though his eyes were used to the darkness, he could not find Roger at first, and would have passed him by had his friend not called again, softly, but with urgent entreaty in his voice.

Abel saw him standing in a pool of shadow formed by an over-hanging solar and the indistinct outlines of a huge heap of refuse.

He was not alone. Leaning against the wall, his head lolling back and forth as he struggled to remain upright, was John Ball.

Abel felt a quick surge of irritation. If he had kept on walking, if he had ignored Roger's call . . . But he could not have done that any more than he could now forsake the priest. He found himself thinking smoothly, sensing that Ball would not be safe in London, reasoning that it would solve no problems to take him back to their village. And all the while he was resenting the presence of the man before him.

Then Ball looked directly at him. Even in the darkness Abel felt the frightful force of the priest's suffering and understood for the first time the full extent of his own.

He put his shoulder under one of Ball's arms and motioned Roger to take the other. They began to walk, and strangely it was Ball, half-fainting and with stumbling steps, who seemed to be leading them.

They had only been walking a few moments when they saw torchlight moving up on them from behind. Ball cried out fearfully, and with suddenly reviving strength darted away from them into an alleyway. Abel was about to follow, when he saw that the men overtaking them were not soldiers but a dozen Essexmen, who told him they were on their way out of London.

He sent Roger after Ball, and they joined the group. The priest was stronger now, capable of walking unsupported. But Abel, watching his face and continuing to observe the torment there, felt a wave of vicious and totally unfamiliar anger sweep over him. He slammed his fist into his palm several times before it passed, and through tears of rage saw Ball looking at him with a frightened, wondering expression.

After a while the priest said in a voice so low and uncertain that Abel had to strain to hear him, 'Perhaps . . . if we had killed . . .'

The Essexmen were looking for Aldgate, but none of them knew exactly where it was. They found the wall and followed it eastward, knowing this would eventually bring them right. The gates they came upon stood open, and as they passed through, Abel suddenly realized where they were, and that it was not Aldgate.

His throat went dry. He scarcely dared to look as the outline of the chestnut tree grew in the glow from the torches.

25

THE morning after the defeat of the rebels he was watching some servants carry damaged furniture and bits of debris out of the White Tower when a suave voice said, 'My good Lord Salisbury . . .'

He turned to see Courtenay regarding him mournfully.

'You're back,' said Salisbury tonelessly.

Courtenay sighed. His fleshy face creased. 'I hastened to return the instant I heard the news.'

'Which news?' asked Salisbury.

The Bishop's tone was bland. 'That the rebels had entered London, of course. A great pity that urgent business took me away just before . . . and news does travel so very slowly, you know. I only heard of the misfortunes the day before yesterday . . . poor Sudbury, poor Hales . . . and I came back as quickly as I could.'

'Your Grace,' Salisbury said icily, 'has a most fortunate sense of timing.'

Courtenay put his hand on Salisbury's arm. 'I can understand that you should be a trifle resentful. Believe me, I shall regret always not having been able to share the burden all of you carried so admirably. I understand His Majesty acquitted himself with particular courage. Had it not been for his bravery . . .'

'Your Grace would still be away.' He knew he was speaking rashly, that Courtenay was provoking him, but as usual when he first encountered the man, he could do little about it.

Courtenay's hand tightened on his arm. 'Salisbury,' he said reproachfully. Then his tone became brisk, 'Well. We shall have work to do.'

'Shall we?'

'Indeed! My poor dear predecessor Sudbury relied heavily on you. I trust I shall be able to count on the same loyalty, or perhaps just a tiny bit more – in certain areas, that is.'

Salisbury stared at him without speaking.

'Yes, my lord,' said Courtenay, smiling at his astonishment. 'You see, I have only now come from conferring with His Majesty and the Princess. Of course, this is most confidential, since the announcement should come from the King.'

Salisbury managed to say, 'May I offer congratulations, my lord Chancellor.'

'Thank you,' said Courtenay, still keeping his hand on Salisbury's arm, 'but we shall reserve the amenities. As I have said, there is much to be done. You will forgive me, but I feel that if I had been in London . . . well, let us not trouble ourselves too deeply over that. The crisis is past, for the time being. We should take steps to ensure it does not arise again. The ringleaders must be sought through every shire and put to death.' He moved his hand slowly, absently, along Salisbury's sleeve. 'You will forgive me again, dear Lord Salisbury, but I find it a trifle shocking that John Ball was not apprehended at once. Doubtless by now he has left London. Shocking, to say the least.'

And of course, thought Salisbury, the most shocking part of all is that he's right.

Walworth slowed the progress of his horse across the Moor, hesitating between the Moorgate and the Bishopsgate, finally entering the city through the latter.

Just before he reached the gate he passed a large chestnut tree, saw a partridge and considered flying the peregrine at it. But he had already flown her at half a dozen grouse, and she had acquitted herself beautifully. Neither her skill nor her ferocity had been in the least diminished by her unsettled existence over the past week.

He had found the other hawks in sad condition. One of them, the merlin, was dead of starvation. The rest were feeble, but they would recover.

He was particularly pleased with the falcon's performance. It had done much to take the sting out of a troubling morning. Troubling in one sense, yet happy enough in another.

Margaret was back. She had been sitting at the table in the common room when he returned from the Wardrobe, and had greeted him calmly, casually, as if nothing untoward had occurred since they had last seen each other. He had waited for her to say where she had been, and when she did not, he had told her of his being knighted. She had seemed genuinely pleased, and again he had waited for her to tell him what he wished to know. Margaret had fallen silent, regarding him in her composed, grave fashion, and he had not been able to ask her the all-important question.

His weakness had infuriated him, and when he saw some of the servants creeping back into the house, he had stormed at them. Then he had gone to fetch the falcon.

He rode down Bishopsgate Street, and when he had almost reached the Cornhill, he saw Courtenay coming toward him, beautifully robed in a red velvet habit with pink shoulder-straps, mounted on a giant grey charger.

The Bishop said at once, smiling, 'I understand congratulations are in order, Sir William.'

Walworth did not reply, and Courtenay said, still smiling, 'Come now, Sir William, an earldom is not yet impossible by any means, though it will probably take somewhat longer to achieve than it might have otherwise. However . . .'

'You got back in perfect time,' said Walworth.

Courtenay continued smiling, but his eyes were shot with anger. 'I must confess,' he said, 'that I find such talk a trifle tiresome. First Lord Salisbury, now you. I would suggest you wait a little longer before pursuing the subject. Then, when you have heard the news, if you still wish . . .'

He stopped, and the anger left his eyes. 'But why should I be cross with you, Sir William? And I am not. Indeed I am not! I'm very happy for you. I was pleased to hear of your having been knighted. And . . .' He jockeyed his horse until his lips were close to Walworth's ear. Then he said softly, 'And I am most happy to hear that you have recovered your wife.'

26

THE idea began gaining favour with them even during the first few days, in their encampment among the yews and oaks of Epping Forest.

There were more than a thousand of them, chiefly Essexmen, but the ranks, if one could still apply a military term to such a bedraggled company, also contained a number of men from Kent.

When they heard that the King and his Council were at Waltham Abbey, less than five miles away, they argued the matter more seriously. Still, no one really thought of pursuing the idea beyond the discussion stage. Talk was a way of passing time, and it helped to divert the conflict which flared up sporadically between Essexmen and Kentishmen.

John Ball did much in the beginning to discourage the line of action they were considering. 'The charters,' he said, 'are worthless. They meant little when they were first sealed. Now . . .' He shrugged.

But the notion had enough enthusiastic adherents to keep the issue alive. The gist of their reasoning was that the King would prefer a peaceful commons to one in continual ferment. While he might not ratify all the terms of the Mile End charters, possibly he would agree to certain concessions, and even a few were better than none.

Eventually Ball changed his mind. One afternoon, nearly a week after their arrival in the forest, he sat for a long time, alone, preoccupied, looking down at the pike he had found on the highroad outside London, and kept near him at all times now. Abel, watching him, noticed how the priest's face had altered. The deepset eyes harboured a haunted, flickering anger; the mouth was hard and twisted; now and then a muscle in his cheek convulsed violently. Toward evening, Ball approached one of the larger groups congregated on the bank of the stream running through the camp. 'Perhaps . . .' he said thoughtfully. 'We can lose nothing by trying.'

'Except our lives,' Abel murmured.

Ball heard him. 'Are they so important now?' he asked harshly.

'On days when we eat berries and roots, no,' Abel replied. 'But the roast boar the day before yesterday gave me the peculiar feeling there was still a little blood in my veins. Now if there were only a drop or two of ale to quicken the flow . . .' He sang, with appropriate gestures, the rhyming little plea, 'Back and side, go bare, go bare, both hand and foot go cold. But belly, God send thee good ale enough, whether it be new or old.' Ball smiled wearily.

The priest's support crystallized the feeling that they should act at once. Two of the Mile End charters, grimy and tattered now, were brought out and read over. The encampment selected a delegation of five, Abel among them, to journey to Waltham the next morning and request an audience with the King.

Roger expressed a desire to go along, but there was immediate and vociferous objection from the Essexmen. One of them, a squat, bristle-faced fellow, said loudly, 'Bad enough that we send one Kentishman to represent us. Two might talk us all into chains.'

Roger's fair skin mottled, and he crouched to spring at the Essexman, who reached for his knife. Abel jumped between the two, seized them and held them apart while he sang a paraphrase of his ale song: 'Essex and Kent, be bent, be bent, but neither the twain be broke. And nothing mends a bend so quick as a hearty, happy soak . . .'

He shoved the pair of them into the brook, and when they turned on him, spluttering, he jumped in himself and kept splashing them until their anger cooled amid the general laughter.

Later in the evening, Ball also talked of going with them to

Waltham. Abel told him bluntly, 'They may have our heads, but they'll get small use from them. Yours has a special attraction. Your friends prefer to see it remain on your shoulders.'

Ball muttered to himself and chewed on a thumbnail. But in the morning, when they departed, he remained in camp.

They made their way through the forest, passing under sheltering oaks, detouring around thick growths of hawthorn and holly, and finally came out into the hot sun. With some trepidation they walked along the sloping street which wound through Waltham and approached the Abbey gateway. A soldier in armour listened to their request, then went away without replying.

They settled down to wait. Noon came and went. By mid-afternoon they were hungry, thirsty and apprehensive.

Then they saw the King coming, accompanied by the Lord Mayor, the grey-haired nobleman and a well-fleshed churchman in a splendid blue habit. A large company of soldiers trailed after them, and suddenly helmeted heads began appearing at the windows of the two watch-towers flanking the gate.

'If they mean to impress us,' said Abel to the man next to him, 'I think it most likely they'll succeed.'

The King and his advisers rode through the larger of the two pointed archways and halted, looking down silently at the five emissaries, who dropped to their knees.

Somewhere in the cloister a pair of birds began to sing. Abel, to still his uneasiness, raised his head and looked past the gateway at the square Abbey tower topped with the four tiny turrets. The birdsong ceased; there was a distant whir of wings, and the sunlit stone face of the tower was momentarily dappled by streaking shadows.

He looked back at the King. Richard's nostrils were quivering. The Lord Mayor hawked and spat, and the fleshy churchman put a hand on his shoulder. The grey-haired man smiled faintly, as if at some private joke. Then Richard began to speak.

'Miserable men,' he said, his face crinkling with distaste, 'hateful to both land and sea, unworthy even to live, you ask to be put on an equality with your lords. You deserve to be punished with the vilest death.'

Abel felt the men on either side of him stir fearfully and thought: indeed we do deserve it for being foolish enough to come here.

'However,' continued Richard in his high, childish voice, 'because you have come in the character of messengers, you shall not die at once . . .' He paused, and the man on Abel's right gasped. 'You shall live so you may take this answer to your fellows.'

I believe, thought Abel, we've already had our reply; but then, a King may repeat himself if he wishes.

One of the Essexmen made a motion to depart, and the Lord Mayor called out, 'You there . . . the King is speaking!' The man sank back shivering to the ground.

The churchman handed Richard a scroll which he unrolled and began to read. 'Serfs you were, and serfs you are. You shall remain in bondage far viler than any you have ever known. For so long as we live and rule by God's grace over this kingdom, we shall use our sense, our strength, and our property to place you in such slavery as will make you an example to posterity. Those who come after you and may be like you will always have your misery before their eyes, as if they were looking into a mirror. They will have reason to curse you, and they will fear to do things like those you have done.'

He rolled up the scroll carefully and handed it to the churchman, who used it to probe the dimple in his chin as his lips developed an oily smile.

Suddenly Richard screamed venomously, 'Serfs! Miserable pigs! Foul dirt . . .' and burst into tears.

The Lord Mayor began to laugh; the grey-haired man started toward the King, his expression appalled. But the churchman's sleek smile neither deepened nor waned, nor did he so much as turn his head.

Abel and his four companions scrambled to their feet and ran as quickly as they could toward the Waltham market-place and the forest which began just beyond.

27

'THE reason I shall never go home,' Roger said gravely as they worked at chaining carts together around the camp, 'is that I want to be free.'

'The only thing you've ever been free with is Barbara,' said Abel, 'and if Elias hasn't killed her by now, you'll still find her in the village.'

Roger brushed his words aside. 'Before I left, I thought I knew what I wanted. I didn't know why, except . . .' He stopped, frowning, and swatted at a swarm of gnats hovering above them in the twilight.

Abel dropped the chain he was looping about a wagon-tongue and put his hands on Roger's shoulders. 'If you were a clown like me, boy, it wouldn't hurt so.' Then he said, 'What a bloody lie that is.'

'I feel,' said Roger, 'now I've had a taste of it, that I've never known anything else but freedom. And now that we can hope again . . .'

Now that they could hope again.

Abel looked around the encampment. The original thousand had more than trebled. Four hundred had joined them that morning, and they had decided then to move to a more central location. The choice had been a forested area just northeast of Billericay called, for some unknown reason, Noisy Wood.

The King's rejection of their request had been the turning point. Their anger, blazing progressively brighter these four days since Waltham, had burned away lethargy and annealed a new spirit. Groups of them had been roaming the countryside gathering those who, like themselves, had not gone home but had been uncertain what to do.

They were certain now. With more joining them every day, they would soon have a force with which they could challenge the King's vicious decree, fling it back in his sly face. At least this was what Ball had been saying. This time, the priest would mutter grimly, there will be no childlike negotiations, no trusting acceptance, no chance for regal treachery. This time they would win, and there was only one way to achieve victory. Ball would thrust his pike into the soft forest earth, his eyes glowing with a wrathful light. . . .

An Essexman came through the dusk to tell Abel there were only enough carts to barricade the camp on three sides.

'Tomorrow,' Abel said. 'Tomorrow we'll have enough carts to finish the job.'

'And soon,' murmured Roger, 'let's hope we have enough men.'

Ball woke in the faint grey glimmer preceding dawn and immediately felt around him on the ground for his pike. His hand closed tightly over the metal tip, cold to the touch, and he thought: soon you will speak, soon, for dead Wat and live commons.

His bones ached from lying on the damp earth. He stretched, and rubbed his legs to ease the pain. Not another winter, he thought, I won't be able to endure another winter of this.

He remembered the winter before, his wanderings and his appearances before the people. What a fool he had been then, how naïve

271

his plans and fears. To spurn violence, to scruple over its use against adversaries who had no such qualms. . . .

Not another winter, he thought again, and this time it was a promise.

An owl hooted, and Abel Threder, lying nearby, laughed in his sleep, then mumbled, 'I'm a clown, my lady. . . .'

The wind of dawn brushed through the treetops. He thought he heard Wat's voice, the bass notes thick and muffled as they had been that night on the wharf when he had looked down at his hands and said: I've begun to believe the way you believe about killing. . . .

How miserably he had failed him in every way: exerting his own devious influence against the bright clean strength, crippling and corrupting it. . . .

An odd vibration rose against the breeze, fell away again. He strained to hear, his heart beating rapidly, knew it was not Tyler's voice he had heard, or any other figmented sound, but the soft thudding of horses' hooves approaching from downwind.

He cried out, grasped the pike and struggled to his feet. Some of the others around him were doing the same, peering about in sleepy confusion.

But not nearly enough of them were up and prepared before the soldiers were upon them in a welter of shouted commands and whinnying horses.

The attackers, both horsemen and foot soldiers, were using swords and lances, laying about them in a whirling slaughter, shrieking as the blood lust took hold of them, their own voices rousing them to greater carnage.

Ball saw a swordsman bearing down on the fair-haired boy, the friend of Abel, who was fumbling frantically with an arrow, striving vainly to fit it into his bow. He could see the soldier's gaze fixed on his intended victim and knew he could intercept the man's running charge. He gripped his pike tightly, raised it high . . .

. . . And found he could not strike. He stood motionless, powerless, as the swordsman rushed by.

Abel paused at the edge of the clearing, looking around carefully to make sure the last of the soldiers had gone.

Perhaps, he thought, he should not have left Ball, but the priest had promised to stay where he was.

The sun was barely up, but the air was already warm over what had been their camp, and the flies were beginning to buzz and circle thickly.

Abel stepped around and over bodies. Later he would try to find enough men to see to burial, though he doubted if many of those who had escaped would return.

Then he saw what he was seeking and had feared he would find. He sat on the ground, took the blond head between his hands. Did death always make a person look smaller?

How shallow we find our knowledge of those we love. He had seen the face before him surrender its bland innocence to savagery, and then change again . . . to what? Eyes on the brink of some discovery, voice the uncertain but eager echo of a probing spirit?

Abel knew he had understood little of what had been taking place in the heart of his friend.

Had he been afraid to understand?

28

SALISBURY set out from Waltham at daybreak, accompanied by Thomas and a dozen armed men.

He knew where he would begin his search. The soldiers returning from Billericay spoke of having seen a priest in the rebel camp. Perhaps it was Ball, perhaps not. If he had been there, he would in all likelihood have fled by now. A full day had elapsed since the crushing rout described by the soldiers. Yet there would be traces, the starting point of a trail, and eventually he would find Ball.

Courtenay's urging was one reason why he had volunteered for the mission. Behind the Chancellor's suave but pointed chiding, Salisbury had detected an almost desperate anxiety to have the priest in custody.

In setting the trap at Smithfield, Salisbury had been forced to make a choice. He knew he had decided wisely. Tyler's death had been essential. It had not been possible, with all the uncertainties involved, to dispose of Ball at the same time.

Yet Courtenay had made him aware how miserably he had erred in allowing Ball to escape after the triumph at Clerkenwell.

Without Tyler the revolt would not have got as far as it did. But without Ball there would have been no Tyler, at least not the Tyler they had known.

Salisbury realized now that as long as Ball remained free, he could never feel secure.

He would find him.

29

Most of the morning it rained heavily. The copse where Ball was hiding offered scant shelter from the deluge, and before long his cassock was sodden.

During the afternoon the sun emerged, hot and fierce. Ball ventured out to the mouth of the thicket and sat gazing at the walls of Colchester in the distance, wondering what night would bring. Now and then he looked down at his hands, contemplating them sombrely. Once he burst into bitter, uncontrollable weeping, and he stuffed the hem of his cassock between his teeth to muffle the sound, though he knew no one besides himself could hear.

At sundown he saw someone approaching and scurried back among the shielding branches, where he remained until he was sure who it was.

Abel threw himself onto the ground, wiped the sweat from his face, took a chunk of bread from his pouch and handed it to Ball. 'The news is bad,' he said.

Ball chewed on the bread. He had almost expected this. 'They won't support us,' he said dismally.

'In London,' said Abel, 'the men of Colchester made a fine loud noise. We're from the city of Wat Tyler and John Ball, they said, and strutted about like bailiffs at tallage time. Today I had a hard time finding any who'd admit they'd even been in London.'

'In time . . .'

'In time you'll find none. I don't blame them. The word of what happened at Billericay, the King's troops in and out of the gates, galloping through the streets.' He paused, went on in a low voice. 'Some of them were looking for you.'

'Yes,' said Ball.

'There was talk of a man named John Wrawe.'

Ball felt hope beginning to stir. The Suffolk leader, and the thousands he had mustered with his fervour and energy. Perhaps then in the north there would still be a chance. 'We'll go there,' he said.

'If you do, you'll find yourself in interesting company.' Abel's tone grew brutal. 'Wrawe surrendered and turned informer.' He said more softly, 'Time to give it up.'

Ball shook his head stubbornly. 'We still have over a hundred men . . .'

Abel laughed, and a rook roosting in the branches above their heads flapped its wings and squawked sleepily. 'An hour ago there were seventy. I told them to go their separate ways.' Ball looked sharply at him, and he shrugged. 'If I hadn't, they'd have been gone by morning anyhow. I agree with them. I've had enough myself.'

'Why did you bother coming here?'

'I intend to stay with you,' Abel said simply.

'I don't want you to.'

'What will you do?'

'I don't know yet.'

'Then I'll stay with you.'

'No,' said Ball quietly.

Abel looked at him for a while. 'All right. No. Will you take some good peasant advice?'

Ball raised his head.

'Give it up yourself. Find . . .' He hesitated, then went on. 'Find a village where you can live. You deserve some peace.'

'Peace,' repeated Ball, looking down at his hands. He curved his fingers into fists, let them go limp again. 'I've told you, if I hadn't . . .'

'It wasn't your fault,' said Abel. 'Only give it up.'

'You've given it up?'

'I have.'

'Will you do one more thing?'

Abel's eyes went opaque with the sly suspicion Ball had often seen in peasant faces.

'For me personally.'

Abel nodded slowly, and Ball told him what he wanted.

The moon, a little better than a quarter full, shone steadily on the flintstone turret of St. Mary's. Ball found the place in the wall he was seeking, scrambled up over the top and dropped, breathing heavily, into the darkness. He listened for some time, knowing he had made a great deal of noise, certain he must have aroused someone. But the churchyard remained quiet.

He made his way toward the priory, hugging the wall, tripping now and then over the protruding roots of trees, scratching his face on bushes. He waited at a corner of the building, leaning against the rough stone, peering around, seeing no one.

Perhaps Abel had not delivered the message. Perhaps they had been followed and had not dared to meet him. Perhaps they had not wanted to come at all.

275

Then he saw them, standing together in the shadow of the priory wall, only a few paces beyond him.

They started when he whispered Christiana's name. She came to him and took his hands. 'You're cold,' she said. 'How can you be cold on a night like this? And you frightened me. I didn't hear you coming.'

He felt himself smiling. It was an unfamiliar feeling. 'With all the noise I made?'

'Did you make a noise? I suppose I was listening too hard. When you listen so hard . . . John . . .'

He took her in his arms, kept her close to him for a moment, then gently put back her hood and held her away to look at her. Even in the moonlight he could see the lines of exhaustion in her face, but somehow they only made her appear more beautiful.

'You've scratched yourself,' she said.

'Yes.' Suddenly he was in a panic. If they had been followed . . .

'We made sure no one saw us,' Christiana said quietly.

He glanced toward Isabella. 'Is she . . .'

'Talk to her now.'

Christiana turned and walked a few steps away, and Isabella drifted to him wraith-like, looking more fragile than ever.

Ball did not know what to say. He had lost the power to comfort. He wished he had not asked her to come with Christiana, but if he had not, there would always be Tyler's dying wish, unfulfilled. Finally he said hoarsely, 'Your name was the last word he spoke.'

She sighed, a slow, whispering exhalation, as if she had been holding her breath a long time. Then she said suddenly, angrily, 'Why did he do this to me? What I had was not enough, but I had learned to live with it. In a way I was even content. Then he . . .' She was silent for a moment, then her lips curved in a small, secret smile. 'At Maidstone he said , , ,' The smile hardened. 'Why did he not let me be? Why did he have to waken me to . . .' She made a helpless gesture. '. . . to this?'

He wanted to explain to her what Tyler had come to know before his death. More than anything he wanted to give her this. He could feel their love for each other flowing through him. But he himself was dead and lost, so where was love? Then he became aware of Christiana watching him, and he put his hand on Isabella's shoulder. When she looked up at him, he saw that she understood. She stumbled away from him blindly, but even in her agony there was a softness about her movements that made him know she would be able to mourn now, fully, as he had not yet been able to do.

Christiana came close to him and said in a lifeless voice, 'You'll stay with me.'

'You know I can't.'

'Then I must come with you.'

He looked at her without speaking for a long time, storing up the look of her against absence. It was difficult, because her beauty was painful to him. She studied his expression, smiled sadly and said, 'Thank you, John Ball.'

He was able then to tell her some of the things that had happened. When he spoke of the attack at Billericay, and what he had done, she averted her head, and he stopped speaking, for he saw she was weeping.

After a while she asked, 'What will you do?'

He shrugged.

'Take me with you.'

'Christiana . . .'

'I'll be your wife. I'll live with you wherever you go. And when you're ready to begin again with the things you must do, I'll help you. I'll . . .' Her shoulders slumped, and she was silent, watching him. Then she said in an almost inaudible voice, 'Strike me.'

He stared at her.

'Strike me!'

He continued to look at her, horrified, but gradually he understood what was in her eyes and reflected: who am I to withhold peace from another? He did as she had asked. She cried out sharply, then turned and ran. He watched her join Isabella in the gloom at the far end of the priory. She took the younger woman by the arm, and they were gone.

It was only later, after he had scaled the wall and was hurrying through the darkness away from the town, that he realized it was not for the sake of her own peace that she had made him strike him.

JULY

I

SALISBURY considered the man standing before him: the half-closed eyes, the slack, brutish mouth, the arms hanging slack.

'When did you last see John Ball?'

'Who?'

The market-place was hot. Thomas standing beside him was breathing heavily, complainingly, and the sweat was rolling down his face, but Salisbury could not get warm. The chill seemed to be with him always now, deep in his bones, and his stomach protested constantly against the indigestible fare it was forced to endure. He would have liked nothing more than a bowl of soup or porridge, but when they stopped for the night at some priory or manor house, the host felt constrained to lay a festive board. Often he departed earlier than he had intended the next day, to avoid facing the hearty, grease-laden morning meal.

He sighed and looked round the market-place, let his gaze rest on the wattle-walled huts deflecting the heat in shimmering waves, the clump of people watching him with identically dull and impassive expressions, his soldiers lounging beside their horses in the sparse shade. He turned again to the peasant he was interrogating. 'John Ball the priest. I know he came through this village. How long ago? Yesterday? This morning?'

The man shook his head stupidly.

He was lying, of course. They all did, and it was only by employing a combination of sensitivity and artifice that he was able to obtain enough information to keep the trail relatively fresh.

The woman in Colchester was the worst, from every point of view.

She was undeniably attractive, full-figured and sensual, and she moved with an indolence which was at the same time irritating and disturbing. For a few moments he had believed her when she said she did not even know John Ball: it had seemed incongruous that she should. Then, after a question which had been intended more or less idly, an inquiry as to when Ball had last visited her house, he had seen her lips part slightly, and tremble for an instant before she could bring them under control.

Once she had sensed that he knew she was lying, she had continued to deny having seen Ball, but she had looked at him defiantly, her eyes shining, letting him know plainly her love for the priest. And he had been forced to leave her then, for he had feared that if he stayed the agitation which suddenly buffeted him might become too apparent.

The chill and his protesting innards had begun to plague him particularly from then on.

Thomas said, 'Will I fetch another one for you to question, my lord Salisbury?'

'No,' he replied. 'This one hasn't told me all he knows.'

The man shuffled his feet. For the first time Salisbury saw a trace of expression in his eyes . . . fear, or simply cunning? 'Master, you won't beat me, will you?'

Fear then. 'I might.'

'I don't know this priest fellow. Believe me, I've never seen him.'

Salisbury sighed. He had been sighing, he suddenly realized, a great deal of late.

'I wouldn't know this priest fellow if I came face to face with him.'

This was one of the more talkative ones. He might betray enough emotion to warrant trying one of the cruder, but often effective, devices.

He looked around. There were three roads leading out of the village. Watching the man's face carefully, he pointed to the easterly one and asked, 'Did he leave by that road?'

Indicating each road in turn, he repeated the question twice more, then sighed and dismissed the man.

He told Thomas to assemble their men-at-arms. When they were mounted, he led them along the way which ran north-westward out of the village.

2

B ALL awoke before dawn, and when he heard the bell ringing in the distance for Morrow Mass, he performed the Divine Office.

The chancel was overgrown with tall grass and weeds; the transept walls existed only as tumbled heaps of shattered, weathering rock, but he found this not at all distressing. Nor did he mind that there was no roof, for the rains which fell every few days filled the two depressions he had laboriously hollowed out in the ground: one to serve as a font, the other to provide him with water for drinking and washing.

Days he spent meditating, walking slowly up and down the rubble-strewn floor of the nave, considering the twisted beauty of the oak projecting gnarled branches through one of the arched windows, sometimes but not often speculating on what had caused the church to fall to ruin. Mostly he would think over all that had happened, before and after the commons marched to London: slowly, with great care, ascribing to each event its individual significance and its importance to the whole.

At night after Vespers he would venture out into the town in search of food. In the beginning he had found it difficult to obtain enough to eat. The refuse heaps yielded only scraps, though one night someone had flung a bone with quite a bit of meat left on it into the street, and he had scrambled for it, seizing it with a triumphant flourish from under the noses of two dogs who followed him, whining, almost all the way back to his church.

Then, prowling behind an inn one evening, he had come upon a woman standing hoodless, humming softly, her face turned up to the last deep blue of the twilight sky. He had tried to retire without being seen, but his usual clumsiness had betrayed him, and when his foot struck a piece of wood she had broken off her song and retreated fearfully toward the door. Then she had come back a few steps, examined him with a long searching glance. When she disappeared, he had thought of running, had decided instead to wait, and in a few moments she had returned with a bowl of steaming barley soup, which she put down on the ground. He had gone back the next evening, and after a while the woman had come out, holding the bowl of soup and peering around. He had smiled his thanks at her, and she had placed it on the ground without a word. When he saw her waiting for him the third night, he knew the problem of food was solved.

Once, as he was returning from the inn, something had happened to terrify him.

In one of the narrow lanes about halfway to his church, he had tripped over the body of a man. Thinking he was dead or injured, Ball had bent down and then had caught a pungent whiff of ale. As he was about to move on, the man had mumbled something. He had knelt to listen and had heard '. . . beware or ye be woe, know your friend from your foe, have enough and say ho . . .' spoken in a hollow, uncertain voice, and had suddenly recognized the words of one of the letters he had written. Before he could stir, the man had opened staring eyes and cried out, 'John Ball has rung your bell . . .' and he had run wildly through the streets, not pausing until he had reached his church and fallen, sobbing from exertion and fear, before the altar.

But that had been some nights before, and though the memory had not faded, he was no longer frightened by it.

And gradually now he felt something like peace descending about him. Something like peace only, for there were still many things lying unresolved in his mind, and he sensed it would take more time than he had to find peace itself.

So, this morning, as he completed the mass and turned from the altar, he felt disappointment but very little fear and no surprise at all when he saw the grey-haired nobleman and a company of soldiers standing at the far end of the nave.

'Wait!' he called, then walked unhurriedly toward them. 'I would not have wanted to force you to violate sanctuary,' he explained as he reached the grey-haired man.

'My lord Salisbury . . .' said a young man, his pale eyes growing troubled, but the nobleman motioned him to silence.

Ball smiled. 'Something I would be grateful if you would tell me . . . you see, I've not been able to ask . . . which town is this?'

'Coventry,' replied Salisbury.

'Coventry,' Ball repeated wonderingly. 'Then I must have had it in mind to return to York. . . .' He shook his head. 'Whatever for? Did I believe that by going back . . .' He smiled at them again. 'Forgive me. Being alone I've grown used to talking to myself. There's something else. You see, I'm afraid I've lost count of the days.'

The young man rolled his pale eyes fearfully. He believes I'm mad, thought Ball, and the notion amused him.

After a moment Salisbury said, 'It's the ninth day of July.'
Ball stared at him. 'No,' he said flatly. 'It can't be.'

'It is,' said the young man softly.

'But . . .' His head was swimming. Objects began slipping out of vision. 'I know I was in Colchester at the end of June, and I've been here . . .' It must have taken him five or six days, possibly as much as a week, to make the journey from Colchester to Coventry. That meant he could only have spent a few days here. Then the weeks he thought had passed . . . the nights of scavenging for food, the woman outside the inn, the drunkard in the dark lane . . . had they been illusion? And if they were, what of the contemplation, the calm and lengthy self-examination he had undertaken. . . .

No, he decided, whatever tricks the twisted juxtaposition of time and events had played on him . . . at the moment he could not be sure what had been reality and what fantasy . . . the reflection itself had been valid and painfully true. A measure of serenity began to return.

'We'll not need the irons,' the young man said quietly.

'No, Thomas,' said Salisbury, 'we'll not need the irons.'

Ball turned for a last look at his church. The morning sun, pouring in suddenly over the roofless walls, bathed the ruined pulpit in red-gold light. He sighed, and heard Salisbury beside him also sighing.

Together they walked toward the horses.

3

THOMAS came back to them near Dunstable after having been gone only a day and a night and reported that Richard and his entourage would be arriving that evening at St. Albans. They would welcome the appearance of Salisbury with his captive.

He listened absently as his squire told him how the King had proceeded as far east as Chelmsford, where he had made a speech to the populace formally repudiating the charters sealed at Mile End, and now would be visiting the Abbey to mete out punishment to the St. Albans rebels. Actually, Salisbury was thinking more about Thomas than about what the lad was saying. His manner was quieter now, less callow, and he sometimes came close to being perceptive. In London he had for the first time in his life grappled with true fear. How he assimilated the experience could very well dictate the quality of his eventual maturity.

Since they were only a few miles from St. Albans, Salisbury ordered a halt. He did not wish to arrive at the Abbey before the royal party and be forced to endure the company of Abbot de la Mare alone.

They rested in a quiet glade with the somnolent noonday hum of the forest all about them. Salisbury sat down next to Ball. When he had first seen the priest in the ruined church, he had thought that he was mad. He had realized his mistake quickly enough. There is a certain type of lucidity so stark that it can easily be confused with madness and is often more terrifying.

Perhaps this was the reason why he had avoided anything more than casual conversation with the priest. He had expected to feel respect for him; he had not known that he would like him. Yet, though he was drawn to him, he was also frightened by him. He was not sure why. Certainly there was no sense of the physical menace he had felt from Tyler. The priest was thin to emaciation, skin stretched tightly over his bones in yellowish translucence; his hands trembled; he seemed in constant danger of collapsing, exhausted and vulnerable.

Perhaps it was in this vulnerability that the enigma lay, in some netherland where weakness and strength swirled as shadows, defying identification with harrowing elusiveness.

'Supposing,' said Salisbury abruptly, 'I allowed you to escape?'

Ball glanced at him. 'If you had intended to let me go, you would never have taken me from my church.'

'But if you were free now, what would you do?'

'That is something,' said Ball, 'I've not yet decided.'

Salisbury persisted, probing for something just beyond his understanding. 'Would you, if you had a decade or more of your life to live over . . . would you do again what you have done?'

Ball smiled. 'Is my lord already presiding at my trial?'

'Would you?'

'I made many mistakes. Like any man, I look back with regret on some things I have done.'

'Then you would not, for example, incite people to rise against authority.'

'I didn't say that.' He paused, went on in a low, wistful voice. 'Nor could I yet. My lord did not allow me quite enough time.'

'Perhaps if I had not found you . . .'

'My lord Salisbury,' said Ball, 'you had to find me.'

They reached St. Albans toward evening, rode along beside the

284

Cathedral with its massive Norman tower and entered the monastery enclosure through the vaulted gateway.

On the green, Walworth was showing a hawk to the gargoyle-faced Abbot, who was clapping his hands delightedly. A few paces away stood Courtenay, surveying them with an expression of distaste. Then the Chancellor looked toward the gateway, and as soon as he saw Ball he came forward, his eyes alight.

'You've done well, my lord Salisbury,' he said, never removing his gaze from Ball.

Salisbury's reply was interrupted. De la Mare was rushing at Ball, shrieking in a harsh, ragged voice, 'This is the traitor! This is the beast who . . .'

He did not finish, for he had reached Ball's side. He seized the priest's leg, dragged him off the horse and onto the ground, began kicking him. Ball scrambled to his feet, but made no effort to defend himself as the Abbot continued to pound him with his fists.

Salisbury wanted to go to Ball's assistance, but he could only watch, sickening, as blood spurted from the priest's nose and mouth.

Then someone stepped between the two men. Salisbury stared unbelievingly as Thomas, pale and obviously frightened, placed himself squarely before the priest and confronted the Abbot.

De la Mare's snub nose remained dead-white, lending his otherwise florid face an increased malevolence. 'This is my monastery,' he gasped. 'You'll be in the gateway prison along with him.'

'This man,' said Thomas in a shaky voice, 'is a prisoner of the King, my lord Abbot.'

The Abbot's expression clotted with hatred. 'You should tell your young man,' he said to Salisbury, 'to be more respectful.'

Salisbury looked at him for a moment, then said quietly, 'I only wish I had learned at such an early age to be so respectful.'

4

BESIDES himself, there were sixteen of them crammed into the tiny cell. They had no space to sit or lie down, and they stood, hour after hour, bodies pressed together in the blackness. The meagre ventilation did nothing to carry off the excretory stench, and the odour of eructation had long since been added to the others. Under ordinary circumstances the night would have seemed interminable. Now it was passing far too quickly, for at daybreak all of them were to be executed.

The Abbey prison was located in the wall of the gateway, and at intervals Ball could hear the portcullis grind upward to let a solitary horseman pass in or out, then rumble down into place.

'Almighty God,' said Grindcobbe in his matter-of-fact tone, 'if they had not tricked us . . .'

They had taken Grindcobbe and his key leaders by a series of subterfuges, brought them to the Abbey for imprisonment three days ago. Ball considered himself more fortunate in this respect, since this was only his second night in the gateway dungeon, and he had spent some of the day between at his trial. However, in the manner of death there was little to choose between his prescribed fate and that of the others. They were to be hanged and drawn, their bodies to remain on the gibbets until only skeletons were left.

'John Ball,' Courtenay had intoned in that smooth and curiously powerful voice, 'you will be hanged by the neck, and drawn according to custom, after which your body will be divided into quarters and dispatched in each direction throughout England, thereby to serve as an example.'

One of the St. Albans men groaned and asked, 'How much of the night?'

'The better part,' replied another voice, 'whether it's ahead or behind.'

A wave of cackling laughter undulated from one wall to the other, rallying the stinking air in its wake.

'John Ball,' Courtenay had said, 'you stand accused of extraordinary treason against the crown and realm of England. How do you plead?'

'I am in no position to plead for anything.'

'We are not assembled here to engage in word-play,' Courtenay had rapped out sharply. 'Did you not commit treason against England?'

'No, my lord.'

'Did you not arouse the serfs and lowborn freemen to active revolt against the King?'

'It was never our intention to rebel against the King.'

'Did you not, wilfully and with malice, attempt to disrupt the established order, the harmony of man ordained by the Lord God in His wisdom at the very moment of Creation?'

'I did what I had to do.'

'Then . . .' softly, waspishly, 'we shall do what we have to do.'

In a corner of the cell a young voice wrenched itself through a fit of strangled, chromatic weeping.

'There's a lad,' said Grindcobbe. 'If I could only do that . . .' In his careless, offhand way he went on, 'The worst part, you know, was to see them bringing our handmills back to the Abbey. Not a single sack of corn did we have a chance to grind in our own homes.'

The tearful voice in the corner was subsiding, settling into a soft, regular whoop like the cry of an owl. Some of the others cackled again, and Grindcobbe murmured musingly, 'Birds of a feather . . .'

Salisbury, the Lord Mayor, the Abbot de la Mare, they had all been present in the musty, high-ceilinged chamber. The King, seated beside Courtenay, had studied his nails practically all the time Ball had stood before him. Only once had he glanced up to ask, 'Why is it taking so long? Can we not execute him now?'

'In good time, sire, all will come right,' Courtenay had replied, looking at Ball. 'We are not animals. Before a man is punished, he must have a trial at which he may defend himself. Defend yourself, prisoner.'

There had been a peculiar expression on Courtenay's face, confusing to Ball: something gentle and angry and anguished all at once. But it had been fleeting, and the voice had continued, suave and supercilious, 'The prisoner has nothing to say. How remarkable! Would he perhaps be more articulate if we were to exchange our robes for rags?'

The cell was becoming so stifling that Ball felt each breath he drew as a kind of personal triumph. He wondered if dawn were near, and the same man who had inquired earlier asked again, 'How much of the night?'

'Oh my God,' said Grindcobbe, 'I do so love to live.'

The very casualness of the words contained an agony more acute than an outcry, and for a moment there was not a sound in the cell. Then the chorus of laboured breathing resumed, and the soft hooting grief of the youth in the corner.

Ball must somehow have fallen asleep, and so must some of the others, one leaning against the next, for when the Cathedral bell began a steady clangour almost directly overhead, he felt himself start violently, and at the same time was conscious of the responsive wakening tremor of those on either side of him. Someone coughed and set off an imitative refrain which ran back and forth, criss-crossing the cell, until the bell stopped tolling.

A key chattered in a lock, and the door swung open. They filed out, stood dumbly in the half-light of the gateway, blinking at one another and gulping great breaths of the fresh air which tasted acrid after their confinement. 'Not you,' said a voice, and hands seized Ball, thrust him back into the rank darkness. The cell door banged shut.

He did not try to understand. It was enough that he was alive, and each time his muddled thoughts began to shape themselves

287

toward reason, he deliberately rescattered them, for he sensed calamity in comprehension.

He felt rather than heard the cell door open and turned to face it. A familiar voice said calmly, 'They're dead, John Ball,' then, 'Come out . . .'

He stumbled toward the light, attempted too late to keep his feet from tangling and sprawled onto the stone paving of the gateway passage. The fall did not hurt him, but for the first time he felt the ache of the beating he had received from de la Mare.

He picked himself up. Standing close, very close to him, a faint, sickly smile on his lips, was Courtenay.

'The bodies are hanging in Sopwell Lane,' said the Chancellor, 'only a few moments' walk from the Abbey. I had intended to take you to see them, but for two reasons I have changed my mind.'

Ball waited, striving to hold reality on an even plane. They were strolling, actually sauntering, for he found himself having to fall in with Courtenay's leisurely pace, across the monastery green. They might have been two scholars enjoying a brief respite from solitary studies in the peaceful morning sunlight.

'In the first place, I think I would become ill if I were compelled to look again at that gibbet fruit. Even so, I should do it readily enough if I believed it would be useful. However, I feel now that it would only make you angry, and so make it more difficult for me to accomplish my purpose.'

Ball moistened his lips. 'And what is your purpose?'

Courtenay smiled but refrained from answering. They were walking along a path winding among the mossy stones of a cemetery. Courtenay led Ball to the wall of the Cathedral and in through a small doorway. A litany was being chanted by monks congregated at the ends of the transepts, and the throbbing resonance of the antiphony evoked feelings of grief and remorse in Ball, along with the memory of the soaring, turbulent moments at Canterbury.

The Chancellor, watching him, said close to his ear, 'I shall persuade you to recant, to make a public statement renouncing all your actions as traitorous and heretical.'

Ball replied irritably, 'If I did not do so at my trial . . .'

'At your trial,' said Courtenay, 'it was impossible for me to apply pressures . . .'

Ball stiffened. 'If you intend to torture me . . .'

'Torture you? My dear man . . .' Courtenay laughed, and the sound rose sharply in the silence between two responses. 'No. I shall bribe you.'

Ball swung away indignantly, then felt himself turning back, drawn inexorably by the Chancellor's eyes, which seemed to have absorbed some coercive light from the radiance streaming through the great stained-glass windows. 'I shall make you an offer in exchange for what I ask. Ultimately, you will not be able to refuse.'

'The Abbot . . .' Ball heard himself mumbling. 'Many months ago . . .'

Courtenay laughed again. 'Yes, the Abbot. But, you see, he approached you out of a variety of motives. The one which defeated him was his friendship for you. We, you and I, will not be hampered in our discussions by sentiment.' He touched the dimple in his chin, let his hand slide down to caress the glossy material of his habit. 'You might be interested to know that the Abbot will soon become a Bishop.'

Ball thought of the face of his friend as he had last seen it: ageing and resigned, the eyes bearing a mournful knowledge of their own destiny.

'Had he urged you more effectively . . . for despite his ability, I place the blame for your refusal on him, not you . . . had he been less blinded by his feeling for you, it is probable that you would be assuming the position he will vacate in York.' He held up his hand as Ball started to speak. 'Never fear. I shall not be so crude. There are better methods of convincing you.'

He was silent then, and for a time the two of them stood listening to the pure notes of the litany swelling out of the transepts, rolling down the nave to lose themselves lingeringly among the cavernous pillared bays.

Courtenay motioned Ball to follow him. At the end of the nave they entered a tiny passageway and climbed winding stairs to an oaken door which the Chancellor opened, admitting them to a luxuriously furnished series of chambers. 'Abbot de la Mare's private apartment,' he explained, and when Ball looked around with trepidation, he laughed and said reassuringly, 'He's not here now. He has a special task to perform this morning.'

A servant moved toward them with noiseless steps across a huge rug fashioned from the sewn skins of bears.

'Is his bath ready?' asked Courtenay, nodding at Ball.

'Yes, my lord Chancellor.'

'What bath?' asked Ball.

'What bath?' repeated Courtenay, mimicking viciously. 'The bath you're going to take, my dear man.'

They were facing each other in dead seriousness, but Ball became aware of the grim and paradoxical humour even as he said, 'I don't need a bath in order to die.'

'Of course not. But then, you're not going to die just yet, are you? You're going to live and recant. And the first link in the chain I shall forge for you is a cleansing and a change of clothing.'

'I'm content with what I'm wearing.'

'To be sure,' said Courtenay, all at once appearing highly amused. 'Oh, I'm certain you are. But I shall not allow you to be. You see, you were too close to death, and in all likelihood too well prepared for it. One luxury you shall not be permitted now is that of self-mortification.' His voice hardened. 'Go with him, and bathe, or I shall call soldiers to force you to do so.'

Kneeling in the wooden tub, he could muster no resolve against enjoyment of the warm water the servant was laving over him. Once he went to sleep and woke shuddering, dreaming he was being led to the gallows, but it was only the gentle pressure of the servant's hand on his arm, helping him from the tub. Very well then, he thought, with what he knew was childish truculence, but no one can force me to wear one of those many-hued satin cassocks. No one did. The habit presented him was of rough russet, much like the one he had discarded, but of course clean.

Courtenay entered just as he had finished dressing, looked at him a few moments without comment. Then he came to Ball, placed a hand on his shoulder and said, 'When I was twenty-five years old, I was Chancellor of the University at Oxford, where I had several years before received degrees in law and theology. At the age of twenty-seven I was Bishop of Hereford. I have still to celebrate my fortieth birthday.' He regarded Ball solemnly. 'I tell you this not to impress you with my precocity, but rather to be perfectly honest with you. I know that I have unusual capabilities. I intend to utilize them all to obtain the statement I have requested of you. I want your recantation. I need it.'

'Why?'

'I am quite sure you are not as stupid as your question indicates. You know as well as I the effect your repudiation will have on the people whose discontent you have nourished. Your death, of course, would have the undeniably direct and salutary result of removing you. But when you have recanted and still live . . .'

Ball felt as if he were sinking slowly into a morass from which he could never extricate himself. 'Why did you not kill me this morning? Why?' His voice, hoarse and cracked as it was, rose soft and muted in the tapestry-smothered room.

Courtenay's smile reflected both satisfaction and triumph. 'You see? My methods are effective. And I shall explain each step to you as we proceed. Already you are less willing to die, whereas a few hours ago . . . You know, it has been said that each man . . .'

He stopped talking and became at once alert, listening, then went to a window and with sudden soft jubilation called, 'Come . . .'

Ball was puzzled. The Chancellor was looking toward the gateway, plainly visible through the open window, but the tranquil beauty of the vast monastery enclosure was undisturbed. In the distance two monks were hurrying toward the Cathedral. Other than these he could see no one.

Then he heard the faint sibilant shuffling and watched, apprehension mingling with curiosity, as the first men appeared at the mouth of the vaulted tunnel and plodded reluctantly toward the centre of the green and a wooden platform Ball had not noticed before, urged on by soldiers with unsheathed swords. The procession continued to pass through the gateway, row after row, trudging with the same weary, shambling gait.

'Every male,' Courtenay said quietly, 'within a radius of ten miles of St. Albans. Every male between sixteen and sixty. I should say there are at least four thousand, would you not agree?'

Their appearance, their sullen dejection . . . not since the days when he had first begun to preach had he seen such disheartenment.

From a massive stone building far across the enclosure emerged two figures, a little in advance of a troop of soldiers. Ball could see that one was wearing a cassock, the other robes of some sort, but he was unable to identify them.

'The King,' said Courtenay, 'and your dear friend the Abbot de la Mare.'

They made for the wooden platform, mounted it, and at once de la Mare called, his harsh voice carrying clearly, 'Down on your knees, oxen!'

The people knelt, and Ball's heart ached.

'You have committed grievous crimes, all of you, against the King and against me, your Abbot. I shall not forget it, nor shall you.' There was a pause, and again the voice cried, 'Nor shall you.'

A very soft, lamenting wail floated above the heads of the people, feather-light and yet filled with such intense despair that Ball involuntarily moaned after them. Courtenay made an oddly commiserative gesture but said nothing.

'Now,' barked de la Mare, 'you will give evidence of your everlasting loyalty to His Majesty King Richard and to the Abbey of St. Albans. Swear!'

Their response had the muttering quality of spent thunder. 'We swear . . .'

'Again!'

Obediently they repeated: 'We swear.'

Richard and de la Mare descended the steps of the platform, and the multitude, rising, faced about to flow like some murky, sluggish stream back toward the gateway.

'You have seen,' said Courtenay, turning from the window and shepherding Ball ahead of him. 'There is no need for me to point the moral. Now we shall speak of you.'

To his dismay Ball discovered he was listening with an interest verging on eagerness.

'The offer is a simple one. I shall not promise you wealth or position, though it is within my power to confer both. You would accept neither, and I would not wish to demean myself by bargaining with you after you had refused. So we shall come at once to conditions I know will be more suitable. You will first of all remain alive. This is the essence: alive and able to spend the rest of your days without fear. You will be given an annual stipend to provide, amply but not luxuriously, for you wherever you may wish to settle.' He paused for just an instant, then said with delicate emphasis, 'There is a woman, Christiana I believe her name is . . .'

Ball struggled against the tears which sprang to his eyes, for until he had controlled them he could not trust himself to speak.

'You need not reply now,' said Courtenay. 'In fact, I do not even wish to hear your answer before Vespers. Only this I must add. You have been sentenced to death. If you refuse my terms, I shall have no choice but to order that sentence to be carried out at sunrise tomorrow. You will be confined in a room in the tower across the Cathedral. Not as opulent as this, but clean and well-aired. You will be able to hear the Vespers service quite clearly. At any hour after that I shall be available. When you call . . .'

He stared at Ball with sudden moodiness. 'Between Vespers and Morrow Mass. . . .'

5

THE peregrine soared overhead waiting, circling, lowering a wing-tip in an elegant effortless turn beneath white shafts of fluted cloud.

Across the wide sweep of valley Walworth could see the Abbey, the lines of the Cathedral hazed by distance and the beginnings of evening light. Soon he would have to return.

There had been little to commend the day. In the morning there had been the executions, and immediately afterward he had felt the urgent necessity to be away and had gone at once to fetch the falcon. But in all the hours since he had managed to flush only two rooks and a single partridge.

As he was about to give up, he saw the grouse, huddled motionless between a boulder and a bush, its plumage blending so perfectly with the dark earth that he almost missed it. The bird, realizing that it had been sighted, began skittering off at an angle from his line of approach.

'Hoya!' called Walworth, though he knew the falcon probably would neither hear him nor have need of his summoning cry. 'Hoya . . .'

Even as the peregrine entered her plummeting dive, Walworth perceived that there was something wrong with the grouse. Instead of mounting in the characteristic short but incredibly swift flight, it rose only a few feet and drifted back to earth, one wing fluttering frantically, the other dangling limp and useless.

'Take it, my sweet,' Walworth said disgustedly. 'Take it and we'll go in.'

The grouse was fleeing for the cover of a thicket many yards away. Walworth, measuring the distance with a rapid glance, knew it had no chance of making it. He reined in, watching the falcon's ferocious plunge, waiting for the thud of impact and the scream which would tear itself out of her throat as she sank talons and beak into her prey.

Suddenly the grouse stopped running, took a few disconsolate hopping steps, then remained still. The falcon checked herself, veered off in a confused rush of wings to hover uncertainly above the crippled quarry, which looked up at her, its head swivelling and bobbing awkwardly.

Walworth called to her, urging her on until his voice wore itself to a wrathful whisper. She made one tiny abortive swoop, then swerved away and came to rest on a low bough of a nearby elm. The grouse scurried into the thicket.

Walworth sat looking at the peregrine for some moments. Once he said tentatively, 'My sweet . . .' but the words were like ashes in his mouth. Slowly he dismounted, took a few steps, stopped, then went resolutely toward the hawk, extending his gloved hand and drawing his knife with the other.

293

The Vespers bell was ringing, and Salisbury was halfway across the green on his way to the Cathedral when he caught sight of Walworth riding through the gateway. Without knowing why, he shuddered. Then, as the Lord Mayor drew near, Salisbury saw the stony expression, and only then did he notice that the stiffly outthrust, gauntleted left fist had no hawk perched on it.

6

THE last strokes of the Vespers bell beat heavily against the still air. All the afternoon Ball had chafed at the slow passage of time, waiting for this hour when he would be able to fling his refusal at Courtenay.

He could hear evensong commencing. When it was over he would pound on the door and tell the guard stationed outside that he was ready to speak to the Chancellor.

He went to the window. His tower room projected beyond the main Cathedral wall, and he gazed out along the shadowed buttresses as he listened to the sweet, muffled notes of the service. Soon now.

But when there was silence once more, he remained at the window, watching sunset slip toward twilight and into darkness. Finally, when the light was entirely gone from the sky, he realized why he had not yet summoned Courtenay. If he did, it would only be to accept his proposal.

The knowledge shamed and sickened him, but he could not disgorge it.

In the ruined church at Coventry he had come to grips with much of what had confused and troubled him. He had gathered enough courage to face death, but he had not been able to find strength to deal with what was left of life. Perhaps, if he had only been allowed a few days longer. . . .

Then suddenly he laughed aloud as it occurred to him that he need not summon Courtenay at all. If he made no reply, it would be construed as refusal, and he would merely have the long night to contend with, and the final moment of fear he knew he would feel when they slipped the noose over his head. Surely Courtenay would not importune him on the way to the gallows.

Relieved, he turned from the window and knelt to pray, but he had always found himself reticent before God in exigency, and words would not come.

Nor could he any longer marshal his thoughts to the ordered clarity he had achieved at Coventry. Between him and honesty now hung Courtenay's offer, its tainted beauty tempting beyond reason.

His only defence lay in sleep, and he thought it would not come, but it did, quickly.

When the key turned in the lock, he was awake at once, springing to his feet, only to note with alarm that darkness still shrouded the window.

He heard the dismay in his voice as he said, 'It's not dawn yet.'

Courtenay closed the door, set the brace of candles down and replied, 'It lacks an hour.'

'Why did you not leave me alone until then?'

'Could I have?' There was muted anger in his expression as he faced Ball, but his tone was unruffled, containing no hint of it. 'I hoped I would not be forced to come to you without being called, but I suppose I knew I would have to.'

'If you had allowed me to . . .'

'If I had allowed you . . .' Now the voice coarsened, taking on its note of spiteful mimicry. 'Do you think I am unaware of what you would have done had I not come now?' He waited, studying Ball, then said stridently, 'Your answer. I will have your answer now.' After a moment he spoke again, this time very quietly. 'Your answer, John Ball.'

Ball gasped and averted his head, but as in the Cathedral many hours before, he had to turn back to face the Chancellor's luminous, compelling gaze.

He drew in a trembling breath and replied. Never had he uttered a word with such irresolution and yet such finality.

Courtenay's eyes filled with disbelief. 'You cannot . . .'

Ball felt the fatigue tugging at his limbs and fought against the desire to sink to the floor, for he knew he had to continue standing before Courtenay.

Furious little mewing sounds grew in the Chancellor's throat. He brought them under control and said in a tight, angry voice, 'Why should you be less corruptible than . . .'

And then an anguished tenderness welled into Courtenay's eyes and he said softly, 'Oh, my God . . .'

They stared at each other in the steady candlelight. Looking at him now, Ball saw neither Chancellor nor Archbishop, but only the man and the priest. He understood now the suffering of the one and knew he could entrust himself to the other. 'I would like you to hear my confession,' he said.

When he had finished they stood in silence again. Then Courtenay's features twisted in agony. His head fell forward, and Ball reached out to touch him.

The single racking sob lingered in the air for what seemed eternity.

They paused for a moment in the Cathedral, deserted now and dark except for a few guttering candles. Then Courtenay made a gesture at once pleading and impatient, the soldier escort moved forward, and they emerged into the cold sombre dawn light.

They turned right and commenced the circuit of the Cathedral, swinging wide to avoid the jutting north transept, cutting in again to make for Sopwell Lane.

Courtenay's face had resumed its customary suave, composed expression. He avoided looking at Ball.

They entered the London road, which pitched sharply downward past the Abbey wall. None of the people of St. Albans were in the street. Their defeat and mine, thought Ball, but in addition to failure I also bear the shadow of shame.

Under no circumstances could he now reverse his refusal of Courtenay's offer. This was certainty, and the knowledge endowed him with the calm of resignation. But he was also oppressed by the futility of what he was doing. He had failed, and the true reason for his being able to die was rooted not in courage but in a terror of living surrounded by the evidence of his failure. Twenty-five years he had laboured for freedom and justice, and these he believed in still. Yet for all he had achieved in their name, he might as well never have existed.

Sopwell Lane branched off the London road and ran along the side of the hill. Above, laced by a network of refuse-choked alleys, lay a profusion of crumbling hovels. Below the lane the hill fell away sharply toward a tranquil vista of fields and forests.

A few hundred paces in from the London road the way broadened to an open square, and as they reached it Ball saw the bodies of Grindcobbe and the other St. Albans' leaders hanging in gruesome array. One gibbet was bare except for the looped rope suspended from the crosstree. Beneath it stood a rickety wooden platform.

The King and his advisers were already in attendance, guarded by a company of soldiers. The executioner, wearing a black hood and tunic, lumbered forward. Ball tried not to look at the slender knife the man wore bare-bladed through his belt.

Richard was gazing open-mouthed at the gallows. On Salisbury's face Ball saw both compassion and fear. When he glanced at

Courtenay, the torment in the Chancellor's eyes was so intense he had to turn from him.

The Lord Mayor alone stared directly at Ball, his expression brutal and uncaring, and perversely this made it easier for Ball to step up onto the platform. The executioner bound his hands behind him and placed the rope about his neck.

The sun was just rising, and the rolling countryside below St. Albans lay under a soft purple haze. Ball had a sudden impression that he could see all the way to London, and it became essential for him to do so. He strained forward, peering to make out St. Paul's and the Tower.

The platform teetered precariously, and the executioner cried out as he tumbled off it, sprawling full-length onto the ground. Ball kicked out desperately, struggling to right the platform with his feet, but the wooden surface slid from under them, and he felt the noose take the full weight of his body.

In the fearful darkness just before oblivion flashed a spark of laughter: wild and mocking, the final futility.

Richard spoke to Courtenay as the executioner was drawing his knife, preparing to carry out the next stage of the sentence. 'It was terribly amusing, that, was it not, my lord Chancellor?' Excitement pitched his voice even higher than usual. 'Once in London when three men were being beheaded, my father the Black Prince . . .'

Courtenay turned from him with a strangled exclamation and hurried back along Sopwell Lane. The King's face crinkled with displeasure, which diminished as he resumed his observation of the proceedings. When they had been completed, he beckoned to the officer in charge of his troops, took his place in the centre of the cordon, and marched with them out of the square.

Salisbury curbed his nausea, but he could not restrain the long quavering sigh that burst from his lips. In any event, he thought, it's over; Tyler without Ball, Ball without Tyler, the circle has come complete, and England . . . he glanced uneasily after the departing Richard . . . England is safe, at least for a time.

He and Walworth were alone in the square except for the executioner and the trio of soldiers delegated to assist him. Salisbury turned to the Lord Mayor, who was staring vacantly at the gallows, and was about to speak when the cry stopped him.

It seemed to be rising from the maze of huts banked on the hillside. Harsh with grief and anger, yet pure and clear as birdsong, the words rolled down: 'When Adam delved and Eve span, who was then the gentleman?'

In a panic, Salisbury seized Walworth's arm. The Lord Mayor pulled away savagely.

'Didn't you hear it?'

'Hear what?'

'Up there . . . it came from up there . . .' He motioned vaguely.

Walworth regarded him with an expression empty and at the same time completely ruthless.

Then he realized that the Lord Mayor neither heard nor understood, nor would it have mattered to him if he had. And in that instant Salisbury perceived that whatever happened, Walworth would somehow always manage to survive. But as he continued to look into his companion's face, he knew he would never envy him his survival.

Salisbury turned from the Lord Mayor and walked wearily back toward the Abbey.

7

HE paused on the highroad, looking beyond fields of ripening grain to the southern horizon, the direction in which his village lay. He knew exactly how it would be to walk once more along the street, to enter his hut, to speak quietly with friends, to feel the joy and sorrow of the seasons.

For many moments he remained motionless, allowing longing for all this to probe the tender recesses of his heart.

Then Abel turned and trudged toward the walled town in the distance.

THE END

PRINTED BY PURNELL AND SONS, LTD.
PAULTON (SOMERSET) AND LONDON